SENSE AND SUITABILITY

"*Sense & Suitability* is a sweet, second-chance Regency romance with an Austenesque flair. Pepper Basham brings a modern voice to classic themes, offering keen insights into family and community, while never losing her signature humor. An absolutely lovely read!"

—Mimi Matthews, *USA TODAY* bestselling author

"An utter delight! Pepper Basham's debut into the Regency genre sparkles with deft wordplay and a joyous wit. Simon and Emmeline's story charms on every page, while endearing side characters try their best to steal the show. With clever nods to Jane Austen's classic, *Sense and Suitability* is everything romance readers adore: sweet, swoony, and perfectly bingeable."

—Joanna Barker, author of *A Heart Worth Stealing*

"Wow. *Sense and Suitability* is one of the *best* Regency romances that I've read in YEARS. With her signature humor, Pepper Basham has penned an engaging, dreamy tale with a cast of delightful characters and witty dialogue that absolutely sings! I found myself thinking about the hero and heroine while away from the novel, eager to find out how it all ended. This is a must-read for Jane Austen fans!"

—Grace Hitchcock, award-winning author
of *To Catch a Coronet*, *My Dear Miss Dupré*, *The White City*, and *The Finding of Miss Fairfield*

SOME LIKE IT SCOT

"In *Some Like It Scot*, a travel writer explores her ancestral roots on a Scotland isle through the misadventures of an Edwardian experience. There, she finds a grumpy Scotsman, a charming bookshop, and the courage to write her own life story. Don't miss this lighthearted romp to Scotland, featuring a swoonworthy tale that's rich in legends and folklore!"

—Denise Hunter, bestselling author
of *The Summer of You and Me*

"An utterly delightful read! Basham weaves the perfect blend of charm, humor, and heartfelt moments as a spirited woman and a hot Scot navigate life, love, and the power of faith. Their journey is inspiring and entertaining, offering readers a story filled with laughter and hope. A must-read for anyone who loves characters that leap off the page and into your heart!"

—Kasey Stockton, author of *I'm Not Charlotte Luca*

LOYALLY, LUKE

"Readers, you are in for a pure delight! Luke Edgewood is, in a word, dreamy. At once tough and tender, guarded and vulnerable, he is a book boyfriend to rival all book boyfriends. And despite being a princess, readers will absolutely relate to Ellie's struggle to overcome her past, prove herself to her family, and make the noble choice—even if it means breaking her own heart in the process. Luke and Ellie's love story has the perfect amount of tension, chemistry, and tugging-at-your-heartstrings moments. Simply unputdownable! Even if this is your first trip to Skymar, you'll feel right at home in this funny, cozy absolute gem of a royal romance! To quote Luke Edgewood, 'I reckon the best kind of love is simple in one way . . . Choosing each other over and over and over again.' When it comes to this book (and the series), these will be stories readers choose to read over and over and over again."

—Emma St. Clair, *USA TODAY* bestselling author

"With a hero who's better at texting and a princess who can wield a hammer, *Loyally, Luke* is 'peppered' with Ms. Basham's signature style of swoony romance and charming characters. She's also added a message we all need to hear and believe for ourselves as two unlikely people wonder if worlds can really merge and not merely collide. This will definitely be another fan favorite."

—Toni Shiloh, Christy Award-winning author

"Fans of Pepper Basham's Skymar series will be thrilled and delighted with this much-anticipated third and final installment to the series. In pure Basham fashion, every page oozes with the magic of romance and characters you won't easily forget. *Loyally, Luke* is an escape many readers look for."

—Sarah Monzon, bestselling author of *All's Fair in Love and Christmas*

"Pepper Basham has done it again! The author's sly wit and enduring tenderness make Luke and Ellie's story a (literal) love letter to the power of authenticity, hope, and redemption. *Loyally, Luke* is sure to hook new readers and delight those who already adore the one-of-a-kind Edgewood family. Prepare to fall head over heels for flannel and fishing!"

—Julie Christianson, author of the Apple Valley Love Stories series

POSITIVELY, PENELOPE

"Basham is a rising star. *Positively, Penelope* is humorous and touching, and everything you want in the perfect summer read. Don't miss this one."

—Rachel Hauck, *New York Times* bestselling author of *The Wedding Dress*

"What do you get when you combine a lovable heroine with characters who have mastered the art of witty banter? A charming read. And that is what *Positively, Penelope* is."

—Sheila Roberts, *USA TODAY* bestselling author

"This book is a positive delight from the first line to the last. I adored Penelope in Izzy's book, and she screamed for her own book, so I couldn't wait to dive into the pages of this novel. Oh my goodness, it was a true, laugh-out-loud joy to read this book. The story was filled with twists and hiccups, but there was also such delight and fun. And fairy tales. And princesses. And Julie Andrews. And Gene Kelly. All the things I adore. In one place. And the kissing. Pepper does enjoy writing kissing books. I highly recommend this sweet, fun, romantic romp of a book. It was wonderful!"

—Cara Putman, award-winning author of more than 35 novels, including *Flight Risk*

"Like the character Penelope herself, this entire book radiates sunshine and magic. The banter between Penelope and her siblings kept me smiling. The theatrical references kept me humming and tapping my toes. And the overall joy that Pepper Basham exudes with her unique writing style and voice kept me engaged in a story I never wanted to leave. Simply put, this book is supercalifragilisticexpialidocious."

—Becca Kinzer, author of *Dear Henry, Love Edith*

"You won't want to put this book down! Pepper has a way of creating characters who are disarming and charismatic in all the best ways, while still reflecting our inner selves. Her stories are charming and witty, and I've never laughed so much while reading! You'll walk away with more joy than you came with and a heart full of assurance and encouragement about the power of our heavenly Father's heart for your love story."

—Victoria Lynn, author of *The Chronicles of Elira, Bound,* and *London in the Dark*

AUTHENTICALLY, IZZY

"A long-distance romance anchors this cute contemporary from Basham (*The Heart of the Mountains*) . . . Basham primarily tells her story through emails, texts, and dating app messages, a quirky approach that complements the adorable leads. Filled with humor and grace, this is perfect for fans of Denise Hunter."

—*Publishers Weekly*

What was even more fun was seeing how Izzy and Brodie's relationship grew from a few funny messages to a sweet relationship. I loved how Izzy grew throughout the story and learned to love herself and find her own strength and love. And her cousins were a hoot! Luke was my favorite cousin. His emails and text messages kept me in stitches. I highly recommend this fun and romantic book!"

—Amy Clipston, bestselling author
of *The View from Coral Cove*

"You don't see enough epistolary novels these days, so the format of this being told almost entirely through emails appealed to me straightaway, and I wasn't disappointed! We follow librarian Izzy as she meets perfect-sounding bookshop owner Brodie online and wonders if he's too good to be true. Filled with the wonderfully warm cast of Izzy's family, and the swoon-worthy email exchanges with Brodie, I absolutely loved reading this book and felt like Izzy was a real friend rather than a book character! A book written by a book lover, about a book lover, for book lovers everywhere! I loved it! In fact, the only issue with this book is that my to-read list has grown exponentially from Izzy and Brodie's recommendations! It's a book lover's dream read!"

—Jaimie Admans, author of romantic comedies

Sense & Suitability

OTHER BOOKS BY PEPPER BASHAM

CONTEMPORARY ROMANCE

Stand-Alone Novels
Authentically, Izzy
Positively, Penelope
Loyally, Luke
Some Like It Scot

Mitchell's Crossroads Series
A Twist of Faith
Charming the Troublemaker
A Match for Emma

A Pleasant Gap Romance Series
Just the Way You Are
When You Look at Me

Novellas
Second Impressions
Jane by the Book
Christmas in Mistletoe Square

HISTORICAL ROMANCE

Stand-Alone Novels
Hope Between the Pages
The Red Ribbon

Blue Ridge Romances
Laurel's Dream
The Heart of the Mountains

Penned in Time Series
The Thorn Bearer
The Thorn Keeper
The Thorn Healer

Freddie and Grace Mysteries
The Mistletoe Countess
The Cairo Curse
The Juliet Code

Novellas
Facade
Between Stairs and Stardust

Sense & Suitability

a novel

PEPPER BASHAM

THOMAS NELSON
Since 1798

Published in Nashville, Tennessee, by Thomas Nelson. Thomas Nelson is a registered trademark of HarperCollins Christian Publishing, Inc.

Thomas Nelson titles may be purchased in bulk for educational, business, fundraising, or sales promotional use. For information, please email SpecialMarkets@ThomasNelson.com.

ISBN 978-0-8407-1706-1 (softcover)
ISBN 978-0-8407-1714-6 (epub)
ISBN 978-0-8407-1740-5 (audio download)

Printed in the United States of America
25 26 27 28 29 LBC 5 4 3 2 1

To Becky Monds
Who believed in me enough to bring this story to life

PROLOGUE

E mmeline Lockhart's life teemed with secrets.

Too many secrets for a country gentleman's daughter, but at least it made her parochial life a little more exciting.

Her smile tipped. Very well—a lot more exciting, in fact.

She tugged at her gloves and stared out into the ballroom, the candlelit chandeliers casting an almost angelic glow across Lord and Lady Ruthton's glossy floors. The hosts of the St. Groves Season never failed to fill their palatial home for every one of the balls they hosted, which was a substantial number for the season. Anyone who was anyone clamored for an invitation to the parties of the wealthiest and most influential aristocrats of their flourishing spa town.

But tonight one of Emme's secrets would come to light. A secret she treasured even more than her occupation as a published author. Tonight she would finally become engaged, putting all the nasty rumors of clandestine meetings and covert affections to rest. Tonight Simon Reeves, cousin to the Viscount of Ravenscross, planned to ask her to marry him.

Her!

A woman without rank or riches.

And though her family was highly respected within St. Groves, they held no esteem in the larger world, so the entire romance proved every bit as fantastical as the fairy stories her mother used to read to her.

Men like Simon didn't marry lower gentry.

Especially not lower gentry with an insignificant dowry and a scandalous secret profession. Perhaps if she had written books more sanguine and suitable for gentlewomen—like the anonymous author of *Pride and Prejudice*—her work might be more accepted by society. But her first two stories involved pirates, kidnappings, and other sensational exploits wholly improper for a gentlewoman to read, let alone write about.

And perhaps she hadn't counted the cost of such a secret when her cousin Thomas convinced her to submit one of the stories she'd only ever shared with her family. Danbury and Sons had taken the book and, upon Emme's insistence and Thomas's keen business sense, chosen to keep the authorship of the story shrouded in mystery. Not even her family knew of the first publication, or her newly submitted second.

And neither did Simon.

Her heart fluttered at the very thought of him.

And their engagement needed to begin with complete honesty, despite her fear of his response to her secret. She had every intention of divulging her career to him once they were sequestered alone from the public's hearing. If they determined to keep her writing a secret, it wouldn't dampen his reputation at all.

They could just go on as they were in all of their delightful affections.

And though she had very few dealings with many of his relations, especially his cousin the Viscount of Ravenscross, the title carried esteem she never wished to sully.

"She's already putting on airs," came a loud whisper to her right.

Two ladies, Mrs. Wheaton and Mrs. Low, stood near the archway where Emme waited, doing very little to hide the object of their conversation.

"It truly is appalling the way she's practically thrown herself at him."

Emme increased the speed of her fan to cool the heat in her face and turned her attention away from the women. She'd never once thrown herself at Simon. Stumbled into him, perhaps. Crushed a foot once or twice. But never thrown anything at him, herself included.

In fact, if they hadn't chosen the same hiding spot while attempting to avoid unwelcome suitors, they would likely have never met at all. Rank ruled—quite literally, in some respects—but especially in the social world. Her smile spread at the memory of their amusing attempt to remain hidden and avoid scandal.

That one unexpected meeting began a humorous rhythm of consecutive encounters, which slowly grew into a friendship and then . . . something even sweeter than friendship.

All the rumors of the determined flirt, Simon Reeves, melded into an awareness that beneath the dashing facade lay a faithful heart worth the loving. And despite every sensible notion, every caution of society, every inward warning at the implausibility of the match, Emme had given her heart to him.

From all accounts and to her utter surprise, he'd responded in kind.

However, over the last few weeks, their clear preference for each other had become more apparent, which no doubt led to the newest rumors swirling about the ballroom. Emme hated being the topic of conversation.

"She's only a distraction for him until he finds a more suitable bride. Everyone knows he has no plans to marry until later, as he's so frequently professed," one of the ladies said.

Emme had heard those rumors too. Recognized the stories of Simon charming one lady after another with no real design to match himself to any of them.

But he had told her he meant to propose. *Tonight.*

Professed how she'd redirected his course.

Her face warmed as she smiled. And he'd told her he loved her.

"It would not be prudent to align himself with someone so beneath him," the other woman responded. "A motherless country gentleman's daughter? Lord Ravenscross would never approve."

Emme raised her fan to shadow her grin. But Lord Ravenscross had, by some miracle. In fact, Simon's cousin cared very little for the romantic entanglements of his uncle's eldest son, so without any resistance whatsoever, Simon was moving forward with his plans for tonight, where he promised to meet her in the Ruthtons' garden by the waterfall to make everything official.

She'd become his wife.

An elevation for her family, for certain, but even more than that, a perfect match for her heart.

After all, *he* wasn't a viscount, so at the foundation of rank, for the most part, they were the same: He was a gentleman's son and she a gentleman's daughter.

"Once he drops her, she'll be ruined. Everyone will know she'd chased after him and been found wanting."

Emme stepped away from the women, waving her fan in time with her pulse. She'd fought the worries of his future regret in the inequality of the match, wondered if he'd come to rue her lack of wealth or connections. But he'd quelled her doubts at every turn, promising her that their future happiness would overcome any of the social ramifications.

And he kept proving to be the veritable hero of any good novel.

She sighed. Only her hero wasn't reserved to the page.

The clock chimed the hour, and she turned her attention to the room. She'd not seen Simon since her arrival, but he often arrived late. In fact, she wondered whether he may already be waiting for her in the garden. With a rather saucy glance back to the gossipmongers, Emme slid down the hallway and out onto the steps of the veranda, breathing in the cool March air.

What a glorious way to end her very first St. Groves Season.

She'd barely made it to the steps into the garden when someone called her name.

Turning, she found a manservant approaching at a clipped speed. How very odd. How had he known where to find her?

And then something much less warm and delightful than her previous feelings quivered in her chest.

"Miss Lockhart?" He paused, still in the light of the doorway. "Miss Emmeline Lockhart?"

Her throat tightened. "Yes."

With a bow of his head, he offered her a card. "For you, Miss."

Hesitantly, she took the card, and the man removed himself back into the house. She slid her finger beneath the seal of the envelope and stepped forward into the light glowing from the doorway. The note held only a few words in a dearly familiar hand, but nothing about those words felt dear.

Everything has changed. Please forgive me.

S.

CHAPTER 1

A knock at the front door of anyone's house before ten o'clock in the morning rarely boded well for the home's inhabitants. And in this particular case, it boded abominably for Emmeline Lockhart.

She'd attempted to brace herself for the lengthy intrusion after her father's unexpected announcement the night before. Likely he'd waited until the very last moment to apprise his unsuspecting daughters of their fate.

Father, as good-hearted as he was, had a tendency to avoid conflict at all cost. When pressed, he sprung unwelcome information on people, and then he disappeared into his study or garden or nobody knew where for the aftermath of his revelation. Some people said that the loss of his dear wife after bringing Alfie, the lone Lockhart heir, into the world ten years ago had led him to an acute need for peace and tranquility, but in all truth, Father had fled conflict in every possible way well before Mother died. Over time, though, his tendency had grown almost chronic.

Another sharp knock echoed through the halls, and Emme could practically hear the doorframe flinch. As if everyone else in the house knew the eventual consequences of opening the door, no one did, prompting another impatient assault on the wood. Emme sighed. As the eldest daughter and in the absence of a mother's guidance, the responsibility of dealing with social expectations inevitably fell to her.

Even this.

Her posture wilted for only a second before she rallied.

She'd been preparing for this fateful confrontation since early morning, alternating between fervent prayers and envisioning it all as a comical plight for one of her novel characters. It did help to have an outlet for her frustrations.

Fictional disasters for fictional people were, after all, far safer than real-life ones.

Setting aside her spectacles and tucking away the slips of paper bearing her latest scribbles, Emme pushed her small pile of novels to the desk's corner, except for one—*The Heroine*—which she took in hand, should distraction become necessary.

She'd strategically placed her desk in this spot by the window for two reasons: One, it allowed morning light to bathe her in enough warmth to dampen any chill from the low-lit fires of the night, and two, the location afforded her a view of the entrance hallway if she twisted just so.

Carter, the long-suffering butler, ambled into view, his pace slower than usual, if that was even possible. The dear man had appeared ancient when Emme was a child, but now he seemed to have approached near antiquity, though his wits proved rather alert and his ears even more so, for good or ill.

He cast her a weathered look down the hallway, his jaw set for battle. Poor man. It was moments like this that she was certain he earned every shilling of his somewhat inflated salary.

Emme stood, novel in hand, and drew in a deep breath before the plunge. Once Carter opened that door, her blissfully quiet life would be turned on its head—for the next four months, at least.

Another series of heavy knocks ushered in the entrance of Aunt Albina Bridges, rather unaffectionately referred to as Aunt Bean, whose self-importance rose from the ends of her pearl-tip shoes to the zenith of her long and usually upturned nose.

She and Father failed to resemble each other at all, in looks or comportment. Whereas Father fled discord as a whole, Aunt Bean saw it as her duty to generously find or create crises wherever she went. In this respect, Emme tended more toward her father's disposition . . . and desire.

Unless in fiction, of course.

"It was quite irksome to remain on the stoop like a beggar for so long, Carter."

And the sweet greetings whisked down the hall with the same melodic ring as a new violinist.

"Now, Mother," came a smoother, more amiable voice, one that immediately brightened Emme's mood. Cousin Thomas. "It is still early. I would imagine Carter has been occupied with other matters this morning."

Where Aunt Bean created persistent offense, Thomas smoothed out the edges with wit and voice, a fortunate trait for a clergyman.

"Besides, Carter," Thomas continued in a mock whisper, which Emme heard well enough from down the hall, "it wasn't *that* long."

Emme's smile brimmed . . . until she heard the resounding click of Aunt Bean's cane as it tapped the floor. Closer and closer, like the march of troops advancing in combat. Each click increased Emme's pulse toward retreat.

She glanced around the room, hoping for reinforcements. Aster? Alfie? Even Benedict, the spaniel, would prove a happy distraction, but no, Emme stood alone, left to face the tampering talons of Aunt Bean.

If only Mother were here.

Without a daughter of her own, Aunt Bean relished her role as matchmaker with the fervor of Lady Ruthton's enthusiasm for hosting balls—a zeal so boundless that she had single-handedly transformed St. Groves into a pale imitation of Bath. And her adoring husband spared no expense. They'd even recently built a new hotel, a theater, and even a concert hall.

Her parties last year numbered fifteen!

Fifteen!

Emme's shoulders sagged yet again from the weight of her social future. Though, to be honest, she conveniently dodged five of the fifteen for various real and imagined illnesses or situations. After the difficulties of her first season, Father hadn't forced the issue.

Six clicks later, Aunt Bean came into view with Thomas at her side. In usual Thomas fashion, he wrestled with a smile, which countered the disposition of every previous rector in St. Groves. And if Thomas's youthfulness and temperament didn't spark a great deal of interest, his singleness certainly would.

"Good morning, Emme," Thomas offered before Aunt Bean pounced. "I'm glad to see you are awake and employed already." His gaze dropped to her book, one quizzical brow etching upward. "Devotional reading, I assume? To usher in the day?"

Emme tightened her grip on Eaton Stannard Barrett's entertaining novel and slipped it behind her back. "How could you doubt it?"

"Of course." A twinkle surfaced in his dark eyes before he turned to his mother. "Our cousin is a paragon of virtue, is she not, Mother?"

Not from what the gossips declared, but after almost two years, the tattling tongues of St. Groves had found new victims to exploit, leaving Emme's catastrophe well faded into infamy. Her inability to find a match last season may have resurfaced some murmurings but mostly pity, which likely sparked this very visit.

Aunt Bean heaved a sigh as large as her bosom and studied Emme from the top of her blonde head to the toe of her morning slippers. "Why is it that you are the only one to greet us this morning? Is everyone else inclined toward laziness?"

Laziness? Emme raised a brow, following Aunt Bean's survey of the room. Cowardice, perhaps.

"Actually, I do believe everyone else is otherwise engaged, Aunt." Which was true, even if "engaged" meant Father hiding in the library and Aster out for an extended morning walk. So extended, in fact, that she'd likely made it all the way into St. Groves by now. "Alfie is in lessons."

"Alfie?" Her cane tapped the floor as the name took agitated flight. "I have no interest in your brother. His future is secure. It is you and your sister for which the rescue must be made."

Rescue? Giving Aunt Bean the role of heroine seemed to defy the very definition of the word. At least for those to be "rescued."

But it was so. Gentlewomen had to be rescued by matrimony, inheritance, or death, for they were not usually given a living and were certainly not allowed to earn one.

Unless it was secret.

"Of course. It's just that we weren't expecting your visit quite so"—Emme almost said "early" but then thought better of it—"soon after your arrival. How have you found the rectory?"

Thomas opened his mouth to respond, but his mother overrode his attempt. "Better suited than I expected." Her face softened a little but not enough to garner much hope toward optimism. "I will not be ashamed to remain for the season. Thomas's uncle offered a rectory of no mean salary and situation. What parson do you know with five hundred a year?"

Thomas winced at the blunt declaration of his private matters. True, everyone knew, but the subject of such gossip rarely wished to hear it dangled about like a prize to be won. Or a horse to be sold.

"Indeed. I have no doubt my youngest son will be the talk of St. Groves in no time."

He already was, and none of the single ladies of the parish had even laid eyes on him yet. "Single" proved a powerfully magnetizing word among the Christian and pagan alike, especially when paired with such an income!

Emme raised her brows and smiled at Thomas. "I'm certain the position will make an excellent *match* of its own for Cousin Thomas."

His eyes narrowed in playful parrying as Emme continued. "I would hazard a guess the church will be particularly full this Sunday of people curious to hear from the new rector, especially the young ladies."

"Young ladies?" Aunt Bean's frown expanded her chin to three. "What do we care for other young ladies? We are here to discuss you, Emmeline." She stepped closer, narrowing her eyes and attention with such intensity that Emme's throat tightened. "I give you my word, I will have you married before I return to Bristol to celebrate my first grandchild's birth."

All humor fled Emme's body, replaced instead by a chill that ran up her spine at the determination emanating from Aunt Bean's terrifying expression. Why did the prospect of marriage have to sound more like a threat than a promise? Emme was certain the original design offered much more joy and happiness than whatever gleamed in Aunt Bean's pale eyes.

Thomas stepped in before Aunt Bean could elaborate further. "Mother, I know you are the preeminent expert on finding women husbands, if you *do* say so yourself." He studied his mother, the gleam in his eyes in contrast to his complacent grin. "But must we discuss matchmaking upon our first arrival at Thistlecroft?"

"How can we not?" Aunt Bean's entire body stiffened so fast that her hat shook. "We have much to repair!"

Thank you for the reminder, Aunt Bean. Yet another barb to stick into Emme's lingering incompetence. But she'd learned her lesson. Do not trust intelligence, handsome features, and a quick wit.

Or excellent dancing skills.

And delightful conversation.

Or a tender heart.

She nearly groaned. What on earth was left to rely upon?

"This is of utmost importance to Emmeline's future and weighs heavily on her father's mind."

It was unlikely Father spent a great deal of time considering his daughters' futures, but of course Father could be easily swayed into worrying about something or other, especially to ensure Aunt Bean's speedy departure. How the woman winkled her way into an invitation in the first place probably involved a little bullying, a heavy dose of guilt, and a massive amount of sweets.

"You haven't even met the prospects yet." Thomas cast a sympathetic look in Emme's direction. "There may not be a decent fellow in the lot."

"We are in St. Groves, Thomas." Her nose rose even higher, if that was possible. "Not some backwater country parish. There are plenty of eligible men who will do for Emmeline." Her hawk eyes returned to Emme. "Whether Emmeline will do for them is why I am required."

After another dramatic second of scrutiny, Aunt Bean released Emme from her gaze and stepped, cane in rhythm, to finally be poised in a chair. *Seated* was a much too relaxed word for Aunt Bean's position.

"Whether Emme will do for them?" Thomas's brows rose in exaggerated mock horror before he turned. Cradling his chin with his thumb and forefinger, he examined Emme, his gaze glimmering like the mischievous boy he used to be. "Well, her eyes are tolerably large and her nose has an acceptable slope." He waved a dismissive hand toward her, the dimple in one cheek the only mark of his teasing. "But there is the question of her chin."

Emme nearly lost complete control of her laugh. Thank God for Thomas and his desire to keep the conversation away from the past. Oh, how she'd missed him. Apart from her sister, Aster, he'd been her dearest friend in all the world. "Ah yes, many a marriage has been ruined over an imperfect chin."

"Chins are in fashion, I am told. And yours is suitable enough." Aunt Bean squinted in focused study of the offending protrusion. "But your nose is rather fine too, despite being marred by those unsightly freckles. The waters in Bath would do wonders for your complexion, Emmeline."

Emme bit her smile into submission. Thank the Lord she wasn't wearing her spectacles to complete the ensemble of inadequacies. "I have heard similar tales."

"She's not too tall," Thomas interjected with a lopsided grin. "And she does read devotionally."

Emme rolled her eyes. Trust her cousin to weave such nonsense into her aunt's relentless critique.

"I have every confidence we will secure an excellent match now that I am here to set things right." Aunt Bean raised her cane like a pointer. "We start at a disadvantage, naturally, but despite the mishap of your first season, followed by an unfruitful second, your reputation has only been slightly tarnished. Mercifully, no true scandal has occurred, even if its stench remains."

How reassuring. No true scandal—only mortifying humiliation and the lingering ache of a shattered heart. But what were those trifles when set against the towering edifice of matrimony?

"A woman grows wiser and stronger when thwarted in love," Aunt Bean added, as though dispensing great wisdom. "And the further we stay from scandal, the better your prospects. A faded rose is still a rose."

Encouragement clearly wasn't Aunt Bean's natural gift.

"Mother," Thomas drawled, "I do believe you're verging on sentimental. None of us are prepared for such a shift." With a sly glance at Emme, he added, "However, if I must indulge this rare moment, I'd say Emme's finest qualities are her quick wit and her good heart."

Thomas's gaze searched Emme's, voicelessly seeking her mood, so she offered a small smile in return. Her good heart proved all too naive, leaving her wiser only in the art of heartbreak. However, her experiences had at least lent a certain realism to her fictional tales of rakish heroes, dashed hopes, and clandestine liaisons turned disastrous.

She sighed. While her modest ventures as a novelist fell short of true disgrace, the revelation would hardly enhance her standing, especially in the wake of her first season's embarrassment. Aunt Bean, she suspected, would be positively apoplectic if the truth ever emerged.

With Thomas's help, she had kept her little profession hidden by granting him full control of her business affairs. No one thought twice about a man negotiating contracts and royalties, after all. She didn't even know how much she'd earned from her three books, only that the reviews had softened considerably since her debut effort.

"Don't be ridiculous, Thomas," Aunt Bean declared with the finality of a gavel. "Her best feature is her two thousand pounds. It may not be as enticing as some other ladies' fortunes, but I feel we can use her first season's . . . misstep . . . and last season's reticence to evoke the proper amount of sympathy for her marital plight. It is understandable that Emmeline should fear stepping back out after the blemish to her reputation, which will only increase compassion from the mothers of sons in want of a wife. Her excellent family"—she raised her chin with pride at full tilt—"should elevate her to a competitive standing with at least one marriageable gentleman of the gentry."

Now *she* felt like the mare in a horse race.

"I have made a list of some of the most suitable candidates," Aunt Bean continued, extracting a carefully folded slip of paper from her reticule and handing it to Emme with the air of a royal decree.

"A *list*?" The word burst from Thomas. He cast his mother a sharp glance. "Really, Mother, is this necessary?"

"Emmeline did not have my guidance the last two seasons and look how those turned out," she replied with unshakable conviction. "I shall steer her toward men who are not only upstanding but also well within her means. One of the difficulties with your first seasons, Emmeline, was that you aimed too high above your station, dear girl."

Emme did not feel very "dear" at the moment. "He was a gentleman, Aunt Bean . . . Albina," Emme corrected. "We are of the same station."

Though the word *gentleman* was perhaps a generous stretch. Simon Reeves had charmed her with kind words, unexpected attentions, and stolen moments: a carriage ride alone and—heat rose to her cheeks—a near kiss in the garden.

He had made her believe he cared.

Cared enough for . . . forever.

Then he'd left her to deal with the consequences: whispers of impropriety, the sting of being deemed "tainted," and the bruising weight of a broken heart. She should have known better. Simon's reputation as a flirt was well documented, his name even linked with the likes of the infamous Selena Hemston on one occasion. It seemed he lived up to the charm without any intention of hurting or truly pursuing the ladies involved. And yet, she had foolishly believed he'd been different with her.

That he'd . . . loved her.

Aunt Bean, of course, referred to Simon's newly altered position. When he had courted Emme, their social difference had been present but not insurmountable. He was simply the heir to a modest estate. Yet everything had changed with the tragic deaths of his father and cousin. Now Simon was the Viscount of Ravenscross, the inheritor of an ancient title, an expansive estate, and, if rumor held true, significant debts. His responsibilities—and expectations—had grown exponentially.

"A man in Lord Ravenscross's position will only trifle with the heart of a girl with a mere two thousand pounds," Aunt Bean declared, punctuating her words with an imperious wave of her finger. "He will marry someone much richer. So keep your head this season, Emmeline, and do not let yourself be drawn into another . . . dalliance."

"You have no worry on that score." Emme's words escaped with more force than she intended, her face flaming. "If I never see him again, it will be too soon."

Aunt Bean's dark eyes narrowed. "Do you not read the society pages?"

All heat drained from Emme's face as she looked from Thomas to Aunt Bean. "What do you mean?"

"Rumor has it that Lord Ravenscross is back in St. Groves and in search of a wealthy wife."

CHAPTER 2

"Well, there it is in black-and-white. You must find a wife."

Simon Reeves's body braced against the invisible blow from his so-called friend, Benjamin Northrop, as the man set his glass on the table with as deafening a finality as his words. His reference to the newest tattle in the social pages somehow incited a pain just above Simon's right eye.

A wife. The very word felt like a shackle, the weight of it pressing sharp against Simon's already overburdened chest. It was a notion he had avoided considering for as long as possible, clinging instead to the naive hope that he might find some other way to salvage the future of his estate and family.

But of course the world offered no such reprieve. Not for him. Especially in a set of consecutive tragedies that started not two years before.

"Marry?" Simon placed his own glass down, rolling the word around on his tongue like a bitter draught. "Because the local tattle says so?" He raised a brow and fixed Benjamin with a look. "A fine proposition it would be for some unsuspecting bride: marry into ruin, inherit a family in chaos, and call it happily ever after. A welcome haven for any of Lady Ruthton's protégées."

Yet even as he mocked the idea, Simon couldn't entirely dismiss it. If one of Lady Ruthton's protégées came with a dowry large enough to restore his crumbling estate, perhaps the idea wasn't as preposterous as he pretended. His pride bristled at the thought, but his situation left no room for such luxuries as pride. Ravenscross needed funds, and it needed them urgently.

"The last lot," Simon continued, tone dry, "did little else but talk nonsense, fret over lace, and read Gothic novels."

His thoughts stammered against his own words. Except one.

The familiar burn of shame twisted through his chest. What a fool he'd been. An arrogant, reckless fool. He had never intended to meet Emmeline Lockhart, let alone court her. Their first encounter had been entirely unplanned, a serendipitous meeting that left him unexpectedly disarmed. Against all sense and propriety, he had let himself care for her. And when he should have walked away, he continued, unwilling to release the sweetness . . . the authentic nature of their connection.

And then she'd become the first casualty of his world falling apart.

She deserved far better than a man forced to choose duty over affection.

"Needs must, Simon," Ben quipped, his gaze flicking pointedly toward the threadbare tapestries and the dim, insufficient light of the drawing room. "Gothic novels may well prepare them for your family and estate."

Simon refused to follow his friend's directive. Updates and candles were luxuries that Ravenscross could scarcely afford. They barely had enough in the coffers to pay the remaining servants, let alone fund repairs. And the debts left by his cousin with the estate—not to mention his father—were as numerous as they were insurmountable.

Even after all these months of the truth being thrust into his face on a daily basis, it still felt surreal, this sudden turn of fortune that had made him Lord Ravenscross. Two years ago, the title had been a distant prospect, held by a cousin Simon barely knew, and destined, Simon had assumed, to pass to his cousin's yet-to-be born son from a yet-to-be-wed wife. But then came the letter—the one that informed him of the storm off the Indies that had claimed the lives of both his cousin and his father. How was he to have known his father had gotten himself entrenched in Cousin Rupert's nasty affairs? And how was Simon to have known he'd end up paying for the mismanagement and profligate spending of two men who should have ensured the reputation and future of Ravenscross?

Of course he hadn't known. Hadn't even fathomed.

And so the estate, the title, the responsibility—it had all landed on him with staggering suddenness, shattering the carefree existence he'd once known, altering every plan. The first six months, he'd passed so much time attempting to understand his new role while uncovering the extent of his father's massive loss in trade and his cousin's liberal spending, he'd not noticed his mother's failing health. But when his brother Theodore joined the military ranks to fight the French, it had served as the last loss for his mother. Within months she'd succumbed to illness and grief, which appeared to propel his sister Arianna to run away with her proposed lover.

After all those months, all those heartrending months, Simon Reeves—once carefree and certain of his place in the world—no longer existed. The man who bore the title Viscount of Ravenscross was burdened, humbled, and all too aware of his inadequacies.

"You flatter me, Ben," Simon said with forced levity. "I fear my very real life may exceed the requirements of any Gothic novel."

Ben's smirk disappeared. "I wish it were fiction for you, Simon. God knows I do. But you had no hand in your cousin's decisions or your parents' fates, and you cannot change Arianna's. Besides, you've done all you can to find her. Months of searching. You've kept the estate afloat against impossible odds. But you can't solve everything with sheer will. It's time to think practically."

Practically? He almost laughed. As if the burden of practicality hadn't been thrust upon him from the moment that blasted letter arrived. But what to do? He felt the answer but didn't want to accept it as his only option, so he offered another deflective smile. "I assume the gossip mill has also selected my bride for me?"

And his friend's humor resurfaced with its usual buoyancy. "Not yet, but give it time. They've already chosen your replacements for half the tapestries in this house."

Simon huffed a laugh despite himself, though the sound lacked any real humor. "As if new tapestries will fix anything."

"They might." Ben's tone remained light. "But they'll require a dowry to match. Which circles us back to the matter at hand."

Simon had tried to stall such a decision by learning the hard work of labor. Once, he'd scoffed at tradesmen, but in the past months, he'd known the hand-callousing occupation of mending fences to save the sheep they desperately needed for income. Wool remained an ever-present need and sheep were aplenty. He'd become familiar with the feel of a hammer as he attempted to shore up some loose boards in the stables. And somehow, within the work, he'd learned to appreciate things he'd never even noticed before.

The true value of a coin or a faithful servant or a sturdy wall.

The importance of good people and hard work.

And the realization that desperation truly did lead to ingenuity . . . but also, as he felt it now, resignation.

"If you marry well and a woman of good reputation, it will restore more than the estate." Ben leaned forward, his tone taking on an earnest edge. "It will elevate your family, provide for your siblings, and allow you to hire a proper governess for the younger three."

Simon groaned, dragging a hand down his face. What governess could possibly withstand the youngest three Reeves children? Aunt Agatha was the only one who'd ever managed to keep them in line, and she'd deserted Ravenscross a month ago to visit an ailing friend, leaving Simon to navigate the treacherous waters of guardianship alone.

"The prospect is not so bad," Ben continued. "I hear marriage can be pleasant—with the right person."

Emmeline Lockhart's face flashed in Simon's mind unbidden, bringing with it a familiar ache. As reckless as he'd been with her emotions, his affection had been sincere. He'd cherished their conversations, her laughter, her sharp humor. If things had been different—if his cousin hadn't died, if his father hadn't squandered his fortune, if the title hadn't fallen to him—he would have known a future with someone he loved.

Simon's eyes closed. There was no use torturing himself with what-ifs. He had to turn his mind from Miss Lockhart and face what was.

Now, he was Lord Ravenscross, and duty had to come first.

"Marriage? A pleasant option?" He forced a grin and gestured toward Ben. "Says the bachelor with whom I'll be competing this season. Tell me, will you take your own advice and seek out a wife of good fortune? Perhaps even find this 'right person' you so readily recommend?"

Ben's smile was maddeningly unrepentant. "I'm not opposed to the idea, should the right one present herself. But unlike you, my friend, I can afford to be selective." He stood, looming over Simon both in height and ease of circumstance. "You, alas . . ." He tsked, smile crooked to soften the blow. "But I shall give you first choice since you're desperate and I am not."

"How gracious of you." Simon reached for his drink, letting the sharp tang dull his sarcasm. Desperation was an unsavory word—one he loathed to apply to himself. Yet here he was, neck-deep in it.

God help him. That prayer had become his refrain of late. No one else could help him. Not if he wished to save the estate and marry a woman who would accept his family. It would take a miracle, and he wasn't too certain God had any left to spare for him and his brood.

Simon stood, grateful at least that where Ben bettered him in height, Simon excelled in breadth of shoulders.

"Take heart." Ben failed to control his grin. "Your somewhat . . . colorful past and current predicament lend you an air of mystery. Ladies will find you a vast deal more alluring. Work up a brooding scowl or two, and you're nigh irresistible."

Simon snorted. A scowl? That he could manage. What with a strong-willed brother off fighting the French, a runaway sister, and his three youngest siblings, who were one step shy of feral.

"See, that expression will do quite well." Ben gestured toward Simon's face. "The ladies will swoon."

Simon pinned Ben with a look. "Why are we friends?"

Ben's laugh echoed off the parlor walls and offered a momentary levity, but the respite was short lived.

The library door creaked open, just wide enough to allow twelve-year-old William space to slip into the room. Pale and thin, the boy's pallor had the matrons at church constantly murmuring over his health, but since the sun rarely touched the boy's face, there was no other tint he could possess.

He offered Ben a tentative nod—a small but significant improvement from the last time Ben had visited—before fixing his gaze on Simon.

Simon's chest tightened. "What is it, Will?"

The boy flinched, shrinking under Simon's scrutiny. Simon silently cursed himself. Had he been too sharp? Or was William simply that skittish? Perhaps both. He'd been gone far too long, chasing the faintest traces of Arianna while his youngest siblings grieved and floundered without the proper guidance of their eldest brother. Another failure to add to his growing ledger.

"Lottie's gone missing," he stammered, his words barely audible. "Mrs. Patterson sent me to fetch you."

"Not again," Ben groaned. "Didn't this happen on my last visit?"

Simon refrained from admitting that Charlotte's disappearances were a near-daily occurrence. "Which direction did she go?"

William looked away and shrugged. "I w-wasn't outside."

Of course not. The boy likely had been sitting by one of the upstairs windows reading or painting. Simon placed a hand on William's shoulder. "Thank you for letting me know, Will."

William's body eased under the touch, and he offered the faintest of smiles. It was enough to cement Simon's resolve. He'd failed these children before, but no more. In the absence of their parents, he would do whatever it took to protect them. To be a better man.

He had to. There was nothing else for it.

Simon dashed from the room and down the hall, bypassing the grand staircase to his left, the unused ballroom on his right, and the dining room, which now rarely hosted family members, let alone guests. Ben followed on his heels.

At the main back door, Mrs. Patterson awaited them, her apron streaked with mud and her expression one of weary exasperation.

Oh, dear Lord, Simon inwardly prayed. *Please don't let her leave us.*

Mrs. Patterson was the linchpin holding their fraying household together, especially in Aunt Agatha's absence. She'd been steadfast for years, even when Simon's selfishness before his parents' deaths might have driven her away. Surely the kindly housekeeper could see his efforts to atone for those past failings, even if they didn't always manifest in his siblings' behavior.

"I'm so sorry, Mrs. Patterson. If I'd been here more regularly—"

"Charlotte had her tendencies before you left, sir." She sighed and studied Simon for a moment, those clear eyes softening around the edges. "But it's good you're here now because the more eyes on this brood, the better."

Her ready kindness humbled him all the more. She deserved sainthood, without a doubt. "I'm here to stay," he whispered—the words as much a promise to himself as to her—then stepped back, clearing his throat. "Do you have any idea where she might have gone?"

"I haven't the foggiest, sir." Mrs. Patterson wiped her forehead with the back of her hand, glancing down at the muddy smears on her apron without so much as a sigh. "But let us hope it's not back to Mr. Dean's stables. Last time she went there, they nearly shot her for trying to 'rescue' one of his horses she claimed was being mistreated."

Simon drew in a breath and cast a glance to Ben from his periphery. His friend's look of confusion twisted into a slight hue of horror. A legitimate assessment for someone who hadn't lived through the last few months learning the idiosyncrasies of the lot.

Lottie had gone positively wild since their mother's death, and Arianna's disappearance had only exacerbated her defiance. It was as though Lottie aimed to challenge the entire world.

Beyond the back door, the late-morning skyline stretched before Simon—a pine forest to the left, pastures rolling out to the right, and the Hemston property abutting their land at the far edge. Somewhere past these familiar boundaries lay St. Groves, quiet and indifferent to his mounting struggles.

"Miss Sophia is in the water puddles with the dogs again." Mrs. Patterson looked up at him, holding his gaze. "This time, she's catching frogs and refuses to come inside to be bathed."

Ben's horror must have worn off because he chuckled . . . fueling Simon's growing headache.

"I believe Miss Sophia knows exactly where her sister went and is disinclined to share the information, my lord."

Simon's lips pressed into a thin line. "Is she?" He eyed the overgrown garden, already suspecting the answer.

"But you have a way with her, sir." Mrs. Patterson's voice gentled. "She wants to please you."

The statement warmed a knotted spot in Simon's chest. Could he have some good influence on these children yet? It wasn't too late to redirect whatever path they currently were careening down, was it?

He gave Mrs. Patterson a grateful nod and strode into the garden, a tangled expanse of greenery that once flourished under his mother's loving care. The scene was too much like his own life at the moment to linger on the view.

As Simon reached the nearest bend in the garden path, his gaze fell upon the central fountain, a pair of stone swans poised in eternal embrace. Beyond it, a familiar cascade of wild curls peeked out from behind a cluster of flowering shrubs. Fair hair. Sophia was the only child with such a hue, so like their mother's.

A sudden pang tightened his chest. Grief had an uncanny way of rising at the most inconvenient moments. He refused to succumb to the pull and stepped toward the shrubs. "Fia?" His tone of voice wasn't as gentle as he'd hoped, so he tried again. "Fia, love?"

Perhaps adding the "love" helped a little. Mother always seemed to respond with a smile on the rare occasions Father used it.

Rounding the fountain, Simon found the five-year-old crouched beside the stream, a wriggling frog clutched triumphantly in one mud-streaked hand while the other absently patted Dodger, the ever-loyal hound. Fia had practically lived outside all summer, and even as the season waned, his fairy-sister kept to her routine of earth and sky. Her focus remained fixed on the frog as though the rest of the world had simply melted away.

"Fia," he repeated, and this time she looked up at him, her round face lighting with a toothless grin.

Variations of plant life stuck from the little girl's curls, giving off the appearance of Medusa's snakes. Mud smudged her cheeks, her neck, and the once-white pinafore over her dress.

Perhaps William's look of terror was founded, especially with such sisters.

In fact, the longer Simon lived, the more terrifying women became.

"Simon, I found diamonds." The sweet voice doused some of his ire—the toothless grin probably helped too. "Come see."

The exasperation knotting his chest unraveled slightly. He

counted to ten in the steps it took to make it to her side. How could he blame her? She barely remembered their parents, so the fault for her behavior lay completely on his shoulders.

He was beginning to think his shoulders were not so broad after all.

He knelt beside her. "Show me, lamb."

The endearment somehow had her edging nearer, or perhaps it was the fact she wanted him there. Close?

"Do you see?" She pointed eagerly to a cluster of quartz glinting beneath the water's surface. "Aren't they lovely?"

"They are quite lovely."

"Do you think they can help us pay for the blasted repairs?" She blinked those piercing brown eyes up at him.

The mixture of her repeating his "blasted repairs" sentiment paired with the desire to find a way to help mend their home took all words from his mind. In fact, his throat closed with more emotion than he cared to contemplate.

He lowered his head and swallowed—gathering himself—and then gentled a palm against her shoulder while ignoring the frog, which appeared to be wrestling for its life. "You are so kind and clever, but I'm afraid these particular types of diamonds will not be able to help us."

A frown pulled at her bottom lip.

"But," he added quickly, somehow finding his smile, "they'd make a fine addition to the library table. What do you say I help you collect them after we've found Charlotte?"

Her eyes brightened. "You would help me?"

His mind reared against the request. He didn't have time. Not with all he needed to do, but the hope in her eyes proved his undoing. "Yes, but only after we find your sister."

Sigh. *Yet another sister to find.*

She rewarded him with a double-dimpled grin. "She went that way on her pony." Fia pointed toward the north fields. "But the pony wasn't behaving, so she was fussing at him. Blasted ponies!"

A snort of laughter erupted from behind him, but Simon resolutely ignored Ben's amusement.

"Thank you, Fia." Simon gave the girl a kiss on the one clean spot on her forehead and stood, turning to Ben. "You *really* don't have to stay."

Ben didn't take the hint. "I've grown accustomed to looking for lost people when I visit you, Ravenscross." He shrugged a shoulder. "Besides, it's the most adventure I've had all week."

And to think Simon used to grow bored on nice, quiet days.

Foolish man. Quiet, uneventful days sounded positively divine.

Simon shot Ben a glare before setting off at a clipped pace in the direction Fia had indicated. Fortunately, not a half hour into the walk, Charlotte and her pony came into view as the thirteen-year-old rode back toward home.

With a great deal of effort, Simon curbed his inner fury.

"Did you really have to come looking for me?" she called out as they approached. "I wasn't even a mile away."

Her unrepentant response did little to assist his self-control. "How many times have I told you that you cannot leave the house without alerting someone to your whereabouts?"

Her chin came up, those fiery brown eyes narrowing. "I told Fia."

"Fia is five," Simon retorted, stepping forward to meet her and the pony. "You must inform an adult, Charlotte. I am responsible for your safety."

"No one's safe here," she shot back. "And I've been doing fine on my own while you've been away. Someone needed to look after the younger children."

Her words struck a nerve, their truth undeniable. She had been forced to grow up too quickly. Even with Aunt Agatha's guidance, the weight of responsibility had fallen far too heavily on Lottie's young shoulders.

He shouldn't have gone after Arianna—certainly not for so long. The youngest three had needed him. But well, to be honest, he hadn't known what to do. Perhaps he'd run away as much out of cowardice in facing his impossible future as to find his ruined sister.

"I am here now," Simon replied, his tone firm. "And I expect you to inform an adult when you leave the house."

"I am not a prisoner," she snapped. "You don't ask William or Teddy to report their whereabouts."

"William never leaves the house and Teddy is a grown man," Simon countered, though not certain if the military had reformed or exacerbated his younger brother's rambunctious ways. "I've already failed by losing one sister, Lottie. Do you wish to cause me to lose a second?"

He hadn't meant to voice the words. They'd slipped out before he'd even thought them. But he felt them. Every single day he felt them. Arianna's disappearance haunted him, like so many of the other failings flashing before him.

Charlotte's defiance faltered, her expression softening just enough to show she'd understood. She was too perceptive by half, her awareness far beyond any other thirteen-year-old's. He had to be more controlled. More careful. The burden was *his*. Not hers.

Simon shook his head, needing to shift the subject. "Where were you headed anyway?"

Her chin tilted once more, though the fire in her eyes dimmed slightly. "Lord Hemston's son has archery lessons on Tuesday afternoons. I've watched every one."

"You ride your pony to watch Lord Hemston's son's archery lessons every Tuesday?"

Ben feigned a cough to cover his laugh.

"How else am I to learn? You won't teach me," she said with a pointed look.

"I promised to teach you when you got older." However, he inwardly winced at the unfulfilled pledge.

"You always say that," she replied coolly, nudging her pony forward. "But it never happens. Someday I shall dress as a boy and join a hunt myself. Then I'll learn."

She rode past as if she hadn't heightened Simon's concern to near implosion.

"By the way, the sheep are getting out over the back fence into Lord Hemston's pasture." She tossed a haughty smile over her shoulder, her dark hair fluttering loose in the breeze. "I thought you'd want to know."

Lord, help me. He wanted to throttle her.

If Simon's shoulders could have descended any farther while he stood upright, they would have. He couldn't continue living life like this—for his own sake as well as for his siblings'.

As if reading his internal thoughts, Ben stepped up beside him and exhaled audibly. "You need a wife, Simon." Ben shook his head and studied Lottie's retreating frame as if the girl had taken on terrifying qualities. "Or her money, at the very least." He met Simon's gaze. "You really have no choice."

CHAPTER 3

S imon was back?

Emmeline's throat squeezed in a breath as she ushered all her strength to maintain a neutral expression. *Simon.*

Her heart pitched again. Perhaps if she stopped referring to him as Simon, it would help. "Lord Ravenscross" felt suitably distant—less personal, less capable of conjuring a roguish smile or tender look. She had thought herself well on the path to conquering her feelings, of moving beyond him, but the mere prospect, after all this time, of seeing him across a ballroom or theater sent her composure to tatters.

Her fingers pinched around her book to the cramping point.

"I have already encouraged your father to purchase a subscription to the season, particularly to the fancy balls." Aunt Bean smiled, or so Emme thought, but Aunt Bean's smiles never seemed to understand the full intention. "Eighteen this year."

Eighteen? Emme wrenched her thoughts from striking blue eyes and shattering humiliation to focus on her aunt's words. Eighteen fancy balls? She had barely survived the ten she'd attended last year, and that had been when Simon wasn't even present. The thought of enduring such a parade of insipid introductions, relentless chatter, and suffocating crowds—this time with Simon likely among them—was enough to wither her to the floor.

Surely there weren't even enough eligible men in St. Groves to warrant so many balls.

Perhaps if she managed to offend everyone by the fifth ball, she could graciously bow out of the rest, leaving Aster to secure the next family wedding.

"We will succeed, Emmeline Lockhart, if it is the last thing I do." Aunt Bean's penetrating gaze locked onto hers, as if the sheer force of her will could extract all resistance. And despite the chill running up Emme's arms at the sight, she realized she'd just uncovered marvelous inspiration for a new character in her latest novel.

The readers would be duly terrified.

Thomas, bless him, stepped forward as if to intervene in the hypnotic moment. But a noise from behind turned everyone's attention toward the hall, where Emme's father attempted to disappear into his study through the back stair.

"John, is that you?" Aunt Bean's voice sliced through the air with the precision of an expert arrow, freezing Father mid-step.

Father turned, eyes as wide as a barn owl's, brown brows quivering upward. He paused, sent a longing look toward his study door, and then, with a deep breath that straightened his entire body, he turned.

"Bina, you've come already?" He failed to add any surprise in his tone.

"Of course I've come." Aunt Bean also failed to notice. "How could I not, given your evident desperation?"

Desperation? Even Emme, whose situation could be charitably described as precarious, found the word overly dramatic, but the drama appeared to work wonders to encourage a deepening of the wrinkles around Father's eyes. He blinked behind his spectacles, and Aunt Bean took that as her cue for clarification.

"We have no time to lose. Emme has already endured two failed seasons, complete with public humiliation at the hands of a rake, and she is nearly twenty with no prospects in sight."

If trusting Simon Reeves had been Emme's great mistake, she had little faith in society's judgment to steer her toward someone better. How was she to trust herself in the brutal machinery of the marriage mart again? Simon had seemed so different—gentle, charming, impossibly dashing. No one had warned her of his tendency to flirt to the edge of propriety and then drop the woman like a stone—or so that was how it felt as she stood alone in the garden two years before. And he hadn't seemed the sort. Not once she'd gotten to know him. Not once he'd become her friend.

"Mother, if I may clarify," Thomas interjected, stepping to Emme's side and resting a reassuring hand on her arm. "The rake in question succeeded only in revealing his own deficiencies, earning Emmeline nothing but sympathy from those who matter. His true colors came clear in the end."

"Which is all the more proof of why I am needed." Aunt Bean sniffed, tapping her cane sharply against the floor. "Sympathy is cold comfort in these matters. A lady's reputation is a delicate thing, Emmeline, and even the faintest breath of impropriety can leave an indelible mark. Society does not forgive indiscretions, no matter how undeserved. I have ample lessons for both you and your sister on how to catch an appropriate husband."

Husband catching? Aunt Bean mentioned catching a husband as if it were like catching a cold. If a man required catching, perhaps it was better to let him escape entirely. Indeed, with the memory of Mr. Reeves—or rather, Lord Ravenscross, as he was now—and the quiet hope inherent in her little secret, perhaps marriage wasn't a necessity at all. Couldn't real life echo the gumption of one of her fictional heroines?

Could she be . . . brave enough to strive for independence?

Thomas coughed into his hand and then gave a slight dip to his head. "Well, Uncle John, while you and Mother discuss the very serious sport of husband catching, would you mind if Emme gave me a tour of your garden? It's been a while since last I saw it, and I believe it may provide some inspiration for my own improvements at the parsonage."

The corner of Emme's lips twitched. She could certainly appreciate this sort of rescue.

Father, well aware of Thomas's gallant intentions, paused. His shoulders slumped slightly at the prospect of being left alone with Aunt Bean, but with a sigh, he stepped forward with reluctant resolve. "Of course. I am certain the garden will provide ample . . . inspiration."

With a slight bow, Thomas offered his arm, and Emme walked with him toward the back of the house.

Once they were outdoors, surrounded by sunlight and the whisper of late-summer birdsong, Thomas broke the silence. "I feel as though I owe you an apology." His playful tone contrasted the contrition in his words. "If I hadn't taken this appointment so near to St. Groves, it wouldn't have brought Mother—and all her glory—down upon you."

A laugh bubbled up despite herself, a much-needed release from the tension coiling her stomach. "How could you not take it? Your uncle's rectory is a most generous offer, and as a third son, your options were . . . limited." She shrugged, following the garden path away from the house toward a gazebo at the edge of a hedgerow. "At least you love the church."

He gave her a half smile. "I'm obliged to say so after earning a bachelor of divinity in addition to my other degree."

She squeezed his arm with her hand. "You jest, but underneath all your teasing, I know you are really happy."

He responded with a good-natured shrug, though his eyes betrayed his contentment. As they rounded a curve in the garden path, placing them out of view of the house, he reached into his coat pocket and produced a thick envelope. "Speaking of happiness," he said, "I thought some additional pin money might benefit you and Aster as you launch into the upcoming season."

Launch? What a word! But before Emme could reply, Thomas pushed the envelope into her hand. The paper bulged from the contents. "What is this?"

"Money, clearly." He lowered his voice. "Your earnings."

"Oh, Thomas!" She pressed the envelope back toward him,

glancing around as if the entire household were spying from the windows. "I thought we agreed you'd keep it invested until I was ready to tell Father."

"It's been over two years, Emme. Three books. At some point, you must tell him."

"Must I?" Her grip on the envelope tightened. In reality, how long could she keep this secret from her father?

"Why not? It's 1813." His palm came up as if the declaration changed everything. "There aren't a great many, to be sure, but more women are writing novels than ever. What about that woman who wrote one of your favorite books? *Pride and Prejudice*? At least she reveals herself as a lady, even if she doesn't use her name."

Emme tilted her chin, staring out at the rolling green hills. "Because anonymity suits my purposes. My pseudonym brings no scandal, no suspicion. And with the shadow of my failed seasons still looming, the timing couldn't be worse. Can you imagine Father dealing with the potential conflict of such information when he's already shouldering the work of a single parent to three? And after my first season's disastrous—"

"Mr. Reeves . . . Lord Ravenscross," Thomas spat out the correction. "His actions were not your fault and no one of consequence thinks so." He steadied his serene eyes on her. "The right man will encourage your pursuits, Emme. He'll support you—writing and all."

Would it were true. Why did she feel as if young women were poised on the edge of a knife and one wrong step easily led to eternal disaster?

And a well-positioned and respected gentleman supporting a bride who wrote novels? She refrained from rolling her eyes. Not everyone was as clear sighted or open minded as Thomas Bridges.

They walked on in silence a little longer. "I would help you tell your father if you—"

Her palm raised, stopping his words. "Please, Thomas. Not now.

Besides, I think I am better off writing for the joy of the story than considering profit and loss. The less I know, the easier it is to pretend that E.K. Winsome is someone else entirely and solely separate from me, which will serve all of us better for Aunt Bean's husband . . . catching."

"Very well. Then I'll quit my argument for now." He held her gaze and narrowed his eyes. "For now. But when you are ready, your accounts and"—he gestured toward himself—"your favorite cousin will be at your service."

The silence slipped between them as they stepped up to the gazebo to take a seat inside. "I do wonder, Emme, if it might not do you some good to write a story with less . . . shadows."

She looked up from the envelope she'd just discreetly tucked into her book. "What do you mean?"

"Well, these books by the anonymous lady are laced with real life and humor. They still include the romance you adore but with, dare I say it, a subtlety of heart?" His smile crooked in an encouraging way. "I believe your wit and clever observation of the world around you would fit a similar style."

Write of real life? Emme frowned and looked back at *The Heroine* in her hands. She readied an argument on her tongue for how uninteresting such a book would be, but then her disagreement died when she reflected on both *Pride and Prejudice* and her most recent read, *Sense and Sensibility*. They'd held her interest but also left her with the most glorious sense of happiness at the end. As if she could step right into that story, meet the characters, and engage in conversations.

Could she write something so . . . familiar?

"Clearly, your current novels are doing well, but perhaps you could think about broadening your skills. Many ladies of your acquaintance are more likely to live lives similar to a country gentleman's daughter than"—he gestured toward her—"your mysterious Arabella Somersby."

He referenced the heroine of her latest book and the poor woman's plight from housemaid to stowaway to captive in a castle before finding her dashing romance on the far side of the sea.

"I'll think about it." She raised her book to him, nodding toward the envelope. "And thank you for this. I suppose if I am to catch a husband, having a new gown or two would meet Aunt Bean's approval." And perhaps help Emme stop pairing each of her current dresses with an event in time associated with Simon. "And Aster would delight in some new things." She breathed in the plan, especially if it meant promoting her sister. "She captures the room wherever she goes, even when she doesn't want to. I wouldn't be surprised if she's not swept up into a lasting romance long before me."

Thomas's hand rested briefly on her arm. "Lord Ravenscross does no credit to his sex, so do not measure yourself by his standards."

Her throat tightened as she absorbed his words all the way down to her wounded heart. How could she have been so blind? Surely, not having a mother to guide her had led to some weakness on her part, but she had been such a fool. In fact, she'd written about such cads in her novels. How had she failed to recognize the signs in real life?

She paused on the thought. Perhaps there was some benefit in writing real life after all. She knew heartbreak. Knew scandal, unfortunately. Could those elements inspire an engaging story that reflected the loves and losses of a regular life?

"I can't imagine there being a great deal more marriageable options than last year, Thomas." She forced lightness into her tone. "It's not London." With the envelope in hand, however, the heaviness of the daunting task lifted a bit more. "But at least I have options. Marriage isn't the only path forward, which is always an improvement over feeling desperate."

"Undeniably."

"And I'll play the part for Aunt Bean."

He grinned. "Though I expect you'll disappear from every ball as quickly as decorum permits."

She raised her brows in mock innocence. "A lady is expected certain allowances, cousin-dear."

"Hmm." He shook his dark head, his grin growing. "Now you're taking advantage of being a woman, are you?"

She ignored his sarcasm and stared ahead, a sweet sense of opportunity dangling before her with each book she published. Though she adored the idea of a family of her own, perhaps marriage wasn't her only option. Her shoulders pinched at the thought. But if a man couldn't accept her as an authoress, would she be willing to give up writing?

If he loved her.

Her jaw tightened. Yes. Only love would induce her to marry.

"If I can use writing to become independent, then I can earn a choice very few women of my station or reputation have." She turned to him, drawing in a freeing breath. "I will hold out for love or become an independent and happy spinster. Either way, I'll settle for nothing less."

Lights and music spilled into St. Groves' illustrious Assembly Rooms, the premier setting for the season's most sought-after balls. Simon Reeves paused at the threshold, tugging his cavalier vest into place beneath his tailcoat. Doing so allowed a few more moments to compose himself before stepping into the fray.

The last ball he'd attended, he'd arrived with the single purpose of proposing.

And she'd looked radiant that evening—utterly spellbinding in her pink gown, her hair a crown of golden curls, and that ever-present quirk of her lips always ready to deliver a teasing remark at his expense. He almost smiled at the memory, before the low-lying ache that accompanied every remembrance of Emmeline Lockhart quashed it before its taking root.

He'd wronged her. Treated her poorly. Like a coward.

Left her standing on the veranda waiting for him.

He'd almost made it to the garden, barely a few steps behind her. Almost voiced his desire to make her his.

But a servant had rushed toward him, delivering news of the shipwreck that had claimed both his cousin's and his father's lives. And he hadn't known what to do. How to think. What to say.

So he'd written the simplest of notes and left.

Their deaths had not been an uncomplicated tragedy; it had been the unsealing of Pandora's box. Stories of his father's misdeeds surfaced, each more sordid than the last. Debts came crawling out of hidden ledgers, dragging their talons through the estate's fragile coffers. One wound after another created more and more distance between his failed proposal and an explanation to Emme.

Until he didn't have any heart to confront her at all.

So he'd run away.

He had justified it to himself as the distraction of responsibilities and funerals and a search for Arianna. But he knew the truth.

He'd been a coward.

Not only of coming face-to-face with Emme, but of embracing the mantle of Viscount of Ravenscross. But time and relentless hardship had forged in him some semblance of strength and wisdom—perhaps even a bit of courage.

Until now.

Until this moment, standing on the edge of a crowded ballroom, his gaze fixed on the gilded chandelier while his courage threatened to desert him altogether.

The sound of familiar laughter drew his attention to the dance floor, and the din around him blurred into silence. Emmeline Lockhart danced with a gentleman Simon didn't recognize. She wore a confection of deep green, her golden hair spilling from her coiffure. His breath caught. Had she become more beautiful in the span of nearly two years?

Without thinking, he stepped behind a nearby pillar, shielding himself from view but not from the ability to observe.

That smile—he'd welcomed it into his dreams more times than he could count. Sometimes it felt as though he lived off the hope it gave him, foolish as the notion might be. She held kindness and strength in her countenance, and so many times he'd needed both.

Even if only in a dream.

Yet now, she was smiling up at her partner in that same way she had once smiled at him—wholly engaged, her bright gaze sparkling with unspoken wit.

His eyes closed, shutting out the sight and the ache that accompanied it.

Another loss. Another piece of his shattered world he had no power to reclaim.

"Lord Ravenscross." Benjamin Northrop appeared through the crowd, his grin as irrepressible as ever. In fact, he looked like he wanted to laugh, which for some reason tightened Simon's posture from toe to forehead in defense. "The hunt begins in earnest now, does it not?"

Simon had the sudden desire to hit his best friend in the chin. "If you're referring to my search for a wife, Ben, perhaps we could discuss it without the theatrics?"

"Theatrics?" Ben raised his brows, feigning innocence. "I'd never. I'm merely the messenger tonight."

Simon didn't trust the gleam in Ben's eyes, but it proved a helpful diversion from his attention roving back across the room. "What message, precisely?"

"Well . . ." Ben's grin widened. "Since you've been away from St. Groves' society for a while and rather occupied—what with your heroic efforts to salvage Ravenscross and raise your siblings—my sister has taken it upon herself to assist."

Simon's face went cold as his fingers balled into fists at his side, almost teasing him to act out his desire to place a dent in Ben's grin. Nora

Northrop—now Chawley—blew into people's lives with the purpose of a hurricane. Oh, her intentions were good, but her methods . . . "What have you done?"

"I've done nothing." The man had the effrontery to raise both palms in the air in declaration of his innocence. "But my sister, *as I said*"—Ben exaggerated his repetition—"has compiled a list."

"A list?"

"Indeed." Ben pulled a folded sheet of paper from his pocket, offering it with all the flourish of a courtier presenting a royal decree. "Allow me to clarify: This was entirely Nora's doing. I am but the delivery boy."

"And yet you're enjoying this far too much," Simon muttered as he accepted the paper.

"You wound me, truly." Ben smirked, palm to his chest with continued theatrics. "In fairness, Nora claims she's saving you from wasting time and effort on unsuitable matches. A noble gesture, don't you think?"

Simon shot him a withering look. "I think meddling is the favorite pastime of women with too much leisure."

"And my sister is quite at her leisure, so I assure you, she was most thorough. This list"—Ben tapped the paper now tucked into Simon's coat—"could rival the naval records for precision."

Simon pinched the bridge of his nose. "And what am I to do with this . . . gift?"

"Why, use it, of course!" Ben gestured to the room. "You're in desperate need of a wife with a dowry that could outshine the Bank of England. The ladies on Nora's list meet all requirements: wealth, family connections, and presumably some tolerance for your peculiarities."

"Peculiarities?" Simon's brow arched as his glare fixed on Ben, who, predictably, remained unfazed.

"Former rogue, tragic history, lonely guardian of your siblings, vast and haunted country house . . ."

Simon's lips twitched in reluctant amusement. "Haunted country house?"

Ben shrugged, thoroughly enjoying himself. "Tragic houses must have tragic ghosts, don't you know, Simon? Everyone else seems to."

"And who, pray tell, is haunting my country house this time?" People were exhausting. And he threw Ben squarely into that lot.

"I believe the latest rumor is that the ghost belongs to your mother."

Simon ran a palm over his mouth, attempting to relax his ever-tightening jaw. "Well then, if Mother is haunting Ravenscross, I do wish she would deign to offer some practical advice while she's at it."

Ben chuckled. "Ah, but that wouldn't suit the Gothic narrative, now would it? A brooding viscount with a crumbling estate, three unruly charges, and a reputation just scandalous enough to make you the toast of the town? Why, Simon, it's impossible not to find you utterly fascinating."

Fascinating, indeed. Simon rolled his gaze skyward. Reality and fiction chronicled two vastly different tales. He was well aware of his new reputation: "The Raven of Ravenscross," they called him. Some of the gossip was close to the mark: ruinous debt, a dilapidated estate, and a viscount whose disposition leaned toward the surly. Other rumors, however, bordered on absurdity. Haunted houses, murdered mothers, and—most ludicrous of all—that he was some kind of vampire. Simon gave his head a slight shake. What a bunch of rubbish. "Am I supposed to thank you for that summary of my shortcomings?"

"I live to serve." Ben bowed with mock humility. "Besides, as Nora put it, one of these prospects should prove savior to Ravenscross, so what harm could a curated list do?"

Simon sighed, tugging at his cravat. A "savior" for Ravenscross. *Heaven, help me.* The very idea of marrying for wealth and conveni-ence, rather than affection, struck far too close to the unhappy union of his parents. Perhaps that was why he had clung to harmless flirtations and fleeting connections until . . .

His attention flitted to the dance floor, chest tightening at the sight of her. *She* would not be on the list. No wealth, no status—nothing society deemed suitable for a viscount.

But for him, the man?

A wry laugh escaped before he could stop it. He hadn't even known he wanted someone like her until she'd come into his life. Witty, kind, companionable—dare he say, a friend?

Yes, a dear friend. And more. A sliver of longing clawed its way up his throat before he crushed it. *You must push her from your mind, Simon. Emme isn't an option.*

It was time to bury any fanciful notions of a match with her. He no longer had the luxury of marrying for himself.

He dragged his focus back to Ben, a deep sigh pulling at his shoulders. "Who would your sister suggest first?"

Ben nearly stumbled in surprise. "Pardon?"

"No doubt you've seen the list." He gestured toward the room. "Which of the ladies do you think I would have the most possibility of winning with the best financial remuneration?"

"Well, that does cut out the frills, doesn't it?" Ben drew in a deep breath and surveyed the room with exaggerated deliberation. "Miss Algerton?" he announced at last, gesturing toward a brunette in pale blue. "Nora's words, mind you: 'Tell Simon she's well tried—third season, you know.'"

Well tried? Simon's eyes slipped closed. "How delightful."

"But between us, though"—Ben leaned in conspiratorially—"I suspect there's one name on the list you'll want to avoid."

"Do I dare ask?"

Ben gestured toward Simon's jacket, as if referencing the list. "Selena Hemston."

Simon resisted the urge to retreat outright. "Let me guess. She still believes Ravenscross should be hers?"

"Determined as always, I'd wager."

"It's the *always* bit that keeps me up at night," Simon countered, stilling a shiver at the thought of the woman. "I'm certain Mr. Hemston would like nothing better than to have his daughter permanently connected to the land adjacent to his own."

"He makes no secret of his wish for it, I'm afraid," Ben admitted. "A title *and* influence over the extensiveness of Ravenscross through an heir. Just imagine . . ."

Simon's jaw twitched from sudden tension, and he almost turned and left the ball altogether, but that would succeed at nothing. If he failed to secure a bride soon, Ravenscross itself might be lost. Would it fall to auction? To Mr. Leo Hemston's hands? The thought turned his stomach. Simon would not fail at this.

He couldn't.

Though Miss Hemston brought a dowry the size of which would restore Ravenscross and care for his siblings, she proved as boorish and arrogant as her father. Most likely she wished to remake Ravenscross and Simon too.

Six dances and a mounting headache later, Simon wondered if selling Ravenscross to a tradesman might not be preferable. Just as he sought solace in a drink, a pair of dark brown eyes locked onto his. Her lips curled into a predatory smile, and she began weaving her way through the crowd like a cat stalking its prey.

Miss Selena Hemston.

"Dash it," Simon hissed under his breath. He'd thought for certain Selena was still abroad.

Oh, how the past brought claws with it. Long, feminine-looking claws.

He'd made many mistakes in his life, usually involving women or horse racing. But encouraging any acquaintance with her had been the worst. Indulged, determined, without any comprehension of the word *no*, she took his harmless flirting and massive estate as her personal challenge to gain.

And now? With a title to win? She'd prove intractable.

"Lord Ravenscross." Selena's voice, one he'd learned to locate in any crowd in order to avoid her, cut the room like a knife.

He turned, intending to escape, but she intercepted him with envious speed.

"It's been too long. Two years?" She blocked his forward retreat, thrusting her amply revealed neckline in his direction. "I thought you may have forgotten about me."

He inclined his head and averted his eyes. "I believe that would be impossible."

"I've been told I make quite the impression, by you even." Her fingers wrapped around his arm, nails pinching just a bit as if to literally make an impression. "You've been back two months and not once called upon me. I feared you were avoiding me."

"I fear that may also be impossible."

A fire lit in those dark eyes of hers. "You could just make everything easier on both of us and marry me. Clearly, your little flirtation two seasons ago failed to satisfy, and whatever you've been doing since hasn't led to matrimony." Her gaze roamed over him with shameless intent. "It must be a sign."

"A sign?"

"That we would be a most advantageous match."

Dropping all pretense of civility, he replied, "Whose advantage?"

Her smile never faltered. "For us all, of course. I conquer you and gain a title, which would be immensely gratifying. My father gains access to Ravenscross, which he desires. And you, my dear Simon, gain the funds to restore your family's estate and live as a gentleman of leisure." Her brow rose in triumph. "A perfect situation."

"Conquer me?" He straightened to his full height, heat rising to his neck. "You mean to exact your revenge for a perceived slight years ago?"

"It doesn't have to be a punishment." Her smile turned razor sharp. "In fact, it could be delightful—if you would temper that iron will of yours." She took a deliberate step closer. "Your father was always rather nasty to my father, and I must admit to a small bit of Hemston pride in knowing I could secure the old man's estate as recompense." Her tone was silk, her brow arching higher. "I am quite determined, my lord."

The sheer audacity of her ambition left him momentarily speechless. The very thought of Ravenscross in Hemston hands was an affront he could not abide. The threat hit his pulse. And as far as his will was concerned, she'd only ensured that it remained ironclad.

Before he could voice a scathing retort, his name rang out to his right, saving him from further engagement. A lady approached with a train of companions, their bright eyes alight with purpose. Another called from his left. A third followed suit, her entourage not far behind, all eager for "a conversation," "a little more information," "tell us about your sister . . ."

Simon bit back a groan. He needed escape. Now.

The throng of women surrounded him, asking after his family, his plans, his very existence as though he were some prize bull at market. As the clamor grew, he spotted salvation—a set of glass doors leading outside, he hoped. And to escape.

Taking advantage of the ladies distracting Selena, Simon ducked into the crowd, but their voices pursued him, with Selena at the helm. Mr. and Mrs. Craven appeared at his left, calling his name to introduce him to their daughter. Mr. Lund did the same. He'd never experienced such a quest before, except when in pursuit of a rather muddy Sophia through the garden on a rainy day with the dogs in chase.

Did becoming the landowner of Ravenscross truly produce such pandemonium?

As if on cue, Ben stepped out of nowhere, garnering the attention of the throng with some redirection at just the right time for Simon to turn the corner of a pillar in the room, duck down behind a nearby plant, and slide out the doors.

Ah! A balcony.

Fresh air. Freedom.

Veering left, he pressed himself into the shadows of the stone wall, another step away from the door. Relief surged—until he collided with something soft.

Not stone, like the railing he'd expected.

"Oh!" A feminine cry pierced the night.

Simon's arms instinctively wrapped around the woman to steady her, her precarious balance sending her teetering toward the railing. He pulled her close, the scent of apples enveloping him like a spell—a deliciously familiar spell. It fogged his thoughts and mingled too well with the fit of her softness against him. Dancing didn't allow for this sort of embrace.

"Pardon me, Miss . . ." He steadied her, the light from inside casting a halo down on the woman's face.

All heat fled his body and then surged back through him in a second.

"Emmeline." Her name escaped on crushed air.

Her pink lips opened in surprise, and only a wisp of breath released, but he nonetheless felt the touch of it against his chin. So close. Too close.

And yet his arms only tightened.

She stared up at him, her wide eyes betraying a flicker of vulnerability before cooling to ice. "This . . . this is *my* hiding spot, Sim—Mr. . . . Lord Ravenscross." The sentence wobbled from her lips in halted puffs.

Beautiful lips. Lips he'd dreamed of kissing dozens of times.

"And . . . and you're going to attract attention," she hissed, pushing back from him only to nearly tumble over the edge again. "Making my attempts utterly useless."

He wanted to smile. Smile at her ridiculous sweetness after racing from Selena's claws. Smile at her trying to hide from the guests at the halfway mark of every ball. Smile at the fact he actually knew about her hiding.

He kept his arms around her. "Emme."

Those beautiful lips parted again, only to firm back into a frown. "If you recall, you forfeited the right to address me on such intimate terms, *Lord Ravenscross*." Her gaze flashed back to his, searching his face, hesitating a second to stare, before snapping to attention. "If you would be so kind as to release me."

Her emphasis distanced them with formality, her volume assured them of discovery, and her reminder of what he'd lost gutted him.

"If you wish to hide, you'd best lower your voice."

Her cheeks flushed, but her chin tilted higher. "I'm not certain I wish to hide any longer, especially with you." She moved toward the door and then froze, quickly returning to the shadows of the balcony, her back pressed against the wall.

Simon peered over her head through the glass. A blond man pushed through the crowd in search of something. Simon's attention fell on Emme. Someone?

"Is that Mr. Marshall?"

Her gaze swung to his. "Don't you dare open that door."

"Does he fancy you then, Emme?"

"Stop calling me Emme," she hissed, her voice rising. "We are not on such friendly terms, Lord Ravenscross."

"Shhh." He looked over his shoulder, catching sight of the gaggle of ladies not far from the door. "Mr. Marshall is very near."

"Don't you shush me." She stepped forward, her eyes alight. "You have no right to shush me."

"Miss Lockhart." The male voice was very near the door.

Emme's lips parted for a retort, but Simon silenced her with a hand over her mouth, pulling her deeper into the shadows. Fire lit those eyes, drawing his attention even more to those marble-like hazel depths. Oh, he'd missed her. More than he even realized. And to have her in his arms? His breath lodged in his throat. "I apologize, Emme. But neither of us wants to be found right now, and Mr. Marshall is nearly at the door." Mr. Ezra Marshall? Consummate complainer who found fault with the temperature of the tea, the length of the waltz, and even the alignment of the stars?

Certainly not the right match for her.

She pushed his hand away. "Then leave. I was here first."

Could her voice get any louder? Selena's face emerged from the crowd, along with a small collection of other ladies on her heels. How on earth was he to survive them? "It would not do well to be found out here together alone," he warned. "Stop talking."

"If we are found out, it will not be my fault." She jabbed a finger in the air at him. "You followed me, if you'll recall."

Good heavens, she had to stop talking for both their sakes. He stepped forward, lowering his voice even more. "Emme . . ."

"I said, stop calling me—" She pushed away from his arms too quickly and stumbled, once again, too near the railing. This time, she squealed as her back tipped over the edge.

With another quick movement, he held her against him again, her fists pressed to his chest, her breaths shallow, and her face so close.

Wonderfully close.

He stared down at her, words clogging his throat. So many things to say and none of them sufficient.

She stared back, frown tight, eyes narrowed. And even her scowl lured him nearer.

Thank heavens she wasn't wearing those cursed spectacles of hers. Something about the way the golden rims framed her large eyes in such a bookishly innocent way unraveled every bit of his control. Not that he had a great deal of control right now, because the longer he remained in the presence of her scent and familiarity, the more and more dangerous the seconds grew.

Suddenly, she ceased struggling. Stopped frowning. Heaven help him, was she even breathing? Those eyes changed. The fury dissipated into something altogether more dangerous—hurt.

The look raked over him.

"I'm so sorry, Emme." The apology scraped through his hot throat. "Sorry for all of it."

The words hung between them, raw and unguarded. Her breath caught, gaze softening in some intoxicating way. Then that tempting bottom lip of hers wobbled, and before he could think better of it, he went mad.

He breached the distance between them, his mouth capturing hers, stealing any words in one swift and certain act of lunacy . . . and desperation. For one fleeting moment, she relaxed against him, her hands clutching his lapel, drawing him closer. He thought he felt a quiet hum of acceptance purr from her throat, feeding his impossible hope. The full potency of apples engulfed him like a step into an autumn orchard. Sweet. Alive . . . wholesome.

He'd dreamed of her kiss. Craved it like a dying man for food.

She tasted like coming home, and he wanted to keep feasting.

Then her entire body tensed, and she pushed back.

"How . . . how could you?" she whispered, voice shaking.

And with a flash of fire in those eyes, her palm connected with his cheek, a sharp sting that left him reeling—not from pain, but from the knowledge that he'd just made everything so much worse.

CHAPTER 4

*H*e was kissing her!

Simon Reeves, the man who broke her heart and left her to the gossips of St. Groves and the possible demise of her matrimonial future, was kissing her.

Full on the mouth.

The warmth of his lips seared her fury. Heat unfurled from her stomach to scorch through her middle before racing back to her cheeks.

Very full on the mouth. Warm and strong, his fingers kneading against her back in an almost desperate way.

And once the initial shock faded, two thoughts rose to prominence, jostling for dominance.

The first: She'd been entirely wrong about kissing scenes in her novels. Woefully, inexcusably wrong. How had she reduced this—the strong, urgent heat of his lips, the solidity of his arms encircling her with such strength, the undercurrent of tenderness in his touch—to mere words on a page? She'd overlooked the exhilarating aliveness of it all: the way his scent—a tantalizing blend of leather, musk, and a trace of rosewood—ensnared her. She drew in a deeper breath, a strange sort of whimper slipping from her in appreciation. Her entire body came alive with . . . feeling. And when his palm slid up her back, pressing her to him? Heavens, she hadn't expected to enjoy the sensation of being captured quite so much.

Her fingers twitched, curling into the rough fabric of his coat, just to give her time for a lengthier assessment. He tasted like lemonade—sour with an undercurrent of sweetness? She almost grinned at how close to the mark it fit his personality.

Or the personality she thought she'd known.

Which ushered in the second thought, striking her much harder than the first: How dare he? How dare he! Simon—Lord Ravenscross, she reminded herself fiercely—was quite thoroughly completing his ruination of her reputation. And she'd already indulged in his thorough ruination for much too long. His abandonment had been a betrayal sharp enough to cut, but this? To kiss her now, as if her feelings and her reputation were his to toy with, was beyond the pale.

With all the strength her indignation could muster, she shoved him away.

The cool night air rushed between them, biting against her heated skin and pricking her eyes with traitorous tears.

The audacity. The sheer thoughtlessness and . . . meanness. She'd never expected him to stoop so low. Not the man she thought she'd grown to know, but he'd proven her wrong in every particular once he'd left her standing alone on a veranda with a handful of notorious witnesses and a crack in her heart.

"How . . . how could you?" Her voice, trembling and uneven, betrayed her fury even before her palm cracked against his face with a force that startled even her.

Simon flinched, his hand flying up to his cheek as he stared at her, wide-eyed. Up close, his eyes were paler than she'd remembered, their blue almost translucent under the moonlight.

"Didn't you ruin me enough already?" she demanded, though her voice wavered.

His expression—a mix of shock and something more devastating—stole the edge from her anger. Why did he have to look so . . . so lost? She pressed on. "Are you determined to destroy me entirely?"

He winced, as if her words struck harder than her palm, and his mouth parted as if to explain, though no words came immediately.

The burning in her eyes intensified.

"I . . . I never wanted to hurt you, Em . . . Miss Lockhart."

The formality should have pleased her. But against every shred of common sense, its distance settled in her chest like a stone. She shouldn't wish for intimacy with him! Not after what he'd done, even if the look he currently was giving her—raw and impossibly sincere—nearly had her reaching for a handkerchief to offer *him*. She hardened herself against the rush.

"Kissing me on a balcony at a very public ball certainly suggests otherwise."

To her chagrin, saying it didn't please her as much as it should have. In fact, she felt rather miserable.

"I . . . I was attempting to keep our location secret so that we wouldn't be discovered."

A weak excuse, and from the frown he made, he knew it.

He stepped back, raking a hand through his dark hair in a gesture that was far too casual for her liking. "I wanted to escape my pursuers just as much as you wanted to escape yours."

Emme instinctively shifted farther from the door, her movement betraying her unease.

His gaze flicked toward her, and a ghost of a smile tugged at the corner of his mouth—the kind she used to find maddeningly charming. "You've always had a talent for disappearing at social events," he murmured, his voice quieter now, carrying a thread of something she couldn't quite name.

Her gaze caught back in his, face warming more than it already was. The words struck a nerve, dredging up memories she wasn't prepared to confront. Their first meeting had been during the height of Miss Willow's debut ball, when the aforementioned lady had pursued him into the garden, only for him to trip—quite literally—into Emme's hiding place behind a hedgerow. She, of course, had been evading the boorish attentions of an inebriated Mr. Douglas Clyde.

For some reason, when he'd literally knocked her to the ground, Simon had refused to leave her side, despite her assurances and a few scathing glances from Miss Willow. At the time, the last thing she'd wanted was the attention of the notorious flirt, but one dance and conversation after another, Simon Reeves had begun to change in her eyes.

From stranger to one of the dearest men of her acquaintance.

Or had appeared to.

And then . . . he'd left without as much as a word of explanation.

For almost two years.

A man who could find his way into any number of drawing rooms, ballrooms, or gambling halls surely could have found a pen and paper, could he not?

Her spine straightened, her resolve hardening. "Well," she said, "in the future, would you be so kind as to locate your own hiding spot and leave me and my"—her finger flicked toward her face, cheeks blazing—"lips alone?"

His brows shot up, and his gaze dipped to her lips, lingering there far too long. The tingling warmth that followed infuriated and, to be perfectly honest, fascinated her.

"I've heard where you and your lips have been over the past two years and I'm not interested in . . . in . . ." Her face exploded with warmth. What was she even saying? "The shared experience."

Her words hung awkwardly in the air, and she tipped her gaze heavenward, silently rebuking her own ineptitude. She was far better at these exchanges when they were confined to the pages of her manuscripts.

His attention shifted to her eyes, one brow arching higher than the other. "You've heard the rumors?"

She lifted her chin in defiance, refusing to envision the whispered tales of his exploits—Italy, Scotland, Ireland.

He tipped his head closer, studying her, his expression hardening a little. "And you believe them, do you?"

At the moment, answering seemed unwise, so she merely tipped her chin higher.

He took a deliberate step closer. "My elaborate escape to Italy with an exotic heiress, was it? Or Edinburgh, where I was supposedly womanizing in the company of poets and philosophers?"

Her lips pressed together, but the words slipped out anyway. "And Ireland."

At the darkening of his countenance, Emme wished she'd kept silent, but she'd raised her chin as high as it could go, so she felt she needed to do something.

"Ah, yes. Ireland." His laugh was short and humorless. "Why not add a voyage to the Americas while we're at it? After all, I've so much leisure time and coin to spare."

Emme flinched a little at the fury lacing his words. Could the rumors about debt be true? She'd thought them inconsistent with owning such an estate or traveling in such elegance—or was he trying to weaken her defenses?

"Why wouldn't I prefer the wild and exotic over . . ." He trailed off, stepping closer, his gaze fixed on her with a ferocity that stilled her breath.

"Over?" she whispered, her voice betraying her traitorous curiosity.

He didn't answer. Instead, he moved closer still, the railing pressing into her back as he leaned in, their faces so near that she could make out the tiniest golden flakes within the depths of his eyes. She didn't push away. Didn't wish to move. All she wanted to know was the end of his sentence.

Could he have been talking about her?

And if he was, what did that mean?

His hands caught her arms, steadying her, and for a moment she thought he might kiss her again.

Air squeezed in her chest to the hurting spot. Something between the rumors and his behavior, her heart, and the evidence of her own eyes didn't fit together at all.

His gaze roamed over her face as if attempting to extract something she didn't know how to give. Her breathing shallowed, her mind warring with itself. Would he kiss her again? She tilted her head just a bit as if to prepare.

Research, after all, might justify another kiss . . .

Her cheeks warmed at the memory. And his closeness. And the idea that those rather impressive arms from his rather impressive shoulders inspired a wonderful sense of safety she shouldn't want from a scoundrel.

Yet the way he looked at her in the twilit night didn't resemble anything like a scoundrel. For some reason she couldn't quite define, she wanted to touch his cheek and comfort him.

No! This was madness. Her reputation couldn't withstand the blow.

As if he sensed her thoughts, Simon blinked, his head shaking slightly as though to clear it. He released her abruptly, stepping back, his jaw tightening.

"No," he said, his voice low and firm. "I have nothing to offer you, Miss Lockhart."

His gaze trailed over her face once more, pausing a moment on her lips.

Her breath hitched.

"Perhaps once." His frown deepened, and he released a sigh. "But a lot has happened since then."

And with that, he turned and walked back into the house.

She braced a hand to the balcony railing, her body suddenly weak from neck to knees. How on earth was she going to survive an entire season with the possibility of seeing Simon Reeves at any moment?

"Bina said you left the ball early without telling her."

Emme looked up from her place in the window seat, morning light spilling over her open book and scattering across the loose papers she'd been attempting to write upon. She tucked the pages into the book nearby, her futile attempt at creativity weakened by her weariness. Most of the house still slept, and she'd hoped for some quiet time to write before the day began in earnest. But her thoughts betrayed her, stubbornly circling one man who deserved none of her attention.

True, she had managed to jot down a few scandalous lines about a kiss—one inspired all too easily by memory—and readjusted some of her prose, which in the light of day appeared too harsh on the hero of the story. But she couldn't seem to write beyond that moment and the warring emotions it had inspired. Not yet.

"Aunt Bina said it's good taste to leave a party early rather than late," she replied, attempting to keep the conversation light.

"Hmm . . ." Her father stepped closer, the faint scent of damp earth and rosemary clinging to his crinkled clothes after his morning visit to the garden. "Not as early as last night for you, dear girl. And without discussing it with your aunt?"

Emme flushed, thankful he hadn't mentioned her leaving without a chaperone. No need to add another social transgression to the growing list of her failings. "I left a message with Aster that I wasn't feeling well."

Father lowered himself to the window seat. "I know your aunt can be trying, but she has good intentions . . . and she knows far more of society's puzzling rules than I."

Emme drew her knees up beneath her, leaning her head against his shoulder. "You know of things that matter far more than match-making, Father."

"If only your mother were here." His sigh ruffled her hair. "She'd know best how to guide you in these matters—and your heart."

She shifted to look up at him. "My heart?"

"Aster told me of some of the people who attended last night." He looked out the window, his lips pinching enough to display his discomfort. "I may not speak of it, but I know you cared for him."

Him. Emme stilled against the familiar ache the reference stirred. No need to say his name. Her father knew.

"It doesn't matter now, does it?" She spoke quietly, her words laced with a bitterness she hadn't entirely banished. "He's gone on to find more tempting options—ones who will, no doubt, make him happier in his newfound position."

Even saying it aloud stung, an old wound reopening.

"Perhaps," he murmured. "But Aster said the man looked rather lost."

Lost? That's the look she'd noticed last night too, when her thoughts weren't split between her anger and his devastating kiss.

She shook off the thought and looked up at her father, eager to change the subject. "What happened to the previous Lord Ravenscross? I know both he and the current viscount's father died at sea, but . . . there are other rumors."

Her father cleared his throat, shifting in discomfort. "It is not polite or helpful to dwell on such matters, Emme."

"But there has to be more," she pressed. She had conjured all sorts of lurid scenarios in her mind after Simon dropped her, some of which had made their way into her novel. If her father knew even half of what she'd written, he'd be scandalized. "The sudden deaths of the former viscount and Mr. Reeves, the whispers of ruin they left behind, and then Mrs. Reeves—Simon's mother—passing not long after." She tilted her head, feigning innocence. "They say she was either murdered or overcome with grief when she learned of her husband's rumored debts and indiscretions."

"Idle gossip," her father said sharply, his tone leaving no room for argument. "Mrs. Reeves was a woman of great dignity and kindness. Whatever her husband's failings, it is unseemly to indulge in such speculation. Grief and disappointment may well have taken their toll, but to suggest foul play is ridiculous."

And her father knew all too well the jarring responsibility of a single-parent household. She almost quieted her curiosity at that thought, but the ideas that had been swirling around in her head all night required some answers.

"Then what of Arianna Reeves?" Emme continued. "The rumors about her are far worse."

Her father's frown deepened. "What rumors?"

"That she was taken against her will. Or worse, that she met some grim fate—"

"Emme, it doesn't flatter you or assist in your own healing to indulge in such rubbish." His steely look curbed any further questions on that topic. "Speculation is a dangerous sort of guessing game that, many times, ends in hurting people."

Emme fell silent, her fingers tracing the edge of her book. "But the new viscount," she ventured after a pause, "with his travels and liaisons, doesn't seem as affected by it all."

Her father gave her a measured look. "You don't believe that."

And he was right. If Simon was anything like the man she'd known, he'd care. Deeply.

"I don't know what to believe," she admitted. "He reappears in society as though nothing has changed, yet whispers follow him wherever he goes. And now it seems he's looking for a wealthy bride." Voicing the phrase hurt much worse than she'd expected.

"Lord Ravenscross is a young man bearing the weight of a title he never expected to inherit," her father said quietly. "His circumstances have changed and so have his choices. It is a hard truth, Emme, but one he could not have avoided."

"And yet he could have said as much," she countered, her voice betraying the hurt she had worked so hard to conceal. "Instead, he left me standing on that veranda with nothing but a note and no explanation."

"Perhaps he thought it kinder to let silence speak for him."

But wouldn't the truth have been kinder coming from him instead of some gnawing silence where speculation ran rampant? "Or he was acting the part of a coward." She turned away, the sun's glow from the window almost too bright now. "To disappear from his troubles and indulge in who knows what across the country. It's as if I didn't matter—"

"Emme." The way Father spoke her name felt like a reprimand. "Many a reputation and, might I say, friendship have been ruined over unchecked imaginations." He patted her knee. "Lord Ravenscross's father was not a good man, but his eldest son doesn't suffer from the same reputation. Unchecked in his youth, perhaps, but none of those accounts are recent. The fact he secured even some of your admiration proves the type of man he truly is at heart. You are a clever girl, even if you do allow some of those more fanciful novels too much space in your mind at times. You always come around to your logic." He stood and tapped his temple. "Think with your head, not your hurt. The world is filled with enough people who parade irrationality as intelligence."

She pulled her knees up against her chest as her father exited the room. Simon had hurt her, and she'd created a whole host of horrible reasons just to spite him. She'd even written a novel out of her hurt. A pain squeezed behind her rib cage. Perhaps she'd spent so much time nursing her own heartache, she hadn't considered the possible reasons he left her alone that night on the veranda. But for the first time, a flicker of doubt crept into her certainty about his character . . . his motives.

What had his words been last night?

"I have nothing to offer you, Miss Lockhart."

She shook her head and slid from the window seat, brushing the thought aside. Regardless of his reasons, Simon Reeves, Viscount of Ravenscross, was not her future.

He needed wealth, and she had none to give.

And she had no interest in getting her heart broken again.

So until she could get the memory of his kiss out of her mind, she'd simply have to avoid him.

Emme closed her book with a resolute snap. And she was very good at hiding.

Simon hadn't slept at all.

Which proved advantageous, as it meant he was alert enough to catch Lottie attempting to sneak out at dawn. She claimed she only wanted a morning ride, but Simon doubted it, given the mischievous curve of her lips.

Lately, he doubted everything.

Saving Ravenscross.

Providing for his siblings.

Finding a bride who wasn't Emmeline Lockhart.

He drove the hammer into the board with more force than necessary, the reverberation jolting up his arm. The stables were in dire need of repairs, and though his skills weren't exceptional, he could at least manage to hammer a nail and replace a broken fence post.

He exhaled sharply. He *had* to conquer this affection for Emmeline Lockhart.

Time had done nothing to strip even a hint of his feelings for her.

Last night, he'd entered the ballroom determined to avoid her altogether. He'd even gone so far as to suggest to a few gentlemen that they ought to ask her to dance—anything to keep her occupied and far away from him.

For a time the plan worked. From across the room he tracked her movements like a moth mesmerized by a flame, his resolve weakening with every glimpse. She glided gracefully in her deep green gown, the fabric catching the candlelight with an ethereal glow. At times she followed an older lady—her aunt, most likely—who seemed intent on speaking to every person in the room.

He'd kept out of her line of vision, minimized situations that brought him near her.

And then, like a fool, he'd kissed her.

Kissed her.

Tasted forbidden fruit.

He picked up another nail and beat it until the wood splintered.

The one woman he could see himself spending a lifetime with, and she was entirely out of reach. Not only because she didn't want him—though her words had made that painfully clear—but because her modest dowry couldn't begin to address the chasm of debt left by his cousin and father.

For years he'd believed he could choose a wife, a future, based on his own desires.

But his newfound responsibilities stole such a liberty.

Now he had to choose between his heart and the future of his family—a choice that wasn't truly a choice at all.

"Simon!" Fia's cry startled him upright.

He turned to find the youngest Reeves entering the stables, dirty, with brambles from the top of her head to the bottom of her petticoat. Scratches marred her cheeks, and tears left streaks through the grime on her face.

She ran straight to him and buried herself into his waist, whimpering against him. His entire body caved around her, pulling the little girl into a protective hold without a thought. Of all the siblings, Fia had been the one most ready to transfer her sweet affections, embrace the care he wanted to give. Perhaps she needed as much consolation from all the changes as he did.

Simon looked up to find Mrs. Patterson holding on to the door-frame, breaths coming in spurts. "She went chasing the cat into the brambles, sir." The woman waved a handkerchief, stopping to catch her breath. "And she wouldn't do anything but come to you about it."

The words hit Simon with unexpected force. He nodded stiffly, swallowing against the lump rising in his throat. "It's fine. Thank you, Mrs. Patterson."

The housekeeper heaved a weary sigh and shook her head. "I'll prepare some salve for the scratches."

"I'll bring her to my study." The woman gave a curt nod and disappeared from view. Simon scooped Fia into his arms and settled onto a nearby hay bale, cradling her on his lap. "Where does it hurt most, little one?"

She sniffled and looked up at him with wide eyes watery, the scratches welting. *Poor lamb.* "My cheeks."

He removed his handkerchief and dabbed lightly at one cheek, then the other. "What were you thinking charging into the brambles like that?"

"Midas got caught." Her little bottom lip wobbled. "I had to save him. Blasted brambles."

Correcting her would prove futile at the moment. That cat had more lives than sense. Appropriate that it happened to be Teddy's cat. Two matching personalities.

"Next time, perhaps you ought to ask for help before launching a rescue mission." He tipped her chin up to dab at a scratch across her nose. "Rescues usually work better when there are more hands to help."

How he would appreciate a few extra hands in his life right now. Then his mind went to the blasted marriageable ladies list, and he paused on the thought. Or the right hands, anyway.

Fia sniffled again and reached into her pocket. Simon braced himself. With Fia's penchant toward finding animals, he wasn't sure what to expect, but then she drew a pink rose forward. "Midas found this in the bushes. It's one of Mama's roses."

"It is." Simon's throat pinched. His mother had loved roses. Fragile yet beautiful, they reminded him of her—a beauty too delicate to endure the thorns set against her in such a harsh reality. They'd overtaken her.

With the way of the world and the current status of his life, he had to secure a bride with more strength of character than his dear mother, if nothing else but to survive his siblings.

"Can we put it on her grave?"

The loss stung afresh. A year ago, they'd buried their mother. And he'd spent all that time shoving his grief beneath the necessity of the next thing. He nodded, biding himself time to rediscover his voice.

And then Simon began to doubt Midas's instigation of this plan into the brambles. Most likely, Fia had seen the rose buried beneath the thorns and set her mind to "rescuing" it.

"I need to put away these tools." Simon stood, lowering the little girl to the floor. "Why don't you run ahead to my study so Mrs. Patterson can put some salve on your scratches, and then we can take the rose to Mother's grave."

Her eyes lit, tears still poised on those long lashes of hers. Without a word, she dashed away, nearly colliding with Ben as he entered the stables.

"What happened to that one?" Ben gestured toward the direction Fia had disappeared. "The cat?"

Simon placed the hammer back in its box. "Actually, it was more of a rose rescue gone awry."

"Ouch." His pale hair bobbed in time with the shake of his head. "Have I mentioned how badly you need a governess?"

"If you've come to state the obvious, feel free to leave," Simon muttered, brushing past him.

Ben fell into step with him. "Actually, I came for you to tell me something I don't already know." When Simon gave no response, Ben continued, "Why did you leave the ball so early last night? I've heard of at least a half dozen ladies eager to meet you."

Simon's stomach plummeted at the thought. A half dozen more?

"Some of them were excessively pretty," Ben added with a teasing smirk. Simon shot him a glare, which only brought out Ben's laugh. "I expected more fortitude from you, Ravenscross. Running scared from a ball?" His friend tsked. "After everything you've endured over the past months to build your character?"

"There are some things for which one cannot prepare." The memory of Emme's lips secured his statement eternally. "Or recover." He growled out the words more to himself, but the scoffed laugh from his friend proved he'd not spoken quietly enough.

One day, Simon might truly lose all self-control and give Ben a solid throttling.

"What on earth happened?"

Simon increased his pace.

Ben rounded him to block his progress, the man's usually jovial expression sobering. "You talked to *her*, didn't you?"

The question brought Simon to a stop. How did Ben always know? It was uncanny and, quite frankly, infuriating.

"You did." Ben crossed his arms, studying him with unnerving perceptiveness. "I knew you were avoiding her, but how did you find your way to talk to her?"

Simon drew in a breath and started walking again, this time slower.

"It doesn't matter. I can't pursue anything with her, and she made it perfectly plain she wanted nothing to do with me."

Except for the kiss. And the kiss suggested otherwise.

Ben had been the only person outside his own parents who'd known Simon's plans to propose to Emme. The only person who likely understood the extent of Simon's feelings. And one of the few people who knew the full, devastating impact of Simon's change in position.

Ben arched a brow. "Did she, though?"

Simon ignored the jab, but his mind betrayed him, replaying the kiss—the way she'd softened against him, the way her breath had hitched, the vulnerability and interest in those eyes.

Ben clapped him on the shoulder. "Affections like that don't just vanish, Simon. Even after all this time. Not entirely."

"Perhaps not, but affections can be conquered." He raised his gaze to the house and the grounds stretching back toward the forest, solidifying his claim. "They must."

For the future of Ravenscross and the good of his family, they must.

So he needed either to find a wife as soon as possible so that he could stop attending balls, or never to find himself alone with Emmeline Lockhart again. Affections could be mastered, but Simon was no master of them yet.

CHAPTER 5

As with our previous lesson on catching a husband . . ."
Aunt Bean's voice cut through Emme's thoughts as she gazed out the window toward the garden and wished for escape. Escape, alas, was as improbable as Aunt Bean's sense of humor. Emme's early departure from the last ball fueled some sort of desperation in Aunt Bean to purge every unseemly habit from Emme's person, inspiring additional passion in her instructions.

Emme ought to apologize to Aster.

"You must always allow a gentleman to speak first," Aunt Bean intoned, her heels clicking rhythmically across the wooden floors along with the steady tap of her ever-present cane. "Men do not want assertiveness in the ballroom. You save that for marriage when he can't escape without a great deal of difficulty."

The corner of Emme's mouth twitched, and she shot her sister a sidelong glance.

To her credit, Aster appeared diligent, pen poised as though to transcribe every word of their aunt's lecture. But upon closer inspection, the lines and curves on the page resolved into a map, rather than notes. Aster, always the more elegant and enigmatic of the two, devoted far more energy to charting her grand adventures abroad than navigating the intricacies of the marriage mart. However, with her ready disposition toward falling in love with any man who might promise her a voyage to lands unknown and without an "unsavory" romantic history, she would likely be the one to marry first.

"I would advise you both to ensure your dancing is beyond reproach." Aunt Bean paused midstride. Her gaze swept from Emme to Aster, weighing them with all the severity of the task at hand. "Beautiful dancing is rather thrilling to the opposite sex. Following dance steps with grace suggests you will manage his household with equal ease and elegance."

Emme blinked. *How exactly did footwork translate into financial management and dinner planning?*

"Emmeline," Aunt Bean resumed. "As the elder sister, you are, of course, an example to Aster. However, having endured two seasons without securing a match, the example is somewhat blemished, which is why you must apply yourself with greater resolve toward matrimony."

At this, Aster actually raised her attention from her map.

Not that Aunt Bean required any encouragement to continue. Her monologue, like the inexplorable tide, surged on unchecked and rewarded by its own sound.

"Knowing your predilection for distasteful sarcasm"—Aunt Bean turned fully to Emme, her sharp eyes narrowing to either root out insubordination or encourage cowardice, Emme wasn't quite certain—"I must remind you of three indelible truths every gracious and alluring lady must embrace."

Emme sat straighter, bracing for impact.

Aster tilted her head, watching Aunt Bean like a specimen under glass.

"Poise." She produced the word with such force it practically became visible. "A lady must be calm, controlled, and composed. No matter the provocation, you must not betray that you are, most assuredly, cleverer than the gentleman addressing you."

Aster abandoned her map entirely, her lips twitching at the veiled criticism. Emme supposed it was rather like watching a comedy on the stage.

Unfortunately, Emme had not been poised at all last night. She shifted in her seat, warmth rising unbidden to her cheeks as the memory of Simon's kiss resurfaced.

"Politeness." Aunt Bean raised two fingers, her expression solemn. "The second disposition you must keep in your conversations with a man of interest or any of his family members. Politeness in expression, in manners, and in words. There will be plenty of time to speak your mind after you've secured your future."

Emme had no memory of Uncle Geoffrey, but for some reason, she felt a sudden pang of compassion for him.

"And lastly"—Aunt Bean approached, towering over Emme in her seated position like a large lavender shadow complete with a matching feather flapping from her hat—"and this is the most important for *you*."

The implication pressed Emme back into the chair.

"Silence."

Emme swallowed hard, her independence bristling under the weight of that single word.

"This reiterates the first point. You may lack your sister's effortless beauty, but you are not without your charms." Her gaze swept dismissively from Emme's coiffure to her slippers. Emme fought against an eye roll with all her might. "And you grow considerably more appealing the less you speak. You are decidedly too opinionated and fanciful, Emmeline. Dance steps, the weather, and the host's generosity will suffice as topics of conversation."

Emme schooled her features, though it took considerable effort to stifle a cringe. Memories of the ball resurfaced with alarming clarity: her suggestion to Mrs. Plumfield to eschew orange entirely; her adamant refusal to dance with Mr. Seivers, whose proximity left much to be desired; and her impassioned debate with Mr. Long regarding women's freedom to ride on horseback as they pleased.

Had Aunt Bean witnessed *all* of that?

Emme's stomach churned. *Or the balcony?*

"Make no mistake, my unfortunate nieces." Aunt Bean didn't even look in Aster's direction. "I shall have you married."

One of the saving graces of enduring the season's endless balls was the ambience.

And the music.

And, if one was fortunate enough to be at Lady Ruthton's, the food.

As the unchallenged hostess of the season, Lady Ruthton spared no expense, dazzling her guests with roasted duck, fragrant syllabubs, and a rainbow of custards and cakes. Little wonder she hosted but three balls—one or two near the beginning of the St. Groves Season and one to close it—allowing her guests the full span of months to compare her fare to all others and find them wanting.

Emme stepped through the entry hall into the Assembly Room, its soaring ceilings and white crown molding framing walls of delicate blue. She wanted to take it in fully, allow the beauty of the evening to transport her. But that would mean forgetting her primary objective laid out quite clearly by her aunt: to be charming, poised, and silent enough to secure a husband.

All in one evening. It seemed like a Herculean feat, but who was she to argue with Aunt Bean's matchmaking prowess?

Plus, there was the simple fact that she needed to keep her distance from a certain raven-haired gentleman.

"It's unbearably hot," Aster muttered, snapping open her fan with a flair. The pale blue of her gown set off her fair hair, giving her the air of a debutante who had yet to meet a single disappointment in life.

"Crowds bring warmth," Emme replied, though the warmth in her own face had more to do with expectations than the number of people in the room.

"Well, I prefer fewer people then." Aster shifted her fan over her mouth to catch her words.

At sixteen Aster had more than enough time to grow into the idea of marriage. Whether someone felt brave enough to take on her distractible nature and sneaky ways, only God knew. A twinge of guilt pricked at Emme's chest. Both Lockhart sisters had a penchant for mischief. Aster's was harmless enough. Emme's might have been deemed notorious—if anyone beyond herself knew the wickedness she inflicted upon her characters.

They had not been in the room more than ten minutes when Mr. Henry Marshall materialized at Emme's side, smile too wide to be endearing.

But alas, Emme's may have been too fake to be endearing.

He offered his hand. "Might I have the honor, Miss Lockhart?"

Emme opened her mouth to offer some excuse, but Aunt Bean's eagle-eyed glare from across the room stopped her short. A vintner's vision in muscadine hues, she was easy to spot.

Perhaps Emme could fake a swoon? She sighed. No. Fake swoons must be saved for more desperate times, or people would begin to suspect her subterfuge.

"Of course." She took his hand and allowed him to lead her into a waltz.

At least it wasn't Mr. Rushing. The middle-aged widower constantly smelled of whiskey and tended to hold her, and every other dancing partner, much too tightly. Mr. Marshall's touch was the opposite—barely there, making it unnervingly difficult to follow his lead.

Perhaps it was much harder to be a man than Emme realized, especially if the rules were as tedious for them as for the women, and when the women garnered the rights of refusal. They did have to stick their necks out a bit, didn't they?

"Your aunt," he began, "was most curious about Thornton House."

Oh dear. Aunt Bean had sharpened her matchmaking hooks on

PEPPER BASHAM

him. Emme braced herself for what was certain to be an exhaustive monologue of his darling estate. However, Mr. Marshall's exuberance would certainly keep her from breaking any of the rules Aunt Bean listed about poise and silence.

So Emme merely smiled her response.

Perhaps if she showed Aunt Bean she was trying, the woman would refrain from following Emme like a vulture on its prey.

"As you well know, Miss Lockhart," Mr. Marshall said, chest puffing with pride, "Thornton House has been in the Marshall family for over one hundred and twenty years."

Oh yes. She knew. Repetition hammered the memory interminable. Her smile faltered, but Mr. Marshall didn't seem to notice.

"I've made significant improvements since inheriting. A future bride ought to find her home quite satisfactory, don't you agree? Not that there's much to improve upon at Thornton House—it's quite the gem already. Did you know that Sir Alexander Cochrane himself dined with my father at Thornton House during one of his returns from the war with Napoleon?"

Emme's attention flipped to him. Ah, now here was something interesting. "I've read in the papers that America has declared war against us."

"You read such things?" He blinked, his cheeks reddening a little. "Why would a lady concern herself with war?"

Research, to be honest. However, she chose a nobler answer. "If it involves my country, shouldn't I take advantage of learning what I can?" She shrugged a shoulder. "Besides, it's a topic far more interesting than the weather, though the food is very good."

He gaped, as though she'd just proposed they invade the dance floor with artillery. Emme's satisfaction at her retort was short-lived; Aunt Bean's disapproving glare snuffed it out like a candle in a gale.

She sighed. "I'm sure the gardens at Thornton House are resplendent this time of year."

And with that, Mr. Marshall launched into a description so detailed that she could nearly smell the primroses. As he droned on with the most effusive praise any collection of flora had ever known, Emme caught sight of a very familiar figure on the far side of the room.

Simon—impossibly handsome in a forest-green velvet cutaway tailcoat and those infernally fashionable trousers—danced with Miss Amelia Godspey. His confident gait, swath of dark hair, and strong jawline, along with the elegance of his movements, were simply maddening.

Oh, why did he have to be so handsome? Emme was certain that if he were a little less handsome, he'd prove much easier to ignore.

She glimpsed Simon twice more—once while enduring a dance with dear old Mr. Trundle, who fancied himself in want of a bride but would do better with a loyal hound, and again while paired with Mr. George Armstrong, Aunt Bean's favored suitor of the evening.

Simon had danced with serpentine Selena Hemston and cheerful Miss Croft. Well, Emme wouldn't mind Miss Croft so much for the brooding man. He could do with a bit of sunshine, and Emme's particular brand of radiance clearly hadn't suited him.

She frowned at the idea as she took a sip from her glass. If he weren't so irritatingly captivating, she might have spared herself the trouble of caring at all.

"You're being too obvious, Em."

Emme spun around to find Thomas lounging against the wall near her, looking every bit as polished as most of the other gentlemen in the room.

"I haven't the faintest idea what you mean." She turned her gaze in any direction but Simon's.

Thomas drew in a deep breath, casting a glance skyward as if for divine intervention. "I wasn't here during your first season to witness firsthand, but if he treated you as you claim, why must you persist in courting him with your eyes?"

"Courting him with my eyes?" Emme's voice squeaked most unbecomingly, so she lowered it at once. "I am not courting him in any respect, eyes or otherwise."

Thomas arched a skeptical brow.

A flush crept up her neck. "He did treat me poorly," she admitted. "But not until the very end. I had every reason to believe he cared about me before then."

Thomas studied her, narrowing his eyes as he shifted his attention from her face back across the room. "His reputation as a flirt precedes your . . . time with him."

"I know." She nodded, trying to clench her hurt a little tighter to fight against the growing uncertainty. "And at first, he seemed every bit the sort, but then . . . well . . ." She shrugged. "He changed. Nothing like what I'd heard." Saying it aloud sounded so unconvincing, and she'd nearly gone dotty wondering how she'd misjudged his character so thoroughly, but after seeing him again . . . after speaking with Father, maybe she'd not been shortsighted after all.

Maybe.

"He became my friend, Thomas." How to explain? "There was a sincerity in our conversation, an authenticity, to truly show me who he was, or who I thought he was. And it shifted my affections from a simple flirtation to . . ."

"Hmm." Thomas tilted his head. "You wrote him as Frank James in *The Castle*, didn't you?"

Heat flooded her face, and she glanced away. Writing had been her solace—and her revenge. In the pages of her novel, she'd poured all the fury and hurt her broken heart could muster.

"There was no redemption for Frank James, Emme." Thomas squinted, lips tipped. "In fact, I believe he ended up at the bottom of the English Channel."

She winced and tossed him a glare. "Frank James didn't deserve redemption, but that's fiction."

"And Simon Reeves?" Thomas asked, his brow as pointed as his tone.

Her lips parted, but no answer came. Instead, she worried her bottom lip, her gaze drifting back across the room. "I don't want another chance with him," she said at last. "I just want the truth."

"And if the truth still leads you to wish him at the bottom of the English Channel?"

"Thomas!" Emme laughed despite herself. "I'd never truly wish such a thing on anyone. Besides, you, as a clergyman, should encourage charity and goodwill about this whole thing, should you not?"

His lips quirked and he straightened. "As your cousin, and without an elder brother to protect you, I find my charity . . . tested."

Emme's smile flashed wide. "I wish you'd been here that first season. I could have used your wisdom."

"Well." He sighed. "I'm here now and, in the spirit of charity, I shall do a bit of poking about to see what I can learn of your infamous"—he narrowed his eyes—"Frank James."

"Frank who?" Aunt Bean sidled up to Emme's right. "Is he from the James family of Newcastle?"

"No, Mother." Thomas's eyes lit with their resident humor. "A fictional rogue, from one of those dreaded novels you abhor."

"Then why mention him at all?" Her expression puckered like a withered plum. "Someone might overhear and think you read such drivel. You, a clergyman, of all people."

"Perish the thought." He threw Emme a wink.

Aunt Bean ignored him, turning her sharp gaze on Emme. "I was quite pleased to see you dancing with Mr. George Armstrong. He seemed thoroughly engaged. I do believe my lessons are making their mark."

Gratefully, Mr. Armstrong was a reader and rider, two things Emme enjoyed discussing with anyone. And he was a good sort. The cheerful, lapdog type of man who put everyone at ease except for the most introspective or morose. "Mr. Armstrong is a lifelong acquaintance, Aunt. I should hope I can hold a conversation with him."

"Well, he's not in infant's gowns any longer." She huffed, sending an appreciative glance across the room as George spoke with Miss Wilcox. "Eligible, affable, and wise enough to avoid the likes of Miss Gloriana Wilcox."

Emme exchanged a quick glance with Thomas but held her tongue. Despite being an almost-nonexistent conversationalist, Gloriana Wilcox was a pleasant enough woman and possessed a far better dowry than Emme's. Surely Aunt Bean, who valued social astuteness above all, would approve of *her* silence.

"She's placed her beauty spot on the wrong cheek, poor girl." Aunt Bean raised a brow. "A woman of consequence would know better."

Emme closed her open mouth with a little snap and refused to look Thomas's way for fear of losing complete control of her laugh, but in facing forward, she made eye contact with the disconcerting Mr. Arthur Rushing.

A chill skated down her spine.

Last season, he had begun to show her attention after what society deemed a suitable mourning period for his third wife. This season, his intentions were no secret.

He was hunting.

And Emme, unmarried and of respectable lineage, was prey.

From the gleam in his eye as he prowled the ballroom, his interests had not waned since the prior season. Some women called him a dandy, but Emme could not ignore the arrogance that clung to his every movement. His meticulously tailored attire and genteel manners only emphasized the hawkish intensity of his gaze, as if assessing not just a potential partner but a prize to be won.

"Oh, I see you've caught the attention of Mr. Rushing." Aunt Bean hummed her pleasure. "A worthy conquest, Emmeline. He is wealthy, handsome, and has experience in matrimony."

"How is being thrice married an advantage?"

Aunt Bean conveniently ignored her. "Oh, look, he's coming this way." Her fan tapped Thomas's arm. "Introduce me, won't you? Then I can assess him properly."

Thomas frowned and shot Emme a look. She responded with an emphatic shake of her head.

"Mother," Thomas began, taking her by the arm to steer her toward the approaching Mr. Rushing. "Let us not be hasty." Giving a gesture with his chin—an unspoken command to flee before Aunt Bean's plans solidified—he turned his mother's attention in the opposite direction.

Emme loved Thomas.

And needed no further encouragement.

The arched doorway leading to a side hall caught her eye. With a knowing glance to her sister, she slipped through the crowd, pulse hammering in time with her feet. She knew exactly where to go.

The Ruthtons' library! Its towering shelves and thick drapes had offered refuge on many past occasions.

She entered the dimly lit room and pressed the door closed behind her with the faintest click. The welcome scent of leather and books offered an immediate calm to her nerves. On the far wall, the flickering fireplace cast shadows over the rows of books and the empty room, so she allowed herself a small sigh of relief.

Until she heard the approaching voices.

Who were they? Ladies' voices? Her face cooled. And a gentleman? "Drat!" She hissed, immediately remorseful for using the word she'd learned from her father.

Pushing off the door, she darted toward the window-covered wall of curtains and flung herself into those thick velvet folds only to run directly into a very solid form. With a little yelp, she pushed back to find herself face-to-face with Simon Reeves.

"What?" He barked the word in time with her gasp.

"Are you following me?" she whispered fiercely, stepping back but not far enough to leave the curtain's concealment.

"Following you?" He voiced the question like an oath. "I've been trying to avoid you all evening."

Well, that was incredibly rude. "I've been doing the same with you," she shot back.

"Clearly, we're both excelling at avoidance." He ran a hand through his hair and took another step away, the cool air from around the windows sending a chill over Emme's warm skin. "God, help me."

"Ah." She raised her chin. "Are you a praying man now? I've heard it's a sign of wisdom."

"Or exasperation."

She offered her sweetest—and falsest—smile. "Well, I suppose God uses everything."

His lips twitched as if to smile but flattened into a frown. "Why are you here?"

"Same as you, it seems. Fleeing unwanted company." His musky scent invaded all the air around her, so she tried to breathe through her mouth. "Though I'd wager your admirers are more persistent."

As if to confirm her words, the door opened, spilling a burst of laughter into the room. Emme covered her mouth with her hand and edged deeper into the curtains.

"He's not here," a shrill voice declared.

"Mr. Thompson," came another female response. "You promised we'd find Lord Ravenscross in the library."

Emme raised a brow at Simon, who grimaced.

"I thought for certain he walked this way" came Mr. Thompson's smooth reply.

"Caroline has already had a chance to dance with him, but I've not, and don't you think I'm the prettiest of the three of us?"

"The Levering triplets?" Emme mouthed.

Simon's glare may have felled a lesser woman.

Or a woman who knew him less.

The internal admission hinged on her thoughts for only a second before she dismissed it. She must simply feel sorry for him, that was all.

The triplets—well, except Caroline—were known as the loudest and crudest young ladies of the town. Not even their vast dowries thus far had won them matrimony after two seasons.

"I'm determined to win him." This from . . . Frances? "Conquering a rake has long been a goal of mine."

Emme lost all control of her grin then.

He sent her a warning look.

"Not if I win him first," Margaret answered.

"Any man would be honored to have such fine ladies as prospective wives." Mr. Thompson's voice took on the weight of his arrogance. "If I were still a single man, I can't imagine doing any better."

Emme cringed at the very idea of the sixty-year-old man flirting with these young ladies. Preposterous.

"We should search the gardens," one of the ladies said, with the others giving their hearty agreement. And within the next moment, the door closed.

Emme's chuckle shuddered free into the quiet, leaving nothing but the yawning silence behind to sober her. Simon shifted behind her, rustling the curtains as he moved to give her a bit of space.

The silence crackled with memories, unspoken words, and myriad questions. But rather than succumb to them, she chose a safer topic.

"If you're going to select among the triplets, I'd recommend Caroline," Emme whispered, careful not to look his way. "She's the least insufferable."

He growled under his breath.

Her lips crooked a little. "Imagine Ravenscross filled with that laughter all day long."

"I thought I saw you enjoying Mr. Potter's company earlier," he countered, his voice laced with sarcasm. "Am I to congratulate you on an impending match with the charming octogenarian?"

"Certainly not!" Emme turned toward him then, just so he could see her annoyance. "Marriage is usually between two people, so there is no room for anyone else except Mr. Potter and his eternal devotion to his dead wife."

His lips quirked, the faintest flicker of amusement that she resolutely ignored.

"And who are you avoiding tonight, if not Mr. Potter? Mr. Marshall again?" He studied her with those blue eyes of his. "Mr. Armstrong, perhaps?"

Emme folded her arms across her chest. "You seem remarkably well informed about my associations."

"As I said, I've been attempting to avoid you to keep any possible rumors from starting." He looked away, his jaw tightening. "Not that it would matter, should someone find us now—"

The creak of the door interrupted him. Instinctively, they pressed deeper into the curtains. Emme's shoulder brushed up against his chest, her foot colliding with his. Soundlessly, he steadied her with a palm to her waist, and her breath hitched, betraying her.

She froze.

Simon's arm tightened for a fleeting moment, as if to reassure her, before he eased them both farther into the folds of fabric.

The quiet click of footsteps sounded across the wooden floors, nearing their hiding spot. Simon's chest moved with his breaths against Emme's back, soundless, the rhythm easy, in complete contrast to her clutched air.

The footsteps paused.

"Mr. Rushing!" came Aunt Bean's familiar voice. "Ah, there you are! I'm certain my niece is elsewhere. Thomas thinks she may be enjoying a glass of lemonade."

Emme stiffened, her breath shallow as though Mr. Rushing might hear her through the curtain. A shiver coursed through her at the thought, and Simon's arm briefly tightened again, this time almost protectively. For an unguarded moment, she leaned back into his hold.

The footsteps retreated, and the door closed with a soft thud, leaving silence in its wake.

Neither of them moved.

Or spoke.

The tension in the air swelled to a nearly unbearable level, the unspoken questions between them louder than the music drifting from the ballroom. They were too close, and yet she had to fight the urge to turn to see his face. What was he thinking? Feeling? Surely, a rake would have taken advantage of his position at this point.

She drew in a deep breath. "Why didn't you write to me?"

His body stiffened against hers, his response slow in coming. "I . . . I didn't know what to say. Everything changed overnight."

That wasn't the answer of a rake. She turned to look up at him, her body much too close to his as they stood encapsulated by the curtains. "Did you think I wouldn't understand? That I didn't care enough to try and understand?"

He looked away, but not before she saw an expression in those eyes of . . . pain?

"And so you ran away in your grief to live a profligate life in Scotland or America or wherever?" She searched his profile, her stomach squeezing from the need to know the truth. "Or was it something else, Simon?"

His gaze fell to hers, a flicker of raw emotion warring across his features, before his entire expression hardened. "Your notions are quite romantic, even for a romantic sort of man."

The chill in his tone struck her, and she stepped back, arms folding defensively.

"But you're right, Miss Lockhart," he continued, his words clipped, his cold gaze unswerving. "I'm sorry to state the facts so bluntly, but you seem determined to hear the truth."

Perhaps she wasn't as determined as she thought. She took another step away.

"There are other ladies who took precedence over you and will continue to do so."

The words sliced through her chest. She squeezed her arms tighter, refusing to bend, to wince. Something in his eyes, in his struggle, resurrected every doubt she'd been concocting. She would not allow him such ambiguity in his answer, even if it ripped open her healing heart.

"Which ladies?"

He blinked, clearly not expecting her directness. She internally apologized to Aunt Bean. This time *he* moved away from her, reaching for the curtain's edge.

"Have you suddenly lost your desire for directness, Lord Ravenscross?" She pushed more force into her whisper, refusing to back down. "Which ladies?"

He looked away from her face again, almost as if collecting himself, and then returned his cold stare. "Let it alone, Miss Lockhart. Believe the rumors. It will be better for both of us if you do."

He hesitated for the briefest moment, as though tethered by some invisible force. Then, barely above a whisper, he added, "Let it all alone."

And with that, he pushed through the curtain, his footsteps following the pattern and direction of Mr. Rushing out the door.

Emme braced her hand against the wall, lowering her body to sit in the small window seat within her hiding spot. The murmur of distant voices and music seeped into the room, but she barely registered them.

"*Let it alone,*" he'd said. Emme pressed her palm against her chest and stood. *Oh no.* His avoidance only fueled her doubt. He'd called out the rumors too. Not giving them the validity of truth. Why? It might break her heart all over again, but letting it alone was the last thing she planned to do.

CHAPTER 6

Emmeline Lockhart was going to drive him mad!

Simon marched from the library, his neck still tense from holding Emme so close without succumbing to his rather rebellious thoughts.

For all his good intentions, he couldn't seem to evade the woman. Each meeting tortured him anew with what he could not have—her scent, her conversation . . . and now the taste of those lips. An evening of uninteresting or completely inappropriate conversations from the most eligible of St. Groves' ladies, coupled with a few dodges from less appealing suitors like Selena, had only made those few minutes sequestered behind a curtain with Emme feel like a dagger to his resolve.

He had to make a better effort at avoiding her, or his thinly held control might snap, and he'd find himself right back on the balcony, his lips against hers . . .

"Lord Ravenscross?"

God, help me. Who was this approaching? Tall, athletically built, dressed in the latest fashion. Hadn't this been one of the suitors who occasionally danced with Emme, one of the few to earn her genuine smile?

Simon braced for the art of pretense.

The man had the most alarming green eyes—unsettlingly so— and his gaze flicked from Simon's face to over his shoulder, back toward the library door. "I hadn't expected to meet *you* here. I was searching for . . ." His voice trailed off, then he shrugged nonchalantly. "Are you coming from the library, perchance?"

How to respond? Especially with Emme in there alone, and not knowing this man's intentions. "The Ruthtons boast quite the collection. Always worth a perusal."

Vague was best.

The man raised an eyebrow, sending another glance toward the door before focusing back on Simon. "Forgive me. We've not been introduced." He offered a slight bow. "Thomas Bridges, the new rector of Greenleigh Chapel in Lemmingston."

Simon paused. He'd just prayed for divine assistance, and here was a clergyman. Odd. Was God listening after all? Simon cast a look heavenward. He could use some divine intervention to save his family and his estate, and to find a suitable bride. So far, God had been silent. "I have heard of your arrival. How do you find St. Groves?"

"I'm enjoying the new situation." His expression eased. "I find I prefer country living to the bustle of the city, and the quiet of the rectory to the busyness of town."

Laughter erupted from the hallway leading to the ballroom.

"Quiet, is it?"

Mr. Bridges grinned, and he gestured back with his chin toward the way he'd come. "At the *rectory*, but I must admit the enthusiasm of . . . welcome, especially from the single ladies, is unmatched here."

Simon's eyebrow arched. "Enthusiasm is one way to describe the battlefield of the ballroom. Tedious and infuriating are a few others."

"Without a doubt, I can attest to those descriptions as well." He chuckled. "The . . . vigor at which matrimony is pursued here"—he appeared to choose his words carefully, the glimmer in his eyes only proving he might choose differently but for sheer tact—"is truly astounding."

"I have heard you meet the basic requirements of the ladies."

Mr. Bridges' brows rose. "And those are?"

"Male, alive, and able to provide a living?"

"Ah." Mr. Bridges smoothed his palms down the front of his jacket and nodded. "As the third son, I've always been fond of low expectations, for I am certain to exceed them."

Simon's laugh burst out, surprising them both. "Better than the impossible expectations of the firstborn, I assure you. You will have much freer choice."

Mr. Bridges' attention snapped back to Simon, and then he grinned. "I'm in no hurry to be ensnared." He placed a hand on his chest as if in pledge. "I apologize. Marriage is a holy affair, meant for the mutual enjoyment of all involved, of course."

"Spoken like a dedicated clergyman." Mr. Bridges' ready wit set him apart from his predecessors, not that Simon had known a great many of them well enough to fully say.

"And I stand by it, my lord, especially when it proceeds in all the right ways between the right people." There was a knowing look in his eyes. "With the mutual respect of both parties' futures and reputations."

"Well spoken, again." Simon's smile faltered. What was Mr. Bridges hinting at?

"If you enjoy those sentiments, Lord Ravenscross, imagine how compelling my sermons could be." His steady green gaze didn't waver, but his mouth twitched in amusement. "All are welcome, even the most wretched . . . of the aristocracy."

Simon had expected the sentence to end predictably at "most wretched," but the twist amused him. Then, catching the look in Mr. Bridges' eyes, he swallowed his laughter. Ah, so Mr. Bridges knew the rumors too? Typical man of the cloth to rush to judgment.

"I've not been greatly impressed by your predecessors. They were quick with brimstone rather than mercy, especially for those who needed it most, including the wretched aristocracy."

A glimmer lit Mr. Bridges' eyes. "I haven't been impressed either,

85

but it means the bar is set low enough for improvement." A shadow fell over the man's countenance for a brief moment. "And we all have feet of clay, my lord, rank notwithstanding."

Simon gave a nod, noting the man with renewed interest. "A soured reputation certainly leaves a great deal of room for improvement."

"Humbling too, I should think." The man rallied a crooked smile. "For those clearheaded enough to learn from it."

A rector who was not only astute and personable but clever too. An interesting addition to Greenleigh. "My mother often said humility was the best soil for wisdom to take root."

Mr. Bridges studied him. "A shrewd observation."

"Learned from trial, I suspect." The memory sobered him. His mother, who'd lost heart and fortune yet kept her smile for her children. He'd never treat a woman as his father had. Better never to give his heart at all than to trifle with another's.

"Most wisdom is, I hear." Mr. Bridges' hand rested on his chest, as if the words were personal. What trials had this man faced? Some secret lingered behind that smile; Simon would bet on it. "I hope you take such advice seriously."

The man did know something. "I would not claim to be a paragon of virtue, Mr. Bridges. I believe you may be very aware of that." He raised an eyebrow, holding the clergyman's gaze. "But I am certainly wiser now than I was two years ago, through the very means my mother suggested."

Mr. Bridges' eyes narrowed a moment. "Should you be in search of a balm of comfort"—his grin crooked anew—"or wish to critique my expositional abilities, I hope to see you in church, my lord." He took a step back. "I have it on high authority," he said as he glanced upward, "that church can be a place for those seeking a new direction and fresh start. One must, however, be humble enough to admit it."

Simon glanced back, seeing Mr. Bridges look past him toward

the library doors again. Could Mr. Bridges know of Emme's presence there? Surely not! Unless he was one of the suitors from whom she hid? But even in their brief acquaintance, Simon found nothing to fault in Mr. Bridges, who would be a fine match for Emme in wit and reputation. She deserved more than a dull companion. And Mr. Bridges carried himself with dignity, another point in his favor for Emme, er, Miss Lockhart.

But surely a rector wouldn't partake in a secret rendezvous.

"I look forward to the opportunity, Mr. Bridges."

"Good evening, my lord." Mr. Bridges bowed and turned back toward the ballroom without another word.

Simon followed at a slower pace, contemplating an escape from the bustle of the ballroom to leave altogether. He paused at the threshold, the room as grand as any in London, perhaps even grander. And it was packed.

Full of the crème de la crème of the town, down to the lesser gentry.

"She's on the shelf and we all know it," a woman's voice hissed to his right.

A large fern obscured his view but did nothing to muffle the words.

"Except her, of course," another lady replied, her voice laced with laughter. "With her younger sister married only last spring and her elder expecting a child soon, it's clear which daughter is not the favored one of the Hemston family."

Hemston? Simon raised his attention to the room, his gaze landing on Selena, who stood too close to Mr. Banbury, her lavish gown accentuating all of her luxurious curves. She came with a sizable dowry and the Hemston name. Surely some desperate buck would take her, infamous temper and all.

Simon's shoulders tensed at the thought. Even in dire straits, he wasn't that desperate. Her temper and emotional volatility were legendary in town, though it couldn't be easy watching one's younger sister marry before oneself.

He recalled her challenge.

Her determination.

Could her threat truly have nettles? His own situation was far from enviable. Indeed, he was more vulnerable to losing everything than he had ever been.

Finances were perilously low.

His family teetered on the brink of anarchy.

And his estate stood on the precipice.

He couldn't move fast enough with his plans to salvage it.

Except through marriage.

A warning twinged through him, pricking at his pulse. How desperate was she, and how desperate did she think he was? If Hemston or his daughter was aware of even a fraction of his predicament, could they maneuver him into a marriage or the loss of his estate?

"Today's lesson, my dears, is one of utmost importance," Aunt Bean announced as she seated herself in the drawing room, her gown spreading around her like a conquering flag.

Emme and Aster exchanged a humored glance. Rather than resist these absurd lessons from Aunt Bean—to no avail—they had agreed to treat them as the entertainment they'd become. The sunlit room, with its floral wallpaper and cheerful morning light, seemed an ill-suited backdrop for the lecture at hand. Aster, ever the strategist, positioned her sketchbook in front of her, likely to refine the map she'd been secretly working on for weeks.

Emme folded her hands in her lap and braced herself, especially since most of Aunt Bean's instruction seemed rather pointedly fixed on her.

"Charm," Aunt Bean began, the word lingering in the air like the scent of overly strong perfume. "A lady must wield charm as a soldier wields a sword—deftly, with precision, and always to disarm."

Emme suppressed a smile. Aunt Bean's metaphors were often on the edge of the ridiculous, yet poetically so. As an author, Emme couldn't help but appreciate the exaggeration.

Which was to say, all of it.

"Now"—Aunt Bean lowered her voice for dramatic effect—"there are three categories of charm every lady must master. The first: the art of listening."

Aster, who had perfected the art of appearing engaged without truly listening, did not look up from her sketch, giving off the illusion that Aunt Bean's words were so compelling that they demanded to be recorded.

From the tilt of Aunt Bean's chin, she was clearly pleased with the reverence.

"To listen," Aunt Bean elaborated, "is not merely to nod and murmur. It is to flatter. You must hang upon a gentleman's every word, as though his opinions are both novel and profound—even when, as is often the case, they are neither."

"Even when they are utter nonsense?"

"Especially then." Aunt Bean fixed Emme with a sharp glare. "A man must never suspect he is anything less than brilliant in your eyes. It is his first and greatest weakness."

Emme bit the inside of her cheek to stifle her retort.

"The second category of charm," Aunt Bean said, forging ahead, undeterred, "is the subtle yet effective compliment. You must be precise, yet vague enough to let his imagination do the work."

"Such as?" Aster glanced up from her paper, her tone too innocent to be sincere.

Ah, her sister was catching on to the idea of engagement too.

Aunt Bean waved her hand dramatically, as though brushing

away their collective ignorance. "For example, you might remark upon his excellent posture, the strength of his stride, or the pleasing resonance of his voice. Men are highly susceptible to praise that suggests physical superiority."

Emme couldn't resist. "So we should compliment them on attributes they have little control over, like their natural height or the timbre they were born with?"

Aunt Bean's eyes flashed. "Exactly, my dear! It's not the truth that matters but the flattery. Men are simple creatures—a few well-chosen words, and you've won half the battle."

Aster's pencil stilled, her lips quivering. "What if his posture resembles that of a wilting flower? Or his stride is more of a stumble?"

"Then you admire his determination in overcoming such obvious challenges, but never speak of those unfortunate defects *before* marriage. After you've secured him, you are at leisure to dissect to your heart's content, but never before," Aunt Bean snipped. "A real lady is clever enough to adapt."

Emme pressed her fingers to her lips, pretending to stifle a cough.

"And lastly," Aunt Bean declared, her attention fixed on Emme. "The third and most critical category: restraint."

"Restraint?" Emme echoed, feigning ignorance.

"In speech, in action, in expression," Aunt Bean clarified. "You must never reveal too much of your true thoughts. A man should see you as an enigma—desirable but unattainable, until, of course, he has committed himself to you entirely, and then you are at liberty to hold nothing back. It is his fault, of course, for not doing better research."

Emme drew in a deep breath. "So we are to be simultaneously captivating, complimentary, and incomprehensible?"

"Precisely," Aunt Bean said without hesitation, as though it were the most natural thing in the world. "And do not think I haven't noticed your particular failures in this regard." She narrowed her gaze on Emme. "The incident with Mr. Long at the ball, for instance—arguing about women riding horseback unchaperoned! Do you imagine such talk endears you to a gentleman?"

"Mr. Long seemed rather invigorated by the debate," Emme replied, although the real reason she'd engaged with him with such passion was simply due to the fact she'd seen Simon dancing with the honorable, and rather rich, Miss Steele.

Yes, it was an irrational choice, but there she was.

"Precisely the problem," Aunt Bean snapped. "A man invigorated by your intellect will only seek to conquer it. Far better to leave him enchanted by your silence."

"And if silence fails?" Aster interjected, tapping her pencil against her smile.

Aunt Bean's brows rose to almost touch her hairline. "Then, my dear, you must resort to the ancient art of . . . fainting. Nothing disarms a man quicker than a lady collapsing at his feet. He'll be so concerned with reviving you, he won't notice your intellect at all!"

Emme worked so hard to quell her laughter, she started coughing. Aunt Bean was quite serious. Too serious not to laugh.

With that benediction, Aunt Bean rose, her gown rustling like the wings of an indignant goose. "Remember, my dears, in the battlefield of love, sometimes you must fall back—or fall down—to win the war."

Emme and Aster exchanged a look, barely waiting for Aunt Bean to leave the room before they broke into laughter.

Mr. Donald Tarleton gave Simon the first good news he'd had in weeks.

The prosperous tradesman proposed to buy some of the timber from Ravenscross for a price that, while not princely, would certainly grant Simon the breathing space needed for essential repairs and perhaps a new coat or two for himself and the children. After all, if he were to charm a lady of fortune, he must look the part. In an era where Beau Brummell dictated the very threads of fashion, Simon knew the significance of a well-tailored suit.

Thanks to Nora's meticulous list, Simon had whittled down his pool of potential brides to four promising candidates—each less tedious than the last and, most importantly, financially advantageous. But before introducing them to the rather . . . eclectic state of Ravenscross and his lively siblings, he needed to embark on the delicate dance of courtship.

His thoughts were interrupted by a letter perched precariously on the edge of his desk. Stokes, the venerable, ancient, and underpaid butler, must have placed it there while Simon was busy repairing Fia's swing in the garden. The handwriting was unmistakable.

Aunt Agatha.

Simon's shoulders slumped. His mother's eldest sister, a widow with a fortune, had always been their family's beacon during rough seas, especially since his mother's passing. She had been the first to detect Arianna's unwise affection toward Joseph Leeds and had warned Simon accordingly. However, her scrutiny often left Simon feeling like a disappointing echo of his father, though his flaws lay in arrogance and youthful indiscretions rather than harshness and financial caprice.

Perhaps she'd seen a change in Simon, though. He could only hope.

He needed at least one ally who understood their family to help him navigate this new world. Ben was an excellent sounding board, but Aunt Agatha knew the expectations of title as well as the depths of Father's offenses and the gravity of those to the whole family.

He opened the envelope, skimming over the familiar hand. It wasn't a long missive. A few simple lines alerting him to her arrival.

This afternoon.

He stood abruptly, the word echoing in his mind.

This afternoon?

He read on . . .

She was coming to alleviate some of their financial strain?

For the first time in months, a whisper of relief washed over him.

If anyone had the ability and interest to generously help his family without strings attached, it was his mother's only sister. Perhaps her support could buy him time to put some of his plans into place to save the estate without a hasty marriage.

He rushed from the room in search of Mrs. Patterson, and as he passed the library, he spotted William, absorbed in a book.

"Will."

The boy's eyes lifted, wide and curious.

"Would you lend me a hand for a moment?"

A light bloomed in the boy's eyes, and he closed the book, standing to attention in answer. The response paused Simon's thoughts. Was Will's solitary behavior less about escape and more about seeking purpose? Or not knowing where to find it?

Simon swallowed a groan. Of course he needed a purpose. Why had it taken so long for Simon to see it?

"I've just learned something quite important." Simon passed the letter to Will.

Will's face grew serious, absorbing the news, and Simon resisted a smile. Perhaps he had misjudged his brother's disposition as retreat rather than a silent plea for involvement.

"Aunt Agatha is arriving at Ravenscross today. We should inform your sisters so they can make a good impression, and alert Mrs. Patterson. Don't you agree?"

The boy looked from Simon to the page, blinked a few times, and then the smallest smile creased one corner of his mouth. "Yes, sir."

"It would be quicker if we divide the tasks."

Will's smile grew. "I could find Lottie and Fia."

"Excellent." Warmth branched through Simon's chest at that smile. "And then let us meet in my study to discuss further?"

"Aunt Agatha will want the Blue Room, sir." Will offered back the letter. "She said it was her favorite last time."

"Then we'll make sure Mrs. Patterson knows. Thank you, Will."

Will nodded, his smile now fully fledged, before darting off.

After informing Mrs. Patterson, who always seemed to glow at the mention of Aunt Agatha's visits, Simon tidied his study, the library, and a corner of the sitting room before returning to the study to await his siblings, ready to strategize.

Not two steps into the room, he came to a sudden halt.

There stood Mrs. Patterson and Will, their expressions grave. Fia was there too, more preoccupied with a worm in her hand and what appeared to be a twig in her hair than any current crisis.

"What is it?" But as soon as he asked, Simon knew. One child wasn't among the group.

"Lottie's missing." Will swallowed, his voice growing small again.

"And that's not all, sir," Mrs. Patterson added, her hands wringing together in a manner that tightened Simon's chest. "So is Zeus."

"Zeus?" Simon's face went cold. "Zeus is missing too?"

Fia, seizing her moment to contribute, piped up, "I thought Zeus was your horse, Simon."

Simon exchanged a look with Mrs. Patterson, her pale countenance reflecting his own dread.

Lottie had never dared to ride Simon's spirited stallion. She preferred Cleopatra, her steady mare. But Zeus was built for speed and distance, suggesting Lottie had ambitions to venture farther than her previous escapades.

His shoulders collapsed under the weight of the realization as he turned and sprinted toward the hallway.

Lord, help me.

He couldn't manage another missing sister.

CHAPTER 7

"To be perfectly honest, Emme, I'm not entirely sure what to make of him." Thomas rode alongside her, his gelding a striking golden brown next to her black mare, Portia. "Tortured, perhaps? He's certainly not the cad I expected."

Emme frowned and fixed her gaze ahead. "He has a history as a flirt, especially up to two years ago, before . . . before—"

"Meeting you?" Thomas flashed a crooked grin. "Reputations are slippery things, often shaped by the tongues that spread them."

"How philosophical." Emme raised a brow, but he was right. How much of Simon's reputation was based on truth?

"And maturity," Thomas continued, waving a hand as though to encompass the entire notion. "Or rather, the right connections can inspire a man to change in many ways."

"But changefulness can be just as fickle." Emme sighed, settling the gift basket between her stomach and the pommel of her saddle. Her riding cane rested within easy reach, but Portia knew the path toward St. Groves—and today the Deans' house. "What if his next whim changes him back to a rogue?"

"If he ever was one," Thomas added. "I suppose that's something for the next Lady Ravenscross to sort out and address."

She felt his gaze on her profile, and her cheeks heated.

"Which, after being slighted by him, I can only assume will *not* be you." His tone remained light, but she felt the prick of his implications.

"Of course not. I just feel as though something is unfinished between us, and I can't be settled about it. That's all."

"More fodder for your fictional devices then, I'd say."

She flung him a glare. "Not everything I've written in those books is based on my life, Thomas."

"I should hope not." His brow rose, a glimmer deepening his eyes. "There are too many intrigues and murders to be based on any one person's life, especially a young woman of your situation. If I thought any such inspiration came from your own life, I should not only pray harder for you but remove your siblings and father from the house at once."

"You're hysterical." She shook her head and guided Portia forward. "But I should tell you, I've taken your advice."

"Very wise. Of which of my many suggestions have you acquiesced?"

"I'm only tiptoeing into the idea, mind you, but I've started structuring a story with less Gothic tones and more"—she gestured toward the countryside—"home."

"Ah." His brows rose with sudden interest. "And how does it go?"

"I'll let you know." She shrugged. "I'm still trying to find my story within it."

"It will come, Emme." He flashed her a grin. "You only need the *right* inspiration."

At the crest of the hill, the view of St. Groves unfurled before them in all its glory. She instinctively brought her horse to a stop. Old buildings of yesteryear intertwined with newer constructions, reflecting the town's recent resort status. The Royal Crescent, the Guild Hall, the Pump Room, and, of course, the newly built Ruthton Cross Hospital. The small town of a decade ago had yielded to industry and tourism, and a little part of Emme grieved the loss.

Yet the influx of excitement and new faces did bring with it many opportunities for observation. And observation, as always, led to stories.

"Are you certain you don't mind visiting Mrs. Dean in my stead?" Thomas's question pulled Emme from her thoughts. "Until I have a conscientious Mrs. Bridges to assist me or become more acquainted with my parishioners, I feel less prepared to meet some of the needs specific to the fairer sex. And Mrs. Dean was highly distraught on Sunday."

Emme's attention shifted immediately to the small farm just outside of town, where Mrs. Georgia Dean lived. A widow, Mrs. Dean had been left a comfortable income by her late husband that would support her and her two daughters for the rest of her life. After her death, the land would pass to a distant cousin. However, the dear woman, though kindhearted, was known for her dramatic responses to the slightest provocation.

As well as her excellent hats and murderous hen.

Quite the combination of attributes, but country life afforded all sorts.

Emme knew poor Thomas had likely been flummoxed during his first visit, though he certainly hadn't left without a wealth of biscuits, lavish compliments, and a full recounting of Mrs. Dean's life.

"I don't mind at all." Emme had been preparing herself all morning for the extensive visit. "Most of the time her distress is easily remedied with a visit and some homemade strawberry jam." Emme patted the basket. "Strawberries are her weakness, so you'll know for future reference."

"Well, Mrs. Dean and I are sure to get along just fine, for strawberries are my weakness too."

"Either you'll get along famously or be in competition—especially when we visit Mr. Sutherland's garden party. His family's strawberry beds are quite the legend."

Thomas's smile stretched wider, inspiring her own. Emme wasn't closely acquainted with many men—her circles were typically composed of women—but Thomas set an excellent example of what a good man should be. Not that she wanted a rogue of a man, but knowing her own faults, measuring up to someone like Thomas in marriage seemed rather impossible.

If her future husband was a little bad, at least the expectations as a wife would feel more manageable. "Where are you off to anyway?"

"The Lennoxes." He gave his brows a triumphant wiggle. "I've been invited to tea."

And the couple were certain to lavish Thomas with praise, food, and the exquisite comfort of their new townhome. "How you must suffer for your profession."

"To the heart." He pressed a palm to his chest, then adjusted it to his stomach with a feigned thoughtful expression. "Or . . . to the gut?"

Emme laughed. "Don't become too arrogant about an invitation, Reverend Bridges. The Lennoxes have three daughters who are in desperate need of husbands."

Leaving Thomas with a pained look, she tossed a grin over her shoulder and guided Portia toward the path outside of town as Thomas took the direction into St. Groves.

Emme had never dared ride horseback too near town without a chaperone, but visiting the Deans' farm kept her near enough to home not to seem too improper.

Just a little.

An acceptable little.

This was her home, after all. The world she'd known all her life—the hillsides, the pastures, the forests, the dales. All of it fit her as comfortably as her favorite gloves. And thanks to her mother's reputation and her father's generosity, she was known by most every family in St. Groves, and she knew them in return. Thomas's decision to ask for her help was not only a compliment but strategic.

She knew this world.

And loved it.

But there were times when she longed for a bit more adventure, beyond the fictional realms she created. Since her mother's death, her father rarely traveled to London more than once a year and even less to the coast, much to Emme and Aster's chagrin. She didn't care to live near the coast, but visiting always brought a sense of grandeur, calm, and unexpected creativity. Perhaps she should encourage Father to take another trip soon—if nothing else, to curb her curiosity about a certain viscount.

Her hurt urged her to flee.

Her curiosity pushed her toward discovering the truth.

And her heart? She wasn't quite certain.

At all.

Except that discovering the truth might help her find some sort of closure to whatever had happened between the man she'd, well, come to admire, and the one who had left her in the garden.

As Emme approached the Deans' farm, she followed the lane between a copse of trees. The house, with its regal red brick and stone quoins, stood proudly with a hipped roof, maintaining its pristine appearance despite Mr. Dean's passing three years prior. Apparently, the patriarch had planned so well for his family of ladies that both the gardener and the steward remained on the books until Mrs. Dean's death or her move to live with one of her daughters.

The eldest had married two years ago and now lived twenty miles to the east, but the youngest, Anna, had made her debut last season. Emme frowned as she surveyed the windows of the house. As a matter of fact, Emme hadn't seen Anna at any of the balls this season, and as another young lady who ended last season without a proposal, she had expected the girl to try again.

Had she been ill? Visiting her sister?

Emme deposited Portia in the nearby stables with Mr. Marks,

the Deans' kindly groom, and walked to the front door. The maid announced her presence, and immediately Emme was taken into the arms and conversation of the petite Mrs. Dean.

"Oh, but I didn't hear your carriage, or I would have greeted you myself."

Emme grinned and pulled away from the woman's embrace. "I came on horseback, so no wonder you didn't hear my approach."

"Horseback?" The woman's eyes widened to almost the same roundness as her mouth. "Dear girl, do you think it's safe to travel alone and on horseback, no less? I'm surprised your father allowed it."

"It's scarcely two miles between Thistlecroft and here—hardly a distance to note. Besides, the air is refreshing, and days like this were meant for riding."

"But alone?" Mrs. Dean tsked, her capped head shaking with disapproval. "Two miles or twenty, it's enough for a highwayman or thief to make trouble." She sighed, her disapproving tone giving way to a warm smile. "But I am glad to see you—and to find you so delightfully unmaimed."

Unmaimed? Emme stifled a chuckle. Mrs. Dean always did have a talent for dramatic turns of phrase.

The woman led her to a cozy sitting room with wide windows overlooking the back garden. Rolling hills dotted with wildflowers stretched toward the horizon, the Deans' stables and barn nestled comfortably in the scene.

"I am so very glad you've come." Mrs. Dean gestured for Emme to sit at the small table by the window. "You always seem to arrive precisely when my heart needs you most."

The words, so heavy with emotion, gave Emme pause. It was then she noticed the red rims around Mrs. Dean's eyes and the tight strain pulling at her usually sunny features.

"Reverend Bridges mentioned you seemed unwell on Sunday, and I had to come."

Mrs. Dean sniffled, dabbing at her eyes with a handkerchief. "Isn't he a treasure in a world full of ordinary stones? Such a kind man—attentive and so good-hearted. The sort of man to make a fine husband for a young woman." She waved her handkerchief in front of her face. "And those eyes."

Emme's grin crooked.

"He's just the sort to do right by a young woman." At this statement, her voice broke.

Emme covered Mrs. Dean's hand resting on the table. "Whatever is the matter?"

At the question, Mrs. Dean fully dissolved into tears. "I'm sorry. I . . . I just can't . . . it's too much." She dabbed her eyes again. "What would her father say?"

Good heavens. "Mrs. Dean, what is it?"

"It's . . . it's Anna," she managed through sobs, clutching her handkerchief as though it were a lifeline. "She's ruined."

"Ruined?" Emme repeated, keeping her emotions measured. Mrs. Dean's penchant for melodrama often inflated small concerns into calamities. "Surely it cannot be as bad as that."

"Oh, it is!" The woman sobbed with such force, she shook the table. "It's dreadful—unspeakable! I don't think it could have been worse if she'd been attacked by a highwayman, Miss Lockhart."

Emme was trying very hard to understand, but Mrs. Dean gave little to work with. "But Anna wasn't attacked by a highwayman, I'm assuming?"

The woman looked up from her handkerchief, blinking. "Of course not. She's rarely ever alone outside of this farm."

Emme drew a steadying breath. "Then what is it?"

Mrs. Dean lowered her handkerchief. "Anna is . . . is . . ." Her voice shook, and Emme tried to brace herself for whatever revelation may emerge. "With child."

For the first time since Mrs. Dean's husband's unexpected death at the wrong side of a horse, Emme's stomach lurched for the woman. Anna? With child?

And unmarried?

"It's more than I can bear. My darling girl!" Mrs. Dean lowered the handkerchief and took a sip of her tea, which appeared to calm her significantly, because words began pouring out of her. "I thought I'd sent her to visit her sister three months ago, but no! She had been sneaking off to meet Mr. Chapman in secret, and the two of them eloped to Scotland!" She gasped for air, her hand fluttering dramatically to her chest. "Scotland, Miss Lockhart. A godless place where even children may marry!"

The word stopped Emme's cup to her lips.

Eloped? Scotland?

Oh, how she wanted to visit the wild place of jagged craigs and windswept hills. Perhaps she didn't research travel as much as her sister, but her creative mind craved a little of the broader picture of the world in which she lived. "So . . . she *is* married?"

"Three months ago!" Mrs. Dean nodded with fervor. "And to think she returned here, acting as though nothing had happened. And now they have nowhere to go! His father, a tenant farmer, has disowned him, and her dowry—meager as it is—cannot secure them a living." She continued, as if fueled by her own devastation, while also placing a massive amount of pastries on her plate. "Can you imagine? Living here as if nothing had happened, but sneaking off to be with her *husband* at night?" The bite of scone failed to stop Mrs. Dean from continuing the conversation. "I can't allow them to stay here. Her father never would have approved of such a situation."

The scene slowly cleared in Emme's head. "But Mrs. Dean, they *are* married. Anna is not ruined. Surely the situation carries with it a shadow, but it is not an irredeemable one. Something can be done to help them. Your grandchild should not suffer for their parents' haste."

"Grandchild?" The woman dropped her scone on the plate, eyes growing wider by the second. "My first grandchild." A light dawned in her eyes. "Yes, you are right. Something must be done." She paused, her eyes narrowing in thought. "And after all, they *are* married, aren't they? It's not so scandalous as it seems."

Emme opened her mouth to offer further perspective, but a flicker of movement outside the window snagged her attention. A girl on horseback—wild dark curls tumbling about her face and a vivid red dress billowing in the breeze—halted her towering black horse beside the barn. There was something distinctly furtive in the way she scanned her surroundings.

In fact, the girl had brought the horse around the side of the barn away from the stables and facing the vast empty countryside.

With an agile dismount that nearly ended in disaster—owing to the sheer height of the horse—the girl steadied herself. Thankfully, being the eldest child of the family allowed Emme to refrain from reacting straightaway to the sight. She'd learned the value of controlling her facial expressions, regardless of what antics her little brother might do to nearly kill himself or garner attention.

Pressing her back against the barn wall, the girl sidled along its length toward the open doorway, casting a glance about before slipping into the shadows.

"But they can't live here, can they?" Mrs. Dean continued, oblivious to Emme's distraction. "Mr. Chapman would never choose to settle under this roof, and my late husband wouldn't have approved. Yet perhaps we might find them a suitable place elsewhere?"

Emme wrenched her attention back to Mrs. Dean. "Um . . . perhaps as a tenant farmer? Then they could remain close to you."

"Oh, I don't believe Mr. Chapman's father would agree to that. Working the same land, especially with the father casting out his own son, poor boy." She took a sip of tea, no doubt to wash down her second biscuit. "But we must think of something, mustn't we?"

Mrs. Dean began weaving a narrative, transforming the troublesome elopement into a love story destined to produce the perfect grandchild. Meanwhile, Emme kept her focus on the barn.

The girl reemerged, moving carefully—cumbersomely—and carrying a sack slung over her shoulder. It wriggled.

What on earth?

Emme gave Mrs. Dean a nod so the dear woman could keep solving her own emotional dilemma, while keeping the situation outside in her periphery.

Was the girl a servant? Emme narrowed her eyes. Showing up on such an excellent beast and wearing a dress that, though worn, was of higher caliber, likely negated that idea. Emme's breath caught. A well-dressed thief?

"I know," Mrs. Dean said, taking Emme's gasp at mutual delight in the fact that perhaps this grandchild would be a boy after a generation of all girls. "And wouldn't it be appropriate to name the boy after my darling Charles? It's a strong name, and he would have basked in the knowledge of having his first grandson carry it on."

"Yes," Emme said, drawing out the word, her attention flickering toward the window. "Mr. Dean would have been utterly delighted, I'm sure."

The girl appeared to prepare a nearby barrel to help her mount the horse.

"Mrs. Dean." Emme leapt to her feet, her gaze snapping from the woman's kindly face mid-sentence to the window. There, the girl—now improbably seated atop the enormous horse, sack and all—looked poised for a quick getaway. "Pardon me, but I just remembered . . . something . . . that I must do for . . . someone. And I must go there right away."

"Oh, heavens, child." Mrs. Dean rose at a much slower pace, concern creasing her forehead. "Of course. You must go at once."

"You're too kind." Emme backed toward the door, snatching a

biscuit on her way. "And I will put my mind to some way to help this matter with Anna and Mr. Chapman."

Mrs. Dean followed, thrusting a few extra biscuits Emme's way, which she refused to . . . refuse.

Once out the door, Emme ran to the stables, hurrying poor Mr. Marks along. Within moments, she was astride Portia and dashing after the audacious little thief. The girl's mount, a hulking black beast, made her an easy target against the green hills.

Emme followed at a cautious distance as the girl rode east, a direction rarely traveled by Emme herself. Beyond town lay a smattering of farms and, of course, the absurdly grand Palladian-style home Mr. Hemston had erected in a fit of nouveau riche flamboyance. Could the girl hail from there?

What else lay beyond the forest in that direction?

If the child led her to a gypsy encampment, she'd have time to assess the situation—and retreat gracefully, if necessary. And if not gracefully, at least with enough haste to avoid catastrophe. Besides, such an encounter might provide excellent material for her writing. Who could resist the allure of untamed misadventure?

Her pulse quickened at the thought. Even so, she knew better than to confess this escapade to anyone. Father would disapprove, naturally. And Aunt Bean? Well, she would likely swoon from sheer mortification.

A slow, irrepressible smile curved Emme's lips, and she urged Portia into a faster pace.

They rode through a thinly wooded copse, emerging into a field of wildflowers that framed a serene pond. Beyond it, a gray stone tower rose above the treetops, its aged surface mottled with ivy.

A castle? No, it lacked the grandeur. A manor house then? Certainly old, judging by its weathered facade, and worlds apart from Mr. Hemston's garish monument to wealth.

But this? This was something else entirely. Emme drew Portia to a halt, her gaze lingering on the harmonious blend of tower, pond, and meadow. It was as though she had stumbled into the pages of a fairy tale.

Where was she? And more importantly, who lived here?

Prodding Portia toward the pond, Emme scanned the area. A sudden noise—a crack of a branch underfoot—snapped her focus to the right. Emerging from behind the trees, not fifteen feet away, was the girl—her wild hair even wilder in the breeze, her brown eyes alight with fury, and the sack still in her grasp.

"I'll teach you to follow me!" the girl cried, charging forward like a tempest unleashed.

Before Emme could react, the girl yanked open the sack and flung its contents in her direction.

Two chickens burst out, shrieking their indignation at their imprisonment. Wings flailed, claws struck the air with vengeful precision, and both hens launched themselves in Emme's direction as though they'd been bred for combat.

Portia reared with a distressed whinny, forcing Emme to tighten her grip on the reins, her riding crop hitting the ground. One particularly incensed hen found purchase on Portia's hindquarters, pecking the poor mare with furious determination.

The result was instantaneous chaos.

Portia bolted, her hooves pounding against the earth as Emme leaned low over the mare's neck, doing her utmost to stay astride while also attempting to avoid the furious hen still clinging to Portia's backside.

This was certainly not one of the scenarios Emme had envisioned when she set out on this escapade.

The pond loomed ahead, directly in front of them. Emme had to stop this horse! She twisted just enough to swat at the offending bird with her free hand.

Her first attempt missed spectacularly. The second, propelled by sheer tenacity and a fervent wish to survive, struck true. The hen squawked in outrage as it tumbled to the ground, feathers flying.

But Portia's momentum was unstoppable. The mare barreled nose-first into the pond, her hooves skidding against the pebbled bottom.

Emme's tenuous hold on the reins did her no favors. The abrupt halt sent her sailing through the air with all the grace of a sack of grain, landing face-first in the pond.

Two thoughts wove through her mind at the same time.

First, this was a thoroughly mortifying way to die.

Second, *but what a marvelous scene it would make in a novel.*

CHAPTER 8

Cleopatra didn't like Simon.

As one of their oldest mares, she preferred a lighter mount instead of his massive form flanking her. But needs must. He had to find Charlotte before she carried out whatever scheme had taken root in her overactive imagination. His greatest fear? She might truly intend to run off with the gypsies—or worse, the circus. He could still hear her explaining, with unnerving conviction, how her "expert riding skills" would land her a spot in Astley's circus as a circle rider. *God help me.*

After handing Fia off to Mrs. Patterson, he had rushed to the stables, only to be intercepted by Will, who pleaded to join the search. Simon couldn't say no. After all, he wanted to continue to nurture what threadbare relationship he had with the boy. With two horses to ready, a few questions to pose to the stable hand, and some sleuthing around the barn, they were finally ready to ride.

"I don't think Lottie really means to run away to the circus," Will offered as Simon gave him a leg up into the saddle.

Simon tightened the boy's girth with a wry smile. "If that's meant to be reassuring, Will, it isn't working."

Besides, Simon was fairly certain Lottie did all of this to enact some sort of punishment upon him for the tragedies of the past two years. No wonder parents felt so exasperated all of the time.

As he turned to mount Cleopatra, he caught the mare's baleful glare—or so it seemed. If Simon didn't know better, he might think she was siding with Lottie in this whole fiasco.

Will's voice piped up again. "Do you think she does it because she wants to be noticed?"

Simon paused with his hands on the saddle and one foot on the mounting block. He was learning that instead of directives to these children, sometimes they just needed to feel a part, even in ridiculous circumstances with runaway sisters. "What do you think?"

Will frowned, clearly reluctant to elaborate, but after a moment he ventured, "I think Lottie would rather be noticed for misbehaving than not noticed at all."

The words hollowed Simon. Such honesty, directed with such precision into his already tumbling attempts, did not bode well for any budding confidence. He winced and swung into the saddle, turning to face Will. "Do you really think that?"

Will shrugged, looking away. The boy spoke little but watched everyone—saw things and reactions Simon may have been too busy to notice.

"So many people were . . . gone all of a sudden," Will murmured.

Simon pinched his eyes shut for a moment, the declaration a boulder on his chest. First their father, then their mother. Teddy joining the army, Arianna running off on a secret elopement. People *were* gone suddenly, sending their already disjointed family into deeper chaos and . . . loneliness? Perhaps Charlotte needed someone to notice her pain just as Will did, craving reassurance that they were still part of a family, still seen and loved.

How was he supposed to focus on finding a bride? He glanced skyward, a mix of frustration and prayers on his lips. Couldn't the right bride simply appear, fully equipped to help him heal this broken household?

Then, just as they'd turned toward the back pasture, a scream shattered through the afternoon air. A horse's pained cry followed. Simon exchanged a look with Will, who was as pale as milk, and immediately spurred Cleopatra into a gallop toward the sound. Was Charlotte in danger? Was she hurt—or worse? His stomach clenched as he tore through the trees, breaking into open countryside.

On the opposing hillside, just beyond the pond, a horse and a rider raced toward him . . . and the horse was at a perilous pace.

But it wasn't Lottie, nor Zeus.

The rider's green habit flared dramatically as her mount bolted directly toward the pond. Simon squinted, his mind scrambling to make sense of the spectacle before him. And then he saw it—an unmistakable, flailing appendage clutched against the back of the horse.

Was that a . . . chicken?

His mind drew completely blank. He looked to Will as if the boy might have an answer, but his brother merely stared with a similar expression as Simon must have worn.

He looked again. Yes, a white chicken clung indignantly to the back of the horse, flapping wildly as the rider—good heavens, was that Emmeline Lockhart?—batted at the bird. Her riding hat dislodged, sending a cascade of golden hair into the wind, stripping all doubt of her identity.

Air jolted from his body. Of course it was Emme. Because who else would be tearing across his land in such an absurd predicament directly toward him when she was the last person he needed to see?

There was no time to ponder why Emme was riding through his back field with a chicken attached to her horse, because her horse suddenly rushed into the shallow of the pond and skidded to a stop.

A stop that Emme hadn't expected.

Simon watched in horror as she flew forward, a flurry of green skirts and golden hair, landing face-first in the pond's deeper waters.

He stifled a curse. What was happening to his life?

Nudging Cleopatra into a faster pace, he came to the pond at the same time as Lottie.

"I . . . I didn't mean to kill her." Lottie shook her head, breathless and wide-eyed. "I just—I just wanted to scare her. She was following me from the Deans' farm!"

The Deans' farm? That was three miles away. What on earth had Charlotte been doing there?

But Simon had no time for questions. Emme hadn't surfaced.

Casting off his jacket and boots, he dove into the murky water. It was nearly impossible to see, and his outstretched hands found nothing but mud and reeds. Panic surged. Where was she?

Breaking the surface for air, he realized the pond wasn't as deep as he'd feared. His foot scraped the bottom—and then he heard it. The most unexpected sound.

Laughter. A familiar, effervescent laugh that reached him even through the mist of fear clouding his thoughts. What in blazes!

Simon blinked water from his eyes. There, waist-deep in the pond, was Emmeline Lockhart, soaked, bedraggled, and laughing with such unrestrained delight that he almost forgot his irritation.

Almost.

"A very clever escape, Miss . . . Runaway," she was saying to Lottie. "I don't think I've ever seen something quite so determined in all my life."

Simon scrubbed his hand through his dripping hair, his chest tightening. Emme stood with her back to him, her focus still on Lottie, and at her praise, his sister had the audacity to almost smile. *Smile!* After the disaster she'd caused!

As if sensing another's presence, Emme turned, her radiant grin faltering the moment her gaze met his. "What are *you* doing here?"

Simon waved a hand vaguely toward the pond, still catching his breath. "You . . . you could have—"

Her brows arched in challenge, her eyes narrowing. "Died?"

The absurdity of his own words hung in the air for a moment as she stood before him, very much alive—and looking far too pleased with herself.

"And you decided to become a hero," she added with a teasing lilt. "By diving in to save me . . . in five-foot water?"

He narrowed his eyes at her, pushing through the water to reach her side. With a low growl, he cupped her elbow to steer her toward the shore.

"Oh, don't be cross. It was *my* life that flashed before your eyes after all." She tugged her arm from his hold, shooting him a glare. "It couldn't have been that much of a hardship for you."

All heat fled him.

She couldn't believe that about him. That her life held so little value in his eyes?

He leaned nearer, holding her gaze. "That is not true."

Her frown faltered as her gaze held his. Then she took another step—only to stumble, the weight of her soaked skirts pulling her off balance. He caught her with practiced ease, a self-satisfied smirk tugging at his lips as he righted her—an expression she conveniently chose to ignore.

"I've never been properly rescued before, so I think you should feel quite excellent about your . . . failed attempt."

He didn't trust his voice to remain steady, so he drew in a deep breath and said nothing, refusing to let her cheekiness rattle him. He wouldn't rise to it—not yet. Not until both of them were standing on solid ground. And how dare she presume he didn't care? The truth was far worse: He cared too much. That was the problem.

She still haunted his thoughts—long past the time she should have faded. And as the fool he was, he didn't want her to fade. It was the only time he could see her smile, the only time she looked at him the way she once had. When he truly felt like a hero instead of . . . whatever he had become since then.

Once they reached the shore, Simon released Emme's arm and planted his hands firmly on his hips. "What, may I ask, are *you* doing here?"

She pushed a tangle of damp curls from her face, lifting her chin in defiance. "If you must know, I was chasing a thief." With a pointed gesture toward Lottie, who seemed intent on becoming invisible, she added, "That thief, to be precise."

"A . . . thief?" Simon's tone held a dangerous edge as he turned his attention to his sister. Lottie peeked up at him, her lips trembling, before dropping her gaze to the ground.

Drawing a steadying breath, Simon returned his attention to Emme, determined to get her away from Ravenscross—and the chaos of his life—as quickly as possible. "And what, pray tell, inspired you to pursue this thief?"

Emme's lips twitched, though she held her composure. "What else was I to do, Lord Ravenscross? She'd clearly absconded with someone else's horse, for that animal is certainly not fit for a girl of her size, and I watched her steal those chickens. So naturally, I followed."

There was nothing natural about it. Gentlewomen didn't pursue thieves as a rule.

"And what are *you* doing here, Lord Ravenscross?" Her arched brow and the challenge in her voice nearly made him smile—blast her for that. He had been resolute in his plan to avoid her, to keep a safe distance, and now here she was, drenched, defiant, and entirely too tempting. He would not weaken to this attraction. He couldn't. And encouraging any banter was a very bad idea.

"I live here," he said simply, folding his arms as if to underscore the point.

Those hazel eyes rounded in an unnervingly attractive way. "Oh."

Some of her confidence dwindled with her posture. Was she so disappointed to have run into him? And no wonder, with his brusque manner in the Ruthtons' library. But he had to. For his own sake as well as hers.

Forcing himself to remain detached, he watched as her gaze shifted to the looming gray edifice of Ravenscross, its stone walls spiraling against the moody sky. "So that is the famed Ravenscross?"

"Infamous, more like," he muttered under his breath, following her gaze to the house. With the recent history behind those walls and the current state of the place, fame sounded like much too grand a word.

Lottie's movement to his left caught his attention, as she attempted to disappear back into the woods. At his steady glare, she froze in place.

So Lottie had been caught by the esteemed Miss Lockhart in the act of stealing . . . chickens, and then Emme had followed the girl all the way to Ravenscross to nearly meet her doom in the pond?

Of course. He almost shrugged in ludicrous resignation. Why not?

His life was a madhouse.

Utterly.

And he was beginning to lose his own senses right along with everyone else.

"It's even better than I imagined it to be." Emme turned back to him as her body gave a shiver. "Older homes retain such character, don't they? Such . . . mystery. It's one of the small disappointments Father and I express over the older buildings in St. Groves being torn down in favor of more modern options."

She clipped her lips closed as if she hadn't meant to relax into conversation. But she couldn't help herself, could she? Her heart was much too generous, and he didn't need to tempt her forgiveness any more than he needed to tempt his own desires. If she turned her affections back on him after all he'd done, he might very well give up everything to secure a future with her.

But what sort of future could it be? He had nothing.

And his siblings needed him to keep practicality as a primary motivator.

But she made it so difficult. She swept into his life so unexpectedly, bringing light into the dark places of his heart he didn't even realize he'd had and bathing it with some kind of gentle touch he kept craving over and over.

A desire he'd been attempting to squelch for nearly two years.

And was nigh impossible when she kept showing up in all her loveliness and wit and . . . hope.

Hope for what might have been.

He took another step back from her as another shudder trembled over her body.

"You're shivering," he said abruptly. "We should get you to the house. Can you manage the walk?"

"To go inside your home?" She straightened her spine, her gaze slipping back to Ravenscross, before turning back to him. "Of . . . of course."

His lips twitched despite himself. "Whatever you're expecting, Miss Lockhart, I assure you, you'll be disappointed."

"Miss Lockhart?" Lottie's small voice broke the moment as she inched closer, glancing between Simon and Emme. "You're *Miss Lockhart?*"

Heat climbed Simon's neck. How much had Lottie overheard during his discreet discussions with their parents regarding proposing to Emme? Too much, if her expression was anything to go by.

Her eavesdropping was as notorious as her thievery.

"Well, I'm one of them." Emme's brow creased a little, and she glanced at Simon before turning back to Lottie. "I have a younger sister."

Before Lottie could press further, Simon cut in. "Charlotte, collect Cleopatra and go to the house with your brother. I'll bring Zeus. Let

Mrs. Patterson know to set out some of Arianna's clothes for Miss Lockhart."

"Wait a moment!" Emme pointed at Lottie. "Mrs. Dean's thief is . . . your sister?"

Mrs. Dean? Surely Lottie wouldn't have stolen from her! Fire flew through him. "You stole from Widow Dean?" His tone was low, but Lottie flinched as if he'd shouted.

Lottie held up the sack clutched in her hands. "I overheard Cook say we only had a few eggs, and you mentioned selling trees for repairs. Mrs. Dean has plenty of chickens, so I thought . . ." Her voice trailed off as she tried to hide the sack behind her back. "It seemed reasonable. She couldn't miss them."

"First strawberries from the Sutherlands' field and then apples from the Lennoxes' orchard . . . now chickens?" Heat rose into his face for a whole new reason, and he pinched the bridge of his nose, fighting for control. "We will discuss this later, but on your ride back to the house, I want you to devise a proper apology for Mrs. Dean that you *will* deliver in person."

Lottie's face paled to such a degree, the faint freckles across her nose stood out. If he was going to be forced to face the embarrassment of her choices, then she should feel the sting as well.

Lottie's eyes pleaded. "We could take the chickens back and she'd never know."

"Go to the house." He snatched the bag from her hands and turned to William. "And ask Mrs. Patterson to have tea ready. I'm certain Miss Lockhart will appreciate something to warm her."

Warm her? And their balcony kiss flashed to mind.

Simon marched to Cleopatra and raised Lottie to the horse's back, then patted its haunches to usher it along. Emme's black mare had exited the water and kept close by the shoreline, its ears still poised as if waiting for another mishap. Its entire body edged for retreat.

Well, her horse was not ready to be ridden at the moment.

With a whistle, Zeus left his grazing position by the forest's edge and approached.

Emme reached out to him, and in uncustomary style, he nuzzled her palm.

"Such a magnificent animal is much more fitting for you." Again, her lips pinched into a frown, as if she'd forgotten her anger toward him.

Another shiver shook her body. September hadn't turned cold yet, but it had lost the warmth of August.

Simon stepped up beside her and retrieved a coarse blanket from Zeus's saddlebag, Emme's sweet apple scent slipping within range. His throat closed and he took a measured stepped back. "Charlotte tends to overestimate her abilities."

"That isn't very surprising, considering . . ." Emme seemed to catch her words again.

He studied her, brow raising in challenge for her to finish her sentence, and then he reconsidered.

Her lips crooked before another tremor rippled through her.

Smothering a groan, he stepped closer and draped the blanket around her shoulders, holding the corners longer than was strictly necessary. Yet the sudden awareness of how near she was—close enough to see the golden ring encircling her irises—froze him.

He'd helped her with her shawl once when the wind had caught it during one of their walks near town. Just as now, he'd looked into those lovely eyes and time had stilled. It had been that moment when he knew he wanted to marry her.

But now, as she stared back at him, the current wariness in her gaze gave way to something he didn't fully understand.

Another shiver from her broke the spell, and he relinquished his hold on the blanket. "We must get you somewhere warm."

The words came out sharper than he intended, and she flinched slightly. He gestured toward the path leading to the house. "Please. Your father would never forgive me if you fell ill under my watch."

But she hesitated. "Simon, what about the chickens?"

Simon! She kept calling him Simon, each instance chipping away the distance he was attempting to maintain.

"The chickens?" He coughed out the words.

"We really ought to try and catch them, if we can." She waved her hand from beneath the blanket back toward the forest, where one chicken pecked at the ground. "The poor things might feed a local fox, and then both you and Mrs. Dean would gain nothing. But would you mind going after the larger one with the black speckles? He's rather nasty and has always had an unjust vendetta against me."

Simon blinked a few times, trying to comprehend her request. "You . . . you want the two of us to chase after Mrs. Dean's stolen chickens?"

He narrowed his eyes. Did she hear the ridiculousness of it?

"We can't just leave them out here."

Perhaps everyone else was mad and he was the only sane one. "Miss Lockhart, you just fell into a pond and are now shivering to such an extent that your lips are blue, and instead of seeking warmth, you propose we chase chickens?"

Those lovely blue lips trembled in a very different way, giving off the slightest warning she might laugh. "If you put it that way, the chickens can wait."

They walked in silence a moment before she broke it. "I suppose I ought to thank you for your intended rescue, at the very least." She tugged the blanket closer. "Certainly not the behavior of a notorious scoundrel."

He said nothing, quickening his stride. The sooner he saw her safely inside and dried off, the sooner he could send her home. Let her believe whatever she wanted.

She hurried to match his pace. He instantly slowed.

"I assume William is your brother?"

He gave a curt nod, keeping his gaze forward. "You shall meet him properly once you're no longer traipsing about my grounds in a soaked gown." Which, unfortunately, clung to her frame in ways entirely too distracting. "Mrs. Patterson will chaperone your visit."

"Mrs. Patterson?" Her breaths came in puffs, so he slowed even more. Well, his legs slowed. His pulse still pounded like a hunted buck's.

"My housekeeper," he answered tersely, but she refused to take the hint.

"Oh." She fell silent, mercifully, but only for a moment. "As I recall, you have three sisters and two brothers?"

The question was innocuous enough, yet it edged toward dangerous territory. Two years ago, he might have answered freely. Back when he had trusted her so completely, he'd considered sharing every secret, every burden, every scar.

But not now.

An ache pricked at the center of his chest and spread a heaviness through him.

Now those secrets were his to bear. Alone.

"You'll meet the three youngest inside."

Her smile, so radiant, unexpectedly bloomed at his words and almost undid him.

He had to quell this conversation.

"I imagine Ravenscross has enchanting tales to tell." The lilt in her voice somehow loosened the tightness in his chest. "Old houses always do. Perhaps even a ghost or two?"

He almost smiled at her absurdity. Almost. And then caught himself.

Ah, he knew very well how to redirect the conversation into an argument.

"You've been reading too many of those ridiculous novels."

Her head whipped around, and she came to a complete stop. "And what, pray tell, is wrong with those?"

Perfect.

He turned to face her, folding his arms across his chest to keep from reaching out to brush those absurd curls away from her face. "Vampires?" He gestured with his chin toward the house. "Haunted estates? They are fanciful nonsense, designed to fill women's heads with unrealistic expectations."

Her eyes brightened with fire.

Oh no. He'd not counted the cost of how much he loved watching her fight.

"As a man," she said, with a dismissive wave of her hand, "you cannot begin to understand a woman's life."

"Please enlighten me." His challenge hit its mark, igniting her ire all the more.

"We wait—constantly. For our father to grant us an escort to town. For a suitor to request a dance. For a husband to provide us a home. And heaven forbid a woman act outside these expectations, or she's cast out entirely."

Was she alluding to their meeting two seasons ago?

That meeting had been improper. She shouldn't have come.

But she had.

His defenses began to soften, so he grunted through an eye roll and began walking again. "Men, Miss Lockhart, bear the far greater responsibility in providing for a woman's welfare and safety. Waiting for someone else's initiation seems a small price to pay."

Some ungodly sound erupted from her throat as if she might very well explode on the spot. "And how often have you been on the receiving end of waiting, Lord Ravenscross?"

Ah, she'd reverted to using his title. The distance ought to have pleased him. It didn't. And waiting? He knew it too well. Waiting for his mother's health to return. Waiting for word of Arianna. Waiting for his finances to unravel. Waiting for his heart to stop longing for someone he couldn't have.

"You have no idea of my personal circumstances."

"Nor you, mine." Her gaze locked on his, challenging and captivating all at once. "You, with your estate and your title and your"—she waved her hand, clearly searching for the right word—"man-ness! You have no idea what it's like to feel like a pawn to be bartered or a trophy to be won." She drew a breath and continued, her voice firm. "And as for those novels, I daresay they require great thought and ingenuity to craft. Why not enjoy them? Why not offer adventure where it is wanted?"

He stopped at the bottom of the steps to the back door, turning to admire the full glory of her fury.

"And"—she raised a finger as she hurried to keep pace with him—"not all of them are unrealistic. The lady who wrote novels like *Sense and Sensibility* and *Pride and Prejudice* crafted stories that are both realistic and . . . sensible."

She shook her head and turned to march up the steps—only to lose her footing among the tangle of her wet skirts.

His arms wrapped around her instantly, steadying her against him for only a moment.

But it was enough. Enough to recall a stolen kiss on a balcony. Enough to make him forget every reason he needed to keep his distance.

She stilled, her face so near to his that he could feel the warmth of her breath. Those eyes—how they drew him in like a man parched for water. She shivered, and his hold instinctively tightened.

Heaven and earth conspired against him.

He was lost.

CHAPTER 9

The shivering in Emme's body quelled at Simon's nearness. If his gentle grip on her arms didn't send a budding warmth through her middle, then the look in those familiar eyes certainly did. Concern? Tenderness?

Her breath caught as he shifted a step closer, his hands sliding down her arms to pause at her elbows. She rested her palms against his chest, the heat of his skin beneath his damp shirt seeping into her fingers, igniting another wave of warmth up her chest and neck.

Oh, how wrong she'd gotten those romantic scenes in her books.

Well, not wrong. But not potent or vibrant enough.

Not like this.

Her fingers twisted involuntarily into the folds of his shirt.

His palms tightened on her arms, and the soft fluttering in her chest intensified to that of a veritable hummingbird.

She didn't want to like him. Truly, she didn't. He'd broken her heart. He'd tainted her name. And he'd insulted women and novels alike.

She didn't want to feel his lips on hers again, just to see if the second time would prove as delicious and memorable as the first. And she certainly didn't want to recall the way he'd emerged from the pond, dark hair curling and shirt clasped to his skin in a way she felt certain wasn't appropriate for her very appreciative gaze.

And yet here she was, leaning toward him on the steps of his house, inviting him—encouraging him—to wreak havoc on her heart and reputation all over again.

How had everything unraveled from a simple visit to Mrs. Dean's house?

"Emme," he murmured, his voice low and rough, almost pleading. "I need you to understand—"

But she didn't understand. How could she? How could anyone comprehend why he had left her without a word?

"What is going on here?"

Emme flinched and turned. She'd only met Mrs. Agatha Thornbury twice. Once at the theater and another time during a garden party. On both occasions, the woman had been stiff but polite, her serious demeanor softened only by the occasional witticism.

Now, however, there was no witticism to soften the severity of her expression or the steel glinting in her eyes.

As if compelled by the same invisible force, Emme stepped back as Simon released his hold on her. Oh, what was she doing? This was not the way to protect her reputation.

Mrs. Thornbury muttered something too low to catch before turning with a decisive sweep of her black skirts and disappearing into the house.

Simon cast one look at Emme—apologetic, pained, inscrutable—before sprinting after his aunt.

Oh, what a disaster!

Emme blinked, still trying to sort through the labyrinth of her emotions. After only a slight hesitation, and some encouragement from a breeze hitting her already cold body, Emme followed.

Simon turned a corner in the hallway up ahead, and Emme moved in the same direction, pausing only long enough to take in the dimly lit hall. Beyond the alcove, the ceiling soared into a vaulted foyer with a grand staircase to her left and two sets of double doors to her right. The wood-paneled arches echoed faintly with the sound of voices.

"It is not what you think, Aunt Agatha." Simon's voice swelled from the nearby room, a plea in his tone that drew Emme nearer.

"Was there not an unmarried and—so far as I can tell—unaccompanied woman in your arms on the back veranda?" Mrs. Thornbury's sharp response echoed back.

"She arrived here entirely by accident."

"So she is to blame then?"

Emme's face went colder than it already was.

"No, not at all." His exhalation took on more volume. "She saw Lottie stealing a few of our neighbor's chickens and followed her here."

Certainly, that bit of knowledge would not endear Emme to Mrs. Thornbury. A gentlewoman would have alerted the authorities, not ridden on horseback three miles to uncover the mystery.

"Charlotte stole chickens from one of your neighbors?"

Silence.

"She is positively wild, as are all your siblings," Mrs. Thornbury declared. "My poor sister lacked discipline as a parent, but in her absence, they have become feral. As, it seems, have you—judging by your current state." Her voice reeked with disgust. "Drenched from head to foot, and with an unmarried woman in your house. Have you ruined her?"

"Of course not!" Simon's protest thundered. "She stumbled on the steps, and I was merely steadying her. Nothing more."

Nothing more. Emme's breath stalled. Of course. Why would she expect anything else from him? She was such a fool.

"Her horse spooked and threw her into the back pond," Simon continued, his tone exasperated. "I dove in to assist her. That explains our appearance."

"It is still highly irregular," Mrs. Thornbury countered. "And had

124

I not arrived when I did, only imagine the impropriety of bringing a single woman into your house. You both chose poorly if you wish to preserve your reputations."

A flush of heat crept up Emme's face and neck. Mrs. Thornbury was right. This entire situation could damage not only her reputation but Simon's as well. She raised her gaze heavenward in silent apology. Her mother would be mortified.

"Based on my previous visits and your letters, I had seen your attempts to reform your previous reckless ways. I should like to believe today's display is not indicative of the direction of your life."

"Of course not," came Simon's quick reply. "I have worked—*am working*—to redeem Ravenscross's future, Aunt Agatha. I cannot change the reputation my father left behind, but I am attempting to rectify the future my cousin seemed destined to destroy. I've plans to sell timber from the land, increase profits from wool, and even reinstate some of the tenant farmers Cousin Rupert carelessly cast out when their rents weren't enough to cover his debts. I am not my father or my cousin."

A chill skittered up Emme's arms at the barely veiled fury in his voice, the hard-edged determination in his words.

Not his father.

Was he living in the shadow—and at the expense—of his father? His cousin, the previous viscount? And now, was he also the sole guardian of his siblings?

If only men shared such matters with women instead of leaving them to draw half-truth conclusions in the name of "protecting their sensibilities," surely the world would have fewer misunderstandings.

And what exactly had the late Lord Ravenscross done to leave such a blight on the estate? And to drive tenants away? Emme's thoughts tangled around the questions, the word *tenants* snagging in her mind, though she couldn't quite grasp why.

"You have yet to prove it to me," Mrs. Thornbury replied crisply.

"Especially given the spectacle I encountered between you and this . . . Miss Lockhart upon my arrival."

"As I said before," Simon replied, his tone tight, "there is nothing of consequence between Miss Lockhart and me. We are acquaintances—unexpected ones today—and that is all."

Nothing of consequence. The words lodged in Emme's chest, sharp and unyielding. Of course there wasn't. He'd made that perfectly clear two seasons ago. Then why, despite her better judgment, did she keep tormenting herself with what-ifs?

Ridiculous heart. Ridiculous man.

"And I would hope," Simon pressed, his voice low and steady, "that you still have some faith in me. I will do whatever is necessary to protect the family I still have."

Emme's hand flew to her chest at the unguarded steel in his words. *The family he still had?* What did he mean? This conversation only reinforced how little she truly knew about the Simon she had fallen for two years ago. About what lay beneath his charm, thoughtfulness, and . . . friendship.

But no—she had seen his protectiveness. He had always been considerate, even during their courtship. And today he had not hesitated to dive into the pond for her or steady her on the steps. That part of him remained unchanged.

Something wasn't making sense. Whether that something lay completely between Emme's ears or not was yet to be discovered.

"I want to believe that, Nephew," came Mrs. Thornbury's frosty reply, "which is why I even proposed to help you in the first place. I want to believe there is some trace of my poor sister in you—a commitment to your position and your family."

A hush settled, and Emme edged closer to the door. She caught their reflections in a gilded mirror angled in the corner of the room—Simon, drenched and disheveled, yet somehow still arresting, and Mrs. Thornbury, a vision of impeccable authority in her fine crepe suit and perfectly matched hat. The woman rivaled Aunt Bean in both presentation and sheer intimidation.

Emme pressed back against the wall, guilt prickling. *What are you doing? Eavesdropping, that's what.* Mother would be horrified. Truly, Emme should retreat to the hallway and allow Simon and his aunt the privacy their conversation deserved, but her booted feet refused to heed her conscience.

"But I am not naive to your past, Simon. No matter your promises of reform, I will not contribute to your father's failed legacy."

"Neither will I," Simon replied without hesitation.

Emme's breath hitched. Those words—and the quiet weight behind them—lingered. The rumors of Simon's troubles had never hinted at the full scale of his burden. She'd thought of debt as an abstract problem, something solvable through effort and strategy. But this . . . this seemed near-ruinous. Ravenscross wasn't just struggling; it was gasping for air. And Simon was clearly in need of more than clever ideas. He needed help. And money.

Was this what faced him when he learned of his cousin's and father's deaths? When he realized his inherited title? No, he couldn't have known the full degree of it on that night so long ago. The breadth must have unraveled over months.

Mrs. Thornbury's stare remained unwavering, her jaw as stubborn as his. "I am not given to fits of blind compassion, but I am . . . hopeful." Her words hung in the air, a deliberate challenge. "Hopeful that my faith is not misplaced."

"It is not," Simon replied firmly.

"Hmm . . ." Mrs. Thornbury's skeptical hum lingered. With a rustle of skirts, she finally settled into a high-backed chair near the fire. "If that is the case, then I shall speak plainly. I intend to offer you a monthly allowance. Not a great sum, mind you, but enough to provide remedial support as you continue to improve your situation."

Simon's shoulders eased. He took a seat opposite her. "I cannot express my gratitude enough—"

Mrs. Thornbury raised a gloved hand to halt him. "There are three conditions to this arrangement," she interjected. "The first is immediate and likely the simplest. You must hire a governess *posthaste* to create structure for those children."

A governess? Simon didn't have one already? Emme's brow furrowed as she ducked back away from the doorway, her mind racing. How many siblings was Simon looking after? She'd only met two today, but there was also Miss Arianna Reeves, whose striking resemblance to Simon was impossible to miss. And Mr. Theodore Reeves, whose reputation for rakish behavior could scarcely have been worse.

Was the lack of a governess due to cost? The very thought deepened her awareness of Simon's predicament.

"Of course," Simon answered. "I shall begin inquiries first thing in the morning."

"The second stipulation is that you acquire a suitable bride by the end of the season."

The outlandish declaration pulled Emme back to the door. "What?"

Emme's thoughts echoed Simon's exclamation. *Suitable.* Her stomach dropped. Suitable for whom? And by what standards?

Surely Mrs. Thornbury must mean a woman with wealth and status, possibly even a title.

She pulled herself back away from the door, her frown deepening.

Certainly not an eavesdropping gentleman farmer's daughter with barely two thousand pounds to her name—and a secret, slightly scandalous occupation to boot. No, Emmeline Lockhart was anything but suitable.

She stepped away from the room, steadying her resolve with a tip to her chin. Why should the thought of him marrying someone else unsettle her? She'd already grieved the loss of a future with him.

Her chest squeezed at the internal admission.

Besides, she had no desire for an aristocratic life. Or the responsibility of caring for a gaggle of siblings. Or a brooding, novel-hating, dangerously infuriating, and impossibly handsome man.

Her cheeks warmed. She sighed. No, she was entirely unsuitable.

"Pardon me, miss?"

Emme jumped back, her heart leaping as she turned to find a petite woman with a disapproving gaze and impeccable posture. A raised brow added silent reprimand to the tableau.

The woman's plain black dress and white cap marked her as one of the household staff.

"Yes, hello, Mrs. . . ." Emme grasped for the name she'd overheard earlier. "Patterson?"

The other brow lifted, joining the first. "Yes, miss."

"Miss Lockhart," Emme provided, keeping her voice low. "It is a pleasure to meet you."

Mrs. Patterson inclined her head, though her expression remained cool. "If you'll follow me, I shall escort you to a more suitable part of the house."

Ah, *suitable*. That word again.

Emme glanced down at her soaking gown, suddenly aware of the clammy fabric clinging to her skin. In her momentary lapse into eavesdropping, she had completely forgotten her damp discomfort.

Her face heated.

Yet more proof that Emmeline Lockhart needed to keep her romantic entanglements confined to fiction, and certainly not attached to a viscount. When Simon had been merely a gentleman's son, she could have fit a little better into his world. Besides, a second heartbreak at the hands of the only man she'd ever dreamed of marrying was entirely out of the question.

Marry by the end of the season?

Simon stared at his aunt as if she'd spoken in a foreign tongue. Finding a "suitable" bride was daunting enough without a timeline, but to strangle his choices into a few months? Impossible.

And yet, not entirely impossible.

His thoughts strayed, unbidden, to two seasons ago. He had met Emme Lockhart by sheer chance, and by their second encounter, he had already considered her as his bride. By the third, he had known it.

She had unraveled everything—his plans, his expectations, his carefully constructed future. Her regard had redirected his very existence . . . until that future had spun entirely out of his grasp.

"You need funds and stability, Simon," Aunt Agatha continued, her tone unyielding. "And perhaps some favorable gossip for a change, which brings me to my final stipulation."

As if the bride requirement wasn't vexing enough?

He squared his shoulders, meeting her stare.

"No scandals."

"What do you—"

"At the first hint of a scandal, I will withdraw my support." She drew in a breath as she stood, smoothing an imaginary wrinkle in her gown. "This family has suffered enough disgrace to last a lifetime. If we are to rise above the ruin your father and cousin left behind, your every step must be unimpeachable."

Simon's jaw slacked. Most of the scandals plaguing his life were caused by others, not him. True, he had indulged in the occasional youthful folly, but he had hardly destroyed estates or eloped in secret. How was he meant to enforce a scandal-free existence?

"I understand you cannot control the actions of others," Aunt Agatha continued, stepping closer. Her sharp gaze swept over him from brow to boot. "But I will be watching yours. Should you follow in your father's disgrace or your cousin's extravagance, I will cut all support and seek custody of your younger siblings."

The blow landed with the force of a cudgel. "You haven't the right—"

"I have friends in very high places, Simon." Her brow arched with imperious finality. "But make no mistake—I take no pleasure in the prospect of removing your siblings from their home." Her voice softened, her expression searching his. "Or from you. However, I will not have the youngest three tainted by association if you waver. We have already seen the effects on Theodore and Arianna."

"It wasn't just Father's actions," Simon muttered, his voice low. "When Mother . . ."

The words faltered. Saying them aloud made the truth raw, too visceral. Even now, the memory of his mother's decline into grief and apathy choked him. She had faded into a shadow of the vibrant woman she had once been, retreating from life until nothing remained but absence.

Aunt Agatha's eyes closed briefly, her own grief at the loss of her sister evident. When she looked at him again, the fire within her eyes still flared but less brightly. More in line with the woman who had been a presence and help since Mother's death. "Precisely why the younger children must be protected. They need examples of fortitude, compassion, and strength."

Everything within Simon surged to the defense. He was not his father, and he couldn't have stopped his mother's decline, no matter how hard he tried. And he had tried.

Yet his pride yielded to the weight of his responsibility. He had failed to save his mother, failed to shield Arianna from her own spiral. But he would not let that legacy touch the others. Even if it meant swallowing every barb and binding himself to a woman he did not love.

His mind drifted, unbidden, to Emme. He saw her as she had been, golden curls tumbling in disarray, her wide eyes searching his own for . . .

He exhaled sharply, as if the thought itself had teeth.

His heart squeezed . . . and then released. "I accept your terms."

"Very well." She studied him once again with those perceptive eyes and then extended an envelope to him.

With a careful look to her, he slowly opened it to reveal a note marked with a considerable sum.

"This will support your current endeavors and enable modest improvements to prepare Ravenscross for your new viscountess."

Whoever she might be.

Aunt Agatha turned toward the door, her posture regal. "More will follow as I see how you manage the first installment." She paused on the threshold, slipping off her gloves with brisk efficiency. "My room?"

Simon blinked at the note in his hand, then shook himself free of his thoughts. He followed her into the hall just as Mrs. Patterson appeared, descending the staircase.

"Mrs. Patterson, would you be so kind as to take Aunt Agatha to her room so that she may prepare for dinner?"

The woman's genuine smile unfolded, and she curtsied to Aunt Agatha. "Always a pleasure, madam."

Aunt Agatha had already taken two steps toward the stairs when she turned back, her expression softening—just slightly—with what could almost be called a smile. "And Simon, do hire at least one footman. It really won't do for a viscount and his butler to haul baggage to his own doorstep." Her shoulder lifted in a delicate shrug. "Though I must admit, the exercise may nurture humility. Perhaps it's not such a bad thing after all."

Simon stifled the glare threatening to escape and instead offered her a placid expression. A futile effort, it seemed, for a sound suspiciously like a muffled chuckle followed her as she ascended the stairs.

Beneath Aunt Agatha's steely exterior, he recognized a deeper purpose. She grieved, like all of them. She wanted to set things right—just as he did. Her manner may have been unyielding, but her support was steadfast.

Simon looked down at the note in his hand, wishing the money relieved the ache in his heart with as much ease as it did the hole in his purse.

Choose a bride?

His gaze trailed back up the staircase.

Emmeline waited somewhere within those rooms.

He would have made her his bride on that night so long ago.

But that was before.

He bowed his head, his chest heavy. Despite the fanciful notions spun in Emmeline's beloved novels, reality often had little patience for dreams.

Dreams surrendered. Hearts mended.

Eventually.

CHAPTER 10

Emme gazed out the window of the bedroom where Mrs. Patterson had deposited her. It was a large room with warm-colored tapestries on the stone walls and a canopied bed at the center. Afternoon light radiated through beveled glass windows, casting fractured rainbows across the dark wood floor.

Her fingers idly traced the embroidered edge of the elegant green day dress Mrs. Patterson had left for her to wear. It had been Arianna's, she'd heard Simon say.

Arianna Reeves. An undisputed beauty with her dark hair and eyes a shade of blue matching Simon's. Where was she? What had happened to her?

Emme's thoughts trailed to Charlotte. And why would a viscount's little sister feel the need to steal chickens?

The events of the morning—and everything since she'd seen Simon again this season—swirled through her thoughts in a hopeless tangle, not unlike the garden below. She studied the walled sprawl of vines and flowers, noting where a careful hand had once tried to tame the chaos.

Had that been his mother's work?

Lowering herself onto the window seat, Emme pressed a hand to her chest. What had happened to *her*? How had she died? And how did the trinity of losses—his father, his mother, and whatever fate had befallen Arianna—shape Simon's choices?

Her heart ached with a strange tenderness. Perhaps his reasons for leaving her two years ago held more nuance than she had believed.

It didn't absolve him of not telling her the truth, but it reshaped the heartbreak. Maybe it wasn't that he had rejected her, but rather that he had chosen someone else—someone who needed him more.

Could the "ladies" he'd boasted taking precedence over her have been his sisters? His mother?

The realization settled over her like a long-overdue answer to an unsolvable riddle. The nonsensical suddenly made sense. And despite everything, compassion for Simon Reeves swelled in her chest.

He needed help in so many ways.

A scrape outside the room pulled Emme to her feet.

Opening the door, Emme came face-to-face with a sight that could only be described as the most peculiar kind of adorableness she'd ever encountered. A little girl stood there, no more than six years old, her golden curls a wild tangle accented with a few blades of grass and a smudge of dirt on one cheek. She might have stepped straight from the pages of a fairy tale—if Ravenscross's library contained such stories.

Surely it did. Perhaps not novels, but certainly fairy tales.

At the girl's side was a gray hound, who shuffled forward to sniff Emme's skirts before graciously accepting a pat on the head and returning to his young charge.

"Hello." Emme crouched slightly to meet the girl's wide, fawn-brown eyes. "And who might you be?"

The little girl examined Emme a moment before responding. "I'm Fia."

"Fia?" Short for . . . Sophia, perhaps? "It is nice to meet you. My name is Emme."

Emme's longer name often proved burdensome for little ones and "Miss" seemed much too formal for such an informal introduction. If this was another of Simon's siblings, she looked the least like the other Reeveses with that blonde hair and those large brown eyes. Perhaps through the nose?

Fia's dimpled smile widened. "Are you a friend of Simon's?"

The word *friend* carried a weight Emme hadn't anticipated. "I am."

"Lottie said so." Fia nodded as she pulled something from the pocket of her rumpled dress.

A wriggling something.

A frog-like wriggling something. And from the grip Fia had on the creature, it was likely fighting for its life.

"And you will like my friend."

Emme's stomach twisted, but she managed to keep her expression neutral. "Your friend?"

"His name is Blast." Fia thrust the amphibian toward her. "And Lottie said you'd like him."

Lottie? Hmm . . . Charlotte?

A flicker of movement in the hallway caught Emme's eye, and she spotted a dark head of curls vanishing around the corner. Clearly, little Miss Charlotte Reeves was testing her. But if Charlotte thought Emme would be easily unsettled, she was sorely mistaken. After all, Emme had been the substitute mother to her brother, Alfie, for years, and he had an unparalleled love for nature in all its most . . . unexpected forms.

Half out of spite and half out of compassion for the poor creature, Emme smoothed her hands over the fine fabric of the borrowed gown, then extended her palms to the little girl. "Let's see what you have there then."

"He's a frog," Fia announced, as if Emme didn't know. "He's very happy to see you. Look how he's trying to jump into your hands."

As an escape, no doubt. Emme cupped her palms around the wriggling creature so that his body was free within her hold and his head peeked from between her fingers.

"You must be a very nice person to like frogs," Fia declared with the utmost seriousness.

Emme smiled. "If liking frogs is the measure, then yes, I must be."

Fia's smile widened into a double-dimpled masterpiece, her missing teeth only adding to the effect. For a moment Emme was overcome with the urge to scoop up the muddy, delightful little girl and hug her.

"I had another frog last month. His name was Rufus." She touched a gentle finger to the frog's head peeking from Emme's fingers. "But he fell asleep and wouldn't wake up."

Oh dear.

Fia shrugged, only momentarily bothered. "But I found a new one."

"And why did you name this one Blast?"

"For Simon," she explained. "It's one of his favorite words."

A snicker slipped past Emme's lips this time. "Is it?"

"Mm-hmm." She nodded, her hair bouncing around as if it were as desperate as the frog. "Lottie said that naming him Blast-It-All was too long."

Emme pressed her teeth into her lower lip to suppress her laugh and glanced toward the hallway to the eavesdropper. This time, Charlotte didn't bother hiding but sauntered closer.

"I do believe the shorter name suits such a small creature." Emme returned her attention to Fia.

"That's what Lottie said."

As Charlotte stepped nearer, Emme studied her more closely. What on earth would drive a girl her age to steal chickens? Was Ravenscross truly in such dire straits that even the children felt the burden?

"I suppose we should be introduced properly." Emme offered the poor frog back to Fia, ensuring she assisted the little one in a better grip. Then she wiped her fingers on the tiny—and dirty—apron at Fia's waist before offering her hand to Charlotte. "Emmeline Lockhart."

Charlotte hesitated, her curious gaze sweeping over Emme before finally taking her hand with a confident grip. "Charlotte Reeves."

She couldn't be more than fourteen, but there was gravity to those eyes.

"A pleasure."

"Is it?" Charlotte challenged.

This child was born to star in a novel.

"Perhaps I should say I sincerely hope it *will* become a pleasure," Emme replied, her lips twitching.

One corner of Charlotte's mouth quirked upward, and her deep blue eyes narrowed slightly. "Did you truly follow me all that way just because of some chickens?"

"To be honest, justice for the chickens was only part of it," Emme said, maintaining an air of composure, despite Charlotte's growing grin. "I'm terribly curious by nature, and you presented quite the mystery. So, in hopes of liberating those chickens and discovering your secret, I followed you all that way."

"And you didn't come to see Simon at all?" One of her dark brows rose with more accusation than intrigue. "He has quite a few ladies after his title, from what I've heard."

Oh, she was well aware of Simon's admirers—most of them ill-suited, the worst being Selena Hemston. But there were at least five others who had made their intentions plain, not to mention the hopefuls charmed by the enigmatic Viscount of Ravenscross.

The man could do with a secretary just to manage his romantic prospects.

"You don't like that idea?" Charlotte's sharp question pulled Emme from her thoughts.

This young lady was much too perceptive.

"Well . . ." Warmth crept into Emme's cheeks. "Titles are all well and good, but if they don't improve someone's life or character, I fail to see why they should command so much attention."

Charlotte studied her before offering a reluctant shrug. "I suppose not."

Emme's untamed curiosity leapt to fill the pause. "But surely your brother's travels have yielded better prospects for a viscountess? St. Groves' social pool is rather . . . limited."

"I doubt it." Charlotte's nose wrinkled with her frown. "The only journeys Simon has taken were to pay off debts or search for Arianna. He'd have done better staying here. We needed him more than she did. Arianna made her own choice. The rest of us didn't have one."

Emme blinked, her assumptions crumbling. All the rumors about Simon gallivanting across Europe, womanizing and carousing, were just that—rumors. And Arianna's disappearance? By her own volition? Had she . . . run away?

A sudden cry cut through her musings.

"Blast!" Fia's voice rang out as she dashed down the hall, the unfortunate frog leaping for its life. "Come back!"

Emme exchanged a look with Charlotte, and then they both set off after the little girl, skirts flying as Fia continued her noisy pursuit. The frog sprang toward an open doorway and disappeared under the bed.

"Blast-It-All, get back here!" Fia cried, dropping to her knees to crawl after it.

A highly unladylike snort escaped Emme as she lifted her hem to quicken her pace into the room, only to barrel directly into Mrs. Agatha Thornbury.

"What is the meaning of this commotion?" Mrs. Thornbury's narrow-eyed glare swept from Emme to Charlotte and then to Fia, who was dropping to her knees by the bed.

"Blast-It-All is running away, Aunt Aggie," Fia announced as she crawled beneath the bed.

"Blast-It . . . ?" Mrs. Thornbury looked up to Emme for clarification.

"Fia's frog," Emme offered with a helpless shrug.

"A . . . frog." Mrs. Thornbury pressed a hand to her forehead.

"This household is worse than I imagined. Completely ungoverned." Her sharp gaze skewered Emme. "I suppose you are encouraging this chaos with your rustic manners, allowing children to run amok?"

Heat flared up Emme's spine, and she straightened her shoulders. "Firstly, Mrs. Thornbury, I am not the children's guardian, so their behavior is hardly a reflection on me."

The woman's brows arched in sudden unison.

"Secondly," Emme continued, refusing to lower her gaze from the woman, "I am the daughter of a gentleman—albeit a country gentleman—and in my opinion, such roots are no discredit. Country manners have produced many well-bred, practical, and compassionate individuals in the world."

If Mrs. Thornbury's brows could climb higher, they certainly tried.

"And lastly," Emme concluded, barely hanging on to her smile, "you do not know me well enough to judge my manners. I may lack expertise in managing frogs indoors, but I am well versed in caring for children, having raised my siblings after my mother's passing. A little lightheartedness and imagination"—she gestured toward Fia's wriggling feet—"frogs included, are healthy for any child. Life will force them into adulthood soon enough." Her gaze softened as it flicked to Charlotte. "If it hasn't already."

Mrs. Thornbury's sharp scrutiny shifted to Charlotte and back to Emme. The silence was punctuated only by Fia's muffled struggle with the fugitive frog.

"We met on several occasions a few years ago, did we not?" Mrs. Thornbury's head tilted in sudden recollection. "Your father is . . ."

"John Lockhart," Emme supplied, caught off guard.

"Indeed." The woman's eyes narrowed as if rifling through an index of Lockharts.

"I believe you may have been better acquainted with my mother, Eleanor Lockhart."

"I do remember her, yes." A fleeting softness graced Mrs. Thornbury's features. "She was well known for her grace and poise."

As if pointedly remarking—with Emme chasing a frog through the house in a borrowed gown—that she did not inherit those attributes.

"Yes, and her ready humor," Emme added, just to feel better about herself. "But perhaps you would have known my father's sister." She hesitated, knowing the peril of introducing Aunt Bean's name into any respectable conversation. "Mrs. Albina Bridges?"

Mrs. Thornbury's gaze sharpened. "We studied together. She was always quite . . . ambitious."

It was Emme's turn to noncommittally respond: "Indeed."

Mrs. Thornbury's appraisal turned more pointed. "I recall you being very efficient at croquet."

The remark threw Emme entirely off course. Two years ago?

"At the Conways' garden party?" She blinked, unraveling her wariness over this conversational shift. "You must mean my sister, Aster. She's the more adept player. I'm the one who nearly knocked Miss Hemston's hat clean off."

A twitch betrayed the corner of Mrs. Thornbury's lips. "Exactly." *What?*

"And you had your cap set at my nephew at the time, I believe."

Oh, Mrs. Thornbury had led Emme into this discourse like a mouse to a trap. If she hadn't felt so woolly-headed about it all, she may have taken note for her next matriarchal character. Mrs. Thornbury was positively resplendent.

"Si—" Emme swallowed. "Lord Ravenscross and I did become acquainted then, yes."

The twitch at the woman's lips took a more prominent stretch upward. She'd caught her mouse, and Emme wrestled through myriad answers for possible questions to derail any further inquiry.

"Blast!" Fia's exclamation burst from beneath the bed, echoing Emme's internal sentiments all too perfectly.

"Women of your rank often pursue titled men, so your efforts to secure an advantage are hardly surprising," Mrs. Thornbury mused, stepping closer. "What *is* surprising is that I expected you to be more levelheaded and conscientious than . . . grasping."

Was there a compliment buried in that quagmire? Emme stared back, refusing to kowtow. "I am not seeking Lord Ravenscross's title, Mrs. Thornbury."

"No?" She rounded Emme like a cat on the hunt. "You've come to save him then?"

The barb struck as intended, though Emme refused to flinch. Everyone in St. Groves knew the Lockhart family's modest means. "I should hope I have the good sense to know my dowry could not accomplish that, but the good heart to wish him well in his efforts to rescue his home and family." Her smile tightened as she added, "Do not mistake me for a grasping debutante in search of a title."

"Then why sully your reputation—and his—by arriving at Ravenscross unescorted? Only desperate women stoop to such tactics to ensnare a suitor."

Emme's jaw slackened at the accusation. "I am neither desperate nor audacious enough to throw myself at Lord Ravenscross."

"Oh?" One brow arched northward. "You genuinely like him enough to risk your reputation?" Her frown deepened with warning. "If you truly wished to help him, you'd employ methods less . . . scandalous."

"I had no intention of risking either his reputation or mine. I was merely visiting a widow in the community when I—" Emme caught sight of Charlotte's wide-eyed alarm. "I noticed Miss Charlotte there, unescorted. Naturally, I brought her home." The line between truth and evasion was perilously thin.

And it was still true. In fact, Emme watched Charlotte rather closely all the way to Ravenscross.

Mrs. Thornbury's attention shifted to Charlotte, her gaze narrowing. "Saw her home, did you? And, pray tell, what was my niece doing at this widow's house?"

Charlotte's eyes grew impossibly wider, her lips parting but no sound escaping.

"She was . . . seeing to Mrs. Dean's chickens," Emme offered quickly.

"Seeing to Mrs. Dean's chickens?" Mrs. Thornbury repeated, another twitch pinching up one edge of her lips.

"Blast!" came Fia's triumphant cry from under the bed as she emerged, her hands clasped tightly around the wriggling renegade frog. "Look, Aunt Aggie, I caught him! He's here to meet you."

The woman's face softened enough to reduce her age by a decade. "Darling child, what have you been rolling in to have mud from boots to hair ribbons?"

"The garden is her favorite place," Charlotte said, voicing her first words since walking into the room. "It's where she and Mother passed the mornings."

Emme pressed a hand to her chest, suppressing the ache the words stirred. Oh, how well she understood the longing to revisit places where memories of a mother lingered, trying to feel her near in some way.

"Yes, well, Sophia could do with a bath," Mrs. Thornbury announced.

"And I have already overstayed my unexpected visit." Emme dipped her head politely and began edging toward the door. "It was a pleasure to meet you, Mrs. Thornbury." Her gaze landed on Charlotte, offering her the faintest smile of reassurance.

"I believe Simon has already called for the carriage to take you home." Mrs. Thornbury nodded, the steel from her earlier gaze momentarily absent.

Emme dipped her head again in acknowledgment and left the

room. As she turned into the hallway, she caught sight of the young boy she'd seen earlier with Simon. William? She smiled gently at him, but he quickly looked away, retreating into the shadows of the corridor.

Despite the faded carpets and vacant walls where the outline of paintings once hung, the house retained grandeur and beauty. But the wounds and fear that must run rife within the walls? Children mourning both father and mother, a new viscount grappling with the burden of salvaging a title and estate, and an enigmatic aunt dispensing ultimatums?

Someone needed to help all of them.

Emme had barely reached the bottom of the stairs when Simon approached, freshly dressed, though the damp curl of his hair betrayed a recent swim. Her smile threatened again. Her hurt had lost some of its sting in light of his burdens—his forced choices that had shaped him.

"I've readied the carriage for you." His gaze flicked to hers as he gestured toward the front door. "And your mare—"

"Portia?"

His lips curved faintly, the smallest concession to humor. "Shakespeare?"

Emme shrugged, watching how he fought the smile. "I have a fondness for intelligent and lively heroines, my lord."

His gaze steadied in hers. "As do I . . ." His voice faltered and he looked away, clearing his throat as he gestured once more toward the door. "Your mare is harnessed to the carriage. She will see you home, along with your belongings."

Her heart pinched at the wealth of words left unsaid. Oh, the weight he now carried!

Simon Reeves had made the right choice.

His family. His duty.

All those bitter thoughts she'd nursed against him unraveled in the face of his burdens. He was, in truth, the man she had believed him to be—the man she had loved.

And she had to let him go. To honor his decision.

"Thank you." She stepped toward the door as he opened it for her.

He fell into step beside her, maintaining the careful distance required by propriety, pausing at the carriage to extend his hand to assist her. Emme hesitated. She had left her gloves with the rest of her soiled clothing. Still, there was no avoiding it. With a slight pause, she placed her bare hand in his.

The warmth of his touch jolted through her, the sensation stirring memories she had worked so hard to suppress. He had held her hand before. Touched her cheek. Drawn her close in an embrace that had once seemed unshakable. Her gaze flickered to his, and the intensity in his eyes told her he felt it too.

And then she released him, withdrawing her hand with quiet finality.

The carriage lurched forward, carrying her away from Ravenscross—and from the man who had claimed her heart and broken it in equal measure.

The man she could never have.

Simon stared into the fire, Aunt Agatha's ultimatum still turning over in his mind. It felt as though the embers mirrored the chaos within him. He had seen Emme off only an hour before, yet her image remained vivid—hauntingly so.

There she had stood, wearing his sister's dress, her golden hair damp and slightly disheveled, the wide depths of her eyes searching his.

And her touch—his fingers fisted at the thought of it. That brief, searing connection as she pressed her hand to his lingered with him, heavy and impossible to shake.

It was as though, in that single moment, she had said goodbye.

Charlotte had, of course, wasted no time in recounting her and Emme's conversation with Fia about the frog and the ensuing confrontation with Aunt Agatha. The sparkle in his sister's eyes as she spoke of Emme's defense had said much. It hadn't been Emme's words alone that had earned Lottie's admiration—but had it also been the presence of another young woman? A female mentor for his hurting sister?

"If you're trying to avoid Emmeline Lockhart, you're doing a remarkably poor job of it," Ben remarked from the chair opposite, his words no help at all. He'd arrived a little after Emme had left, passing the carriage as he'd come to the estate, so of course Simon had told him of her . . . unexpected visit.

Simon's attention snapped to his "friend," who lounged as though he had not a care in the world. "Did you hear anything I just said? It was an accident, plain and simple. The last thing I wanted was to see her here."

In fact, seeing her in his home, with his siblings, made everything worse. She fit too well. Brought too much light. Sprinkled her loveliness within the lonely walls.

He didn't need to have that vision in his head.

Nor the sensation of her in his arms, the soft curves of her body shivering up against him.

"I heard"—Ben relaxed back into his chair—"something about your thieving sister, some chickens, and a swim in the pond with your favorite heroine." He paused, adding a shake of his brows. "Very romantic. I daresay your life is nearly novel-worthy."

Simon sent Ben a warning glare, which only bounced off the man's self-satisfied grin. A bruised eye would do a great deal to alter his smug expression. Perhaps a broken nose too.

"Come now. It has all the best parts of those novels. Hero's noble sacrifice for his family, faced with financial ruin, having to choose between love and duty." He waved toward the door, as if to conjure up someone. "You've even got the tragic heroine in the mix."

"If I had the money to spare, I'd pay you to leave right now."

Ben chuckled, entirely unbothered. "Your house is teeming with characters waiting to be written. Speaking of, I ran into the infamous Aunt Agatha as I came in. She gave me a look that could freeze the Thames in mid-July." He forced an exaggerated shiver. "I can't fathom why she doesn't like me. I'm rather charming, if I do say so myself."

Simon, at that moment, found himself fully sympathizing with Aunt Agatha. "Aunt Agatha has little patience for charm, as you well know."

"Her loss then." Ben reclined farther, crossing his arms with a smirk. "I'd be an asset to any dinner party, charming as I am. Is she always so . . . glacial?"

Simon's attention fastened on the note on the side table. "I've known her softer side, though I've not seen it for a few months."

"Ah." Ben sat up, grinning. He always grinned when Simon was on edge. "Why do I get the sense she's complicated matters for you?"

Simon growled, the sound unintentionally revealing.

"And . . ." Ben drew the word out, his grin turning positively wicked. "What is her current method of torture?"

Simon sighed, pinching the bridge of his nose. "An ultimatum actually. I'm tasked with hiring a governess and finding a wife— without causing a scandal—before the end of the season."

"What?" A laugh burst from Ben. "And if you fail, will she send you to bed without supper?"

Simon leveled a glare in his direction. "She's offering an allowance, one that would grant me a bit more freedom to save the estate."

"Is it really as bad as that, Simon?" Ben's expression sobered. "That you must accept her terms?"

Simon rubbed at his temples, the weight of the situation pulling at him like a physical ache. "My cousin was thorough in his debts, my father very close behind."

Ben winced. "Good heavens."

"And Aunt Agatha," Simon continued, "is dangling just enough of an allowance to keep Ravenscross afloat. She's made it clear—if I don't find a bride by the end of the season, she'll end her allowance."

"No wonder you're in a devil of a mood." Ben gave a low whistle, shaking his head. "A bride? By the end of the season? It's absurd."

"Unfortunately, what I really need is time." He ran a hand over his face, giving his head another shake. Time to watch his current ventures expand. Time to see how his investments grow. "Time to make good decisions, not just practical ones."

An uncharacteristic frown played over Ben's features as he studied Simon. "On second thought, practicality doesn't suit you at all."

"I'm afraid that what suits me," Simon replied dryly, "is a dowry large enough to save Ravenscross without delay."

Ben's grimace deepened, before recovering with a glint to his eyes. "Well then, if practicality is all you need, then Mrs. Tewksbury is an obvious choice. She has a fortune, is pleasant enough, and I hear she's rather fond of gardens. You do have a garden, don't you?"

Simon scowled. "Mrs. Tewksbury is twice my age."

Ben waved off the comment with a casual flick of his wrist. "Details."

"And I would like an heir," Simon added. A faint smile tugged at the corners of his mouth. "Mrs. Tewksbury is not an option."

"Then there's Miss Moss, of course." Ben's grin returned, this time brighter. "Didn't you already dance with her? Perfectly amiable, lovely hair, and—most importantly—no scandal attached to her name."

Ah, his friend was trying to lighten the mood. Simon raised a brow. "Miss Moss barely said two words the entire evening."

"Precisely," Ben countered, his grin widening. "Think of the peace and quiet she'll bring to your life."

Simon chuckled despite himself. "Indeed. I shall move her to the top of the list."

Ben stood, clapping Simon on the shoulder as he passed. "Well, I'd offer more advice, but I believe you're beyond saving."

Simon squinted up at him. "Your encouragement knows no bounds."

But the levity had ebbed. Even Ben's steps carried a heaviness as he moved to the door. Pausing at the threshold, he glanced back, his expression unusually grave.

"I know I tease about practicality," he began, hesitating before meeting Simon's gaze. "But you're a good man. One of the better ones, despite my otherwise deplorable taste in friends."

Simon's lips twitched at the poorly veiled compliment.

"And I don't want to see you . . ." Ben faltered, his tone softening. "This is your life, Simon. 'Until death do us part' can be an awfully long time with someone you neither respect nor care for."

The warning struck low and firm, tightening Simon's chest.

Ben patted the doorframe, a flicker of his usual grin returning. "My father once told me that when choosing a bride, I should at least find someone I could stand to be in the same room with."

"Very practical." Simon shook his head, his gaze traveling back to the fire. Low expectations, low results?

But Ben's lingering silence pulled Simon's attention once more, his friend's expression uncharacteristically earnest. "But I'd say it is even better if you can find someone who makes you forget there's a room at all."

With that, Ben stepped out, leaving Simon alone with the gravity of his words. Ben's mother had been a silly, selfish woman who'd cast a shadow over the entire household until her death. Simon had no intention of following such a path.

If he were to choose a bride, it would need to be someone he could trust—or at the very least tolerate without constant friction. But truly respect? That was a high bar in his world.

And yet, only one person came to mind. One person who, against all logic, tempted him to forget not only the room but his very reason for being there.

Simon's lips finally gave way to a faint smile, but it was a sad imitation, lacking the joy it once carried.

What he'd hoped to bring to this family two years ago had to die.

What he needed to bring to this family now must remain his focus.

And he prayed to see Emmeline Lockhart as little as possible during his search because no bride should ever have to compete with another woman for her husband's heart.

CHAPTER 11

Would you mind repeating that?" Thomas stared at Emme, his brow growing more creased by the second.

"We should help Lord Ravenscross and his family." Emme picked at a piece of lint on the settee before raising her gaze to Thomas's. "How could we not at least try after all we've discovered about their situation, Thomas?"

"We?" His blond brows hitched upward.

"He *is* one of the flock in your parish, isn't he?"

"A viscount in financial straits is rather different than a farmer's widow, Emme." Thomas took a few steps closer to her and rested his hand on the back of the chair nearby, as if bracing himself. "I'm not certain how welcome my help might be."

"That's all the more reason to help." She waved a hand toward him, her voice firm. "He's not the sort to ask for it, but that doesn't mean he doesn't need it. And he's not just a viscount. He's also a son, grieving the loss of so much, carrying the weight of responsibility for his family. He could use some encouragement and guidance, I'm certain of it."

"Emme, I don't know that it's wise for you to get involved." His knowing look caused her to glance down at the lint again.

"I don't know what you mean."

His sigh filled the room. "Lest you forget, cousin-dear, he is the man who slighted you, left you to fend for yourself among the social pariahs, and broke your heart. You may not have the clearest vision on this."

"Or my vision is very clear because of it," she shot back, only to meet his knowing look.

She immediately found the lint incredibly interesting again.

"He must make a practical and responsible decision, not a sentimental one, Emme."

Thomas didn't have to go about reminding her. Her heart knew the sting all too well. "Perhaps because I understand Lord Ravenscross better, because I've seen past the aristocratic facade to the man beneath"—an unbidden vision of him in the damp shirt from the pond came to mind, but she shook it off—"I know how best to help him. And . . . well, he has a good heart, and he's found himself in a bad spot. Those poor children, Thomas. I don't want to see him or his family suffer any more than they already have."

Her breath caught in her throat. It was the first time she'd voiced it, this understanding, this admission. And it shook her, because it meant that somewhere along the way, she'd truly forgiven Simon Reeves. How could she feel a twin sense of freedom and grief at the same time? Her heart knew it had to let go, yet still, a part of her wept.

Was that why she wanted to help him so much?

"Emme, in most cases, your desire would be admirable, but with him—"

"How can you say that? You're a clergyman, for heaven's sake." She sent a pointed look from his toes to his hatless head. "You should applaud my decision, especially with someone whom I would have considered nearer my enemy only a few months ago. Where is all your talk about loving one's enemies and forgiving others?"

"He has friends. He doesn't need you getting involved—"

"But I am his friend too," she said, cutting him off, the acknowledgment settling deep. "I heard his aunt's ultimatum and met the children. And I have a very real way we can be of assistance. Besides, he may be more inclined to take advice from a man of God."

Thomas narrowed his eyes, his skepticism clear. "My position is not a game card, Emme. Not everyone is eager for a visit from a man of God." He leaned forward slightly, his sigh revealing the first cracks in his resistance. She thought the "man of God" bit might help her cause, and she shot a glance heavenward in gratitude.

"What exactly are you proposing I do?"

Her smile wavered wide. "Nothing outrageous. Quite the opposite, in fact. Small, sensible acts in keeping with your station." She raised her hands in a placating gesture, as if soothing a skittish horse. Surely Thomas would see the wisdom in her plan. "Encourage him in subtle ways—gifts for his larder, which I mean to provide. And perhaps you might help me persuade him to allow his younger sisters an outing or two under my care. It would provide them a touch of a lady's influence and grant him some relief."

Not to mention, it might keep Charlotte from her light-fingered tendencies.

Thomas tilted his head. "These are tasks you could manage without my involvement."

"I cannot visit him alone," she pointed out, her gaze lifting to meet his with unspoken pleading.

His lips thinned. "What else?"

"I want you to help me convince Simon to take on a tenant farmer or two."

"A tenant farmer? Emme, it is his business what he does with his—" Thomas's words faltered as understanding dawned on him. "You're thinking of Mrs. Dean's daughter, aren't you?"

"It would be a mutually beneficial arrangement," she said. "They need a place to live and work, and Simon needs income and produce. His cousin's poor reputation likely left him with few recommendations for tenants." Perhaps her idea wasn't so far-fetched after all. In fact, she was beginning to feel a little giddy about it all. "And as rector, you're aware of others in need. It's a practical solution that benefits more than just Lord Ravenscross."

Thomas studied her, his skepticism giving way to a wry grin. "I see your plotting isn't confined to your novels."

"Stories are everywhere." She offered him a pleased smile. "Why not use them to work toward better ends?"

Thomas regarded her thoughtfully again, and then, with a resigned bend of his shoulders, he moved to the seat beside her. "You must realize, Emme, he can't choose you for his bride, no matter what you do."

Oh, she knew. The truth had settled over her long ago, and though it ached, it no longer cut as sharply. Perhaps her resolve to help had dulled the pain. "I'm not ignorant of the world, Thomas. Lest you forget, I am embroiled in Aunt Bean's rather inventive campaign to find me a suitable match." She squeezed his hand, her smile tinged with humor. "It was a fanciful notion to think a country landowner's daughter like me could aspire to marry the nephew of a viscount. Even less so now that he's inherited the title."

She exhaled, the weight of reality pressing firmly against her. "I know he cannot choose me, even if he wished it. But that does not mean I cannot help."

"I think," Thomas said slowly, shaking his head, "you show much more Christian charity in this moment than I would."

She chuckled. "Then perhaps extending a little benevolence toward him might ease your ire."

"I still wish to throttle the man," he muttered.

"Then do it with a dose of charity," she teased, giving his hand another squeeze. "Your protective instincts are clouding your godly ones."

"I've been practically a brother to you. It is my right."

"And I'm grateful for it, most of the time."

His grin widened as he released her hand. "Most of the time, we aren't discussing your former suitor. It makes for far less agreeable conversation."

"Then perhaps"—she scooted to the end of her chair, her anticipation nearly shaking her body—"you'll find my next proposal more to your liking."

"Oh no," he groaned. "More magnanimity? I suspect the wrong family member joined the clergy."

"Would you truly wish to hear me preach a sermon?"

He gave her a hard look, a twinkle lighting in his eyes. "Complete with adventure, dangers, mystery, and romance? No, because you may very well show me up, and then I'd have no income."

"Unlikely," she retorted with a snicker, rising to her feet as Thomas did the same. "You are an excellent preacher and, usually, the one proposing acts of service and magnanimity."

"For good or ill, I believe you're particularly inspired in this case." His frown deepened, so she pressed forward quickly with her idea.

"I've written to Miss Lane to see if she is currently seeking employment."

"Miss Lane?" Both of his brows rose in unison. "Your former governess?"

Emme nodded. "With her mother having passed away three months ago, she may be ready to resume a position somewhere. I know her mother did not leave her very much money, and she'd be an excellent recommendation for Lord Ravenscross."

Thomas regarded her for a long moment before shaking his head. "You truly are relentless."

"Determined," she corrected, unable to tame her smile. "And entirely justified."

"Certainly, if anyone knows how to guide fanciful and head-strong young girls into womanhood, it would be the indomitable Miss

Lane." Thomas braided his hands behind his back and started down the hallway toward the door, Emme at his side. "Do you think Lord Ravenscross will agree?"

"Well . . ." Her grin spread as she followed him to the entryway. "It would be very practical and responsible for him to do so." She quoted back his earlier words.

Thomas shot her a mock glare. "I shall remember never to give you ammunition."

"So you will go with me to Ravenscross tomorrow?"

He paused at the threshold, his expression turning serious as he studied her face. "I will. But Emme, this is not one of your stories. The daring hero will not abandon his responsibilities for the lesser-known and poorer damsel. He will choose for status, money, and family. Are you prepared for that reality?"

She held his gaze, embracing reality with a painful hold. "I am."

He nodded and opened the door. "Then I believe I can help you." He hesitated, his eyes narrowing slightly. "As long as there are no other surprises."

"I think those are quite enough, and then I'll know I did my part."

"More than your part." He searched her face with complete skepticism. "And that is all?"

She shifted her gaze away from his. Why was he asking her that as if she weren't being completely forthright? "Of course."

"Just be careful, Emme," Thomas said, his voice low and steady. "Putting your heart on the page is one thing. But placing it close to someone who has already wounded it? That is far riskier. Take care not to step into a situation that breaks it all over again."

A knock at the door pulled Simon's attention from the letter he'd just finished, written to secure a date for Mr. Tarleton to fell some of his timber—the first real sign of hope in his situation. It lightened the tension in his neck, though not enough to fully dissolve the strain of too many problems and not enough solutions.

"Come in."

Mrs. Patterson entered, clearly a bit discombobulated at having to attend the door as well as the rest of the house when Mr. Stokes, the butler, was engaged elsewhere.

"You have visitors, my lord."

"Visitors?" Simon cast a glance at the clock on the wall. Was it noon already? "I wasn't expecting anyone."

"No, sir." Mrs. Patterson dipped her head, almost apologetic. "It is the new rector, Mr. Bridges."

The rector? Why on earth would the man come to Ravenscross without invitation?

"And Miss Lockhart, my lord."

His chest collapsed with a silent exhale. So much for not seeing her often. He pushed the rising interest beneath a shield of iron will and rose to his feet.

"Please lead them to the drawing room, Mrs. Patterson."

"Yes, my lord."

"And Mrs. Patterson?"

She turned back with pale brows raised in expectation.

"Thank you for taking such good care of this household."

Her entire expression froze for a moment, save for a few rapid blinks. Then she pressed a fist to her chest and nodded before closing the door behind her. His words hung in the air, a simple truth that sank into him more than he'd expected. How long had it been since someone had shown true appreciation for the woman?

Two years ago, he would have scarcely noticed her presence, as most servants were meant to be invisible. But since his world had turned upside down, his perspective on everything had shifted.

One trial after another, each pointed to his own insufficiency—his weakness, his lack of wisdom, and the wounds of his own emotions. All those friends who'd once filled his life, aside from Ben, had vanished when his cousin's death had cast a shadow over the entire Ravenscross reputation. Slowly, Simon had come to appreciate the dedication of the few who remained, and the humbling of his pride—though brutal—had pulled out the poison of his father's stubborn blood, bit by bit.

He glanced out the window as sunlight attempted to break through the ever-pervading clouds. Why, he wondered, did the deepest lessons always come through the harshest trials?

A quiet laugh escaped him. Probably because he was the greatest fool of them all, and only the sharp blade of suffering could cut away the disease that ran through his family line. He brought his gaze back to the sky.

"Then cut away, for I would not wish to be like my father."

He sealed the letter to Mr. Tarleton, dropping it on the platter in the hallway on his way to the drawing room. The timber would provide some financial relief for Ravenscross, but it would take time. Perhaps securing another deal, like offering a portion of the estate for grazing or timber rights to neighboring farmers, could help as well. But the idea of Emmeline Lockhart returning to his house after the fiasco two days ago both puzzled and—perhaps—terrified him.

What in the world had brought her back?

They'd courted for only three months, yet he'd learned swiftly that once Emme set her mind on something, it became a matter of when, not if, she saw it through. Arriving back at his house with the clergyman—of all people—meant she'd brought someone to support whatever scheme she had in mind.

A tiny sliver of hope tried to resurrect itself, but Simon swiftly quashed it.

He opened the drawing room door and entered, his gaze immediately finding Emme. It never failed. Even at every ball and gathering, he always sought her first. He noted her clothing, her position, the subtle clues in her demeanor. And there she stood by the window, sunlight catching the rose hues of her blue gown as if she had stepped directly from a dream into his home.

His breath hitched. Despite it all, she'd found her way beneath his skin, into his bloodstream, coursing through him like breath and soul. How was he to still this longing? Now that he had held her again, kissed her, breathed in the scent of her?

How?

It would require, at the very least, the amputation of his heart.

And yet, he must. He must silence the heartbeat for her. Disconnect the gravity pulling him to her.

He shifted his attention to Mr. Bridges and nodded. "Welcome to Ravenscross."

"Thank you, my lord." Mr. Bridges dipped his head and then sent a glance to Emme. "We hope we are not intruding."

"Not at all," Simon replied, though the words were only half-truth. Her presence always unsettled him. "What can I do for you both?"

"We've come bearing gifts and . . . ideas." Emme stepped forward, a large and laden basket in her arms.

Oh dear, she *did* have a plan!

"This holds various jams, a ham, and some freshly baked bread, compliments of Thistlecroft." Her smile bloomed. "And I just delivered a wonderful selection of fresh eggs to Mrs. Patterson in order to keep Charlotte from becoming . . . inventive again."

Simon stared at Emme for a full five seconds as the full weight of her words settled. She'd brought a food basket? Like one might bring to a sick widow? For some reason, he wasn't sure whether to be offended or . . . amused.

"And I thought, if you're amenable to it, I could take the girls out on a few excursions over the next weeks." She thrust the basket toward him, her smile nearly theatrical in its brightness. "It would give them something to do outside of Ravenscross, and perhaps they could benefit from a bit of female company?"

Simon's usually adept grasp of the English language was sorely tested in this moment. Emmeline Lockhart's words seemed to fly at him from unexpected directions, leaving him struggling to keep up.

"Emme, you are confusing the poor man." Thomas stepped forward, deftly rescuing Simon from his turmoil by taking the basket—which Simon had yet to receive—and setting it neatly beside one of the high-backed chairs. He turned to Simon, his expression steady, a calm anchor amid the storm of Simon's scattered thoughts. "Would you mind if we took a seat, Lord Ravenscross? Miss Lockhart has apprised me of certain matters and believes we may offer some assistance—or, at the very least, guidance—should you wish it."

"Rescues usually work better with more hands," Emme offered, looking a little less confident than she had only a moment before.

Had he only recently said that very same thing to Fia?

"Y-yes." Simon shook his head to clear it, gesturing to the chairs. "Of course. Please, do sit."

Simon kept his focus on the rector, though he could feel Emme's gaze on him. Evidently, her presence made him both nervous and an imbecile. Not exactly the mental state he needed for this conversation.

"Miss Lockhart is eager to be of service to your family and has, perhaps"—Mr. Bridges sent Emme a look that incurred an exasperated sigh from her—"moved forward with more zeal than necessary."

She shot Mr. Bridges a frown, which nearly brought a grin to Simon's lips. Why was it so tempting to provoke her indignation? He quickly schooled his features, determined to regain his composure. He needed to marry—quickly, even—if only to avoid further complications with Emmeline Lockhart.

It was a terrible reason to marry, but there it was.

"Forgive me for my forthrightness, my lord," Mr. Bridges continued. "I understand these are private matters, and I do not wish to pry, but Miss

Lockhart and I have a few very practical solutions for you to consider. If you will allow us."

"Solutions?" Simon's voice was flat, though inwardly he bristled. As if he hadn't racked his brain for every conceivable answer from every possible angle.

"It is no secret you have found yourself in a difficult financial situation." Emme's voice was soft, almost consoling. There was no pity in her eyes, but compassion?

His body stiffened at the reminder—or perhaps at the unexpected solace he saw in her gaze. "And how do these matters involve the two of you?" he asked, his tone sharper than intended. Their visit, and especially this line of conversation, was entirely improper.

Well, perhaps not from a clergyman, but certainly from Miss Lockhart!

There. Referring to her as "Miss Lockhart" rather than "Emme" helped create a distance in his mind. This was Miss Lockhart, the country girl currently prying into his personal affairs. Not Emme, his former . . .

He refused to finish the thought.

Mr. Bridges, oblivious to Simon's inner conflict, pressed on. "I can only imagine the weight of responsibilities that have fallen upon you since inheriting your title. Doubtless, you are exploring ways to address your estate's financial concerns."

Simon leaned back in the chair, the space between them now tinged with cool detachment. "I am, but I am still uncertain how those matters concern the two of you."

"Of course." Mr. Bridges' jaw tightened, a clear sign Simon had struck a nerve. "Have you considered taking on tenant farmers? I believe your cousin did so during his time, but not . . . near the end?"

"The numbers had dwindled considerably over the last year of his life," Simon replied. "He wasn't the most generous of masters."

"But you're not him," Emme quickly interjected.

Simon closed his eyes for the briefest moment. *Miss Lockhart. Not Emme.*

"It happens there are several families within the parish who could benefit from tenancy," Mr. Bridges continued, clearing his throat. "Take Mrs. Dean's daughter and her new husband, for example. They need work and a place to live. A section of your fallow land could be farmed, providing produce for Ravenscross, income for you, and a home for them."

Simon regarded the rector, the suggestion digging uncomfortably into his pride. He had entertained the idea briefly, but larger ventures had seemed more pressing. Still, with assistance, this could yield a modest, steady income. "You could provide me the names?"

"Indeed, sir." Mr. Bridges' expression relaxed, almost imperceptibly. "Within the week, if you wish."

Simon's pride took another hit, but it had become so bruised of late, the sting was less severe. "Thank you both for the suggestion and your assistance." His gaze flickered toward Miss Lockhart.

Despite Mr. Bridges' delivery, the idea had been hers, hadn't it? She had seen Ravenscross's struggles firsthand, understood its needs. And despite having every reason to avoid him, she had come—with baskets, ideas, and jam, of all things. His pride crashed to smithereens.

"There is another matter." Mr. Bridges gestured toward Miss Lockhart, who immediately leaned forward in anticipation.

"I've written to my former governess, Miss Lane, to inquire if she is looking for employment. She is a fine lady, matronly in manner, who has . . . personal experience"—she shrugged apologetically—"with girls who may find themselves in more mischief than usual."

Simon froze. She must have heard Aunt Agatha's ultimatum. There was no other explanation for her suggestion. He had not mentioned the need for a governess to anyone but Ben. What else had she overheard?

"If she responds favorably, shall I arrange for you to correspond or perhaps interview her?" Mr. Bridges interjected smoothly, steering the conversation into more conventional waters. His tactful phrasing underscored an unspoken understanding—Simon couldn't correspond directly with Emme.

"I would be grateful, thank you."

Emme's smile was immediate, bright enough to light her eyes. "Your sisters would benefit greatly from her guidance. And it would relieve you of the burden of overseeing their education."

Simon looked down briefly, gesturing toward her with a slight nod. "You've . . . put a great deal of thought into this."

"Well, once the idea occurred to me, I couldn't rest until I'd thought of potential solutions."

"A regular hazard of any friendship with Emmeline Lockhart," Mr. Bridges said, his lips twitching into a smile.

They exchanged a look—a shared understanding—that tightened something in Simon's chest. How close were they?

Why had Emme asked Mr. Bridges to escort her here today and present this plea? Was it simply because Mr. Bridges, as one of the clergy, would be more easily accepted into Ravenscross? Or was there something more between them?

Hadn't Mr. Bridges been going toward the library at the Ruthtons' where Emme was hiding when Simon had first met him? Heat seeped from his body. Could they have been meeting in secret?

And hadn't he observed the rector and Emme dancing together on more than one occasion?

A sharp heat crept up Simon's neck, his chest tightening further.

"There is one more matter on which I feel I can provide assistance," Emme said, drawing his attention back to her. Her fingers were twisted together in her lap, the slightest ink stain visible on one edge of her palm. It was the twisting of her fingers, though, that truly caught his eye. She only did that when she was nervous.

Extremely nervous.

"You do?" Mr. Bridges looked over at her.

She raised her chin, another warning sign. "I do." She drew in a breath. "Considering the circumstances in which you find yourself, and the restricted timeline, I would like to help you find a suitable bride."

CHAPTER 12

"What?"

Both Thomas and Simon jerked their heads toward Emme, staring at her in unison.

And her resolve floundered entirely.

Of course the very barriers that had caused her to second-guess their fledgling connection two seasons ago were now even more insurmountable. A newly titled viscount, laden with debt, did not marry a woman of middling fortune and modest social standing—especially not one who scandalized society by writing shocking novels under a pseudonym. A viscount needed wealth, position, and an impeccable reputation.

It was how the world worked. She'd accepted that.

Her body sagged with a sigh. Until Simon had swept into her life and made her believe in more.

She nearly laughed aloud. Thomas was right; she wasn't living in one of her stories. She should have held fast to her resolve not to meddle, to avoid Simon Reeves at all costs.

Then she'd seen Simon's reluctant gratitude, and she'd caught sight of Charlotte peeking shyly from behind a shelf at the back of the room—a much more experienced eavesdropper than Emme had ever been—and she realized something simple yet undeniable: She was uniquely positioned to help Simon secure a "suitable" happiness for his future.

But as the two men stared back at her, both wide-eyed and

slack-jawed, she warred between backing out of the plan or forging ahead into the madness of it. One look into Charlotte Reeves's large round eyes secured the decision for her.

She had to help him.

No, them.

"I am in a unique position to offer my assistance," she said firmly, summoning confidence she didn't wholly feel. "I know most of the ladies of the ton and have the freedom to converse with them in ways gentlemen cannot."

"Emme, we never discussed you offering to—"

"For example," she said, ignoring Thomas entirely, fixing her gaze on Simon. There was no turning back now. "Miss Lanard, whom you danced with at the Ruthton ball, is the very picture of poise in the ballroom. However, she's an inveterate gossip in private, a trait that would bring untold misery to your household."

"Emme, this is not your—"

"And Miss Pool," she pressed on, "is generous with compliments in public and makes conspicuous visits to the sick, but she treats her servants abominably and the poor even worse when there is no one to witness her 'charity.' Did you know that?"

Thomas sighed audibly, but Emme refused to be deterred. She held Simon's gaze, searching for a flicker of understanding. He stared at her as if she had grown horns from her head.

Sadly, it wasn't the first time he'd looked at her that way.

"I don't presume to know you . . . intimately," she added, clearing her throat. That kiss lingered in her mind, undermining the statement's veracity. "But I do understand your situation better than most, and"—her voice softened, her heart panging for the lost man before her—"I know more of your character than you might suspect."

His attention flickered to hers and then held. "I cannot say it is the most prudent conclusion, Miss Lockhart." His tone was neutral, his expression impassive. But his eyes—they betrayed something deeper, an unspoken connection that surged through her like a silent plea for what neither of them could give.

So, she told herself, she would channel her emotions into a safer, more acceptable direction.

Friendship. Nothing more.

It would have to suffice.

Her newest heroine—a woman separated from her beloved by war only to return and find him married to another—would undoubtedly appreciate the authenticity of such anguish. Research, indeed.

Authentic research, indeed.

She was mad.

"It's a simple start, really." She stood, backing away from him to give her emotions some distance. "In fact, if you'll note from this short list, my first suggestion is Miss Eliza Clayton." She pulled a piece of paper from her reticule. "She's well bred, has a respectable dowry, and she's perfectly amiable. I would even suggest you invite her to the theater this Thursday."

Another puff of exasperated air came from Thomas at her left.

Simon's mouth dropped open as he stood. "You've . . . drafted a list?"

"Of course. You haven't much time."

"Emme, have you gone mad?" Thomas stepped forward, between her and Simon. "What are you doing?"

She stiffened her resolve and met his incredulity with a steady gaze. "Not mad," she said, willing her expression to reflect her sincerity. "Just . . . sensible. And good." Sidestepping Thomas, she placed the envelope in the gift basket she'd brought. "Speaking of sensibility," she added with a bright smile, "I've included some light reading for you in the basket."

"Apart from the list, I presume?"

Ah, Simon had found his voice again. She much preferred this version of him to the one gaping at her as though she'd lost all reason.

"Indeed. To broaden your appreciation for novels. You may find it hits rather close to the mark of reality." Reaching into the folds of the basket, she withdrew a copy of *Sense and Sensibility*.

Before she could present it with dramatic flourish, the door slammed open, and Sophia Reeves charged in.

Today the girl wore a little red dress instead of the blue one from the other day, though the mud splattered across it remained a consistent feature.

"Blast! Come back here."

Sure enough, a frog darted through the door and hopped at a desperate speed toward the shadows beneath the couch.

Everyone froze except Charlotte, who began to rise slowly from her hiding spot.

"Blast-It-All!" came another frustrated cry as Sophia dashed forward, heedless of the adults in the room, her hair as wild as her pursuit.

William appeared next, stumbling into the doorway, clearly giving chase. He stopped when he noticed the audience and retreated into the shadows of the hall.

The chaos of the moment only solidified Emme's decision. This family needed help—whether Simon asked for it or not.

"Sophia!" Simon stepped forward and scooped the girl into his arms. "A lady doesn't use such language."

Charlotte's eyebrows arched nearly to her curls. Emme pinched her lips against a smile, while Thomas's gaze flicked from Sophia to Simon to the frog, now hidden beneath a bookshelf.

"But you use the word all the time," Charlotte piped up, her voice ringing out with all the clarity of an accusation.

Every eye shifted to her.

"Have you been hiding back there this entire time?" Simon's tone was part exasperation, part disbelief as he strode toward his sister, still holding Sophia.

Fia sent a toothless smile over her brother's shoulder toward Emme. "I caught a snake today, Miss Emme."

Emme's face cooled several degrees. "Oh!"

"He got away before I could keep him, so you won't be able to hold him."

Thank heavens.

"I thought Aunt Agatha was watching after you." Simon scanned the room, finally setting his attention on Charlotte, who took a few steps back. "What did you do to Aunt Agatha?"

"Nothing." She shook her wild curls. "She fell asleep while reading *Little Red Riding Hood* to us, so we left her undisturbed."

"She doesn't do the voices like you do, Simon," Fia added with a pout, leaning close to her brother's face. Something in Simon's expression softened, and Emme's heart puddled entirely.

That vision nearly overruled the pond scene.

Nearly.

"She was a horrid wolf," Fia continued. "Will does a much better wolf—he even bares his teeth." She made a face showing what little teeth she possessed, supposedly in imitation of her brother.

From the doorway, William's serious expression broke into a rare grin, evidently pleased with this accolade.

Emme's heart squeezed further. These children might be untamed, but their affection for each other was undeniable. If her sister and brother had been in such dire circumstances, she would have wanted a good friend to step in—even with something as unconventional as matchmaking.

"It seems Miss Lane cannot arrive fast enough," Thomas muttered, earning a sharp look from Simon. He shrugged regretfully, waving vaguely at the room as if to say *case in point.*

"Blast, Simon!" Fia suddenly grabbed her brother's face with both hands, her urgency palpable. "We must find him before he's squished."

"Who?" The poor man blinked, utterly at sea.

"Blast."

"Fia, I already told you, you cannot use such lan—"

"It's the frog," Emme interjected, stepping forward to spare him further confusion, though her smile threatened to escape. She extended a hand to Fia, who squirmed free from Simon's grasp. "The frog's name is Blast," Emme explained, fixing Simon with a look of mock matronly disapproval. "Since it appears to be one of your preferred expressions."

He opened his mouth, no doubt to protest, but no sound emerged. Seizing the opportunity, Emme led Fia to the bookshelf. After some coaxing and an unladylike amount of kneeling, she succeeded in retrieving the errant amphibian.

Fia beamed, holding Blast far more carefully this time. Smart girl.

"Are you staying for dinner?" Charlotte's hopeful inquiry broke the moment, earning a cough from Simon.

The look on the girl's face nearly swayed Emme, but good sense prevailed. "I'm afraid not, but I would like to invite you and Fia to join me at the Sutherlands' strawberry patches tomorrow—if your brother allows it. My sister and I have been invited, and I'm sure they'd welcome more hands to ensure their fine produce doesn't go to waste."

"Strawberries?" Fia exclaimed, clutching the frog with renewed excitement. "Blast loves strawberries!"

Doubtful, but Emme smiled anyway.

"Do you mean it?" Charlotte's voice came quick, her gaze darting between Emme and Simon. "Truly?"

Before Emme could reply, she caught sight of William lingering in the doorway, edging closer. "William is welcome to come as well," she offered. "We shall need a strong lad to help carry the baskets."

Simon narrowed his eyes at her for a moment, but then he drew a deep breath, the corners of his mouth twitching as if to suppress a smile. "You've placed me in a difficult position, Miss Lockhart. How can I refuse?"

"Excellent." She turned to the children's smiling faces.

"Shall I send my carriage with the children to collect you at your home?" His brows rose, a teasing light in his eyes.

Ah, so he still had a way of steering situations to his advantage. Clever man.

"That would suit perfectly," she replied, moving toward the door. Beside her, Thomas shook his head, as though still baffled by her conduct, and . . . perhaps the conduct of the smaller people in the room. She braced herself for a lecture all the way home.

"And I shall join them," a voice interrupted from the secondary doorway. Mrs. Thornbury stepped into view, stately in her unrelieved black, her presence as imposing as ever. "If the invitation extends to me?" One arched brow challenged Emme to refuse.

Emme forced her best hostess smile. "Of course."

"It is far more prudent," Mrs. Thornbury declared, "for the children to have a family chaperone until the governess arrives."

Emme flicked a glance to Charlotte, wondering if her aunt's eavesdropping abilities had rubbed off on her niece.

"Quite so," Simon agreed, his tone studiously neutral. Yet, when his gaze met Emme's, it lingered for a fraction too long. Had he been admiring her? The notion was absurd. She brushed it aside, though her face grew warm.

It didn't matter. It *couldn't* matter.

"Very well." Emme bathed the room in a smile she hoped predicted the future of a glorious outing. "I shall expect to see you tomorrow."

"I still can't believe you offered to help him find a bride," Aster settled on the couch in the parlor and opened her sketch pad, sparing Emme a raised-brow look. "Him, of all people, Emme."

Truly, the idea of helping a man she'd once loved find a bride who wasn't her was one of the most preposterous schemes she'd ever conceived.

"If you'd stared into the eyes of those children like I did, you'd have understood." Emme glanced down at her forgotten embroidery, though her stitches were a disaster—unsurprising, given her thoughts had been anywhere but on her needlework. The last thing she needed was another lecture on how preposterous the scheme was. Thomas had given her a rather lengthy, sermon-worthy speech all the way home from Ravenscross. They'd had an understanding, he'd said. She'd diverged from the plan, he'd said.

"Your compassion overrode sound judgment?" Aster didn't even look up for that reprimand.

"Perhaps." Her voice barely broke a whisper. "And perhaps I know all too well the life of a motherless child."

Aster's gaze shot up, the edge in her expression faltering.

"You know as well as I how difficult it was for us, especially as girls, until Mrs. Lane came to Thistlecroft."

And the governess had become a motherly surrogate, providing not only structure but also an affection and understanding that their dear father had struggled to provide, especially in his own grief.

"I'm certain Lord Ravenscross can find his own bride, Emme."

The sentence pricked at Emme's conscience. Of course he could. But Emme knew the ladies of St. Groves and could provide practical guidance. How could she not help Simon choose the best match from his limited options? For him and for those children. Love could grow in time, couldn't it? The thought stirred an ache in her chest, but she pushed it aside. What they all needed now was hope.

Hope for a world that had been turned upside down more than any Gothic novel she'd read recently.

Or written, for that matter.

"His life is in shambles, Aster. He could use a . . . friend to help him."

"Friend?" Her brow jutted up again. "I saw how his *friendship* broke your heart. As wholesome as your compassion is, you grieved as thoroughly as any heroine in a novel."

A line of worry wrinkled her sister's forehead, and Emme pushed up a smile. "Unlike last time, I go into this choice aware. This time, I harbor no hope of being with him."

But Aster's reference to story shifted Emme's thoughts and her gaze wandered from the hallway—where Aunt Bean was removing her shawl in preparation for the morning lessons—to the novel she'd chosen for the afternoon: *Pride and Prejudice*. She had read it for the first time a few months ago and again last week. Something about its beauty and the vivid authenticity of its characters captivated her heart far more intimately than any Gothic romance had enchanted her imagination.

These epichoric tales pricked her emotions in ways that left her eager to reread and savor them. When she'd first begun writing, she believed only mysterious stories or those tinged with the supernatural could enthrall a reader, but novels like this one—and those by Fanny Burney—had taught her otherwise. Their simple beauty, their exploration of real life, love, danger, and loss, were rooted in truths more deeply than any fantastical adventure ever could be.

Her attention snagged on the stack of papers peeking from beneath the novel—her newest manuscript—an attempt to emulate these stories she'd grown to adore.

"Ladies, I must impress upon you the single most important aspect of your success in society," Aunt Bean declared, sweeping into the morning room like a galleon under full sail—or at least what Emme presumed a galleon under full sail might look like.

Not that she'd ever seen one.

But she'd written about them.

Several times.

"Your choice of suitor," Aunt Bean continued, "will dictate not only your future comfort but also your legacy. Therefore, it is imperative that you are both strategic and shrewd. The wrong man could ruin you entirely."

Aunt Bean ensured the full potency of her stare landed securely on Emme.

Emme needed to break the hypnotizing hold. "Define 'wrong,' Aunt."

Aunt Bean sniffed, as if the very question carried an offensive odor. "Wrong, my dear, is any man without title, wealth, or influence. And ideally, he should possess all three in abundance. However"—she added another meaningful look at Emme—"as you have so unfortunately learned from life experience, securing such a man is not as simple as it appears. You may have to settle for two of the three."

"Of course," Emme retorted, ignoring the critique. "For what is love without an estate to house it?"

Aster smothered a laugh behind her hand, her sketchbook angled away just enough to reveal a caricature of Aunt Bean dressed as a red-coated soldier. How fitting.

"Precisely," Aunt Bean said, missing the sarcasm entirely. "Now, allow me to elucidate the five types of gentlemen you must avoid at all costs."

Emme sat back, fully prepared for the performance. Aster turned her sketchbook over entirely. Truly, this production was too much to miss. And Emme was fully prepared to be slighted by her aunt in at least three of the five "unsuitable gentlemen" listed.

"The first," Aunt Bean began, holding up a gloved finger, "is the pauper pretender. He may possess a charming face and a fine wardrobe, but his pockets are as empty as his promises. You'll recognize him by his penchant for extravagant flattery and his reluctance to discuss anything of substance—such as property holdings or income."

"Ah." Emme tilted her head in thoughtful pretension. "So we are to ask after his finances in the same breath as the weather?"

"No, of course not." Aunt Bean's brows soared upward in indignation. "One must be subtle. You inquire about his family seat or the state of his tenants. A man with nothing to hide will boast freely. One can learn a great deal about a man while letting him boast unchecked."

"Whereas a pauper pretender will feign modesty," Aster added helpfully, sending Emme a grin.

"Exactly," Aunt Bean said, pleased for once. "The second type"—she raised another finger—"is the libertine. He is rakish, untrustworthy, and altogether too appealing. You'll know him by his devilish smile, his penchant for waltzes, and his tendency to whisper compliments that are *just* shy of improper."

Simon's teasing smile flashed to mind, heating Emme's cheeks to the teary point. Oh, heavens, he did wear a rakish smile far too well, though it had been terribly absent since his return to St. Groves. She desperately needed a distraction and quickly cleared her throat. "So, any gentleman who waltzes is suspect?"

"Not *every* waltzer," Aunt Bean replied impatiently. "But the ones who waltz too well. A proper gentleman is slightly awkward in such a dance—it shows he hasn't been practicing excessively."

But she knew many gentlemen of good rapport who waltzed exceedingly well. Thomas, Aunt Bean's very son, was at the top of the list, and he was no libertine.

"The third," Aunt Bean continued, her tone growing graver, "is the eccentric. He may have means, but his peculiarities will prove unbearable. Collecting beetles, speaking to plants, or—God forbid—writing poetry."

"Not poetry, surely!" Emme gasped, looking to her sister for company in the faux horror.

"Is it as dreadful as all that, Aunt?" Aster's features arranged in an artfully contrived look of concern.

"My dear, it is worse," Aunt Bean replied with a dramatic sigh. "Only the worst kind of man believes his thoughts worthy of immortalization in verse. Beware of poets, Aster-dear. They are not to be trusted."

Emme dared not look in her sister's direction for fear of losing all control of her laugh.

"The fourth," Aunt Bean continued, oblivious to their amusement, "is the brute. Wealth and title are no excuse for uncouth behavior. You'll recognize him by his lack of manners—interrupted conversations, loud laughter, or a tendency to overindulge at dinner. There is no revulsion as acute as a man who speaks with his mouth full or drinks to the point of delusion."

Well, Simon didn't really fit into any of these categories. Of course her heart knew that. She'd forgotten beneath the hurt of his rejection, but his current predicament paired with the memory of their time together . . . well, perhaps the only two dangers he posed most of all were to himself and to her vulnerable emotions.

"And the fifth?" Aster's grin crooked for the game of it all.

Aunt Bean's expression took a tragic turn, and she placed a palm to her chest like the most dramatic of all thespians. "The reformer. He is the most dangerous of all."

Emme shot Aster a look and then turned back to Aunt Bean. "A man who . . . seeks improvement?"

"Precisely," Aunt Bean declared with a solemn nod, before she jolted back to attention. "These are the gentlemen who fancy themselves philosophers or philanthropists. They will expect you to share their lofty ideals, dragging you into all manner of schemes—educating the poor, abolishing taxes, or some other nonsense. Such men make their wives miserable."

Aster leaned forward, her look of genuine curiosity an automatic warning. "But wouldn't abolishing taxes and educating the poor be very good reforms?"

The room fell silent. Aunt Bean froze mid-gesture, her eyes widening in absolute shock. "Aster!" she cried, as though her niece had just proposed eloping with a footman to open a pie shop in Covent Garden. "Good reforms? It is not a lady's place to entertain such radical notions, let alone voice them! Clearly, my next lesson must address a woman's proper concerns—running a home, subduing a husband, and extracting critical information regarding local society."

Oh, good heavens. Uncle Geoffrey likely died of exhaustion at having such a wife.

"We shall be sure to avoid anyone with ambition or moral integrity," Emme offered, turning the direction away from Aster's outrageous independent thinking.

"See that you do," Aunt Bean replied, unamused.

Emme decided it was best to end the conversation before Aster's wit tipped the balance. Rising from her seat, she offered a placating smile. "Thank you, Aunt. Your lessons are always enlightening."

"Indeed, almost like . . . poetry to my ears," Aster added, her tone as sweet as honey. "I feel quite transformed already."

As Aunt Bean swept from the room, Emme turned to Aster.

"Well, that narrows our options considerably. Perhaps we should take holy vows and live as nuns."

"Or poets," Aster said, grinning.

CHAPTER 13

Simon sat at his desk, his attention flitting between scattered papers and the small stack of unopened letters that still demanded his notice. It had taken longer than usual to settle Fia for the night. The promise of strawberries tomorrow had fueled her endless stream of questions long after the storybook had closed.

She had insisted, as she had for the past month, that he be the one to tuck her in. To his own surprise, he'd grown to welcome the ritual. Somehow, it fed a flicker of hope that he hadn't entirely ruined every life under his care.

His gaze landed on a note from Mr. Tarleton, the first payment for timber harvested from the estate. The sight buoyed his spirits. Something about earning the sum through his own ingenuity—however modest the amount—stirred a sense of accomplishment.

It was a beginning.

And beginnings, he reminded himself, often led to better ends.

His smile widened as he opened a letter from Mr. Douglas Arden. A chance conversation in the streets of St. Groves had birthed a promising connection. If all went as planned, Mr. Arden would lease a set of stone storage buildings on the town-side edge of Simon's land to expand his cotton mill operations. Combined with the prospect of leasing several acres for sheep, it promised a consistent income—a step closer to the stability he so desperately sought.

And the tenants only offered another. Mr. Bridges had sent a list of at least ten family names of those who may be possible prospects.

None of the ideas drastically changed current matters, but altogether? Over time?

Certainly.

There was also progress with his aunt's stipulations. He'd written to Mrs. Lane and another governess recommended by Ben. If either candidate proved appropriate, it would be the first and simplest of her demands checked off the list.

His gaze fell on a neatly stacked set of gray-bound books at the edge of his desk. The title along the beige spines caught his attention: *Sense and Sensibility*. He rested his chin on his folded hands, eyeing the volumes with suspicion. The three-volume novels he'd perused in the past had often indulged in wild sentimentality and gothic absurdities—vampires, pirates, ghosts, and fainting heroines in flimsy gowns.

He released a sigh as he rolled his gaze to the ceiling and then focused back on the books. But this title didn't fit the usual mysterious nonsense. *Sense* was in the title, after all—a clear attempt to entice more rational readers, or perhaps a clever trick disguising yet another ludicrous tale.

Opening the first volume, he skimmed the initial sentences. A humorless laugh burst from him. The passage about owning an estate resonated—uncomfortably so. But living in "so respectable a manner as to secure the general good opinion of their surrounding acquaintance"? That was another matter entirely. Certainly not with the mess the patriarchs of his family had left behind, compounded by the incessant whispers regarding himself, Teddy, his mother, and of course, Arianna.

"The cheerfulness of the children added a relish to his existence." Simon paused, considering the sentiment. Fia brought her fair share of cheer—along with a generous helping of exasperation—but poor Will and Lottie? Their cheerfulness had been in short supply, at least until today. Emme's invitation to take them to the Sutherlands' strawberry patch had been a rare bright spot.

He read on, gripped by the tale of an older brother whose foppish nature rendered him deaf to decency as his scheming wife persuaded him to abandon his stepmother and sisters with barely enough to live on. Simon frowned, his jaw clenching. What sort of man did such a thing? A selfish, cotton-headed brute!

But the narrative soothed him with Edward Ferrars—a sensible, amiable sort with a clear appreciation for the refined and composed Elinor Dashwood. It provided a glimpse into what could very well be an average day for a family within his acquaintance. No vampires or captured damsels. No ghosts or mad monks. But clever dialogue, wit, and well-drawn characters such as the Dashwood sisters, the genial Sir John, the meddling but good-hearted Mrs. Jennings, and the quietly noble Colonel Brandon. He'd just been introduced to the buck Mr. Willoughby when a sharp knock at his study door startled him.

Glancing at the clock, Simon blinked. Had he truly been reading for two hours?

The knock sounded again, firm and insistent. He turned toward the door. Who could possibly be awake at this hour? "Yes?"

The door creaked open to reveal the one person he least expected: Aunt Agatha. She looked less formidable than usual in her dressing gown, her dark hair threaded with silver and still pinned back. Had she been reading too?

Her expression held a gentleness that Simon hadn't seen in months, possibly years—curiosity, rather than her usual imperiousness. He rose, gesturing toward a chair near the hearth. "I saw your light beneath the door."

"Only answering a few letters and indulging in a book." He gestured toward his desk. "How may I assist you?"

She wore a cautious expression—not a hard-edged one, but as if weighing her thoughts before they spun into words. "I am *for* you, Simon." She paused, holding his gaze. "Or at least for the man I believe you can become."

The words hung in the air, and truth be told, Simon wasn't certain how to respond, so he offered no immediate reply, allowing her sentiment a chance to settle.

Agatha eased into the chair, sitting near its edge as though poised for flight. "You were gone so long in search of Arianna. I feared . . ." She glanced toward the bookshelves. "I feared you had lost your way."

At times he almost feared it too. "Like Father?"

Her chin dipped in acknowledgment. "It is a concern I've voiced before. But I see less cause for it with each passing day. Your care for the children, your work—it speaks to a resilience I had thought lost to you." She drew in a steadying breath. "We have suffered much as a family, Simon, and the Ravenscross name has borne its share. The road to recovery has not and will not be easy."

This was the Aunt Agatha he remembered from before their world fell apart: thoughtful, sharp, and deliberate, with an undercurrent of care. There had always been an edge to her, like a cat basking in sunlight but ready to strike at the faintest provocation. Yet compassion had once tempered that edge—until the loss of her sister seemed to have stolen it away.

"I want to see you succeed." Her gaze fastened on him. "And find happiness. As I do for the rest of your . . . *my* family," she corrected. In fact, the Reeveses were all the family she had left. He knew she felt that deeply. "But the quickest path to securing some semblance of restoration and stability is through an advantageous marriage—to an equal who can elevate both your finances and your reputation. I can only provide a basic sum, but you need more."

Simon's shoulders tensed, bracing for the inevitable.

"Which is why," she continued, her gaze sharp, "I must know the nature of your relationship with Miss Lockhart."

It was not the question he had anticipated, though neither was it a surprise. Of course Aunt Agatha had noticed. After all, the woman had appeared in his pond one day, only to surface days later with a rescue plan in place.

Simon's intentions with Emme had been delicate from the start, which was why he'd protected the information, only sharing his plans with his cousin (out of necessity), his parents, and Ben. He'd never intended to fall in love with someone so far outside his rank and position. Yet Emme had fit him so well, so naturally, that he'd prepared to battle every expectation and argument to make a union happen.

He hadn't needed to see her with his siblings this week to know how perfectly she belonged in his family. Nor did he need to picture her in the halls of Ravenscross to realize she would make the estate a home again. He didn't need to hold her in his arms to understand that her strength and heart would leave an indelible mark on future generations.

He'd known it all already.

But the moment the title fell upon him, everything had unraveled.

How much should Aunt Agatha know?

"I courted her the season the title fell to me with the intention of marrying her."

Agatha's sharp intake of breath cut through the room. "You courted her?"

He nodded, though the admission stuck in his throat. "I had every intention of proposing on the day I received news of Cousin Rupert's and Father's deaths. When the full extent of everything became clear, I knew . . . I couldn't follow through."

"Does she harbor false hope?" Agatha stared at him, still surprised. "Does she believe you might offer her some lesser position?"

"No." The denial came swiftly, almost violently. "Never. She knows I cannot marry her, and I would never insult her by suggesting anything less than honor." He slowly shook his head, attempting to explain. "She . . . she wishes to help, that is all. It's who she is. But her compassion is more for the children now, I think."

Agatha's lips pressed into a thin line. "Take care, Simon. Compassion is well and good, but if either of you still carries a flame for the other, rest assured people will be watching. Scandal is what they'll hope to find."

⌒

Emme quickened her steps along Avalon Street, one hand clutching a bundle of ribbons from Matthews' Haberdashery, the other gripping a pair of gilded hair combs she'd admired in Crown and Comb's window. The combs, embossed with delicate leaves, would make the perfect birthday gift for Aster. No doubt her sister would liken them to some Grecian ideal she'd uncovered in her geographical studies.

Having some extra pin money, especially funds she earned herself, certainly made purchasing gifts more delightful.

She had barely made it past Cole's Grocer when someone called her name. Turning, Emme found Thomas approaching at a near run, his typical smile restored from his previous agitation with her. She loved that about him. He rarely held grudges. It was an excellent characteristic for a clergyman.

"How providential to encounter you this morning, Miss Lockhart," he teased. "I had imagined you at home, preparing for your grand strawberry-picking adventure."

Her smile flared. "Lord Ravenscross's carriage isn't meant to collect me for a few hours yet, so I thought I'd indulge in a little shopping beforehand."

"Making wise use of the spoils of your success, no doubt?" He fell into step beside her, his dark hat casting a shadow over his fair hair.

"There's a certain satisfaction in making purchases with my own money, I must say." She couldn't repress her smile. It brimmed to the point of pinching her cheeks. "Not something bestowed upon me as an inheritance, but wholly mine."

"And there's much more where that came from, cousin-dearest. You are on your way to becoming an independent woman, should you wish it."

She stumbled slightly, the words jarring her. Independent? Such a notion required substantial resources. She had dreamed of it in some distant, uncertain future, but surely not yet. "How . . . how much do I have?"

"Ah, so you *do* wish to know," he said, his eyes gleaming. For nearly a year, she'd refused to let him tell her, preferring to imagine the modest profits of her books without confronting specifics. It felt less humbling.

"I financed it as I advised, and it has been an excellent investment." His grin crooked. "You currently have over three thousand pounds in the funds."

Emme stopped walking altogether. "Three thousand pounds?"

"In the funds, yes." There was no mistaking the pride in his eyes. She almost hugged him there on the street.

"That's over one hundred fifty per annum in income, and the principal continues to grow. It's not enough to live as you are accustomed, but it is certainly a handsome sum."

Three thousand pounds? What on earth had Thomas done with those investments? Her mind reeled. One hundred fifty pounds a year might not rival her current lifestyle, but it was hers. Hers alone. With careful economizing, she could live on it—and on her own terms.

"And since you haven't taken the interest as income," he added, "I've reinvested it to increase your holdings. You should be proud, Emme."

"Proud?" she repeated, a laugh bursting from her lips. "I suppose I am." She pressed a hand to her cheek, trying to take it all in. "It's remarkable. This brings my little stories to life in a way I never imagined, more so even than holding the first bound copy in my hands. And yet . . ." She shook her head. "I cannot share this with anyone but you."

"Which is why I bring my highest enthusiasm."

That something she had chosen to do for the sheer delight of it could yield such an outcome was extraordinary. Of course the income depended upon her continued writing, but for the first time, her future didn't seem quite so dim. If she didn't marry, she had a real prospect of independence.

On her own.

Which meant she had greater freedom to marry for love instead of desperation or expectation. "How ironic," Emme mused. "That this success, which should be a source of pride, could very well ruin my family's reputation. What if it jeopardizes Aster's chances for a suitable marriage? And my father—imagine his reaction to learning that his eldest daughter not only earns a living but does so by writing Gothic romances! He can scarcely endure the contents of the scandal sheets most days."

"Times are changing," Thomas said gently. "There are more women—even among the gentry—who are finding their way behind a pen. Perhaps, in time, you won't need to remain a clandestine authoress."

She offered him a skeptical look but didn't argue.

He reached into his coat pocket and drew out an envelope. "But the reason I caught you this morning . . ." He offered her the envelope. "From Danbury and Sons, sending their own praise, I believe."

She took the envelope with a smile, the flush of pleasure warming her cheeks, and had just opened her mouth to thank Thomas when a third party entered their conversation.

"Good morning to you both." Miss Selena Hemston's voice was as sweet as honey, but there was no sweetness in her eyes.

She stepped forward in an exquisitely tailored burgundy walking suit, the fabric shimmering in the sunlight. Her cream spencer jacket, embroidered with burgundy threads up the sleeves, marked her as one of the wealthiest unmarried women in St. Groves. The ensemble was designed for one purpose: to be noticed.

Especially when Emme, in contrast, wore a simple muslin dress and her two-year-old broad-collared pelisse coat. It was a lovely shade of green, Aster had insisted, but even the most charitable would never mistake it for the height of fashion.

"Is it not a lovely day for a stroll in town?" Miss Hemston inquired, as if she hadn't already decided the answer for herself.

Emme, ever careful not to judge too hastily, nonetheless knew Miss Hemston all too well. They had known each other for years, but not as friends. No, their acquaintance was forged in the social circles of St. Groves—always at a polite distance, as dictated by their differing stations.

"An excellent one, indeed," Thomas agreed, bowing slightly. "Perfect for a morning stroll."

"And intimate conversation, it would appear." Her dark gaze shifted between Emme and Thomas, a serpentine glimmer shining in their depths.

"Pardon?" A warning knot coiled in Emme's stomach. Miss Hemston had never been one for idle chat with those she deemed beneath her.

"Do not look so surprised, Miss Lockhart," Selena cooed, her lips curling into something like a smile, though there was little warmth in it. "I couldn't help but notice how enraptured Miss Lockhart was by your conversation, Mr. Bridges. And exchanging letters? How mysterious. I believe I even overheard the word *clandestine*?"

Emme's blood ran cold. The impertinence of the woman knew no bounds. Any person of respectability would know better than to eavesdrop on an unsuspecting conversation. She sighed inwardly, the memory of her own recent eavesdropping experience still fresh.

Why had neither she nor Thomas considered the risks of conversing in public at this hour? Midmorning in St. Groves was prime gossip time, when the eyes and ears of the town were most alert to any new "information."

Emme glanced at Thomas, who, ever the diplomat, was already smoothing over the situation with a charming smile.

"I do feel as though every personal visit must seem rather *clandestine* in my new role as rector of Lemmingston," he said smoothly, but sent Emme a knowing glance. No, Thomas was not fooled by Miss Hemston's charm. "I am often required to act on others' schedules, rather than my own, as you can imagine."

"So you write secret letters to Miss Lockhart, is it?" The sauciness in Miss Hemston's tone stiffened Emme's spine for a rebuttal, but Thomas took control.

"Of course not." He chuckled. "A mutual acquaintance of ours, whom I happened to encounter in London last week, asked me to deliver a letter to my dear cousin. I was simply discharging my duties."

"None of my cousins have ever inspired such affection in me as I witnessed between the two of you." Her gazes switched between them, one slim brow slowing rising northward. "Incredibly warm . . . loving."

"Then I'm sad for you, Miss Hemston. It is a remarkable privilege to find friendship and encouragement in one's cousins." Emme took Thomas's controlled lead. "And I might add that if you wish to benefit from Mr. Bridges' encouragement, he excels in both wit and words, which are often on display in his sermons. Should you wish to observe them in a more public setting, rather than through the lens of an overheard and *private* conversation."

The slight downturn of Miss Hemston's lips was the only indication that she had caught the reproof.

"I believe you're right, Miss Lockhart. I've neglected a proper study of your *cousin*." She bit into the word. "Especially if he brings . . . intrigue along with him." She waved a gloved hand toward the buildings nearby. "In such a quaint town as this, one is always in search of occupation."

And with that, she dipped her chin with a coy smile that left Emme's face cool, then sauntered away.

"I'm sorry for my timing." Thomas stepped up beside Emme once Miss Hemston retreated. "I should have been more tactful in my choice of when and where to speak with you."

"Do not worry yourself, Thomas." Miss Hemston disappeared around the side of Moss's Apothecary Shop. "I daresay Miss Hemston has little need or desire to bother herself with two people so beneath her."

"Hmm . . ." His response pulled her attention. "I've heard enough about Miss Hemston to not underestimate her desire for information or need for importance. Those who are seeking attention will find ways to obtain it." He held Emme's gaze. "There are some people in life who are merely waiting to be baited to become an adversary. Don't underestimate her."

CHAPTER 14

I appreciate you staying behind from the strawberry patches to assist me, Will." Simon sent his brother a smile as they rode across the field, the afternoon sun warming them against the slight chill of the wind.

"I'm happy to . . . be of help to you, Simon." Will gave a small nod, his dark hair tossed beneath his hat as they kept a leisurely pace, allowing room for conversation.

"You're a great help. Not only is this your home, but I could do with another opinion or two on the matter of tenants."

Simon had spent only a few summers with his cousin, as encouraged by Father under some excuse of building family connection. Not enough to give Simon thorough knowledge of how the estate ran, but enough to bring some awareness of the breadth of the job. Perhaps it was during those visits that Father and Rupert began discussions of shared business ventures.

Father had never discussed such ventures with Simon. And no wonder, from what Simon had unearthed after their passing about the nature of some of their schemes. Smuggling? Exploitation? Even illegal slave trading?

The weight of those wrongs painted Ravenscross's reputation an even darker hue than the two men's reputations alone. Their ventures nearly led to the estate's ruination outright.

And Cousin Rupert clearly hadn't been focusing on Ravenscross, his tenants, or its future. So Simon's "inheritance" had been much more of a shackle than a gift.

"You probably wish Teddy were here." Will's quiet voice carried over the space between them. "He knows more about these things."

Teddy had spent far less time with Rupert than Simon, even.

"Perhaps, but he is fighting the French far away, and besides, you have the mind and ability to render welcome service. Should I ever need you to manage anything, you'll know exactly what it's about."

Will sat a little taller, his hesitant smile becoming fuller.

"Do you usually visit the tenants? To collect their rent?"

Ah, he was already embracing the responsibility. "Do you recall Mr. Starnes?"

Will furrowed his brow, considering, before nodding. "The man with the silver hair and white horses?"

"Yes, though he isn't very old. An illness turned his hair white before his time. At any rate, he is the steward who manages the finances of Ravenscross, as it's not typically something gentlemen do. Though I've done more than my share of it recently." He paused, his tone growing quieter. "His father was steward before him, so he knows our estate and tenants well."

Will's nod encouraged Simon to continue—the additional time with the boy was somehow taking away a little of the melancholy of the last few months. Perhaps, despite the need to marry for money, his family would be all right. Perhaps he could yet make amends for the children's losses and turn their family around.

"Tenants are a primary source of income for an estate, which is why we've been suffering from more expenditures than gains since our cousin's passing," Simon continued. "I had no idea of the extent of our cousin's mismanagement, and I am only glad that we've been able to keep the few tenants we have."

"Why did Cousin Rupert send the tenants away if having them helps provide funds for the estate?"

"Smart boy." Simon's compliment incited a glint in Will's eyes. "I don't know that he sent them away as much as they left for better places. Near the end of his life, he made impossible demands upon the tenants, which drove them to seek better accommodations elsewhere. Only a few of the more desperate or faithful remained." He paused, glancing at Will. "And today we'll be visiting some of them to inform them of new neighbors, who will be arriving soon, as well as assessing two vacant cottages to see if they're ready for immediate occupancy."

"Are we visiting all of the tenants?" Will's eyes widened.

Simon stifled a grin. The poor lad probably thought they'd spend the next three days on horseback appraising properties and meeting strangers—a task neither of them relished. "Not all, but a visit has been long overdue. We're taking some fresh bread from Mrs. Patterson and some jam Miss Lockhart kindly provided to three of our most veteran tenants before we meet with Mr. Starnes to see if the vacant cottages need any repairs."

"How many new tenants do you expect?" Will asked, his curiosity keen.

Ah, yes. This purpose and camaraderie had been what Will had needed all along. "I wish for more, but for now, we have four of the ten families provided by Mr. Bridges, all of whom are seeking immediate residence. I've also written to a few former tenants, hoping they might be willing to return to their places now that I am Viscount of Ravenscross. They've likely established themselves elsewhere, but it never hurts to try."

Silence fell as Will appeared to consider this. Over the last few days, the boy seemed to have aged years, but not in a burdensome way. More in the direction of maturity and—dare Simon think it—confidence? Yes, perhaps a little.

Simon would continue the dialogue if it meant bringing the boy out of his shadowy reclusion and into the light and breath of the real world. He'd been so busy with his bachelor life first and then the estate business, he'd failed to share affection with these younger siblings. The age difference likely helped with the distance.

But he was their surrogate father now, and he would not repeat the same absence or disgrace of that man. No, if he had anything to do with it, their futures would be different. The very thought of Mr. John Dashwood from *Sense and Sensibility*—that self-important man, indifferent to the true concerns of his half sisters—nearly had Simon groaning for two reasons. One, Dashwood was an atrocious figure, and Simon would never accept any comparison to him. Two, why, of all things, had that novel come to mind just then?

"Did Father gamble away all the money?" Will's quiet question brought Simon back to the present. He turned to look at his youngest brother.

He supposed directness was in order.

"No, not all." Simon glanced ahead as the cottage of Mr. and Mrs. Morrison came into view. "After settling his debts, I attempted to invest the remainder to keep it safe, but it is truly my inheritance from Mother that has supported us the past two years."

And it would not last forever.

"And it's not enough?"

How much should he reveal? Simon shrugged. The boy had already seen more than he should through observation alone. "Not at present, no. We lack the investments to secure more income, and much of the revenue we once had from rents has dwindled." He forced a smile. "But those finances will grow. They must. Though not quickly enough to meet Aunt Agatha's demands or the needs of the present."

Which, of course, meant Simon would be attending the theater with Miss Clayton on Thursday.

It was quite possible that Alfie and Fia developed a lifelong friendship over collecting insects rather than strawberries. Alfie, only five years Fia's senior, recognized that she'd replaced him as the youngest of the group and set about leading her along and pandering to her as if he were her very own brother. The boy, with his brown curls and hazel eyes, had always had a deep affection for younger children, and Emme smiled at his ability to exhibit his patience and attention to little Fia, who drank in Alfie's devotion.

His patience was in much less supply during lessons . . . and tidying up.

After a few stiff exchanges with Mrs. Thornbury, Emme offered Aster a grateful smile as her sister launched into a rather animated conversation about all the places Mrs. Thornbury had traveled in her life. From what Emme overheard at a distance, the woman's younger years swarmed with travel since she'd been married to a navy captain, so Aster was at her most inquisitive.

Remarkably, the tight lines around Mrs. Thornbury's face began to soften by degrees—whether from the sweetness of the strawberries, the reminiscences of her adventurous past, or Aster's infectious enthusiasm and attentiveness was anyone's guess. Whatever the reason, Emme was glad to see the transformation. She recalled how Simon, when they were courting, had spoken fondly of his aunt, so Emme knew there had to be more to the woman than frowns and ultimatums.

So it was that Emme found herself in Charlotte's company the most, or as a matter of fact, Charlotte seemed to follow Emme wherever she went.

And the younger girl offered some delightful conversation, speaking of her horse, her nearest siblings, and of course, her favorite books. It was clear that Charlotte Reeves desperately sought a female companion, or perhaps, more to the point, an elder sister.

"Do you think Mrs. Patterson can find a use for all these strawberries?" Emme asked as she dropped another plump berry into the nearly overflowing basket. "She'll have enough to supply the entire village—and perhaps another basket or two, if your aunt and my sister can ever stop talking long enough to pick some."

Charlotte's smile came slowly, but it lit her eyes. "She'll make jam and cakes, provided we don't eat them all first. But you're right, Aunt Aggie's basket is suspiciously empty." She cast a glance toward the animated figures of Mrs. Thornbury and Aster, whose conversation seemed to have reached a particularly enthusiastic pitch. "They seem far better suited to conversing than harvesting."

"That much is plain." Emme chuckled, glancing toward the horizon where the afternoon sun bathed the fields in golden light. "Give Aster her drawing pencils or a willing conversationalist, and she'll happily forgo any sort of outdoor labor. Still, if good conversation is all it takes to win Mrs. Thornbury's favor, then I am perfectly content to let Aster wield that particular talent."

Charlotte's smile brimmed even wider, and more quickly. A very good sign. "It does seem to be working. Aunt Aggie rarely speaks so freely of her past. Your sister must be rather charming."

"Charming," Emme agreed, doing nothing to hide the humor in her voice. "And entirely shameless in her curiosity. Aster has always had a knack for asking questions no one else would dare." She turned back to her occupation. "But I am fond of strawberries and do not think one can have too many." She pinched the green off the top of one and popped it in her mouth. "They are my favorite fruit."

Charlotte's smile fell as she turned back to her work. "My mother and older sister shared a fondness for strawberries. We used to grow our own."

Emme hesitated, letting the silence linger, unsure if the girl would say more. There was no telling what the Reeves children had witnessed or endured in the months after their father's death, followed so swiftly by their mother's. Simon's insistence on discretion had succeeded almost too well, leaving space for all manner of rumors.

"Do you have any strawberry patches now?" Emme prodded gently.

Charlotte picked another few strawberries, deliberately keeping her gaze averted. "We used to have them, but . . . but . . ." The girl seemed to measure Emme and then returned to the strawberry plant. "Not since Mother."

The loss squeezed from the girl's words. Emme kept her eyes on the fruit she was gathering, appearing absorbed in the task. Charlotte, she suspected, would not welcome pity or undue attention. "Perhaps you could plant a new patch in her honor?"

The girl's gaze came up. "I wouldn't know where to start."

"Well," Emme replied lightly, "I happen to know a thing or two about it. My mother and I planted strawberries at Thistlecroft when I was a little younger than you. With the weather being as it is, there's still time to plant for next spring. If you'd like some guidance, of course."

Charlotte didn't respond immediately, but Emme could feel the girl's focus shift toward her, even as she continued gathering fruit. The silence felt familiar—Emme had a younger sister, after all—and she braced herself for the inevitable question.

"Why are you helping us?"

"Why am I helping you?" Emme returned her attention to the fruit she plucked from the current bush, sifting through a suitable answer in her mind. "I should hope I would offer Christian charity to any of my acquaintances who found themselves in need."

"But I don't know of anyone who has gone to such lengths for us. Not even Aunt Aggie would offer to find us a governess, and you not only provided one but brought us on this outing with you today."

The little girl was too astute for her own good, which also led Emme to truly examine her own motives. Was it solely Christian charity? There was, of course, her lingering affection for Simon, but there was more to it. The shared ache of knowing what it was to lose a mother at an impressionable age, perhaps? "Must there be any reason beyond kindness?"

Emme should have known better than to further this subject of conversation, because Charlotte, after only a moment's hesitation, asked, "Because you're in love with my brother?"

The question landed with all the bluntness of youth, and Emme's breath caught. Denying the truth outright would feel dishonest, but admitting too much was unthinkable. She drew a steadying breath and met Charlotte's gaze with equal frankness. "I do admire your brother greatly—for his resilience, for all he has done to see your family through difficult times. Perhaps that admiration inspires my efforts to help." She hesitated, then added, "But I also understand the ache of losing one's mother, and at a similar age to yours."

Charlotte blinked, and Emme returned her attention to the berries, fearing her confidence might waver. "Every girl benefits from the kindness of someone who understands—someone to, well, commiserate with at times." She threw the girl a smile.

"Is that why you didn't tell Aunt Aggie I'd stolen those chickens?"

Emme's body relaxed at the humor lighting the girl's eyes. "Having been a young girl who had her fair share of mischief, I felt it better to encourage a camaraderie than a rivalry."

Charlotte's own smile flared, a mischievous twinkle in those eyes. "It was very good of you." Then she turned back to her strawberry bush, adding in almost a whisper. "But Aunt Aggie already knew about the chickens."

Emme's laughter bubbled up, and with it, her resolve to continue helping the Reeves children. Simon, as a romantic prospect, was lost to her. But doing a good turn for a man she so highly regarded and his siblings she was beginning to care for? That, at least, remained within her power.

"I should like very much for you to teach me how to plant strawberries," Charlotte announced, a little challenge in her look.

Ah, she didn't believe Emme's request was in earnest? Well, Emme saw the request for what it was. More than just mere curiosity—it was an olive branch. Perhaps even a plea for the companionship and guidance of an elder sister.

"I have some seeds at the ready." Emme covered Charlotte's hand with a gentle squeeze. The girl's smile flared, bright and unguarded. "Speak to your brother and see if he might spare you on Saturday afternoon."

Charlotte's expression shifted—wide-eyed surprise, as though the touch had been both unexpected and welcome—and then, a look of . . . longing?

Oh, dear child.

How long had it been since the girl felt such affection? Such care?

Emme turned back to her work just to compose herself.

The afternoon sped forward with continued conversations of lighter topics. Alfie and Fia gathered enough insects to colonize the back garden, and Aster's guileless interest even encouraged Mrs. Thornbury to laugh on two occasions.

Overall, Emme would call the outing a complete success.

When the time came to leave, Emme was surprised to find Simon himself, along with his driver, at the helm of the carriage.

For a journey requiring six passengers, the arrangement should have been tedious at best. But with three of the travelers being children, they all fit snugly yet comfortably, and the short drive to Thistlecroft passed in pleasant company. Fia praised Alfie and his knowledge of insects, while Aster launched into an impressively thorough explanation of Egyptian pyramids. Mrs. Thornbury added her own sly remark about visiting Egypt before Napoleon's campaign, prompting an avalanche of questions and admiration that carried them all the way to Thistlecroft.

It truly had been a good afternoon, on all accounts.

Simon helped Aster from the carriage and then offered his hand to Emme. She shouldn't have hesitated to take it, but he caught her faltering and raised his gaze to search her face. The last time he'd touched her hand to assist her from a carriage, she'd felt the connection from their fingers to her toes, and the reminder of not having him for her own only made such touches more difficult.

Ridiculously difficult, in fact.

Summoning a smile, she placed her gloved hand in his, acutely aware of the warmth of his fingers as they closed around hers. When her feet touched the ground, she managed a steady breath and a polite nod of thanks, quite proud of herself for such masterful composure.

"I trust Will enjoyed his time with you while we were away?" Emme asked, slipping her hand from his and strolling toward the house.

"He did, though I've promised him his share of strawberries once the baskets arrive at Ravenscross," Simon replied, falling into step beside her.

"He should be quite satisfied then, as we picked three baskets." Emme grinned up at him, only to falter as she caught the tender expression in his eyes.

Oh, why couldn't he be a very unlikable rogue? It would make things so much easier.

Simon looked away first, clasping his hands behind his back as their pace slowed. "Thank you for providing this diversion for my sisters."

The low timbre of his gratitude sent warmth rising up her neck, and she suddenly understood why fans were such an indispensable accessory in courtship, especially with voices like his. "It was truly my pleasure. And you should hear from Mrs. Lane within the next few days. She seems most eager to learn more about the position."

"I look forward to meeting her. With your recommendation, I daresay she'll be more than suitable."

"All that remains, then, is finding a suitable bride," Emme said lightly, tilting her head with exaggerated cheer. "Miss Clayton is an excellent option, my lord."

If looks could render a woman breathless, his certainly did. His gaze held hers for a moment too long, the humor fading into something . . . far too intimate. So intimate, in fact, that her breathing stalled altogether.

He cleared his throat and gestured with his chin in the direction toward town. "To that end, I plan to attend the theater tomorrow evening."

Why did being in Simon's presence or thinking about him lead to a war of emotions? She blamed that covert kiss on the balcony.

And his voice.

And likely those devastating eyes of his.

So she rallied her humor to the battle. "Do you?"

Unfortunately, if the glimmer in his eyes gave any warning, he rallied his humor as well. "On the recommendation of . . . a friend."

Her throat tightened, and her reply came out strangled. "Indeed. And are you taking someone?"

"I am," he answered, grin crooked but faintly pained. "On that same friend's advice."

And in that moment, Emme recognized that his struggle matched her own. The conflict between doing what one wanted versus what one must. What would he choose if he had the freedom to do so? Would it still be her? After all this time?

"That friend wants to see you happy, Lord Ravenscross."

His brow tightened and he lowered his head. "I am grateful for such a friend."

She looked away, though her steps continued to grow slower the closer she came to the front door of her house. It was as if her body wanted to hold on to as many of these moments with him as possible because soon they'd be over.

He'd be married.

And any such connection with him would be gone.

"I understand they're performing *He's Much to Blame*," she offered, pausing at the front steps. "It might even earn a laugh from you, Lord Ravenscross. That could do your heart some good."

"Hmm." He turned as if to retreat but hesitated, his gaze finding hers again, this time with enough mischief dancing in those eyes that it mustered her wits to the ready. "I am curious about something."

"Yes?"

"Do you think a shooting jacket is the most becoming style for a gentleman?"

Clearly, her wits were not ready. "What?"

He shook his head with mock gravity. "I suppose any man's jacket might become irresistible, provided it's offered in the rain after a fall."

Her laughter shook loose as his meaning became clear. "You're reading *Sense and Sensibility*?"

"You challenged me. How could I refuse?"

Taking a woman's book recommendation to heart might be one of the most romantic things in all the world. Oh, why did she have to be so poor? "And what do you think so far?"

He glanced toward the carriage, lowering his voice. "The wit is sharp, and the characters are finely drawn. But do women truly think in terms of manly beauty and gallantry?" His attention fastened on her with such intensity, her wits might have flown right out of her ears. "Do you?"

She swallowed, ushering back some sense for the sake of all women. "Since it was written by a woman, I think you already know the answer."

His humor faded into something more searching. "And is that what you thought of me?"

The question struck too close to her heart. Her mind went completely blank. With his dark hair waving back from his impressive forehead, the structure of his jaw and cheeks almost like someone carved them from marble, and eyes so dark blue that one wished to peer a little closer to see if the shade wavered into other hues, it was difficult to think of him as anything except arrestingly handsome. But despite her current insanity—which she blamed entirely on him—she'd learned a great deal about governing her own emotions. Learned that hopes did not necessarily lead to realizations.

And those eyes weren't meant for *her* adoration.

Schooling her features, she took a measured step back. "Why indulge your self-importance with such a reply? A man's actions— not his appearance—prove his true worth, don't you think?"

He released a pulse of air as if her words struck deeper than she'd intended. What had she said? And then realized he may perceive them in light of their failed courtship, and she quickly added, "And yours are commendable—your hard work, your sacrifices for your family. I have every faith you'll find happiness, Simon."

She shouldn't have addressed him so familiarly, but the name fell much too easily from her lips. However, the comment did not resurrect the glint in his eyes. He searched her face for a span of time much longer than appropriate, shallowing her breath with each prolonged second.

And she reminded herself.

One did not always get what one wanted.

Parents died.

Finances diminished.

Loving someone didn't necessarily secure a future with them.

With a faint smile, he tipped his head. "You are wise, Miss Lock-hart, to temper my pride." His lips crooked a little as if trying to find their former humor. "Though perhaps, in the future, I might find occasion to don my shooting coat more often."

To torture her, no doubt.

She rolled her eyes in plain sight for him to see.

She stood and watched the carriage disappear down the lane, the longing for the impossible turning her thoughts toward prayer. If Simon Reeves could not become the hero of her story, she hoped he might become the hero of his own.

CHAPTER 15

S imon had taken her advice to read *Sense and Sensibility*?

Emme took another spoonful of her soup, unable to suppress the smile tugging at her lips. From all appearances, he not only endured it but also seemed genuinely engaged. What would he think of Edward Ferrars' secret? Or Colonel Brandon's steadfast devotion? Or Willoughby's betrayal?

Her spoon hovered midair as doubt crept into her satisfaction. Two seasons ago, she and Simon had formed an attachment she had believed to be one of the dearest of her life. The ton had interpreted their actions—though more restrained than Marianne's and Willoughby's—as a declaration of intent. But like Willoughby, Simon had left her without explanation.

Now she understood the necessity of his actions, yet the sting of disappointment, the whispers of society, and the wound to her heart remained. Had she unwittingly handed him a book that might cut too close to the quick? She had no intention of hurting him, especially with fiction!

"What is this I hear of you taking the Reeves children to the Sutherlands' this afternoon?"

Emme blinked at Aunt Bean's sudden inquiry. Thus far, their conversation had touched only on the weather, Thomas's forthcoming sermon, the Langston boy's cough, and the state of the roads. All fine topics. Pleasantly safe from Aunt Bean's critique.

The narrowing of Aunt Bean's eyes, however, suggested the current topic was anything but safe—for Emme.

"I thought I might do a good turn for the girls, Aunt."

"Now, Bina," Father offered, his tone mild but his gaze pointed. "Emme has always been inclined toward acts of charity. Surely you wouldn't fault her for such a thing?" He gestured toward Thomas with his spoon. "A most Christian endeavor, wouldn't you say, Reverend?"

Thomas's lips twitched at the timely use of his title before sending a glance to Emme. "Indeed, it is." He raised a brow. "Usually."

"You know I am the very model of charity, John," Aunt Bean countered, lowering her spoon with a decisive clink. "But one must not confuse charity with folly. I suspect there is more behind this particular display than meets the eye."

Emme refused to lower her gaze under Aunt Bean's scrutiny. "Those girls are in need of a young woman's friendship, particularly since their mother can no longer provide it."

Aunt Bean's eyes narrowed to such a degree they almost closed. "Attempting to curry favor with your former suitor through his sisters will not achieve the desired effect. Frankly, I am astonished. Real ladies resort to such schemes only when there is *actually* a chance of success."

"Mother, I must protest," Thomas interjected, though his tone held more exasperation than outrage.

"Do you not recall what became of you the last time you set your cap at a gentleman well above your station?" Aunt Bean continued, undeterred. She sipped her wine with deliberate precision, her gaze steady over the rim. "And with the very *same* man."

"I am not setting my cap at him." Emme dabbed at her mouth with her napkin to give her fingers something to do. "I saw a need and sought to meet it, as a friend might."

Mostly true, though some of her thoughts about this particular "friend" had ventured dangerously close to the scandalous.

Aunt Bean sniffed, her skepticism unabated. "Friendship between a single gentleman of title and an unmarried lady of no consequence is folly unless it leads to matrimony, an inheritance upon his untimely demise, or favor with his mother. Since he appears in robust health and his mother is, regrettably, departed, I can only assume your aim is marriage."

"Mother," Thomas admonished.

"It is simply the way of the world, dear," Aunt Bean replied without so much as a glance his way.

"Perhaps we might aspire to something nobler than the way of the world," Thomas said, leaning back in his chair.

Father muffled a chuckle behind his napkin, though Aunt Bean seemed impervious to her son's rebuke.

"My intentions"—Emme held Aunt Bean's stare, refusing to bend—"are purely out of goodwill. Have you considered that possibility?"

Aunt Bean gave a faint, disbelieving snort. "Women in your position, Emmeline, with a prior attachment to said gentleman, do not squander their goodwill on an impossibility." She paused briefly. "I hear his estate teeters on ruin, thanks to his cousin's unorthodox business patterns and overindulgent spending. With no fortune of his own and little hope of inheriting from his late father's dissipations, Lord Ravenscross cannot afford to marry for sentiment, even if"—her lips curled faintly—"such sentiment existed."

"Oh, I think sentiment is very much present," Aster chimed in sweetly, her youthful grin belying the mischief in her words. "You should have seen how he looked at her."

Emme shot Aster a warning glance. Not helpful.

"What man wouldn't show some gratitude for a woman who is taking his siblings from under foot for an entire afternoon?" Aunt Bean countered with another weighted look at Emme. "Mark my words, he will take your kindness, and you will be left with nothing for your trouble, just as before."

The barb might have struck deeper if Emme still nurtured hopes of marrying Simon. But she didn't. Couldn't. Truly, there was no way forward for them. Which meant her charity was entirely . . . well, *mostly* . . . charity. She almost smiled at the realization—Aunt Bean's criticism lacked its usual sting.

"Did you find the Sutherlands well?" Father redirected smoothly, tipping his glass toward Emme. "I believe Cook has prepared a dessert using some of your spoils."

Emme thanked Father with a grateful smile.

"Strawberry trifle, I believe," he continued, patting his stomach. "And I, for one, plan to benefit from Emme's *goodwill* in bringing those strawberries for our enjoyment."

"I second that, Uncle," Thomas added, turning to Aster. "Aster, how did you enjoy your visit to the Sutherlands'?"

"Exceedingly." Aster dabbed her serviette against her smile. "Mrs. Thornbury was a wealth of information—she's traveled more places than I've even read about."

"Mrs. Thornbury?" Aunt Bean's head jerked up with such suddenness, the feathers on her head gave a violent shake in protest. "Do you mean Mrs. Agatha Bennett Thornbury?" The name was produced with enough venom to add a little hiss on the sibilant sounds.

Aster froze, her cheer dimming under Aunt Bean's thunderous glare.

"Bina, there is no need to—" Father began, but Aunt Bean plowed ahead.

"No wonder Emmeline is behaving so rashly!" She shook her head, her feathers quivering with each emphatic motion. "That woman is notorious for stealing eligible gentlemen right from under more deserving ladies' noses. Spending time in her company has clearly influenced our dear Emmeline."

It was remarkable how Aunt Bean could distort the meaning of the word *dear* in the way she spoke it.

Thomas groaned, while Aster exchanged a wide-eyed look with Emme.

"That was years ago, Bina," Father said. "And—"

"And," Aunt Bean interrupted, "she ruthlessly pursued a man already interested in another woman."

"As I recall"—Father stared at his sister meaningfully—"the lady in question did not return his attentions, which led him to look elsewhere for a bride."

Aster's eyes widened further, and Emme felt her own mirroring the expression. What on earth was this thinly veiled conversation referencing? A former suitor of Aunt Bean's?

She glanced at Thomas, who had taken to massaging his temples.

"But if I'd known!" Aunt Bean burst out, her indignation bubbling over. "If I'd known he'd become a wealthy naval captain, I might have mustered a great deal more interest!"

The table fell silent. Even the servants at the sideboards seemed to pause.

Aunt Bean surveyed the room, her indignation faltering in the oppressive quiet. Finally, as if the silence itself challenged her, she declared, "John, I forbid you to allow Emmeline any further association with that family. Their lineage is riddled with villainy! From the late Lord Ravenscross's excesses to the current Lord Ravenscross's fickleness, they are nothing but a blight on society."

"Bina, you are letting ancient grievances cloud your judgment," Father said, which, coming from him, was practically a rebuke.

Had Aunt Bean once fancied Mrs. Thornbury's husband? And regretted slighting him now?

"Mark my words, Emmeline." Aunt Bean's gaze bore into her. "Any continued involvement with that family will ruin your reputation—and when it does, I will not vouch for your matrimonial or social future."

Emme sat in bed later that evening, absorbed in Maria Edgeworth's *The Absentee*. The tale offered more than a commentary on one woman's relentless pursuit of status and its ruinous effects on her weak husband's finances; it also provided a poignant exploration of estate management and a charming glimpse into the lives of ordinary Irish folk.

It was another quiet encouragement for Emme's current novel-writing endeavor.

A soft rap at the door pulled her from the page. Before she could respond, Aster slipped in, her hair wound into cloths for curling. She crossed the room with soundless steps and perched on the end of Emme's bed, her expression pensive. "Do you think Aunt Bean could still be in love with Captain Thornbury?"

Emme placed her book on the bedside table, a grin pulling at her lips. "I think Aunt Bean may still be in love with the status and money Captain Thornbury would have brought to her, not necessarily Captain Thornbury himself."

"It is rather difficult to imagine Aunt Bean in a swoon from love." Her smile flared for a moment before she leaned in. "I asked Father more about the story after Thomas and Aunt Bean left. Evidently, Captain Thornbury—though not yet a captain at the time—was merely a merchant's son with his looks and charm as his chief assets. Aunt Bean, as you know, was a gentleman's daughter, though not an especially wealthy one."

"Ah, the requisite disparity in rank," Emme said dryly, though she felt the words to her heart.

"Precisely. Aunt Bean, of course, refused his attentions. He eventually turned them toward someone more amenable."

"Agatha Bennett," Emme supplied, trying to imagine a younger Mrs. Thornbury. She must have been a great beauty—she still retained a certain elegance despite her stern demeanor.

"Exactly. Mrs. Thornbury spoke of him with such fondness today. It's clear she adored him, and from all accounts, the feeling was mutual. With no children to occupy them, they seemed to have poured their affections entirely into each other. It was quite moving, really." Aster's face softened. "If Captain Thornbury once harbored feelings for Aunt Bean, it only proves love can happen more than once in a lifetime."

Emme studied her sister. What had drawn Aster to her room at this hour? Was she trying to comfort her? To remind her that, despite Simon's absence from her future, love was not an impossibility with someone else?

"I'm sure it can, though not all novels are inclined to admit it."

Aster's gaze drifted to the window, where the moonlight painted the panes in silver. Emme knew that look well—a quiet longing for something far beyond the edges of St. Groves. Her sister's dreams often strayed to exotic lands and distant adventures, not the parlors and polite dances where eligible matches were expected to be made.

She turned back to Emme and took her hand. "There is someone out there for you, Emme. A man who could hold your heart with the same devotion."

Ah. So Emme had guessed correctly about her sister's motives. "And I do hope to find him one day." She forced a lightness into her response she did not entirely feel.

For it was true, wasn't it? Love could happen more than once in a lifetime.

"But there is no doubt in my mind Lord Ravenscross still harbors feelings for you." Aster leaned forward, her eyes aglow in candlelight. "Yesterday, as he walked you to the door—"

"Aster." Emme's face splashed with a sudden warmth. "He is a friend. That is all." She forced meaning into her stare. "That's all it can be. Put those thoughts from your mind for my sake, if not your own."

Aster sighed and stood from the end of the bed, walking slowly toward the door. "I know we, as women, especially as women of smaller means, have little choice in making our fortunes match our hearts, but I do wish money didn't play such a large factor in everything." She leaned her head against the spine of the door as she lost her thoughts in a distant look again. "How I would love to see the world."

With Father so devoted to his land and still mourning their mother's loss, Aster's world had been a small one, apart from her traveling through books and maps.

Emme offered a gentle smile. "Perhaps you will find a husband who wishes to see the world too."

One of Aster's brows tipped northward. "Not from our current options. Not one of them is touched by wanderlust."

"For this season, but you are not even seventeen. There is still time for you."

Aster held Emme's gaze, brow perching high. "There is time for you too, Emme. Twenty does not make you an old maid." Her frown deepened, and she added hesitantly, "And . . . perhaps your heart is not so broken that you couldn't find love with someone other than Lord Ravenscross."

Emme's lips faltered, though she managed a nod. She did not share Marianne Dashwood's dramatic views on heartbreak, after all. Too many stories, both fictional and real, offered proof of hope beyond the loss of a first love.

But if love never came her way again?

Her chest squeezed at the thought. Independence would be a fine achievement, certainly. But the idea of a family—a home bustling with life and love—was as dear a dream as her writing.

"Then it seems we both have cause for hope, don't we?"

Aster tilted her head, her small smile weakening. "Sometimes, don't you wish life turned out as easily or as beautifully as it does for women in novels?"

Emme almost revealed her own literary endeavors then and there, but instead she said, "The women in novels must endure a great many trials before reaching the beautiful part, I think."

Aster considered this, her gaze turning thoughtful. "I suppose love is worth it, if one can find it."

Emme took a deep breath, her heart responding with an answer she wanted to be true. "I want to believe, Aster, that love is always worth it."

The theater hummed with busy tattle breeders and marriage seekers, who spent more time watching prospective suitors than the thespians on the stage.

From his box seat, Simon surveyed the bustling crowd and the stage below, the entire room sizzling with the energy of "the hunt"— whether for gossip, a match, or a possible scandal. There was no want for any, he was sure, and he—his frown deepened—likely provided a solid amount of the fodder.

Miss Clayton sat at his side, her posture impeccably straight, while her sharp-eyed mother perched like a vigilant sparrow just behind them, keeping watch.

The younger woman was, as Emmeline had so generously professed, "*perfectly amiable.*" A compliment that was entirely correct yet entirely uninspiring. She was, no doubt, a handsome woman—her dark green gown offset her soft brown eyes and matching hair beautifully. And she conducted herself with unflappable agreeableness. In fact, her conversation and opinions were so obliging that the dialogue ended within two turns at most.

A desperate man might overlook such things. After all, Miss Clayton brought two thousand pounds a year to a potential marriage, and he was, by all measures, a desperate man. But desperation did not erase memory, nor did it dull the sting of longing.

He had once tasted the rare delight of a match forged in shared wit, intelligence, and a generous heart. After that, even the most mercenary arrangements felt unbearably hollow.

Besides, a certain amount of cleverness was necessary to survive or even outwit his siblings and probably, at times, himself. Miss Clayton's complacent temper and obliging nature might leave her thoroughly hoodwinked—or overwhelmed—before the week was out.

About halfway through the first act, the uncomfortable sensation of being watched placed him on alert. Of course he shouldn't be surprised at garnering some attention. Besides the scandals around his parents' deaths and his sister's disappearance, he was also the walking equivalent of a placard reading "Poor Viscount Needs a Title-Seeking Wife." And from the many glances he caught throughout the first of the evening, many unmarried women—or should he say, many mothers of unmarried women—found him fascinating.

He turned his head away from the stage and scanned the crowd with practiced subtlety. Nothing seemed amiss until . . . he caught sight of a very familiar silhouette, lovely in deep blue, and staring directly at him through a pair of theater glasses.

Emmeline.

He blinked, not necessarily at seeing her in the audience, but her not-so-subtle way in attempting to . . . spy on him?

A laugh tangled in his throat, so he coughed to disguise it.

"Are you unwell, Lord Ravenscross?" Miss Clayton inquired.

"Quite well," he replied quickly, clearing his throat. "Merely a small irritation." He sent the final word silently toward Emmeline, though he knew she couldn't hear him. His lips twitched anyway, fighting another laugh.

Miss Clayton offered him a puzzled glance but thankfully refrained from further inquiry.

Simon, however, couldn't resist looking across the crowd again. Sure enough, the moment their eyes met—well, the moment her *glasses* met his eyes—she quickly lowered the glasses, feigning a sudden interest in the stage.

Another cough slipped from his pressed lips, and he rubbed a hand over his mouth, suppressing a smile. Miss Clayton resumed discussing the intricate embroidery on one of the actress's gowns with mild enthusiasm, though her words barely registered. His attention strayed, unbidden, back to Emmeline. At his pointed stare, she lowered the glasses again and feigned innocence, her expression a picture of surprise at having been caught.

His heart expanded with emotions he dared not acknowledge, pressing against his rib cage to the painful spot, threatening to spill over into words and actions and completely irrational decisions.

He loved her . . . still.

The internal admission settled through him like a deep ache, a soreness that had crept into his bones, but no less real for its quiet persistence. How could loving her but not having her be his future? Was financial success worth the devastation of his heart?

Simon sighed inwardly, struggling to regain some semblance of control over himself.

And furthermore, why on earth would Emme want to be with him? He'd already slighted her once and then took her up on this ridiculous matchmaking scheme of hers, when the very idea had him wanting to hit his head against the nearest wall. If she, of all women, wanted to help him find a bride, then she'd clearly moved beyond any attachment.

And Emme had insisted on Miss Clayton as a choice, but instead of drawing his emotions further away from a very unsuitable match, the only thing it seemed to do was drive deeper the painful clarity of how no one else could ever be Emmeline Lockhart.

As the first act ended and the curtain fell, Simon turned to Miss Clayton. "Are you enjoying the performance, Miss Clayton?"

The woman turned her face to him, her smile already in place. "Oh yes. Quite."

A turn of silence followed, and Simon prodded a little further. "And what have you enjoyed thus far?"

"The acting is fine." She nodded. "And of course I have enjoyed the costuming."

He pushed his smile wider just to try and encourage her to talk. "Yes, the embroidery, I believe."

"Oh yes." Her eyes lit. "I've been fascinated with embroidery since I was a girl. I've never been very good at it, but I do so admire it."

Simon nodded, though his knowledge of embroidery was limited to the fact that it was something he thankfully never had to endure himself. He wasn't sorry for that, but Miss Clayton seemed to notice something behind him and blushed, quickly turning back to him. "But you were speaking of the play, of course. Not embroidery."

Simon studied her a moment, then glanced over his shoulder, catching sight of Mrs. Clayton's pointed expression toward her daughter. Once she noticed Simon's attention, she feigned ignorance, but Simon was no fool. Was the mother coaching the daughter along?

"Have you enjoyed the storyline of the play?" Simon turned his body slightly to keep Mrs. Clayton in his periphery.

"I have," Miss Clayton replied with another wide smile, though it faltered slightly as her brow furrowed. "Though I must admit, I was having some trouble following along with the banter. Sometimes it sounds as if the characters are rather rude to each other, yet the crowd laughs all the same."

"Indeed," Simon agreed, watching Mrs. Clayton's movements from the corner of his eye. "The humor does tend to be rather sharp."

"But I adore funny plays," Miss Clayton added quickly, her cheeks flushing. "So much wit, don't you think?" She forced a small laugh at the end, as if to emphasize her point.

Good heavens, the poor girl either was so nervous that she had to rely on her mother for help with the conversation or lacked the wit to form her own opinions entirely. Yes, she appeared compliant and subdued—qualities Ben had once insisted were ideal in a wife—but Simon knew better. He wanted more.

Emme would have challenged the themes of the play, sparking a lively debate over the characters' choices, and pointed out some of her favorite humorous exchanges.

Simon's chest tightened again. But desperate viscounts, it seemed, had to make practical choices.

The orchestra resumed, playing a light melody to accompany the intermission, and the audience began to rise from their seats. Simon stood, offering Miss Clayton his arm. "Shall we take a turn about the hallway?"

Miss Clayton nodded graciously, slipping her hand onto his arm. "How kind of you, my lord."

They moved into the bustling corridor, mingling with the other attendees, the murmur of voices and rustle of gowns filling the air. Simon made polite conversation with Miss Clayton as they walked, but the comparison with Emme kept distracting him from his focus. There was something both absurd and endearing about her blatant attempt to observe him from afar. Did she doubt his ability to court a woman? Or was she merely assessing the success of her matchmaking scheme?

Or—his thoughts rushed to a halt—could Emmeline be jealous?

He frowned, shaking the thought from his mind. No, of course not. The entire idea to court Miss Clayton had been hers, after all. Jealous women didn't orchestrate such things, did they?

"Lord Ravenscross." Selena Hemston appeared at his side, her presence commanding as always. "How delightful to see you this evening."

Simon straightened, his face and expression cooling as he dipped his chin. "Miss Hemston."

Selena offered him a slow, practiced smile, the kind that was meant to disarm, to charm. And she was charming, in her own way—polished, confident, and unmistakably beautiful. She knew how to dress to turn heads, and tonight was no exception. Her deep red gown shimmered in the candlelight, and her dark hair was styled to perfection, every curl a testament to her calculated allure.

"Are you acquainted with Miss Clayton?" Simon turned toward the young woman on his arm. "Miss Clayton, this is Miss Hemston."

Selena trailed an unwelcome look over the woman. "I believe we've met once or twice before."

Miss Clayton wilted beneath the stare. "Good evening, Miss Hemston."

If Selena could reduce the woman to a mere shadow of herself with a look, a few weeks with Simon's siblings would utterly annihilate her.

Miss Clayton's attention shifted to something behind Simon, and she gave a polite curtsy. "I shall leave you to your conversation. I should greet my father before the next act begins."

She slipped away, leaving him alone with Selena, whose smile only deepened, feline in its satisfaction. "I couldn't help but notice you and Miss Clayton," she purred. "Such a practical choice for you, wouldn't you agree?"

Simon held her gaze, unwilling to fall into her trap. "How are you enjoying the play, Miss Hemston?"

"Ah, not quite the conversational partner you were hoping for, I take it?" Her laugh was light, but there was an edge to it. "Why continue playing this ridiculous game and torturing yourself longer than you must? There is an easy, quite willing solution to all your difficulties, Lord Ravenscross. All you need to do is say the word."

Getting caught in her claws was a terrifying prospect for any man. He tilted his head slightly, his eyes narrowing. "I'm assuming, then, that this comedy is not to your liking."

Selena's jaw tensed for the briefest moment before she took a step closer, her lilac scent filling the air between them. It was a scent he knew well—strong, potent, undeniably hers—carefully chosen to make her presence known. "I'm suggesting, Simon, that we both know you need not only money to save Ravenscross but someone with the fortitude to help you rebuild. I can provide both, and you know it."

"I appreciate your magnanimity to my plight, Miss Hemston." Simon offered a slight nod before stepping back. "And I am sorry to appear unobliging, but I do not believe we are well suited."

"Why not?" Her fan flicked open with a flourish, the feathers brushing against her wrist with practiced elegance. "I come from a family of influence. My father is well known"—though Simon wasn't certain of how well respected—"and with my dowry, you could more than secure your estate. Together, we could ensure your legacy. I have ambition, Simon, the kind that aligns perfectly with your needs."

And with her own.

Simon's jaw clenched against her offer. The very thought that a child born of their union would inherit Ravenscross, under the influence of her shrewd, coldhearted father, sent a chill through him. No, his family would never accept it—not even his astute Aunt Agatha would stand for such an arrangement. But he knew Selena well enough to sense her determination. The viscountcy of Ravenscross might not be the most powerful title in the land, but it carried with it prestige—prestige that Selena longed for to rise above her father's shadow, to win his affection.

Well, if she was determined to be direct, then so could he.

"You seek a title?" Simon asked, cutting to the point. "To win your father's favor?"

Selena's eyes flickered with something unreadable. For a fleeting moment, the confident mask slipped and her smile quivered. "What of it?" Her reply took on a sharpness. "You think I'm the only one with something to prove? You need this just as much as I do. I'm offering a partnership. One where we both get what we want."

"You want my title, and in exchange, I'm supposed to marry a woman whose loyalty is to herself, not my family."

Her eyes flashed. "I am loyal—to my future. And if you think for a second that I wouldn't be loyal to you, you're wrong. I've always respected you, Simon. I wouldn't be standing here making this offer if I didn't believe you were the best match for me. We could be powerful together. Don't you see?"

He saw it, all right. She was pragmatic, just as he was. Her offer wasn't born from affection, nor from passion—it was a calculated arrangement, a way to rise, to secure power and influence. But ambition alone couldn't sustain a life.

"I'm sorry, Miss Hemston." He softened the edge in his voice and drew in a deep breath. "I cannot build my future on ambition alone, no matter the cost."

"No matter the cost?" Selena's expression darkened, her mouth tightening as she snapped her fan shut. "You think you'll find something better? With Miss Clayton, or"—her lips curled—"a country gentleman's daughter?"

Simon flinched at the mention of Emme, and Selena caught the movement, her eyes narrowing with a predator's satisfaction. "You're not as insensible as that, no matter your emotional entrenchment. Besides, rumor has it your dear Miss Lockhart has found a new interest of the clerical variety."

Simon's heart stilled at her words, and though he fought to keep his expression neutral, he could feel his features betraying him. Her smile flickered, sharp and knowing. "Ah, I see you haven't heard the latest. I've even witnessed their exchange of letters firsthand."

Letters? Would Emme resort to such a breach of propriety? Unless there was some truth in Selena's words.

He stilled against the swell of disappointment. But why shouldn't she find someone else? He'd given her no reason to hope for him, despite every fiber of his soul praying for a miracle.

"I fail to see how Miss Lockhart's personal matters have anything to do with me, Miss Hemston."

"Of course not. But as a *friend*, I wouldn't want your hopes to be misguided." Her eyes gleamed with a knowing look. "Why do you fight my offer with such tenacity, Lord Ravenscross? No one else can give you what I can."

The weight of her proposition pressed into his good sense. One answer would change his fortune forever.

But it would also ruin his life.

She leaned in ever so slightly, her voice dropping to a dangerous murmur. "If we both learn to play nice, as I know I am quite capable of doing, it may become more than an alliance. It could become a real connection."

Simon steadied his expression and studied the woman's face, nearly strangled by the urge to call her out for her forwardness, for her breach of propriety, for the fact that a marriage started on such animosity from his part and self-interest on hers had very little chance to be much more than indifference at best or utter torture at worse.

"Miss Hemston, I would encourage you to find someone who values the same things you do because I am not that man." He dipped his head to leave. "Forgive me."

Simon caught the glare she sent him as he turned, but he would not stay for more. Already, his extended conversation with Selena would likely raise some eyebrows, and if there was one thing Simon knew well, it was how easily the gossips could spin a simple conversation to their favor.

He was working hard to repair his family's reputation, to restore the estate's solvency with his own efforts, rather than relying solely on Aunt Agatha's charity. The last thing he needed was anything that could complicate that. His family's future depended on it.

CHAPTER 16

Miss Clayton was an excellent match for Lord Ravenscross. Emme repeated the sentiment to herself, as though it could somehow make it truer, the image of Simon sitting next to the quiet young woman at the theater ever fresh in her mind. They made a charming pair—both handsome and composed. Their children would be stunning.

Her throat tightened. Surely, if she called upon her most sensible side, as Elinor Dashwood might, she could accept what must be. It didn't dull the sting of knowing that someone else would capture his fancy, that someone else would claim the future she'd imagined. Yet there was some small comfort in the knowledge that Simon was doing what was best for his family and his legacy. For future generations. It didn't *erase* her heartache, but it softened it.

Especially the part about the children.

Miss Clayton would be permissive but kind. And they needed kindness.

She probably wouldn't know what in the world to do about Blast or Charlotte's outspoken nature, but at least she could help offer some stability for the entire family. That would have to be enough.

And Emme would go on, finding another dream, another path. Still, there was a part of her that longed to mourn with all the fervor of a fictional Marianne so the world might see just how thoroughly she understood the plight of the brokenhearted. But what would that signify?

It would change nothing, and it would profit her nothing—save for a headache and a concerned visit from St. Groves' Ladies Society.

However, even from her perch in the theater, she could tell Simon wasn't really applying himself to the wooing process. He'd done a much better job with her. The right looks, the dedicated attention, the smiles. Her pulse quivered into a faster pace at the memory of basking in those smiles. He'd given her one when he'd walked her to the house from his carriage yesterday. Emme had felt something pass between them. Aster had even noticed it.

Oh, she must stop this torture. Besides, if Aster's perception was accurate, Emme was only complicating matters for Simon by her insistence on helping. As delightful as resurrecting his feelings for her sounded in the moment, in reality it would only prove much more difficult for both of them, especially when he needed to marry someone rich!

No, if she cared about him and his family at all—charitably or otherwise—she needed to distance herself.

Her mother's sister had long wished for Emme to visit them in Yorkshire, an invitation Emme had not acted upon. Perhaps now was the perfect time. A lengthy trip, long enough to help Simon develop an alliance with a bride and for Emme to move forward with whatever plans she chose to make without him.

Yes. The idea took root. It was a good choice—for both their sakes.

"I would encourage both you and your sister to wear your hair higher on your heads." Aunt Bean's voice broke into Emme's thoughts as she swept into the parlor without ceremony to continue another husband-catching lesson. Evidently, Emme's behavior in helping Simon and avoiding other suitors hadn't encouraged Aunt Bean's confidence, so the Lockhart girls required further instruction.

Emme really should apologize to Aster.

"The higher the hair, the more elegant the neckline, and any man worth having knows the value of an excellent neckline."

Aster's laugh burst from her, but she quickly turned it into a cough as Aunt Bean's attention flashed in her direction. "You must remain healthy, Aster. No man is tempted toward a weak wife who sounds as if consumption is her next illness, unless he's prone to melodrama or, even worse, requires the constant need to rescue something or other."

Emme immediately thought of Simon jumping into the pond after her. The vision of his fine form emerging from the water, his hair curling over his forehead, increased the temperature in the room. She shook the image away. Mostly.

But not before lingering on it just enough to encourage a sigh.

Besides, Simon wasn't prone to melodrama, but having a man who cared for the safety of his family sounded like an excellent trait. Perhaps Miss Lawson would be a better choice for Simon. She was always tripping on something.

"Emmeline." Aunt Bean rapped her cane against the floor, pulling Emme's attention back to the present. "Are you listening to a single word of my instruction?"

Emme scrambled to recall Aunt Bean's lecture. "The importance of necklines?"

Aunt Bean narrowed her eyes before pointing her cane at her. "I believe it is my duty to inform you of some difficulties you, in particular, will face in securing a husband."

Emme braced herself. The list was likely two pages long.

"First of all, your wayward mind. You must overcome this deficit, at least until matrimony—or perhaps until you produce an heir. After that, I dare say, your husband won't care a great deal where your attention lies."

Emme pinched her lips together to contain her grin.

"Secondly, you cannot continue associating with Lord Ravenscross. It will only discourage more appropriate suitors from attending to you. I strongly advise you to avoid him altogether, if possible, and speak only of dull topics in his presence, such as your favorite muslin gown, the meaning of flowers, or the prospective suitors of your sister."

Aster's eyes widened, and she shook her head as though to deny any such suitors—or perhaps to protest Emme mentioning any to Simon.

"Some men—blessed few—are truly drawn to a woman of intelligence or wit. I believe Lord Ravenscross may be one of them. To deter further attachment, you must avoid highlighting those qualities. There are many eligible men who would appreciate your pretense of dim-wittedness, for it allows them to feel superior in saving you, of course." She waved a dismissive hand. "Not to worry. Once you are married and he has 'rescued' you from your ignorance, he will congratulate himself on your sudden ascension to brilliance as you manage your new home and entertain your guests as hostess."

Emme truly had no response to this. Not even in her mind.

Aunt Bean's low opinion of men was well known, and Emme often wondered how her sons had managed to grow into men at all, given the constant barrage of such thinking. Thankfully, Mr. Bridges hadn't passed on until all three sons had reached adulthood, so his influence—rational and measured—had managed to temper some of his wife's more . . . extreme views. At least that was true of the eldest and youngest. The middle son, Harry, was more inclined to his mother's disposition.

"I have every intention to give Lord Ravenscross a wide berth from this point forward." The declaration solidified her plan. Distance. "I . . . I do wish him the very best of happiness."

"Hmm." Aunt Bean grunted in response, a sound more dismissive than contemplative. "The fact that you're still even remotely interested in his well-being shows either a great deal of stubbornness or a woeful blindness to the true nature of the social world." She gave a sharp sniff. "However, if you are determined to turn your attention away from a man who is clearly well above your notice, I would strongly advise against being so particular with the bachelors who remain. All this nonsense encouraged by those dime novels about romance is highly overrated. A woman of strength can manage a marriage just as well without affection. In fact, she'd be wise to choose it, for emotions only cloud one's judgment and lead to an overindulgence in fainting salts."

Aster's cough resurrected.

"The right novels can lead to far better things than that," Emme shot back before stopping herself. In many ways, her earlier novels would have fit everything Aunt Bean despised in fiction, but this current one of hers . . . it was different. It hummed with something deeper, with heart, reality, and—dare she say it?—hope. "I've read books that made me more compassionate toward others in situations I hadn't experienced, or helped me find courage when the characters displayed their strength. I've even found encouragement when I've felt disheartened and—"

"Things better discovered in your Bible than in make-believe stories," Aunt Bean interrupted with a huff.

"The Bible is one grand story, Aunt Albina. And though it may not be fictional, there is a clear celebration of how stories impact us within its sacred pages. If our Lord can use stories to inspire others, surely He can create authors to do the same."

"Nonsense," Aunt Bean retorted with a tap of her cane. "Utter nonsense. No more of that." She struck the floor again, as if to punctuate her authority. Taking a deep breath—one so exaggerated her bosom shook—she steeled herself. "You've distracted me enough from the lesson. How will you ever find a husband if you don't listen?" Another sigh escaped her, large enough to stir the air. "Let us address the proper tilt of a chin for maximum advantage."

Emme cast Aster an apologetic look and then closed her eyes. Though most of what Aunt Bean spoke was utter nonsense, a thread of truth wove through the sentiments and confirmed Emme's thoughts. If Simon still harbored feelings for her, her very presence would only hinder his progress toward finding a more suitable match. So . . . she needed to focus her attention elsewhere, at the very least to ensure that he would continue his pursuit of Miss Clayton or another young lady.

She lifted her gaze to the ceiling, considering the options. Miss Johnson was, of course, a splendid choice with her five thousand pounds and generous annual allowance—though Emme had the distinct feeling that her laugh could scare small children. Still, Fia was old enough to overlook such things, surely.

Stop it! She scolded herself internally. Clearly, it did no good to stay close enough to Simon to know about his life. The temptation was far too great to either help or see him. When he'd been gone those two years, she had almost moved beyond her affection for him.

Almost.

So it was proof enough that time and distance could help remove him from her heart—and hopefully, though the thought was a painful one, her from his.

It was truly time to leave St. Groves.

⁓

"Bina means well, you know."

Emme turned from her writing desk to find her father standing in the open door, his arms crossed and a pipe resting at the corner of his lips. Society may have spurned pipe smoking in public spaces, but in the privacy of their home, it was a familiar comfort.

She smiled in greeting, and he stepped farther into the room, removing his pipe with a small, indulgent sigh. "She will be gone soon.

Her daughter is nearing her time of confinement, and then you will not bear the brunt of her goodwill any longer."

Emme's grin stretched wider. "I must admit, there are few people who bestow their"—she raised a brow—"goodwill with such fervor."

Her father chuckled low, the sound filling the room as he leaned against the mantel, the firelight catching his blond hair, now speckled with silver. "I should have encouraged her to leave sooner," he mused, his gaze softening with the memories. "But your mother always offered such charity to Bina, despite all her idiosyncrasies. She was the most generous of ladies."

His voice grew tender, and Emme felt that known ache in her chest at the mention of her mother. It had been ten years since her death, yet her father still spoke of her with such reverence, as if his heart had never moved away from its devotion.

Nor would it, she imagined.

Theirs had been a love match and a sweet example of what could be.

His gaze shifted to the envelope on Emme's desk—the one she'd just finished addressing. Her mother's sister's name and address marked the front.

Father raised a brow in silent inquiry.

"I was going to ask you about it before posting the letter." She sighed. "I'm thinking of distancing myself from St. Groves for a while." Emme tapped the envelope lightly. "Aunt and Uncle have wanted me to visit for some time, and I never have."

"Distancing yourself from St. Groves?" He nodded slowly, his gaze holding hers. "Or from a particular someone *in* St. Groves?"

Why she sometimes mistook Father's reticence to talk about things as a disinterest or unawareness humbled her. He rarely spoke of matters of the heart, suitors, or future marriages, yet this one observation told her he had watched, and understood, far more than he'd ever voiced.

Emme looked toward the window, the long shadows of evening noting the late hour. But she had much more to do. More words to write on this new story that kept pulling at her heart more than any other she'd ever written. "I don't want to love him, Father. Not at all. It's been terribly inconvenient to love him."

He gave a low laugh, though there was no mirth in it. "There are few people I know whose love came in a convenient way. Not real love. It usually sweeps in like a gust of wind, knocking you off your feet." His voice grew distant with his gaze, and then he turned back to her. "Does he return your affections?"

"It doesn't matter, does it? I can't give him what he needs, and I'm no viscountess." She gave her head a little shake, swallowing through the painful admission. "But I do want what's best for him."

"As your father, I would attest that you would improve any man, and you are certainly intelligent enough to take on such a role. In fact, you'd only improve whatever house you enter, my dear, pauper or king."

"Thank you, Father." A puff of a laugh escaped her lips. Her father's faith in her was insurmountable. "But deeply caring for someone doesn't make money suddenly appear. And I fear his heart may turn from me soon enough when the needs of his estate prove too great."

His entire expression softened, and he lowered himself to the settee at the end of her bed. "Emmeline."

His gentle use of her name pricked her heart. "I will be fine, Father. I just think some distance will help the process along."

"Even after everything, you still care for him?"

"I don't agree with the way he ended things between us—not telling me why." She sighed. "But I believe he is still every bit the man I thought him to be. Perhaps even better now, after all he's endured. And in the throes of affection"—the memory of the balcony kiss flashed to her mind—"it would be easy to forget what is best."

"What is best for whom?"

Emme looked away, the question so pointed that it pricked at her heart.

Father stepped closer, his gaze falling to the papers scattering her desk with her newest manuscript. She rarely hid them in her own room in the evening because no one, except Aster, usually visited her there, and Aster never showed any interest in what Emme had on her desk. But Father's gaze sharpened.

"Working on the next novel, are you?"

Emme's bottom lip dropped. "What?"

He smiled, eyes alight. "I've read them all, you know. Every terrifying adventure."

Emme blinked a few times, absorbing her father's words. "You . . . you know about my novels?"

He shrugged as if his admission hadn't just shocked her senses. "Just because I've never mentioned it doesn't mean I haven't noticed. I supposed you'd tell me when you were ready for me to know."

She struggled to collect her thoughts. "All this time, you've known?"

He gave a calm nod, as if it were the most natural thing in the world.

After all her worry over his response? "And . . . and what did you think?"

Her father raised an eyebrow, clearly amused at her response to his revelation. "Well, you're certainly an excellent writer. You always were, even as a child, constantly spinning stories for the rest of us."

An excellent writer? A sweet warmth pooled through her. Oh, how long she'd wanted to tell him. How much she'd craved to have him approve. And now—he had known all along. Not only had he known, but he thought her an excellent writer. Tears stung her eyes. "And the stories?" Her voice wavered a little. "Did you like them?"

His hesitation was slight but enough to temper her rising elation.

"Stories of pirates and haunted castles are not my usual fare, though I must admit you wrote them exceptionally well. I prefer tales that reflect more of what I know, but"—his lips twitched in a teasing smile—"they certainly held my attention."

She couldn't help but laugh, though his words reminded her of Thomas's. Her gaze fell to the papers on her desk, and a small, unbidden idea took root. Carefully, she lifted the corner of a page left out to dry before glancing back at her father. "I'm . . I'm working on something new," she said, her voice dropping as though others might overhear in the privacy of her room. "Something different from what I've written before."

Father inclined his head. "Are you now?"

She nodded, hesitating before her courage finally overcame her. "Would you . . ." She took a breath, steadying herself. She'd never shown anyone her work before she'd finished it. Not even Thomas. "Would you like to hear a few pages?"

For a moment he simply looked at her, his blue eyes infused with a warmth that soothed every lingering uncertainty. Then, with a broad smile, he gave a firm nod and moved to a chair near the fire. "Indeed, I would."

He tucked his pipe into the corner of his mouth and offered her a most encouraging smile. "Begin whenever you're ready."

He should be happy for Emmeline Lockhart.

It would be the noble, self-sacrificing thing to do.

If she'd formed a new attachment, even if it were to the newly installed rector, Simon should feel nothing but contentment at her chance for happiness—just as she appeared to wish the same for him.

But blast it all, he wasn't.

Crossing his arms, he stared out the window at the cloudy afternoon. A sheen of rain lingered on the grass, and the air carried a sharp coolness, foretelling the turn of seasons. Not that he cared for the weather. Autumn might as well rage into winter if it pleased. The only thing weighing on him now was the truth pressing against his chest.

He loved Emmeline Lockhart.

He wanted to marry Emmeline Lockhart.

And up until Selena Hemston planted the idea of Emme having feelings for Mr. Bridges, he'd thought she may still harbor some affection for him. He lowered his fist to the windowsill. But why? Why should he seek her attention? He had nothing to offer her. He'd broken her heart once. He had no money to marry her now, or at least not enough to save his estate *and* marry her. No, Emmeline deserved someone unencumbered by financial woes or family scandals. Someone like Thomas Bridges—witty, intelligent, wholesome.

Unshackled.

Blast!

His interview that morning with Miss Lane for the governess position only kept Emme even more forward in his thoughts. Miss Lane had impressed him with her intelligence and disposition, meeting every qualification he sought in a governess. She was sharp-witted, good-humored, and precisely what his siblings needed. He'd hired her immediately.

And she was set to begin within the week!

One task checked off Aunt Agatha's infernal list.

One month remained to secure a bride.

He frowned. He already knew who he wanted for a bride, but Aunt Agatha's standards—and his own circumstances—rendered Emmeline unsuitable. Perhaps, he thought grimly, the word *suitable* needed redefining.

A glance at the copy of *Sense and Sensibility* on the side table deepened his mood. Willoughby's character only grew more suspect with each chapter, and Edward Ferrars seemed to be teetering on the brink of some wretched secret. The steadfast Elinor Dashwood and dignified Colonel Brandon were the only reliable souls in the narrative. Everyone else was as unsettling as Simon's own predicament.

Why did he care so much? Yet he couldn't put it down. It felt too familiar—the tension, the longing, the quiet suffering. It was as if he were peering in on the inner workings of St. Groves. Perhaps that was it. The story felt real. Especially right now. With Emme possibly making a connection with someone else. He felt very much the plight of Colonel Brandon, except Simon deserved his disappointment. Brandon didn't.

"Still brooding, are you?" Ben strolled into the room, heading straight for the drinks tray.

Simon spared him a look.

"Oh, indeed." Ben poured himself a glass, his tone dry. "That furrowed brow of yours could frighten the rain away. Or is it a certain *someone* troubling your thoughts?"

Simon's jaw tightened. "I wasn't brooding until you barged in."

"Ah, of course." Ben took a deliberate sip. "Nothing to do with the fact that your heart and your head seem to be engaged in a duel, I'm sure."

Simon glared. "It's just—" He broke off, dragging a hand through his hair. "It's just—it's so blasted infuriating."

"I can imagine." Ben leaned casually against the table. "But perhaps you're making it harder than it needs to be."

Simon let out a weary sigh. "What do you want me to say, Ben? Yes, she's . . . everything. But Ravenscross needs more than affection. It needs funds, repairs—"

"You're not destitute, Simon." Ben waved his glass toward the

Great Hall. "If you fail to resolve Ravenscross's finances through some neat marriage contract, you may have to endure a few lean years, but you won't be utterly ruined. And as for the ancestors' dour faces glaring at you from their gilded frames—well, they've had centuries to perfect their disapproval. I daresay you'll survive it." His tone softened as he straightened, setting down his glass. "My father married for money and status, and I grew up in a home where my mother neither respected nor cared for my father or her children. We endured years of quiet misery, especially Father. Wealth isn't worth a lifetime of regret."

Simon arched a brow. "Wasn't it you who delivered your sister's infamous list of potential suitors at the season's first ball?"

Ben shrugged, entirely unbothered. "I've said many things I'd never act upon. You, of all people, should know me well enough to ignore my worst advice and enjoy my best mischief along the way."

Simon rolled his eyes heavenward.

"There is no guarantee that my efforts with tenants and businesses will make the needed difference for this estate without a rich wife, Ben." His hard work had proven successful so far, but he had much more work to do to become independent enough to not rely on Aunt Agatha's help. "I need to know I've secured the estate and my siblings' futures."

"And you need more than a convenient marriage," Ben interrupted, his tone pointed. "There's more to a family's future happiness than ready cash and a title. What would it look like to have a wife who would stand beside you—not just in the ballroom, but here, in the work? A woman willing to help you save this estate?"

Simon began to shake his head, but Ben pressed on.

"You're stubborn, but you're not blind. I've seen how you look at her. It's not mere admiration. It's something more."

Simon's chest tightened, warmth threatening to betray him.

"It doesn't matter what I feel. She deserves better than to be tied to a man drowning in debt. I won't deceive her into believing our marriage could fix what is broken here."

Ben was silent for a moment, then spoke softly. "Perhaps she doesn't need to save your estate, Simon. Perhaps she only needs to save *you*."

Simon's breath caught. Ben's words struck deeper than he cared to admit. For a moment he allowed himself to imagine it—Emmeline at Ravenscross. Not merely as a comforting presence for his siblings but as a partner, a force of strength and steadiness.

Could she bear the strain of rebuilding alongside him? Would she shoulder the inconveniences of a salvaged estate, the gradual work of making Ravenscross whole again? A part of him believed she would. Yet he couldn't allow himself the indulgence of hope. Not when she might have already turned her heart toward another.

He forced her smile, her laugh, from his mind. "She's not an option," he muttered, almost as if convincing himself.

Ben stepped forward, clapping a hand on his shoulder, his voice low. "I think the real question is, do you want her to be?"

Simon didn't answer. His gaze returned to the rain-slicked lawn, the droplets sliding down the glass panes like his own thoughts—scattered, relentless. Want and need were two very different things.

And yet, for the first time since he'd returned to St. Groves as Lord Ravenscross, he began to wonder if the best hope for him and Ravenscross was the one person he'd been refusing to consider all along.

CHAPTER 17

S imon hadn't intended to be in town this morning.

He hadn't planned on witnessing Emme and her sister, Aster, strolling alongside the new rector, all engaged in an animated exchange punctuated with smiles. If not for the errand to collect a package from the post, he might have missed this . . . charming tableau entirely.

His frown deepened. How delightful.

Did they often walk together? Did Mr. Bridges enjoy the privilege of Emme's smiles on a regular basis? Could there truly be merit to Selena's insinuations that an attachment was forming between them?

Before Simon really understood what his feet were doing, he'd quite intentionally redirected his path to walk directly into theirs.

The trio came to a halt as he approached, and though heat rose uncomfortably to his face at his unplanned intrusion, Simon removed his hat and offered a courteous bow, focusing his attention on Mr. Bridges, of course. "Good morning."

Mr. Bridges raised his brows briefly, his expression settling into a polite smile. "Lord Ravenscross." He dipped his head. "A fine morning to you, sir."

Simon turned his gaze to the ladies, inclining his head again and catching Emme's wide-eyed reaction.

"I wished to congratulate you, Mr. Bridges, on your first month as rector of Lemmingston. Your reputation for compassion and eloquence has already reached me."

"High praise, my lord. Thank you," Mr. Bridges replied, the

corner of his mouth curving with amusement. "Yet I must ask—why rely on hearsay when you might experience my unparalleled oratory firsthand? Your attendance would doubtless be a boon to the community and might even encourage some of your tenants to return to church."

"Not to mention, greatly enhance his spiritual life," Aster added, her large eyes a darker hue than her sister's, but with the same intelligence.

A soft snicker came from Emme's direction, though she quickly covered her mouth with her gloved hand, her expression one of mock innocence.

Simon cleared his throat and offered Aster a smile. "Miss Aster, your counsel is duly noted. I shall endeavor to attend on Sunday in eager expectation of being transformed."

The halts and stops of air coming from his left increased in volume and Simon's chest tightened. Her laughter—at his expense, no less—had always been as infuriating as it was endearing. Her humor, her light, and her comfort enough in their friendship not only to laugh *with* him but *at* him only dug into his desire to make her a permanent part of his life.

Surely, with her kindness and selflessness, she'd make an excellent clergyman's wife. But—he cast a glance at Mr. Bridges, who was really too handsome and charismatic to be a rector—would she really be happy? Would he engage her wit? Comfort her in her sadness? Make her laugh?

The thought settled uneasily in Simon's chest.

Giving her up had seemed possible and necessary when the distance of months and his own stupid rationalization of the situation kept his mind fully occupied, but the longer he spent time with her, the more his arguments teetered into forcing possibility.

Could he? What sacrifices would he have to make? What promises?

"Ah, well, I don't know that I'd place my abilities into the transformative category, Lord Ravenscross," Mr. Bridges offered, his gaze measuring Simon as it had during their first meeting. "But perhaps the Good Book would provide the proper impetus for the right encouragement."

Whether it was the fact that the man was a clergyman or a possible suitor of Emme's, Simon wasn't certain, but something about Mr. Bridges kept Simon guessing. He was friendly but carried himself with a quiet confidence few men of his age possessed.

An attractive quality in any man, but particularly so for an intelligent woman like Emme. His shoulders slumped.

"Have the new tenants settled in, Lord Ravenscross?" This from Emme, whose smile drew him a step forward.

"Bit by bit, I believe." He cast his nod to the trio. "The two families who have already moved into the cottages have made quick work of starting things well, and I mean to have two more cottages ready for occupation by end of next week."

"Excellent, sir." The rector's praise somehow made Simon stand a little taller. Perhaps it was merely because the man had some sort of special connection with the Almighty. "I shall continue to send more names as you need them, if you wish."

"I do. As I make the cottages habitable, I have every intention of filling them." And a genuine smile spread across Simon's face, not just at his own pride in his work, but in the welcome light in the rector's face. He was a good sort. Blast it. "Thank you."

"And your family?" Emme continued. "Are they still enjoying the strawberries?"

"Indeed, they are." His body eased into the dialogue. "And Fia cannot stop singing Alfie's praises."

"They did become quick friends, didn't they?"

His gaze paused in hers. She was beautiful. Absolutely. The

light in those eyes, the turn of her chin. He couldn't pull his attention away.

And then he realized in the middle of his adoration, Aster had taken Mr. Bridges' arm at some point, and they'd begun walking along the pavement. Simon gestured forward to Emme, who fell into step beside him, her pace deliberately slower, as if inviting a more private exchange.

His pulse quickened. He shouldn't want this. Neither should she.

And yet, if he could steal one more moment with her, he would. For however long it lasted.

For a few beats, they walked in companionable silence, the sound of their steps muted against the pavement. Emme's hands tightened slightly on her reticule, and Simon wondered if she was deliberating her words as much as he was. It seemed too strange that he had so much he wanted to express, so many forbidden thoughts and feelings, and yet, he couldn't.

Shouldn't.

But they were nearly strangling him to get out.

Clearing his throat, he managed, "I . . . wanted to thank you for your recommendation of Miss Clayton."

Brilliant, Simon. A masterful way to woo the woman you love— praise another.

Emme's brows rose. "Truly?"

"You doubt me?"

Her lips twitched, her eyes narrowing as she studied him. "Well, appearances might suggest otherwise."

"Is that so?" The sunlight danced across her golden hair, but it was the gleam of mischief in her gaze that truly held him. From the first time they'd met—when she'd teased him mercilessly in the Ruthtons' library—she'd been utterly disarming.

She hadn't known who he was . . . and she'd just been her charming self.

Unlike other women, who charmed with calculated poise, Emme's wit struck like lightning, quick and natural. She was a force entirely her own.

And heaven help him, how could he marry anyone else?

"How very . . . observant of you."

One corner of her mouth edged a little higher as she stared up at him and then laughed, shaking her head as she did so. "Was I so obvious?"

"Painfully," he shot back. "Especially with those theater glasses of yours."

And then, to his own surprise, he laughed. Not a polite chuckle or a restrained smile, but an unguarded, genuine laugh—the kind he hadn't indulged in for far too long. His body relaxed, his burdens momentarily forgotten in the comfort of their familiar banter. "I believe some training in covert skills would be in order."

"Indeed." She glanced ahead as they continued their walk, the distance between them and Mr. Bridges with Aster widening. "But how could I help it? The play was diverting enough, but I confess your performance was far more compelling than the actors on the stage."

"My performance?"

"Between your rather uninspired courting of Miss Clayton and the grand scene with Miss Hemston during intermission . . ."

"Your theater glasses extended all the way to the lobby during intermission?"

Her smile dropped wide and she looked away, a bloom deepening her cheeks again. "I took a stroll, as many others did, to refresh myself after sitting so long."

"And just happened to witness my exchange with Miss Hemston?"

She avoided his gaze, the blush deepening, and his grin only grew.

"It was quite the spectacle," she admitted. "Poor Miss Clayton looked positively ruffled by Miss Hemston's theatrics. It was all very dramatic."

Why did she care? Unless . . . could the idea of her being jealous hold some truth? He slowed his steps, her reaction feeding a flicker of hope. Perhaps Miss Hemston's earlier insinuations had been wrong—or intentionally misleading.

"It's wise to consider one's options when contemplating matrimony, wouldn't you agree? Focusing solely on Miss Clayton when Miss Hemston is so very . . . insistent seems rather inefficient."

"Inefficient?" Her lovely bottom lip dropped, but she rallied within a second, her cheeks heightened with color. "You're far too intelligent to entertain Miss Hemston, Simon Reeves. And you care too deeply for your family to make such an error."

"Giving my family and estate what they need is of prime importance." He kept his face forward to hide his growing amusement. "She brings a great deal of wealth."

"And an even greater measure of misery," she shot back, her steps quickening before she turned to face him, her expression fierce. "She's selfish and manipulative. Can you imagine how she'd treat Fia and her frogs?"

Simon nearly winced, but her passion kept him entranced.

"And poor William. I don't know him as well as the girls, but can you even contemplate such a harsh woman in his life? Or Charlotte! She'd try to hold her ground, but Miss Hemston's years of practiced haughtiness would crush her spirit entirely."

He stared at her, his heart nearly leaping from his chest. How could one woman understand his family so perfectly? How could she care for them as much as he did? He almost grabbed her and kissed her in the middle of one of the main thoroughfares in St. Groves.

"I must choose someone," he said, his voice low.

Her brows knitted together. "I've given you a perfectly acceptable suggestion in Miss Clayton. Surely she deserves better than a suitor so easily distracted during a performance."

He wasn't distracted by Miss Hemston.

"If this is your idea of courting, Lord Ravenscross, I'd say you're in dire need of instruction."

On instinct, he reached for her arm, stopping her mid-stride and drawing her closer. "I recall a time when you found my courting skills more than satisfactory."

Her eyes widened, her breath catching as her cheeks flushed deeper. "That . . ." She hesitated, her gaze imploring him for mercy. Tugging her arm free, she whispered, "Everything was different then."

She turned and resumed her walk, her pace brisk, leaving him no choice but to follow.

"If Miss Clayton is not the conversationalist you desire," she said, her tone deliberately light and her smile as thin as parchment, "perhaps Miss Perkins might suffice?"

"She's barely sixteen."

"And men your age have married sixteen-year-olds before," she retorted, waving a hand. "She has some spirit—perhaps like Marianne in that novel you're reading?"

"I am not as old as Colonel Brandon," he huffed, "though I do admire his character. But sixteen and eight-and-twenty is far closer than sixteen and five-and-thirty, wouldn't you agree?"

Her eyes lit as she paused her walk and turned to face him again. "You must be enjoying the story to have remembered such details."

"I am, but I'm afraid business has slowed my progress."

She resumed walking at a more leisurely pace, her face tilted toward him. "Good business, I hope?"

"Very good." His expression softened at her sincere interest. "Every small, sound decision matters."

"Indeed. An excellent life motto for anyone."

His gaze narrowed in mock suspicion, which only deepened her grin. If he were truly keeping his aunt's stipulations in mind, he would end this conversation and suppress the pull of her presence. But her sunshine—the pure, uncalculated brightness she brought to his life—felt like the only thing tethering him to sanity.

Her.

Ben's words came back to mind. *"Perhaps she doesn't need to save your estate, Simon. Perhaps she only needs to save you."*

A dangerous idea unfurled in his mind, nudging aside his fears and the prescriptive future he had resigned himself to. His trials had shaped him—his cousin's negligence and debts, his father's ruin, his mother's death, and Arianna's disappearance—all forging his courage in ways he'd never expected.

Could choosing right for his heart also lead to what was right for everyone else he held dear?

"And what sort of business?" she asked, breaking the silence. "With wheat prices as they are, have you sought alternative sources of income?"

Trust her to dive straight into the heart of practical matters. She'd become her father's confidante after her mother's death, and her aptitude for sensible discussion was just another admirable quality.

"Besides implementing your suggestion about the tenants, I've acquired sheep, sold some timber, and leased some larger buildings to Mr. Arden for his expanding mill."

"Oh, that's an excellent choice," she said brightly. "His opinion carries weight among the tradesmen. Have you approached Mr. Jenkins? I know he's seeking more space for his fringe and lace business. And Mr. Leeds's warehouse is nearly bursting."

The urge to kiss her surged again, stronger than before. He was clearly losing his mind—and his battle with restraint.

When he failed to respond immediately, she took a cautious step back, a fresh rush of color highlighting her cheeks. "I'm sure these aren't the most ladylike topics to discuss, but—"

"They're excellent suggestions. And I thank you for them." He split the distance between them, taking her gloved hand in his. "Truly, Emme. Your kindness is . . . overwhelming."

A pair of ladies approached, and Simon released Emme's hand, doffing his hat and offering a welcome smile as the women passed. The younger of the two nearly turned all the way around as she walked, her smile anything but demure, but the fan she had in her hand took on new speed.

Emme chuckled softly, drawing his attention back to her. "You have quite the effect on the ladies, Lord Ravenscross. I daresay she nearly swooned at your smile."

"Did she?" He turned his focus to her, the corners of his mouth quirking upward. "Does my smile induce swooning from you, Miss Lockhart?"

There it was—he'd danced far too close to the line, and he knew it.

Despite the momentary redirection of her gaze, she rallied her response. "Well, besides being undeniably handsome, you do have a certain dashing quality. Rather like John Willoughby as I imagine him in your current reading."

"Ah, I see." His confidence wavered. "I should much prefer to be viewed as honorable. Like the colonel."

"Oh dear, but wouldn't the combination of the two make the most delightful hero in a novel? Dashing *and* devoted?" She sighed wistfully, her voice dipping as though she spoke to herself. "Imagine scripting such a character."

He studied her profile as they resumed walking, the haberdashery now distressingly close. "You speak as though you've plans to create such a hero yourself."

She faltered slightly but recovered. "Why not? You're reading and enjoying a novel written by a woman, are you not?"

"I am. And the author's talent is beyond reproach. But she is wise to keep her anonymity. A lady taking to writing as a profession is often viewed . . . poorly."

Her expression hardened slightly as she turned her attention ahead. "What an unfortunate reality. Gentlemen inherit fortunes by virtue of birth, yet ladies cannot earn honest money without their reputations suffering." She turned her gaze back to his, her look piercing. "Does that not strike you as terribly unfair?"

"There are many injustices in the world, I'm afraid."

She tilted her head, her expression adorably stubborn. "Perhaps. But in our small part of it, I think we ought to make things right. Even in the everyday choices we make for the people we love."

For the people we love. The words echoed in his mind, a pang of longing sharpening his awareness of her. *Would that I were one of those people.*

"Which you do so naturally," he said, his voice softer now. "In that, you remind me very much of Elinor Dashwood."

Her smile bloomed again. "Oh, I'm not so levelheaded, I'm afraid. But I do hope my heart is as compassionate as hers. She has a strength of character I greatly admire."

"I'm afraid I must disagree with you on the matter of strength. You've borne your share of heartache with exceptional grace, and I'm ashamed to say I've been part of that."

She looked down but did not respond.

"As for characters," he continued, returning to a lighter refrain, "my confidence in Mr. Willoughby is waning considerably."

Her brow arched slightly, her expression teasing. "Oh? And what has brought on this sudden concern?"

They were now within sight of the haberdashery, where Aster lingered in the doorway, watching them with obvious anticipation.

Still, Simon longed for just a few more moments. "I find myself impressed by Colonel Brandon's steady nature, and Mr. Willoughby's relentless criticism of him has begun to grate on my nerves. Something about it feels . . . off. And then there's the matter of Lucy Steele."

Emme's laugh bubbled out, warming him like fresh sunshine. "Is there?"

"You know precisely what I mean. She's a meddlesome young woman with a silly sister. I had high hopes for Edward Ferrars, but I'm finding myself increasingly vexed by his inconstancy. In fact, I'm much angrier at him than Elinor appears to be."

Her expression sobered, forehead crinkling with her frown. "Perhaps she understood him in ways others didn't. Believed in the man she'd come to know." She drew in a breath and looked up at him. "She must have realized a deeper reason for his apparent inconsistency of character, don't you think?"

Was she speaking of Elinor and Edward or of him and her? "And . . . and she forgave him?"

They were only a few steps from the haberdashery, but he couldn't end the conversation without knowing her answer. Without understanding her. One touch to her arm paused her steps, and when she turned to him, her eyes held a quiet intensity.

"I . . ." She hesitated, a watery sheen filming over those eyes. "I don't agree with the way Edward handled things. That he didn't explain, didn't trust Elinor to understand. But as she gained hindsight and the story offered her more perspective, I believe she saw that the heart of his character never changed. Only his circumstances did."

She *did* know. She saw it. Felt it. Believed in him—and forgave him in ways he had not dared to imagine or ask.

Aster moved at the edge of his vision, but he seized the moment, refusing to let it slip through his fingers. "His feelings were constant, Emme. Elinor came into his life so unexpectedly, and once he began to care, he never stopped. How could he stop? She was perfect for him."

"Not quite perfect." Emme offered a small, wistful smile. "Not enough."

The words struck him like a blow. Not enough. No. She was

more than enough—always had been. Blast the money. Blast society's insufferable expectations. Didn't love matter at all?

"Emme—"

"Pardon me!" Aster approached, her tone playful as she glanced between them, her smile just shy of teasing. "I'm so sorry to interrupt your conversation, but you did promise to help me choose a hat. And Thomas has quite finished indulging me."

Emme pulled her gaze from his, nodding to her sister before returning her attention to him, smile sad. "Good day, Lord Ravenscross. I do hope you enjoy finishing the book—particularly to see what becomes of dear Colonel Brandon and Edward Ferrars. I think you'll be pleased."

With that, she stepped into the shop, leaving him standing on the street, her words and their implications echoing through him.

She'd forgiven him.

She'd seen past his failures and his missteps, and she believed in him despite them.

And he knew now that his next choice would be the one either to keep her in his life—or lose her forever.

He would take every ounce of courage he'd learned from the past two years and fight for her. For them, if he had a chance to win her. He just had to make a plan.

He'd made it halfway down the street back toward his horse when Selena Hemston emerged from around the corner of Rosewood Tea Rooms, her determined steps aimed directly at him. He dipped his head with the full intention of a quick greeting and escape, but she stepped directly in his path.

"What are you doing?"

Simon attempted to bypass her, but she slipped in front of him again. What was she playing at? "Walking to my horse."

"You do realize, Lord Ravenscross"—Selena narrowed her eyes—"that it would be folly—utter folly—to reintroduce *that* attachment."

"That attachment?" He arched a brow, his patience fraying at record speed.

She gestured back toward the haberdashery, her meaning clear. Had she been following him? Watching his interaction with Emme? What absurd game was she playing?

"To which attachment are you referring, Miss Hemston?" he asked. "The gossips have been rather industrious with my name of late. I'd like to ensure I'm addressing questions about the proper lady."

"Don't play coy with me," she retorted, her tone clipped. "You know perfectly well to whom I refer. Or has your memory become as unreliable as your judgment?"

Simon's mouth twitched, though not with amusement. He forced a mock smile that bordered on a grimace. "Your concern is noted, Miss Hemston. However, I assure you, my affairs—whether social or financial—are entirely mine to manage."

Selena took a measured step closer, her voice lowering, almost taunting. "Then be responsible, Simon. Think carefully about what you're throwing away—what you and your family stand to lose." She tilted her head, her tone honeyed yet edged with steel.

Her words grated against him, but Simon held her gaze without flinching. "And you, Miss Hemston, need to understand that not all things can be claimed by mere assertion. Now, if you'll excuse me—"

But Selena didn't step aside, her lips curving into a smile that was all calculation. "Miss Lockhart may present herself as innocent and charming, but I suspect there is more to her than meets the eye. And rest assured, I will uncover it. I only hope it is before you make an unalterable mistake."

Simon's jaw tightened. "Jealousy, Miss Hemston, is a poor companion to civility. I suggest you dismiss it." He barely kept his tone measured. "Your insinuations do not reflect well upon you, and I have no intention of forming an alliance—of any kind—with someone who behaves in such a manner. I must insist you refrain from involving either myself or Miss Lockhart in your future schemes."

Selena's smile barely wavered. "I'm not going anywhere, Lord Ravenscross. And neither are your problems—until you begin making wiser decisions. This is not a difficult one, but sentimentality could cost you everything."

Simon exhaled slowly, his mind clearer than it had been in days. The certainty of what he needed—and whom he needed—settled over him with newfound resolve. Yes, it was time to revisit his plans, adjust his estate's financial strategy, and above all, convince Aunt Agatha that his choice was the only sensible one for Ravenscross, the children, and himself.

For a moment his gaze locked with Selena's in a silent battle. She, no doubt, was accustomed to winning such exchanges within their social circles, leveraging her father's influence and her own cunning. But she held no power over him—not truly. Her threats were hollow, her confidence built on sand.

With a crisp touch to his hat, Simon stepped neatly around her, his tone polite but final. "Good day, Miss Hemston."

As he strode away, determination replaced the frustration Selena had stirred. Now it was time to focus on how to make Emmeline Lockhart his bride.

CHAPTER 18

E mme should have feigned sickness for this evening, she supposed. That would have done her heart better than to see Simon gliding so beautifully on the ballroom floor looking every bit the hero in his black cutaway coat and trousers.

He certainly waltzed well.

She almost grinned. Aunt Bean's instruction on the matter came back to mind. *The rogue.*

To complicate matters further, this was Emme's penultimate ball in St. Groves before she left for Yorkshire. The plan had been simple: keep to the periphery, reduce prolonged conversation, and above all, avoid Simon.

But they always seemed to find each other, even if merely a glance.

Their encounter on the street a few days prior had left her more certain than ever about her plans. His words—veiled though they were—had carried the weight of truths she could scarcely believe. He still cared for her.

His earnest expression filtered back in her mind. Deeply. She pressed a palm to her chest. Beautifully.

And now, to see him move with effortless grace, his hand steady at the waist of Miss Lucy Thompson? Her breath pinched for release. The admiral's daughter had risen from obscurity on the swell of her father's naval success and was now as admired for her quiet beauty as her father was for his victories.

Emme's smile faded. A good choice for him. Kind. Quiet. Dependable. Of her wit or fortitude, Emme knew little, but such things could grow in time, because Simon would be the sort to nurture them.

The acknowledgment stabbed through her, but she braced against the ache and sought some semblance of contentment in the knowledge he was doing his duty, caring for his family.

Simon spun nearer, his attention catching hers in a way none other could. His gaze for a breath too long, a moment too deep, and the air seemed to thin.

This—this was why she had to leave St. Groves.

Her very presence in his life distracted him from what he most needed to accomplish.

And she needed to make it through only one more ball after this before she left for Yorkshire.

She turned sharply, heading for the sanctuary of solitude on some private balcony or in an unused closet. But before she could escape the crush of the ballroom, an iron cord of fingers gripped her arm, holding her in place.

"Emmeline Lockhart, I will not have you scurry away to some hiding spot for the remainder of this ball. We haven't much time left." The intensity in Aunt Bean's eyes, not to mention her solid grasp, held Emme to the spot. "I know of a gentleman who has every intention of speaking to you on a rather particular matter this evening."

On a particular matter? Oh, heaven help me! She knew exactly what that meant.

Aunt Bean's sharp gaze latched onto a figure across the room, and her entire demeanor shifted to one of triumphant anticipation. "Ah, there he is."

Mr. Marshall.

Of course Emme had wondered if he'd offer himself, but in all truth, he seemed enamored with so many ladies, it was difficult to tell.

"Tonight I will fulfill my promise to you, dear girl."

Again, the word *dear* felt anything but.

So that explained the half hour Aunt Bean had spent adjusting Emme's gown, tweaking a ribbon here and a curl there, all while grinning like a cat with a canary firmly in its sights.

The last thing she wanted to do was cause a scene, but she had to end Aunt Bean's mission now, especially with Emme leaving St. Groves' social scene in less than five days. "I'm sorry for all the trouble you've gone through, Aunt, but I cannot marry Mr. Marshall."

Aunt Bean leveled Emme with a look of utter frustration. "You can and you must."

"No, I do not have to marry someone just because he asks me. Or because he fits some sort of social expectation."

"A girl in your situation must take what she can, and he is much better than what I expected you to be able to find given your overt flirtation with a certain viscount."

Emme refused to allow guilt to be her deciding factor and pulled her arm from her aunt's hold. "If Mr. Marshall asks me to marry him, I will refuse him."

"Refuse?" Aunt Bean's voice rose a notch, though she kept her tone just shy of a scene. "Four thousand a year! An estate, respectability— everything you could ever want. He is your rescue."

Heat burst up through Emme's chest. "I don't *need* to be rescued." Emme kept her voice at a much more private volume than her aunt. "Especially by someone who sees me as a convenience or an adornment. He barely knows me, and what he does know he does not particularly like."

"Those novels of yours have done you an immense disservice." Aunt Bean's fan took on the wing patterns of a hummingbird. "Marriage isn't about liking each other! You think I married your uncle because he was charming?" Her voice dropped, and she cast a furtive glance over her shoulder before continuing in a fierce whisper. "I married him because he had land, connections, and a respectable name. Did I overlook innumerable flaws? Of course. Did he spend more time away than at home? Yes, and the better for it. But I gained security and standing. All the things you'll throw away with your reckless whims."

"I suppose I am reckless," Emme countered. "To prefer true affection over companionable indifference, at best? To seek a little freedom over four thousand a year."

Aunt Bean snapped her fan shut, pointing it at Emme as though it were a sword. "Freedom won't save you when the ton finishes devouring you. Have you heard the whispers about you and Lord Ravenscross? Because I have. And they aren't kind. That man is your ruin, Emmeline."

Emme's cheeks flushed, but she refused to let Aunt Bean see her falter. "Lord Ravenscross is an old friend, nothing more. Our shared past lends itself to exaggeration, but as you can see, he's well on his way to finding a bride"

"Nonsense." She narrowed her eyes at Emme. "It is as obvious as the exaggerated pineapple on the dining table that you are still very much in his thoughts, but he has no power to do anything about it, does he? Which lends itself to the worst rumors. Whispers have already begun. Speculations about what Lord Ravenscross may offer you instead of a ring."

The implications scorched Emme's cheeks. "He would never stoop to malign me in such a way."

"It doesn't matter what he will or won't do. It is all about what people think and"—she waved her fan toward the room—"see. Do you understand? *No one* will have you after this."

"Then no one shall have me," Emme ground out, lifting her chin, the confession burning through her like fire.

Aunt Bean's laugh was sharp and mirthless. "You jest, but spinsterhood is not the grand adventure you imagine it to be. It is a slow, cold descent into irrelevance," she hissed. "You may rid yourself of Mr. Marshall and his ilk, but you will also rid yourself of invitations, allies, and respect. Society is unforgiving to those who break its rules."

Aunt Bean opened her mouth to say more, but before another syllable escaped, she gasped. The sound was so uncharacteristic that Emme startled, turning toward her. The woman even turned three shades paler, which was a feat of science.

"What is *she* doing here?"

Emme followed her aunt's gaze across the ballroom. There, standing amid a group of similarly distinguished women, was none other than Mrs. Agatha Thornbury, Simon's formidable aunt.

The emotional ricochet of Emme's day—the threat of a proposal from Mr. Marshall, Aunt Bean's relentless critique, and . . . Simon—had left her reeling. Now, the sight of Mrs. Thornbury only added another wild volley to an already unpredictable match.

She looked rather lovely in her simple blue gown, giving off a much gentler appearance than the almost militant walking suit she'd worn the day they picked strawberries. The look didn't make Emme feel at ease per se, but it certainly didn't enhance the tension.

Emme moved her attention from Mrs. Thornbury to Aunt Bean's vibrating fan, which seemed on the verge of taking flight. "What is wrong?"

Aunt Bean turned to Emme, her expression both incredulous and affronted. "How dare she show her face in polite society? That woman has done more to sully the Thornbury name than a thousand scandals could ever hope to achieve!"

"From what I've observed," Emme murmured, attempting to sort out the dilemma, "Mrs. Thornbury seems to manage herself—and her reputation—quite well."

Aunt Bean bristled—her feathers, quite literally, ruffling in indignation. "You've no idea, Emmeline. No one knows the truth like I do. That she stole a man who I was practically engaged to marry. *Stole* him. And then proceeded to marry him within three months' time. Likely to secure him and spite me. That's why. That woman—she . . . she . . ."

"Yes?" Emme prompted, raising a brow at her aunt's uncharacteristic floundering.

Without any explanation, Aunt Bean swept forward, her fan snapping open again as she marched across the ballroom, gaze locked on Mrs. Thornbury.

Oh dear. What sort of scene would Aunt Bean create now? The irony was not lost on Emme—the woman who prided herself on instilling decorum in her nieces was about to create a spectacle. Emme was sure of it.

Mrs. Thornbury must have turned at the unmistakable rhythm of Aunt Bean's cane, the sharp *click-click* cutting through the soft hum of the crowd. If she felt any apprehension, it didn't show. Instead, Mrs. Thornbury dipped her head, offering a reserved smile that was just warm enough to convey politeness but stopped short of invitation.

"Mrs. Bridges, what a pleasant surprise to see you this evening."

"Mrs. Thornbury," Aunt Bean replied, her fan slowing to a calculated flutter. "I had not realized you were in town. What a . . . fortuitous encounter."

Mrs. Thornbury's brow lifted ever so slightly, her expression steady and inscrutable.

There was something almost heroic in the way Mrs. Thornbury met Aunt Bean's barbs without flinching. Her quiet confidence, her unshakable composure—it was, Emme thought with reluctant admiration, inspiring.

"Indeed. My nephew persuaded me to rejoin society for tonight.

It has been a pleasure to reconnect with old friends—and to meet new acquaintances."

At the mention of Simon, Aunt Bean's fan paused midair before snapping shut with an audible *click*. "Ah, yes. Lord Ravenscross. A young man with many responsibilities—and, one might say, many challenges."

Oh, good heavens! Emme needed to concoct some plan to get her aunt away from Mrs. Thornbury and further embarrassment. Perhaps this was a perfect time for a faint?

Mrs. Thornbury's smile remained in place, though there was an undeniable steel behind it. "Lord Ravenscross bears his responsibilities with admirable fortitude, though I am certain you, with your extensive experience in such matters, might have a great deal of advice to offer."

Emme bit back a smile, silently marveling at how effortlessly Mrs. Thornbury deflected her aunt's jabs. Truly, if one aspired to grace under pressure, Mrs. Agatha Thornbury was the pinnacle. Perhaps society brought out her best.

"I would offer advice if it were sought," Aunt Bean said with a sniff. "But the younger generation often prefers to chart its own course, heedless of the wisdom of their elders." At which time, Aunt Bean did nothing to hide her rather pointed look in Emme's direction.

Mrs. Thornbury's gaze flicked to Emme, her expression softening. "Miss Lockhart seems quite capable of determining her own path. I have always admired a woman with a sense of purpose."

"Purpose is admirable," Aunt Bean said, her tone sharpening. "But purpose without propriety is another matter. My niece has grown beyond her silly connections of youth, and she has no regrets related to previous attachments, I assure you. It is clear she can do much better."

"Aunt," Emme warned, but her intervention was futile.

"And I would encourage her to steer clear of families who seem to inherit poor judgment, deception, and inconstancy in relationships,"

Aunt Bean continued, her words aimed like arrows. "I am sure you know such legacies quite well."

Mrs. Thornbury's calm remained unbroken as she replied, "Regret, Mrs. Bridges, is a most peculiar thing. Some are plagued by it; others learn from it and move forward. I suspect Miss Lockhart is wise enough to choose the latter." Mrs. Thornbury offered a slight nod to Emme. "From my brief acquaintance with her, I feel she knows her place and her own mind."

Her place? That, Emme thought bitterly, made Mrs. Thornbury's opinion of her and Simon's potential future quite clear. Yet her own mind was precisely the problem—it knew the painful truth all too well. It was her own heart that was causing the indecision.

Aunt Bean's lips tightened. "Wisdom in youth is often a matter of luck rather than merit. Tell me, Mrs. Thornbury, did your husband share your philosophical outlook?"

No! Aunt Bean did not just bring up Mrs. Thornbury's heartache.

A shadow flickered in Mrs. Thornbury's eyes, but her tone remained steady. "Captain Thornbury's outlook was one of optimism and constancy. He was ever guided by his heart and his sense of honor. A rare combination, I must say."

Emme's breath caught. What happened when the heart and honor were in conflict? Did honor always triumph?

The implication was clear, and Aunt Bean bristled. "Rare, indeed. Though one might wonder if such qualities are valued as highly as wealth and connections. The heart is rarely a trustworthy appendage, except in hindsight."

"Albina"—Mrs. Thornbury's tone dipped with tender entreaty—"it was a long time ago. Whatever grievances you may carry, they do not serve either of us now."

"Grievances?" Aunt Bean's cheeks flushed bright red. "I hold no grievances. I merely observe that some choices are made without proper foresight."

This conversation really needed to happen elsewhere instead of a crowded room. So much for all those lessons on propriety!

"Your foresight in rejecting him was most acute, I am sure." Mrs. Thornbury tilted her head, her gaze steady. "But you chose someone else that better met your desires, which left dear Captain Thornbury to find me." Her smile softened, though her eyes remained steel. "And for that, I owe you my most heartfelt gratitude."

Aunt Bean sputtered a few seconds, the feather in her hair dancing a rather unruly rhythm in response. "Gratitude," she snapped, "is an easier sentiment to bear when one has gained everything they wished for."

"Not everything." Mrs. Thornbury's quiet response carried the faintest edge.

In that moment Emme remembered Simon mentioning how his aunt and her late husband had been unable to have children of their own. And now, to lose someone she evidently loved so dearly—two decades into their marriage—would surely weigh heavily on a heart.

Loss came in all shapes and sizes, didn't it? The way of the world.

"Life takes its toll on us all, Albina. You and I are not exceptions. Perhaps it is time to let the past rest."

Aunt Bean sputtered, her voice tangled in her protest, but Mrs. Thornbury did not wait for a response.

"Miss Lockhart." Mrs. Thornbury turned her attention fully to Emme, her smile welcome. "You remind me very much of your mother. She, too, had a remarkable strength of character. I am certain you will navigate these waters with grace, no matter what the gossips say."

Emme inclined her head, uncertain whether to be encouraged or chastened by the comment. Mrs. Thornbury's words, though kind, carried an unmistakable point in them.

With a polite nod to Emme and a final deliberate glance at Aunt Bean, Mrs. Thornbury stepped away, leaving the elder woman to stew in the wake of her remarks.

But Emme wasn't finished. How could she leave Simon's aunt to think Emme held any similar view to her own aunt?

It was only a moment before Emme followed. "Mrs. Thornbury," she called softly, hastening after her. "I must apologize for my aunt's remarks. Her opinions are her own and do not reflect mine."

Mrs. Thornbury's brow arched slightly. "Do they not?"

"No." Emme's cheeks warmed beneath the woman's steady gaze. "I hold Lord Ravenscross in the highest esteem."

Mrs. Thornbury's expression revealed nothing, though a flicker of interest danced in her eyes. "The *highest esteem*," she repeated, her tone so neutral that it left Emme wondering whether she was amused or incredulous. "So much so that you would assist in finding him a bride?"

The question, posed with disarming calm, caught Emme off guard. Still, she refused to look away. "Yes, though not solely for his sake. His siblings—his family—deserve security and comfort. A strong and thoughtful alliance would provide that."

Mrs. Thornbury regarded her, the silence stretching just long enough to make Emme's pulse quicken. "A strong and thoughtful alliance," she echoed softly. "Indeed, you are not wrong. But you must know, Miss Lockhart, that the history you share with my nephew is not easily forgotten—by society or by Simon himself."

Emme straightened, refusing to let the words unnerve her. "I understand the risks of gossip, but I assure you, my intentions are honorable. It is because of our shared history that I wished to help. I understand . . . him and the situation with a unique perspective."

But even her attempt at an explanation failed to convince her own heart. She'd offered, in part, with selfless motivation, but in hindsight she'd wanted to be near him—and perhaps somehow make amends for all the horrible thoughts she'd had about him in his absence, before the truth of his situation became clear. She almost laughed in her realization. "Helping him find happiness offers me some measure of perspective as well. It's terribly inconvenient for my own hopes. But I see the good of it for everyone involved, especially Lord Ravenscross."

Wasn't that the essence of love? To find joy in another's happiness even at the cost of your own heart?

Something shifted in Mrs. Thornbury's gaze—so slight Emme might have imagined it. "Your loyalty to him is . . . notable. And yet, loyalty can be misconstrued. Have you considered that your efforts, however well-meaning, may complicate his path forward?"

Emme merely nodded her head in assent. She hadn't voiced her plans to anyone but Father and Aster. "I plan to leave St. Groves by the end of next week."

Mrs. Thornbury blinked, the faintest hint of surprise softening her reserve. "Leave?"

"Yes." She forced a smile. "It has never been my intention to cause rumors or to distract. I have family up north I've neglected far too long. A lengthy visit will do me good."

The older woman studied Emme, her gaze probing. "You are leaving St. Groves," she said slowly, "for my nephew's sake?"

"It is the choice of a . . . friend." Emme lowered her gaze, the bridge of her nose tingling with warning. "A friend who wants what is best for him and his family."

At the sudden silence, Emme raised her gaze and found the woman studying her with an unreadable expression. Finally, Mrs. Thornbury's lips curved into a faint, almost imperceptible smile. "You are an intriguing young woman, Miss Lockhart. I can see why my nephew speaks of you with such admiration."

Emme's breath caught, but before she could respond, Mrs. Thornbury inclined her head, her voice returning to its composed, measured cadence. "I do hope your path leads you to happiness, wherever it may take you."

The words, though kindly meant, were like a dagger to Emme's chest. She nodded politely, refusing to betray the sudden pain coursing through her. "Thank you."

Barely waiting to regain her composure, Emme fled around the corner of the hallway into a small alcove. Fresh evening air wafted in through the open window, carrying the scent of hyacinths—likely the blue ones the groundskeepers nurtured at the base of the Assembly Room stairs. A humorless laugh shook from her. Blue hyacinths meant sincere care.

Sincere. And if she cared sincerely, she knew the good of her choice.

Emme exhaled, sagging against the wall and stilling the tears threatening release.

She'd experienced almost every imaginable emotion within the span of an hour.

No wonder she detested balls.

But amid the turmoil, a quiet certainty settled within her, ringing louder than any whispered gossip or distant sweet memory.

Goodbye, St. Groves.

Simon's happiness and her own fragile heart demanded it.

CHAPTER 19

Aunt Agatha had agreed to meet with Simon alone after dinner that evening.

He would make his case.

He'd dutifully played his part at the last ball, dancing with a veritable parade of suitable options she'd brought before him. Dutifully, he'd returned with his observations—polished, diplomatic, and entirely detached. Yet none of them, not one, could compare to Emmeline Lockhart.

Some had their merits, he supposed. A few came with fortunes large enough to settle Ravenscross's debts outright; others displayed a measure of charm or kindness. But how could he transfer his affections, like a ledger entry, from one lady to another when his heart so clearly, so immovably, belonged to Emme?

In truth, Simon felt like Edward Ferrars, caught in the aching dissonance between duty and love. He recalled Elinor Dashwood's quiet anguish upon hearing of Edward's engagement to Lucy Steele. Elinor's outward composure had masked a torrent of heartbreak, but Simon suspected her suffering paled in comparison to Edward's torment—trapped with a woman he could not love, while loving a woman he could not claim.

That would not be his fate.

Not if Aunt Agatha accepted his terms.

And not if Emme would have him.

That morning's ride to visit his new tenants had only solidified his resolve.

Mr. Chapman and his young bride, Anna—formerly Miss Dean—had taken up residence in a modest cottage at the edge of the estate. They had gone about their union in an unconventional way, eloping to Scotland, much to the shock of her family. Yet as Simon observed their quiet joy, the way they seemed to exist entirely for each other, he couldn't help but feel humbled. They had no grandeur and no fortune, but their affection for each other was wealth enough.

Then there were the Pooles, who had been tenants for little more than a week. Decades of shared hardships had forged a partnership of seamless understanding. Their cheerful camaraderie, their unspoken harmony in labor and life, was a quiet testament to the power of true companionship. Simon left each visit more heartened by their example than by any encouragement he had offered them.

It was those moments—simple yet profound—that assured Simon he was making the right decision.

The only decision.

Colonel Brandon had been mocked for his steady nature, his lack of flamboyant passions, yet in the end it was his constancy, his unwavering devotion, that laid the foundation for his happiness. Brandon had waited, endured, and hoped.

Could Simon not do the same? Given time, could he not earn his own happy ending?

He had no Lucy Steele forcing his hand, no clandestine engagement threatening to undo him. All he needed was time—just a little more time.

Emme wasn't merely the best choice for him, she was the best choice for his family and for Ravenscross. As a wife, a guardian to his siblings, and a viscountess, she would bring warmth, intelligence, and resilience to their lives. She would be the anchor they all needed.

The estate was improving. The new tenancy agreements were

yielding profits, modest though they were. The timber management, carefully overseen, had already begun to show promise. Even the wool production—a venture Aunt Agatha had been skeptical of—was on a steady upward trajectory.

If Aunt Agatha could be persuaded to grant him the freedom to delay his choice, he could build enough financial stability to relinquish his dependence on her allowance. They might endure a leaner season or two, but in the end, his decision would secure their future.

Surely Aunt Agatha would see reason. She was a practical woman—sharp-tongued, yes, but not unfeeling. He would present his case with logic, clarity, and with any luck, a measure of humility that might soften her resolve.

This wasn't merely sentiment. It was strategy. For them all.

Simon straightened his cravat in the mirror over the mantel in his office, holding his own gaze with a promise. Tonight he would make his aunt see.

At that moment the door burst open, and in ran Fia, a cat slung over one arm and a crumpled paper flapping in her other hand. She stopped abruptly in the middle of the room, her little face scrunched into a frown. It was clear she hadn't even noticed him.

Midas, the long-suffering feline, hung limply, resigned to the whims of his pint-size captor. The poor creature likely had no illusions left about dignity.

Two more days. Just two more days until Mrs. Lane arrived to impose her miraculous order upon the household. Emma had praised Mrs. Lane's ability to somehow wrangle chaos into something resembling routine, while still allowing the children their games and whims. Simon raised a thankful gaze to the ceiling.

Oh, happy day.

"Are you looking for me, Fia?"

Her head snapped up, and her face lit with a wide, toothless grin. "Mrs. Patterson said you were here, but then you weren't." She shuffled forward, and Simon lowered himself into a nearby chair, bringing himself to her level.

Of course she had a story to tell. Fia always did.

"Midas brought me a bird," she announced with the solemnity of a royal decree. "But it was very asleep, so I took it to Mrs. Patterson." She nodded, her eyes wide with the weight of her tale. "But she said it was a very special sleeping bird and needed more rest, so she put it outside again."

Poor Mrs. Patterson. Simon bit back a laugh. "Very wise of Mrs. Patterson. I've heard those sleeping birds are not very good at managing either cats or the indoors."

Fia tilted her head, considering this, her curls bouncing with the movement. "Then I do hope Midas stops catching that sort. They're no fun to play with at all."

"Indeed, I imagine they aren't." His lips twitched as he glanced at the paper clutched in her small fist. "Was there something else, lamb?"

She beamed at him, her dimples carving into her cheeks, her golden curls framing her face like a cherub in a painting. With that combination of a toothless grin and earnest eyes, she could melt the heart of the sternest curmudgeon.

Fia skipped over to him, unceremoniously releasing Midas, who bolted for the safety of a nearby chair. Then, without so much as a by-your-leave, she climbed into Simon's lap. "Lottie asked me to give you this very special letter."

And just like that, Simon's smile faded.

A letter.

Arianna's farewell had come by letter too. Its brevity had been as cutting as its contents—irrational and emotional, its cruelty sharpened by the whispers of a flatterer who'd preyed upon her grief.

He shook the thought away and forced himself to focus on the scrap of paper Fia now held aloft like a prize. With a steadying breath, he unfolded it.

The words were written in a childish scrawl, their content equal parts innocence and impudence:

I've gone to Miss Lockhart's house to learn about strawberries. I didn't ask because I knew you would say no, which would have been a very bad idea as Miss Lockhart has been so kind to us. Perhaps someday you'll remember how to be a gentleman, but I don't care to wait until then.

Simon suppressed a groan, his jaw tightening. *The little imp.*

"Thank you, Fia," he managed, though his voice sounded strained even to his own ears.

He stood, setting Fia gently on her feet. Would he have refused Lottie's request if she'd asked? Likely not. The idea of building a stronger relationship between Emme and his sisters might have felt dangerous—not only because he hadn't secured any acceptance from Aunt Agatha, but also because every additional moment he spent with the woman only made him want to spend dozens more without a certainty of their future—but for Lottie's sake, he might have relented.

Now, it seemed, she had taken matters into her own hands. *Typical.*

Tucking the note into his pocket, Simon sighed. His little sister's audacity had certainly been inherited from somewhere—though at the moment, he wasn't particularly inclined to take credit for it.

He glanced at Fia. "Anything else you'd like to confess, lamb?"

She shook her head solemnly, then beamed up at him again, her smile entirely guileless.

"Good. Now I must ride to one of our neighbors' houses." Simon reached over to ruffle her curls. "Do you think you can manage to stay out of the water puddles while I'm gone?"

Fia nodded, though her expression wavered as though the promise might cost her dearly. "But sometimes, they're so big, they find me."

"Understandable." Simon pressed his lips together as though

weighing her predicament. "But perhaps you could stay inside, just for a little while, and search for"—he glanced around the room, desperate for an idea, until his eyes alighted on the carved ravens perched over the doorway—"ravens. How many ravens do you think there are in the house? Count them all, and when I return, you can tell me the number. If you're very thorough, I daresay we'll have strawberry tart to celebrate."

Fia's face lit with delight, her previous hesitation vanishing. She followed his gaze to the carved ravens, her brows knitting with determination. "I am very good at finding things."

"I know." Without a doubt, and many times things he'd wished she hadn't.

With that, she scampered off and Simon marched to find Mrs. Patterson. Who knew whether Emme had actually invited Lottie or if his sister had concocted the scheme entirely on her own?

After notifying Mrs. Patterson and Aunt Agatha of his plans—"a quick ride to a neighbor's estate, back by dinner," he assured them—he saddled his horse and set out toward Thistlecroft House.

And yes, he could have stayed home. He could have waited for Lottie to return, heard her story, and avoided yet another interaction with Emme Lockhart.

But what would that accomplish?

Yes, calling on her at her home was ludicrous. Borderline improper, even, considering his supposed search for a different sort of bride.

And yet, the memory of her antics at the theater rose unbidden, warming him in a way that made rationality seem wholly overrated. Add to it her veiled conversation, telling him she'd forgiven him? Well, there was nothing else to do but to attempt to ascertain her feelings.

And if he had to use Lottie as an excuse to do so, well, so be it.

"You cannot be upset with him," Aster announced, not looking up from her sketch. She lounged on a garden bench near the roses, her lap scattered with pencils and paper.

Emme had spent far too much time in the garden that morning. For some reason, her creativity had dwindled overnight, and unfortunately, it seemed to begin and end at the theater and then the ball.

"I am not upset with him." She clipped a full chrysanthemum, the shears in her hand as precise as her tone.

"No, of course not." Aster's attention flicked up from her drawing. "You're merely sulking like a governess left out of the nursery party."

Emme spun around, spectacles nearly toppling from her nose. "I am not sulking!"

"Good, because it would be terribly hypocritical of you." Aster raised one brow. "You're the one who sent Miss Clayton his way in the first place."

"I did no such thing," Emme countered, her voice lightening as she feigned detachment. Though, in all honesty, she did do such a thing. "And I'm not upset. Miss Clayton is exactly what Lord Ravenscross needs."

Aster studied her, a smirk tugging at her lips. Very unsisterly of her. "I'm so glad you didn't take to the stage, Emme. You would have failed miserably."

"I beg your pardon?"

"If you're attempting to look unaffected, you're doing a poor job of it."

Emme huffed, looking directly at her sister and snipping an aster bloom with more force than was strictly necessary. "What do you expect me to say? That I'm pining for someone I cannot have? That I wish the world worked differently?" The conglomeration of floral scents wafted on the cool breeze, tousling tendrils of hair across her face. She brushed them back with a sigh. "The truth won't change the fact that he requires something I cannot provide." Her voice hitched as she turned back to snip another chrysanthemum, its rich pink hue and voluminous petals offering a charming distraction. "All I can do now is leave to let nature take its course."

"I understand why you're leaving, but I don't like it." Aster harrumphed, a sound that did nothing to calm Emme's mind—or heart. "It's not fair."

"Not everything can be resolved as neatly as in a novel, I'm afraid. We must accept it . . . and move on." Even as she spoke, the words tore at her. Oh, she had wanted to assist Simon, but perhaps more selfishly, she yearned to remain close to him just a little longer. What a dreadful decision! It only complicated matters further. She really should've let him alone from the very beginning.

At least when Colonel Brandon asked Elinor Dashwood to talk to Edward Ferrars about a job as curate on his estate, Elinor had possessed undeniable purpose in seeing and helping Edward. Emme had just thrust herself on poor Simon at cost to both of them.

She inwardly groaned. How could she have been so rash? Good intentions without wisdom rarely boded well.

"Can't there be another way?" Aster's eyes, which could shift from blue to green with the hue of her gown, studied Emme with evident disapproval. "He still harbors feelings for you. And I know you feel the same."

"It's not enough, Aster." Emme averted her gaze, adding a rose to her bouquet. "Yes, I care for him. But we must accept the reality." She met Aster's gaze, her voice dropping to a pained whisper. "We must."

With a deepening frown, Aster crossed her arms. "Your plight almost persuades me to accept Mr. Todd, who only desires a pretty arm ornament but promises to let me travel the world. Clearly, love need not be a priority."

Emme's lips tipped the slightest at her sister's attempt at levity. "Mr. Todd is old enough to be your grandfather."

"And yet, that does not detract from my point," Aster retorted, her brows arching in challenge.

Before Emme could respond, the sound of the garden gate creaking open made them both turn. Simon strode in, his coat undone and his cravat slightly askew—an uncharacteristic look for him, but not one she necessarily disliked. She swallowed. At all.

"Sim—Lord Ravenscross?" Emme corrected herself. "What are you doing here?"

"Pardon my intrusion, but I need to find Charlotte." He strode toward them, his attention fixed on Emme in such a way that her throat closed just a little.

"What do you mean?" Emme's face cooled at the statement, nearly losing her grip on her bouquet. "Is she missing?"

Dear heavens! Like Arianna?

"You've not seen her?" He raked a hand through his hair, mussing it even more. And still, she didn't mind the look. "She left a note saying she'd come here to learn how to plant strawberries."

"I offered to teach her, but I insisted she must ask your permission first." She sighed, reading the worry on his face. "I assume from your scowl and the desperate flight here, she did not follow my advice."

The scowl softened considerably. "She isn't very good at heeding instruction, I'm afraid."

"Well, at least she's among good company," Aster quipped before casting Emme a pointed look.

"Is that so?" He dipped his head to Aster in greeting.

"How can you doubt it? You know Emme." Her sister only tipped her brow higher, needling the reference to Emme and Simon's past. "She's always been a little too opinionated for her own good, setting off into ridiculous rescue plans without thought."

Aster's implications, and in front of Simon of all people, were too pointed.

"You're one to talk, sister." Emme's face grew sunburn hot, but she pushed up a grin for diversion, if nothing else. "It's no wonder Charlotte felt a kinship to us then, is it?"

"No wonder," Simon murmured, his gaze lingering on hers just long enough to set her pulse skittering before he shifted his focus. "But if she isn't here, where could she be? I came directly from the estate."

"She's likely on her way." Emme was thankful her voice sounded much calmer than the tremor of her pulse. "Perhaps you traveled faster than she anticipated."

"Yes, that's quite possible." He exhaled with a nod, scanning the garden again. "I rode Zeus. Her mare is not the fastest animal."

"Given by design, I'm sure." Emme allowed herself a small, teasing smile as she snipped another chrysanthemum, only to realize—too late—that Aster had vanished, leaving her alone with Simon.

Her breath hitched. *Dear heavens.* Aster had abandoned her with the one man she had no business being alone with. What *was* her sister thinking?

"I apologize for interrupting your"—he gestured to the bouquet—"artistry?"

"Bouquet for the dining room," she managed, adjusting the flowers as though they would shield her from the effect his nearness had on her thoughts, pulse . . . emotions. Good heavens, all of her.

He didn't stand terribly close, but her desire for him to step closer was a traitorous thought. It really wasn't fair for him to show up in her garden looking this handsome. And if it wasn't incredibly inappropriate to tell him, she would have said so. "Chrysanthemums are in such abundance this year, and they carry a lovely meaning of . . ." Her gaze settled on the red one in her hand. *Love.* She hesitated. "Good fortune."

"Good fortune?" He stepped nearer, inspecting a flower with a half smile that made her knees feel rather unsteady. "Is that so?"

"Mm-hmm. An excellent flower for you, Lord Ravenscross, to inspire the best of luck."

His lips crooked further, and her heart stammered rigorously in response.

She wouldn't have to feign a faint at all if he kept this up. Heaven help her!

All she needed to do was make it through this week, and then she would be gone.

She turned back to her work to keep her face from his, taking the opportunity to pluck a late sunflower next, sending him a grin over her shoulder. "Sunflowers for determination, in honor of Charlotte."

His chuckle warmed the space between them, sending a lovely tingle up her neck, despite the high collar of her jacket. "Determination, indeed. She has that in spades."

Emme was certain she was disproving Aster's assessment of her acting abilities with each moment she passed in Simon's presence. But whatever skills she did possess were beginning to weaken with each grin or look he sent her. Something new hid in those eyes, and her heart nearly lurched from her chest attempting to seize it.

She shifted a step to the right, plucking a white rose. Relatively safe. "Gathering bouquets is one of my favorite tasks. Not only do they make a room more cheerful, but the aromas sweeten any space."

"Indeed." His voice brewed low, nearer. "And what does the white rose signify?"

Her breaths grew shallower. She cleared her throat and then almost whimpered. Love, also. But she sifted through her mind for a safer meaning. "Loyalty, actually." How on earth were the plants even conspiring against her?

"Loyalty?" At this, he'd drawn too near, his presence entirely too much. Oh, why was he torturing her so? Hadn't Miss Clayton supplied ample distraction? Or Miss Thompson, for heaven's sake?

To keep from turning toward him, Emme reached for another bloom without looking, but instead of a chrysanthemum, her fingers closed around a sprig of nettles.

"Ah!" She snatched her hand back and dropped her shears altogether.

"Nettles?" Simon's concern gave way to a wry grin, his brow arching. "What subtle message were you hoping to convey with those?"

Cradling her stung fingers, she glared weakly at him. "Perhaps 'keep your distance' would suffice."

"Ah, but I've never been one to heed instruction well either." His voice swooped low, reverberating somewhere inside her—the teasing look in his eyes disarming her entirely. In fact, she hadn't realized he'd taken her hand until she saw him lifting her fingers for inspection.

They hadn't been this close since the balcony—or perhaps his veranda at Ravenscross. And they certainly hadn't been this close since she realized just how much she'd never stopped caring for him. How bothersome feelings were—especially right now, when her body wanted one thing, and her mind—*bless it*—proved entirely useless at forming a coherent thought, let alone mounting a defense.

Clearly, her sense was no match for a pair of familiar blue eyes, a velvety voice, and the gentleness of his touch. He studied her fingers with care, his brow furrowing as if this small injury were of the gravest importance. Then, without breaking eye contact, and with an infuriatingly tender slowness, he brought her wounded fingers to his mouth, brushing a feather-light kiss over the reddened area.

Sweltering heat rushed to her hairline, her heart stopped, and the world shrank to this—the press of his lips to her skin, the look in his eyes, and the brush of his breath over her wrist.

And she knew that as long as he was anywhere near, there was no escaping him.

Or this overpowering love she had for him.

"Blast it, Emme," he whispered, her name slipping past his lips like a plea. His gaze traveled over her face with a look so endearing, she stopped breathing altogether. "Why did you have to wear those ridiculous spectacles?"

A helpless laugh bubbled from her lips, barely a sound. He'd always weakened in some mysterious way when she'd worn her spectacles. Distracting, he'd called them, which, in truth, had caused her to wear them all the more.

Her free hand reached for his chest, an instinctive move to steady herself, but the quick rise and fall beneath her palm only drew her nearer. His unoccupied hand slid gently to her cheek, his thumb grazing her skin in a way that unraveled her. How curious it was to love and loathe the effect someone could have on her in equal measure. It never made sense, but at that moment, logic was clearly irrelevant.

There was no mistaking their intentions this time. No hiding behind convenient interruptions from suitors or overbearing aunts. This was madness, pure and unbridled.

Would he kiss her again? Here in her very own garden?

And what about Miss Clayton? And the money?

But as his head dipped closer, the world seemed to fade until there was nothing but him—his eyes, his touch, the heat of his breath against her lips.

Dear heavens, who cared about Miss Clayton or the money?

And then—

A sneeze shattered the stillness.

They froze, heads snapping toward the shrubbery.

Simon recovered first, his jaw tightening as he called out, "Charlotte."

Charlotte? What on earth was Charlotte doing hiding in Emme's garden . . . witnessing a reputation-ending kiss?

Or near kiss.

And Emme wasn't certain what was worse. Kissing Simon Reeves for the last time.

Or not getting the opportunity of another kiss at all.

CHAPTER 20

Good heavens, he'd nearly kissed Emme. In her own garden. When he knew perfectly well that he had no freedom to pursue her.

Not yet.

He could blame the spectacles, but that would be a lie—and he despised liars, especially when the truth was so painfully clear. It was her. It had always been her. No amount of logic or time could diminish the pull she had on him. Every other option, every other path, seemed pale and lifeless by comparison.

And it was driving him mad.

Mad enough to nearly ruin her reputation in broad daylight. At her own home. What in the devil was wrong with him? How had he let himself become so utterly undone?

He was a cad. A heartless rake.

Turning back to Emme to beg her forgiveness, a movement in the shrubbery caught his eye. Charlotte rose, her grin utterly unrepentant as she picked a stray leaf from her skirt, her dark hair in disarray.

"What on earth are you doing hiding in Miss Lockhart's garden?" he demanded, striding toward her with barely contained exasperation.

"I came to learn how to plant strawberries," she replied, brushing off her sleeves with a flourish, sending him a knowing look that no thirteen-year-old sister should ever dare to flaunt to her utterly flustered elder brother.

Imp!

Then a thought struck him. Had Lottie meant for him to follow her to Emme's in order to . . . he shook his head. Surely not. His sister wouldn't concoct some sort of plan like this, would she?

Simon had little time to consider it because just then another figure emerged from the shrubbery, her honeyed hair gleaming in the sunlight.

His face went cold. "Miss . . . Miss Aster?" The words came out strangled, choked by his own surprise.

"It seems wrong to allow Lottie all the fun," Aster said, shrugging a shoulder as if entirely unaffected. "So I joined her and"—her brows wiggled—"it was quite the show."

"Aster!" Emme's hand fluttered toward Simon, her gaze catching in his for a moment, heat rising back into those lovely cheeks, before she snapped back to her sister. "This was not what it should have been. And I would hope"—she threw an almost matronly look at the girls despite the chirp of her pitch—"that you would keep this private exchange to yourselves. Spying is hardly an appropriate pastime for a lady."

"We weren't spying," Aster corrected, a mischievous glint in her eyes. "We were . . . observing." She smiled just slightly, and Simon realized for the first time that second-born daughters may be creatures unto themselves, no matter what household they abided. "There's a difference."

Lottie nodded solemnly, as if this were a perfectly reasonable excuse. "Precisely. Observing. For . . ." She paused, glancing at Aster for an answer.

"Horticultural inspiration," Aster supplied with a wink.

"Ridiculous." Emme crossed her arms over her chest as she moved to Simon's side to create a united front, he supposed. "At your age."

"Horticultural endeavors are excellent at any age, I hear." Aster gave her sister a syrupy smile that did nothing but tighten Emme's posture. "In fact, sister-dear, I'd always heard that a white rose meant love," she continued. "And a red chrysanthemum as well." She paused with a deliberate shrug, her eyes twinkling. "And even—"

"Aster." Emme stepped forward, thrusting the bouquet of flowers into her sister's hands with remarkable finality. "Take these inside." Her brows rose, her lips pinched. "Now."

Love? Had Emme been avoiding saying the word to him? Despite the absurdity of the situation, Simon couldn't suppress the slight tilt of a smile.

Aster offered a sweeping curtsy, taking the flowers with an exaggerated air of graciousness before disappearing through the path.

With arms still folded, Emme turned to him, brow raised in expectation.

He'd almost kissed her. Catastrophic, really. Dangerous when there was no understanding between them.

He'd already been the rogue. The unintended rogue, but one nonetheless. He would convince Aunt Agatha to allow him time to choose a bride, and then—then he'd marry Emme and kiss her whenever and however often he wished.

With a quick turn, he faced Lottie. "Am I to think that you dragged me to Thistlecroft under false pretenses?"

"Drag you here?" Lottie blinked up at him with wide eyes, all mock innocence. "Me? You mustn't give me so much credit. You're the one who followed me."

"Followed you?" he repeated, his voice rising.

"And I'd been invited," she added. "Miss Lockhart invited me to teach me how to plant strawberries, as I'd mentioned in my letter."

Simon let out a slow breath, dragging a hand through his hair. "But you knew I'd follow you."

She smiled all the more, not an ounce of remorse in her expression.

"Lottie, we will discuss this later. At length." With a resigned sigh, Simon shot her a hard look before turning to Emme.

But the tender look she'd given him a moment ago had vanished, replaced by a wariness that made his chest tighten. And he hated it. He hated that he had caused it.

"I apologize, Miss Lockhart," he said softly, searching her face, pressing his deeper meaning into his expression.

Sorry for nearly kissing you again, for wordlessly promising something on which I could not deliver just yet, for losing control of my senses and nearly wounding you all over again. His eyes searched hers, trying to convey the depth of his regret. It was a silent apology for the unspoken promises he had made in his mind, ones that he knew he could not yet fulfill. "Please," he began again. "I would be grateful for the opportunity to speak with you—properly—at another time."

Her gaze flicked to his lips for the briefest moment before returning to his eyes, her expression shuttered, those faint traces of warmth now veiled. He nearly groaned from the wound.

"Emme, forgive me."

Her brow creased, and she took a deliberate step back. "I believe," she said, her voice steady but with an undeniable quiver beneath the surface, "that particular conversation may not be the most fitting for me, my lord." Her eyes held his for a heartbeat too long before darting to the ground. "But I am certain there is another lady more suited to it."

No!

He couldn't lose her again.

And at his own hand.

If only she knew what he intended, how he planned to resolve this madness. His family, his obligations—they would all fall into place soon enough. And then—then he could pursue Emme properly, without shame, without guilt.

But she didn't know that, and he couldn't tell her until there was some hope to offer.

"Emme," he began, his voice rougher than he'd intended, "please don't—"

"I'd better bid the two of you good day." There was a finality in her words, a decision to retreat, and Simon hated it. "Perhaps Lottie can return at another time." She glanced toward the cloudy sky. "But I believe we may have lost our opportunity today."

The door to retreat was being closed—and she was locking him out.

He wanted to protest, to stay, to explain the confusion and the rush of emotions that had nearly made him act as a fool in front of her. But there was nothing he could do now except to accept it.

"I understand." He paused, waiting for her attention to shift back to his. He had to promise something. "But I *will* attempt to remedy this. You have my word."

"Emme, I'd wondered about his feelings from the start, but the ball last night and his behavior in town yesterday morning only proved my suspicions." Thomas shook his head and sank into a nearby chair. "He is still in love with you."

Oh, she knew. This afternoon in the garden had only proved it. Her face grew warm at the memory of how close his lips had come to hers, how gently those same lips had skimmed across the skin of her fingers.

And she, no less at fault than him. Hadn't she all but begged him, in her silent way, to bridge the distance between them? His words as he departed to remedy things still echoed in her mind. Remedy what? His situation? Her heart, which had broken in so many pieces? Or perhaps it was his little sister, the budding matchmaker, who had forced this all into motion.

She tucked her dress around her as she drew her knees onto the window seat and looked away from Thomas, unwilling for him to witness the effect his declaration had on her. The way her heart had twisted with those very words he'd spoken.

And though she should have felt a sense of triumph at the knowledge Simon still cared for her, she couldn't embrace it. Yes, knowing his heart had remained the same somehow confirmed her greatest hopes and worst fears. They were both as trapped as ever.

Simon's needs and expectations hadn't changed.

Her dowry and social status hadn't changed.

"I know you may object," Thomas continued, his voice a little too knowing, waving a hand as if to dismiss her likely protestations. "You may argue that the faithfulness of a man's affections is of little importance in fiction, but I dare say, Emme, you must admit—that man's heart may prove as constant as yours."

If only that were cause for joy. If only it could be enough.

For heaven's sake, they had nearly kissed in her garden. *Kissed!*

Reality doused the sweet flutterings the thought sparked. The prospect of loving him without any assurance, without any notion of securing her future, terrified her. If she loved him—if she truly loved him—and if she respected herself . . .

"I'm leaving, Thomas." Her voice broke the silence, almost defiant as she wrapped her arms tighter around her knees. She met his gaze across the room. "I can't stay."

Thomas raised a brow. "That's not usually the way romance goes, my dear cousin. Not to gain a happily ever after."

"You *must* see it." Emme narrowed her eyes at him. "How can he have a happy ending if his estate is in jeopardy? And the more I've written this new story, the more I realize how I've been pouring my imagination into fantastical tales that failed to celebrate the simple, everyday choices—the decisions made for the good of those around us, not just for the breathtaking, pulse-pounding possibilities in some other realm." She let out a long breath. "You were right. There are plenty of real-life moments that can make a story come to life in ways my other novels did not. Perhaps I'm meant to write those . . . and accept that future."

Thomas moved beside her on the window seat, his gaze intense. "And perhaps you're meant to do both."

She leveled him with a glance. "His thoughts are clear on female writers. And with his family's reputation already in disrepair, my little secret would only bring more scandal upon him and his family. I can't do that to him."

"Are you certain you are not underestimating his ability to accept you with your secrets as willingly as you have been to accept him?"

"It's not the same thing." She looked back out the window. "I am not a viscount or a man. And those two elements make all the difference."

The room fell silent, the weight of her words settling like dust. A small ache pressed into her chest, and she stole a quick glance at Thomas. She'd known he couldn't fix the situation—she hadn't expected him to. But a small part of her had hoped he would offer some divinely magnificent solution, some eloquent remedy. Instead, his quiet only needled the impossibility of it all deeper into her heart.

"My mother's family in Yorkshire invited me to stay with them for a few months." Emme kept her focus on the horizon. "I plan to take them up on the offer now. It will give me a chance to see a different part of England, write another novel, and perhaps make decisions about using my writing funds to become independent."

At his silence, she looked over at him.

For a moment surprise flickered in his eyes, but it was quickly masked. "So you're going to leave me here to deal with Mother's failure to procure you a husband, are you?" His gentle grin almost inspired hers. Ah, he'd accepted her choice without argument. "That is not very gracious of you at all."

"You know as well as I do that within a few weeks, she'll be so overcome with the birth of her first grandchild, her disappointment in my romantic future will be duly eclipsed."

"For now." One of his brows quirked upward.

Emme smiled faintly, then turned back to the window. Perhaps her perfect match would always remain a dear memory—or a fictional creation, but nothing else.

"Emme." His gentle voice carried a note of reprimand. "You sound as though you're giving up on matrimony altogether."

Was she? Her heart ached at the thought, and she closed her eyes for a moment, steadying herself. "Perhaps I should shift my focus away from matrimony for now. My name is already tainted, and I'm certain the gossipmongers are weaving new, unflattering tales this season. And leaving will allow Simon to focus on his future instead of being plagued by his past feelings for me."

Thomas nudged her shoulder with his, a look of mock reproach on his face. "I feel certain 'plague' is not the descriptor Lord Ravenscross would use in regard to his feelings for you."

Her lips quivered upward at the corners. "Regardless, after the Ruthton Ball on Tuesday, I leave for Yorkshire. Sometimes, no matter the affection between two people, we cannot get what we want. And then . . . well, we must turn to a different dream."

Thomas slowly nodded, though his gaze remained locked with hers. "And will that different dream be enough to overthrow the old one?"

"It must, Thomas." She lowered her head onto her knees, a prayer for help in her mind. "It must."

Willoughby was a scoundrel.

Simon had taken up the book after putting Fia to bed, and then he had finished some evening correspondence and business inter-actions, with the intention of reading only a few minutes while he awaited his meeting with Aunt Agatha. An hour later, he sat staring at the book, wondering if Marianne would live, if Edward would fol-low through with his loveless marriage, and if Colonel Brandon and Elinor might end up as a pair.

Books should not cause such emotional distress. These people weren't real! Why were they taking up so much of his mental faculties? It was ridiculous.

A rap on the door pulled him from the pages and alerted him to the time. He'd planned to speak with Aunt Agatha about Emme a half hour ago. He needed to send a letter to his steward in regard to Mr. Arden's approved lease of the buildings as well as take up Emme on her advice regarding Mr. Jenkins's needs before anyone else reached out to him. Those would be two large leases along with the—hopefully—growing number of tenants on his property.

How could he have gotten lost reading . . . fiction?

He gave his head a shake and stood from the desk, calling for the person to enter.

To his surprise, Charlotte and William stepped over the threshold, their faces both sober as they entered.

"Aren't the two of you supposed to be in bed?"

Lottie shot her brother a look before stepping farther into the room. "We . . . we needed to speak to you, Simon."

Simon's body shot to alert, but he'd learned over the past few months to guard his reactions. These two siblings were incredibly ob-servant and incredibly responsive to his moods. He gestured toward the chairs nearby, taking their request as seriously as their expressions communicated. These two siblings had grown up the most in the last months.

Perhaps because he'd grown too.

"What would you like to discuss?"

Lottie looked over at Will and he nodded for her to begin, so she straightened her posture and gave Simon a very businesslike look. "First of all, we wanted to tell you how much we like Mrs. Lane and are looking forward to her starting as our governess."

Praise, indeed. Simon managed a small smile. "I'm glad to hear it. I certainly want to ensure that you are as invested in your future as I am."

Lottie gave a curt nod. Will smiled.

"And we know finances are bad," Lottie continued.

"And you must rely on Aunt Aggie's allowance," Will chimed in with equal seriousness . . . and bluntness.

Information they really shouldn't know, but Lottie's keen observation and propensity for snooping left little to secrecy.

"And we know," Lottie continued, "that you are under obligation to marry someone before the season is out in order to keep Aunt Aggie's allowance."

Why did this sort of conversation from his two younger siblings feel both humorous and highly inappropriate? Well, there was no use denying what they clearly knew. A reluctant chuckle bubbled up in Simon's throat. "That is true, unfortunately."

Lottie, ever the strategist, glanced at her brother, as though for reassurance, before continuing. "Well, we have a suggestion for you."

Simon leaned back in his chair, raising an eyebrow. "Do you now?"

"We don't mind being poor," Will offered with surprising conviction. The words struck Simon like a blow, a reminder of how much they'd already sacrificed. They weren't destitute, of course. They had Aunt Aggie's allowance, Simon's inheritance from his mother, and what little he'd invested from his father's remaining funds. In addition, his business ventures were each proving beneficial enough to truly make significant changes in their financial future. Slowly but significantly.

"And we don't mind helping you by working hard." Lottie folded her hands in front of her. "But what we *do* mind is you making decisions to help all of us without considering that we have opinions on the matter."

His brow shot high. "What decisions exactly?"

"Well, of course, the governess," Lottie started, suddenly a bit uncertain. "Of which, you did ask our opinion."

"And the tenants, which you've discussed with me," Will offered.

Not truly his responsibility as yet, but Simon certainly appreciated the boy's perspective.

"But there is the matter of a wife for you, Simon." Lottie tipped her chin and studied him as if she'd brought a little of Aunt Agatha's spirit into the room with her.

"And that decision needs your intervention as well?" He wasn't sure whether to grin or groan.

He loved them. More than he'd even understood a year ago. They'd all born their heartache together, and even in their mishaps and misdirection, they were slowly rebuilding their family into something, he hoped, much healthier.

Something Arianna had needed before she'd decided to forfeit her future.

Something good.

"Well, *we* won't marry her," Will stated, as if that had been an option.

"But we will be living with her," Lottie added, her tone carrying the weight of a serious negotiation. "And between the two of us, we agree there is already a perfectly suitable option."

Simon had an inkling where this was going—and wholly agreed with their recommendation—but offered noncommittally, "Really?"

"And it's not the Selena woman," Will burst out, his voice carrying surprising conviction. It even caught Lottie off guard.

"Miss Hemston?" Simon looked to each sibling. Why, of all people, did they mention Selena Hemston?

"But I told Will," Lottie said, undeterred, "that you're too smart to ever consider someone like her."

Well, at least after all his blundering, his siblings still had some confidence in his mental faculties. "Why did you think Miss Hemston was even an option?"

Lottie and Will exchanged a look before Will spoke up. "She came by earlier today while you were out."

"And stayed long enough to find out where you'd gone," Lottie continued. "But it took her a good fifteen minutes because we wouldn't tell her."

"Because she wore a pretend smile and reminded me of Hamish."

Simon narrowed his eyes at Will, attempting to match the reputedly beautiful Miss Hemston with their old, rather grumpy hound. Clearly, Will hadn't grown enough into manhood to be distracted by peripheral things, because there were some qualities in Selena that reflected, quite well, Hamish's personality. Ill-tempered being one.

"When Mrs. Patterson wouldn't tell her and neither would we, she became angry," Lottie continued, her arms folded across her chest in a most adultlike fashion.

"And Blast did jump on her dress," Will offered, looking oddly unbothered by the entire incident.

"Then she screamed at Fia, who was just trying to catch him," Lottie added with a touch of indignation.

Simon's blood pressure spiked. "She did what?"

Both children's eyes widened at the sudden growl-like words that erupted from Simon's throat.

"Where is Fia?" he demanded, half rising from his chair.

"She's fine now," Will replied quickly, clearly sensing Simon's rising fury. "Aunt Aggie came to the rescue."

"And nearly throttled Miss Hemston." Lottie grinned, enjoying the memory. "Gave her such a tongue-lashing that the lady left in a hurry."

Simon's pulse returned to normal, and he lowered himself back into his chair. "I wish I could have seen that." He chuckled. "And what would make the two of you think I planned to marry Miss Hemston?"

"Aren't you?" Lottie's eyes grew wide. "She seemed set on it."

"I told you Simon wouldn't be so daft." Will rallied in Simon's defense.

Simon's smile brimmed.

"He was daft enough *not* to marry Emme."

And . . . the smile completely disappeared. "Are the two of you settling my future then?"

"Aunt Aggie said you liked Emme before." Lottie's look brooked no denial. "And I think you like her still."

"Which only proves he's not daft." Will nodded, giving Simon a reassuring look.

Lottie shot him a look of no confidence. "That all depends on what he does next."

Ah, had these two jumped inside his head and tinkered with his thoughts, or did they see in Emme what he'd fallen in love with long before? Did they recognize what a good fit she'd be for . . . all of them?

"First of all, I appreciate the two of you coming to me with your concerns, and I want you to know that I have no intention of marrying Miss Hemston."

Will sighed, but Lottie remained vigilant. "But you must marry someone. We know what Aunt Aggie said about the allowance."

Far too many people knew the particulars of his life, and even more projected about his future. "And why do you suppose I should marry Miss Lockhart?"

"Because you like her," Will answered, quite plainly.

And it was the truth. Simon didn't only like Miss Lockhart—he loved her, ardently.

"Because she's kind and smart." Lottie spit out the words like a challenge. "And she likes you back, which is why we are trying to tell you quite plainly that we don't care about the money."

The realization pressed through Simon's stubborn mind—Lottie and Will wanted to rescue him as much as he longed to rescue them. Even Fia, with her sweet "diamond" offering that day at the stream, had shown him that his little ramshackle family was perhaps not as broken and disconnected as he had feared. They all wanted the same thing for one another, and it wasn't to restore Ravenscross to its former magnificent glory.

It was to find love.

His throat tightened as he looked from Will to Lottie, struggling to work the words through his emotions. "There's a very real chance Miss Lockhart may not wish to marry me."

"She's too clever for that," Lottie replied without hesitation. "I know she likes you. I saw the two of you—"

"Yes, quite," Simon interrupted, his voice smooth as he stopped her from recounting the near kiss in the garden. "But I've hurt her."

"You've done things to hurt us, and we've forgiven you," Will said, the guileless look in those earnest eyes closing off Simon's throat.

"And I've done things to hurt you, and you've forgiven me," Lottie confessed, still in her defensive stance. "And Emme . . . well, she seems to be the sort who would forgive you too."

And she had. But like a fool, he'd hurt her again.

How could he experience such profound gratitude for these children and such fearful loss of Emme all at the same time? Was his heart even big enough to hold it all? He shot a glance heavenward, his heart sending a half cry, half thanksgiving, before he gathered his wits to address those in the room.

"Well, then." Simon stood, attempting to find his voice. "I . . . I suppose I must find a way to prove I'm not as daft as you think."

Both children grinned. Lottie even giggled, and the sound hit him in the chest.

And then, as if the only response for the moment demanded it, he opened up his arms. With only a slight hesitation, Will ran to one side and Lottie to the other, both burrowing into him as if they'd been waiting for this moment as much as he had.

All ability to speak was stripped from him.

This . . . this was what Ravenscross needed most of all.

Before Simon could compose himself, with Will and Lottie still clinging to him, there was a knock at the door. Aunt Agatha entered in a dark blue dressing gown. Her brows rose as she took in the sight of the three of them, attempting to blink the scene into comprehension.

For a moment silence stretched, and then she cleared her throat and stood taller. "Children up at this hour? It is past ten o'clock."

Simon gave the children a final squeeze. "I usually enforce bedtimes, Aunt, but"—he shot his siblings a wink—"Charlotte and William were sharing some important information with me, and I thought I'd make an exception this once."

Aunt Agatha looked unimpressed, but there was a faint softening around her lips.

With a turn to his siblings, he gestured toward the door. "Off to bed now."

Lottie and Will gave him another long look, Will even sliding in another hug, before they slipped past Aunt Agatha and disappeared into the darkened hallway. Aunt Agatha pulled her dressing coat around her and took a seat in the spot Lottie had just vacated, her chin at almost the exact tilt as her niece's.

It was no wonder from where Lottie inherited her particular feistiness.

"The children told me of your unexpected visitor today," Simon began, eager to address the matter directly. "I'm sorry for her intrusion and presumption."

Aunt Agatha studied him, her dark brow arching. "Does she have reason to presume?"

"No, but that doesn't stop her from taking every opportunity to do so."

One corner of Aunt Agatha's lips quivered. "It sounds as if the only way to stop her wrongful assumption is to take on the right bride."

Simon drew a deep breath, steeling himself for this confrontation. He had faced his emotions before, but now his heart was set. Though the road ahead would be difficult, filled with months of uncertainty as he worked to restore his family's fortune, it was a price he was willing to pay. For Emme.

And, as Will and Charlotte had made rather plain, for the children.

But he couldn't do it alone. Without Aunt Agatha's support, all his plans would falter.

An estate didn't run on goodwill and affections alone.

"I must return to London tomorrow," Aunt Agatha continued, as if she were in complete control of the conversation. "To attend to some pressing matters at my house. But I leave you in much better shape than when I arrived." Her gaze lingered over him with that appraising look.

"I believe things are much improved," Simon replied. "You're aware of the business ventures I've taken on."

"Hmm." Aunt Agatha gave a slight nod. "And you've also secured a governess, who I trust will prove capable. I also appreciate your involving me in the interview process, which reflects well on you. That shows humility—a valuable trait in any man of the gentry." She paused before adding, "And since she arrives in only a few days, I feel confident that my absence will not be felt too keenly."

"Your absence is always felt, Aunt Agatha," Simon said, attempting to lighten the mood.

Aunt Agatha's eyes narrowed, but the faintest twitch of a smile gentled the look. "Flattery will not work on me, Simon."

"I would never presume, Aunt." Simon hazarded a grin at the playful tension between them.

Her lips twitched again before she mastered her expression, her voice dropping to something more serious. "You've made good progress in several areas, I'll admit. You've stayed clear of scandal, for the most part." She studied him a moment, clearly referring to his interactions with Emme. "But the season is nearly over, and I've heard no word of a bride."

Here was the moment. The chance to change his own future.

He drew in a deep breath, accepting his fate. He would not be Willoughby. Let rumors and difficulties fall as they may. "I should like to offer you such news about a bride, but I should like clarification first."

Both her brows rose.

He continued. "What do you consider . . . suitable?"

"I should think you are old enough to sort that out yourself."

"I am, indeed." He held her gaze. "But my definition of 'suitable' may not align with yours."

Something flickered in her eyes—an awareness, perhaps, and then she sighed. "How so? Do you wish for someone to make Ravenscross a home instead of a crumbling stone pillar? Do you want someone who will raise the reputation of your family because of their character and family status? Do you wish for someone who will care for your siblings and protect them and the family's name with as much intention as you?"

She didn't mention money. Not once.

"Those are exactly the qualifications I'm seeking as well."

She tilted her head, studying him, expression softening. "Simon, your attachment to Miss Lockhart and hers to you is plainly evident, but . . ." She paused, lowering her gaze for a moment before meeting his again. "Financially, she can offer you so little."

"But as you've said before, money is only one piece of a larger puzzle in matrimony."

"One piece for *most* marriages."

The implication cut.

"But you are not at liberty to follow your heart so easily." Aunt Agatha searched his face with a calculating look. "Your responsibilities—"

"I take my responsibilities very seriously." Simon's tone was firm. "Not only have I increased financial gains for Ravenscross in a short period of time, but my business ventures are showing steady growth. If given enough time, I could make Ravenscross independent of your support. As is right. I just need *time*."

Her silence seemed to halt the words she might have spoken, her lips pressed into a thin line. He continued, his voice soft but determined. "Money nor status brought my parents the satisfaction of a happy marriage, Aunt. I want more than that. I think Ravenscross needs more than that, and I am willing to work as hard as necessary in order to achieve that future with the right bride by my side."

"And reputation? Your father maligned this legacy long before your cousin's indiscretions came to light. Miss Lockhart's influence is rather small in the larger pool of the social world." She narrowed her eyes and then sighed. "I do not doubt her character, Simon, except perhaps when it comes to you."

He opened his mouth to defend Emme, but Aunt Agatha raised a palm to stop him, her smile flickering on one corner. "No doubt your charms overcame her, I am sure. But the gossips are still quite attached to your pairing, in part, due to some mild indiscretions and clear partiality that you have for her."

"I'm not ashamed of being partial to her." He sat straighter in his chair. "I am partial to her. Utterly."

Her hesitation threatened his confidence a little, but he rallied internally to plead his cause. He'd not give up so easily. This was the right choice.

"There is a great deal to overcome, as you well know, and I would prefer you choose a woman whose reputation was not only impeccable, but whose influence spanned a wider berth."

"The influence that matters most is the one that happens inside these walls. Because that effect will carry beyond Ravenscross to impact years in the future." Simon held her gaze. "And if I had the time and freedom to choose anyone in the world to influence the people who matter to me most within these walls, it would be her."

She stared at him, her hands folded in her lap and posture impeccable, and then without answering, she stood. Simon followed, readying to confirm her approval when her attention fell to the desk. There, nestled against the corner, was *Sense and Sensibility*, just where he had left it.

"You're reading this?" She tapped the cover with her finger and looked over at him. "Surprising."

"It was a recommendation from a trusted source."

"Hmm . . ." She took the book in hand and flipped through the pages. "What on earth would propel a lady to risk her reputation in order to become a novelist? Such a dangerous undertaking in our world of social expectations."

Strange, but Simon found himself defending the author. "Perhaps there was nothing else for it. She had a story to tell, and it must be told."

"Well, at least the woman had the foresight to remain anonymous. For her family's sake, if nothing else. Novelists—especially among the gentry—are rarely seen in a favorable light. All those absurd tales of pirates and . . . undead." She shuddered slightly.

"I think, Aunt Agatha"—Simon drew in a breath—"you'd actually enjoy this one. It's a look at regular life among the gentry. No pirates in sight. And you'd appreciate the humor, I think."

"Humor?" She glanced back at the book and, for the briefest moment, hesitated before placing it gently back on the desk. Simon noted the subtle shift, a quiet indication that his words had stirred her curiosity.

"You might find it surprisingly refreshing. Perhaps I can finish it tonight and you can take it with you when you leave tomorrow."

Aunt Agatha said nothing, but the silence between them felt like approval.

"Mrs. Patterson told me that she has never had a master show such gratitude to her as you have." Her lips offered the smallest smile but enough to gentle her entire countenance.

Mrs. Patterson had said that? Simon blinked in surprise. He had thought he'd nearly frightened the woman away with his clumsy attempts at kindness.

"That is a sign of good character, Simon. An example of not only who you are at heart but of who you've become. The right woman will make you even better."

"Then trust me to know who that right woman is."

Aunt Agatha regarded him for a long moment before she tipped her head, a whisper of a smile in place. "There is nothing wrong with a good, *honest* country gentleman's daughter."

Simon's heart gave a lurch. Did she mean . . . ?

"But if you make that choice," she added, her tone becoming more serious, "you both must also accept the consequences that come with it, great and small." She moved toward the door. "You both will have an uphill battle before you, in reputation and finances."

"I understand and I've weighed those choices." He stepped with her toward the door, wavering on asking the next question, but he had to confirm. "And your allowance?"

She stopped and turned back to him. "You've chosen a governess and evidently a bride." She peaked a brow. "As long as you remain free of scandal, then you will have it. Good night, Simon."

Her words, though reluctantly spoken, carried the weight of her blessing. With a soft nod, she stepped into the hallway and the door closed behind her with a quiet finality.

Simon stood there for a moment, taking in the unexpected turn of events. The door had barely clicked shut when he stumbled back into his office, his breath escaping in a soft laugh. Then he collapsed back into his desk chair and raised his gaze to the heavens, his heart full, his hopes even fuller.

Tomorrow night at the ball, no matter what it took, he was going to ask Emmeline Lockhart to be his bride.

CHAPTER 21

Clearly, possible scandal was not enough to deter some men from their unwanted pursuit.

Emmeline's shoulders stiffened at the thought of Mr. Rushing.

He was relentless.

And unnerving.

And completely dismissive of her disinterest.

She had managed to avoid dancing with him for the first half hour of the ball, even going so far as to accept the offer of the septuagenarian widower, Mr. Roth, who'd mistaken her attempt to hide behind him as a subtle request for a partner. The smile on his face had been her reward, and despite the social faux pas in the elegant Assembly Room, she couldn't truly regret it. The elderly gentleman may have been several decades her senior, but he was nimble on his feet, and his attentions kept her safely on the opposite side of the ballroom from Mr. Rushing.

The latter had already secured one unpleasant dance, gripping her far too tightly. Each word he slurred was laced with whiskey, and he made certain to lean in so close that Emme felt as though she were being swallowed whole by the overpowering scent of alcohol. She had no idea what the dance must have looked like from an observer's perspective, but she'd leaned back so far at one point, she thought she'd almost gone horizontal.

Oh, if only Thomas were here to rescue her! He had come to her aid at two previous balls, but he'd been called away to visit a sick family.

Most of her other dance partners had already been claimed, and she could hardly blame them.

And Mr. Marshall, who had clearly heard of her intent to refuse an offer from him, had only regarded her with glares from the opposite side of the room, which meant he would not be a possible partner to escape Mr. Rushing.

She sighed, resolutely avoiding Mr. Rushing's gaze. At least this would be her last ball in St. Groves for a while. In her absence, she hoped he would find someone else to unnerve. Most likely at this point in her third season, he thought her desperate enough to succumb to his . . . charms.

She hoped never to be that desperate.

But where to hide now? She glanced around the ballroom for any route of escape. The lights flickered in the grand chandeliers above, casting a glow over the swirling couples, but her focus was locked on the man moving toward her with single-minded fervor. Perhaps finally, she'd found a perfect time for a solid faint.

Her pulse quickened as he closed the distance. She scanned the area around her, looking for a soft spot to land should she decide to take such drastic action.

Mr. Rushing's grin twisted with ruthless interest, the glimmer in his eyes promising the verbal battle ahead.

Before she could summon an excuse—or muster the courage to swoon—a dark figure stepped in, cutting through her view of Mr. Rushing. The air around her shifted, warmed by the sweet leather and fresh cologne that heralded only one man.

Simon.

He looked maddeningly handsome, dressed to perfection in a black tailcoat and matching trousers, with a dark blue waistcoat that almost matched his eyes. But what truly disarmed her was the *way* he looked at her—not with the gawk of Mr. Marshall, nor with predatory intent, like Mr. Rushing—but with something infinitely more dangerous. Tender, warm, and so full of unspoken emotion that she dared not meet his gaze for too long, lest fainting become a genuine possibility.

"Miss Lockhart." His voice was low as it wrapped around her name like a caress. "I believe you promised me this next dance." Simon smoothly extended his hand as he cast a cool, dismissive glance at Mr. Rushing.

And, as if her body and mind took a sudden disconnect from each other, she placed her gloved hand in his. The man truly shouldn't hold such power over her mental faculties.

But something in his demeanor, in the secure way he drew her onto the dance floor into one of the triple minor sets, proclaimed a confidence she'd not seen since . . . her face grew cold.

Since when she'd thought their futures aligned.

But not now! Dancing with him could only invite gossip, and gossip could ruin everything for him.

What was he thinking?

"What are you doing?" she whispered as they took their positions, grateful they were the third pair in the set, affording them a measure of privacy. "This is not a good idea, Lord Ravenscross."

"Saving a lady from that walking cask of brandy is always an excellent idea." The teasing quirk of his lips failed to match the man she'd spoken with in the street only a few days earlier.

It fit the man in the garden, though. Too rash. Too unguarded for his own good.

Had he lost his senses again?

And she wasn't certain whether to very unfashionably run from the room or reprimand him for being so unguarded. Well, since it would cause a greater scene to leave the dance floor, she acquiesced to the moment. Perhaps this could be her goodbye—a memory to carry with her as their paths inevitably diverged.

"You've taken to heroics this evening, then?"

"Heroics?" Their turn came, drawing them into the steps, away from each other for only a moment and then back together, his gaze finding hers at every turn. "Oh yes. I have my sights set on being a hero, Miss Lockhart."

His palm warmed her waist through the fabric of her gown. No other dance of the evening had her responding in such a breathless way, no matter how intricate the footwork. "And is there a reason for this sudden devotion to gallantry, my lord?"

The strong muscles of his arms tensed at her back as he steered her through the steps, their bodies closer. Kissing-close with just the right angle.

What a thought! Her cheeks heated. And yet, her attention dropped to his lips as if to ascertain the exact trajectory.

Have mercy! Perhaps she should leave the room straightaway! She stumbled a moment, barely noticeable, but Simon noticed.

"I've finally gotten the proper perspective, Miss Lockhart. And I must say, it's been difficult to put my transformation on display for you because you've been in such high demand tonight."

"Hardly," she countered, averting her gaze from the intensity in his eyes. What was he doing? He seemed almost . . . giddy. "One persistent suitor is scarcely a testament to my popularity."

"A persistent suitor?" His lips twitched up on one corner as they drew close again. "I suppose then that you could say the same for me."

"You?" She nearly missed her next step. What did he mean? He was certainly no Mr. Rushing. The heat in her cheeks clearly attested to that fact. "Except, unlike Mr. Rushing, you would not risk propriety in front of an entire ballroom."

His grip tightened subtly, almost as though he were pulling her just a fraction closer, his eyes darkening with something unspoken. "Perhaps I've grown reckless."

Her breath hitched. There was something in his tone—something

298

simmering beneath the surface. She could feel the warmth of his body acutely now, the rhythm of their movements a magnetizing force with every step.

"Or perhaps," she ventured, her voice barely audible, "you've forgotten what's at stake."

"I haven't forgotten, Miss Lockhart. If anything, I've realized what truly matters." His gaze trailed over her face as though committing every detail to memory. "Or rather, who."

Her heart trembled at the intimacy of his words. For a fleeting moment, she forgot everything—his aunt's stipulations, their differing social standings, the curious eyes around them. Even the music faded into a distant hum.

What was he saying?

They parted again, allowing the other two pairs a turn as they stared across the short distance between them. His smile faded, replaced by an expression so earnest that it left her more unsettled than ever. Then the dance brought her back to his arms. "I know I hurt you, Emme."

And as strange as it sounded, the music gave them an intimacy and freedom little else could. Distracting others. Crowding over their conversation so that only they could truly hear each other as the others danced their part. She studied his face, trying to make sense of his behavior. She read his expressions and lips as he continued, "I was lost and afraid. Overwhelmed by responsibilities I hadn't expected. And I failed. I failed everyone, but most of all, I failed you. I should never have acted on my feelings in your garden without being able to offer you a future. Forgive me."

Their turn came to an end again, and she hesitated to follow the dance rules, her mind reeling. He stood only a short distance across from her, dancers framing them on either side, but only his eyes communicated with her, inspiring a hope she didn't fully understand. Finally, with a quick step and a touch of hands, they drew near each other again. "I did little to discourage the rumors about my romantic exploits because I thought, in time, they might lessen your regrets."

What? He'd wanted her to hate him in order to protect her? What an idiot! She fixed him with a glare. "So you thought turning yourself into a rake would help me?"

"I've been a fool in many parts of my life, Emme." Simon's voice dropped as his hand steadied her through the allemande turn, his gaze never leaving hers. "But this reluctant, misguided, cowardly fool has never stopped loving you." He was so close that his breath fanned lightly against her cheek. "You alone have always held my heart."

Every word fled her. Breath evaporated from her lungs. She would have stopped entirely if his hands hadn't guided her seamlessly into the next steps. Her emotions splintered—love, frustration, and longing all battled within her. Why was he confessing this now, when they could do nothing about it?

"I know I don't deserve your forgiveness, let alone your affection," he said as they danced toward each other again. His words pulled her in as much as his arms did. "But you have shown me nothing but grace, even when I gave you every reason to despise me. You should not have a man who has been so careless with your heart."

Their movements carried them apart again, and she used the reprieve to gather her thoughts. He gave himself far too little credit. She'd seen a glimpse of his life now, heard the ache of impossibility in his voice. When they came together once more, she met his gaze, her defenses rallied. "You have not been care*less*, Simon." Her voice steadied. "Fumbling, perhaps, but I believe you've had so many cares that the last thing you've been is careless."

Their turn ended and they took their spots across from each other again, waiting for the other two pairs to have their turn.

But he pressed on, relentless. It was as if he'd been waiting years to speak and not even the distance of a dance and a room filled with ravenous socialites would stop him. "At first, I didn't think it was possible for you to forgive me or for me to even pursue you."

At first? Had something changed in his circumstances?

"I didn't want to hope for it, only to break your heart."

"Break my heart?" She forced a light laugh, though her voice wavered. "You've already done that, Simon, and I survived."

The words seemed to hit him with the same force she'd felt moments ago. He blinked, then softened his expression into one of such unguarded adoration that she very nearly *did* swoon. "Yes," he said quietly. "Strong enough to survive, care for my siblings, and even help me find a bride. Emme . . ."

She'd never heard him cradle her name as he did in that moment, half in plea, half in reverence. With all of his struggles, of which she knew only part, he also carried this affection for her, which he'd beautifully confessed. An affection that held him back.

"I think the real problem is that you're willing to break your *own* heart. I see you struggle with what you want to do and what you *must* do. And that hurts me far more than your leaving me ever could." Their turn came again, drawing them back together. "Any woman would find a generous-hearted, intelligent, and witty husband in you. Whoever you choose, Simon, if you determine yourself, you can have a happy marriage. And the children will be happy to see you so."

He completely stopped in the middle of their turn, tightening his hold on her waist. "I want *you*, Emme." His gaze burned into hers. "I've always wanted you."

She only stared, barely believing her ears. Or eyes. Or every other sense.

The next couple nearly stumbled into them as they paused mid-step, forcing Simon to resume the dance, but Emme barely understood how her feet worked. Why did he have to make it so hard to leave? She'd determined her heart. She'd accepted it all last night. She'd grieved the loss of him again. And now, to have him express such sweet affections, such passion for her. It was too painful.

But at the next available moment, as she searched for words to say, he continued, "From the first moment you startled me with your wit, I was captivated. You walked into my world with charm, light, and beauty. I went from finding joy in your company to seeking you out—and finally to needing you as if you were the air itself."

She couldn't breathe.

"And you loved me as I was," he said, his tone thick with emotion. "You loved my family. And I will not forfeit a future with you. No matter what I must do or sacrifice, you are the best choice for me."

She had read about men going mad for love, but Simon had never struck her as the type to lose his senses completely. Yet here he was, defying reason and reality all at once.

"But your family?" It was the only thing that came out of her mouth. A hundred things danced in her head, a hundred objections, but this one emerged first.

"My family"—his lips curved into a smile—"would gain far more from having you in our lives than any wealth could provide."

Why did there have to be so much space between them? It was barely two feet, but it felt like a mile. She wanted to be close to him to try to understand. After months of attempting to accept a future where he married someone else, was he . . . changing everything?

"Emme, I will not be Willoughby. Not anymore. I will not be ruled by others' expectations or the fear of financial ruin. Not if I must give you up." He drew her back into a turn. "But . . . but you must know, it's not going to be easy. I can only offer you the simplest life for now. But with hard work, solid investments, and time, I know we can move beyond my current menial funds to restore much of what my cousin and father lost. And then I can give you more of the life you not only are used to but deserve."

He was speaking as if he intended to marry her. *Her.* The daughter of a country gentleman with a modest two-thousand-pound dowry.

"What . . . what are you saying?" Her breath shook out the question.

"Marry me." The words burst through his smile. "Marry me, my darling. Allow me to love you freely and openly before the whole world. To care for you. To laugh with you. To grow old together."

Tears stung her eyes. "Simon . . . we can't. I won't destroy your dear family. You'll come to resent me when life is hard and we are poor. I can't bear that thought."

"My family is accustomed to struggling with our finances at this point, but it is unanimous among the entire household that we'd rather have you, with all your sunshine and joy among the walls of Ravenscross, than make sure the carpets are new. Even Aunt Agatha has agreed to maintain the allowance to enable us to marry . . . well, because she likes you. And she knows you and your family bring with them a reputation that can only strengthen Ravenscross."

The warmth that had been brimming through her chest and into her face suddenly stilled, a painful icy shroud dousing the internal glow. Reputation. Everything hinged on her reputation?

Never had her secret as an authoress shot through her with such searing pain. Right here, right now, she had the prospect of a future with the man she loved. He'd asked her to marry him—the words she'd longed to hear two years ago.

"Simon—"

"Would you do me the honor of becoming my wife, Emmeline Lockhart?"

The music came to a stop, along with her hope. "Simon, I will not . . . I cannot continue this conversation in the middle of a ballroom. It's . . . there's too much to say."

"Yes." He nodded, looking up to search the room as he linked her arm through his and led her toward the edge of the ballroom. "We need privacy." His grin flashed wide again, so much joy dancing in those beautiful eyes of his that her heart ached all over again.

Perhaps she didn't need to tell him about her books. In fact, she could stop writing altogether if it meant being with him. She loved him, as much as ever, and if he was willing to sacrifice the money for her heart, couldn't she sacrifice her talent for his?

She could still write, for herself and the children. Tell them the stories, couldn't she?

But how long could she live with the shadow of this secret looming over them in the form of what she'd already published? Even if he shared in the secret, there was no guarantee the truth wouldn't come out someday—and then . . . what?

He'd have no escape from being linked to her. No way to salvage the damage her profession might do to his name. No, no, no. She'd lost him once by no fault of her own.

And now, would she lose him all over again?

"I'll meet you in the garden," he whispered, nodding toward the glass doors. "This time, darling, I won't leave you waiting."

Darling. Her eyes withered closed as the endearment hurt.

And he did love her. It was the entire reason she'd planned to go away.

She saw it. Felt it. Nearly stepped back into its familiarity as if they'd never been apart. But love only grew as strong as the truth that bound it.

And—she turned toward the garden doors—sometimes, as she'd come to accept, love alone wasn't enough for a happy ending.

Sometimes love demanded the hardest sacrifices of all.

CHAPTER 22

He'd asked her.

The words had been clogging Simon's throat for almost two years. Now, he'd finally voiced them. He felt as if he could vault the room, his grin entirely untamable as he approached his friend. Ben stood back, surveying the dancers with the air of a man contemplating his next chess move—or perhaps his next victim.

Simon knew exactly who he'd be asking for the rest of his life.

"Well, what sort of mischief has you looking like the cat who got the cream?" Ben raised his glass, one brow quirked in mock suspicion. "A certain dance partner, I should guess."

"And you would be correct." Simon took a glass from a passing tray and tipped it slightly forward, as though to toast the entire room. "You once told me, in one of your more sentimental moments—"

"I have those?" Ben's brow furrowed. "Are you sure it was me?"

"Entirely." Simon grinned, his gaze flicking to the doorway leading to the garden. "In one of your rare lapses into wisdom, you advised me on the matter of marriage. You quoted your father, who said to at least find someone you could stand to be in the same room with."

"Ah, yes. That sounds like him."

"And then you added, in your own words, no less," Simon continued, his smile widening, "'*But I'd say it is even better if you can find someone who makes you forget there's a room at all.*'"

Ben pulled a face of exaggerated disgust, though the twinkle in his eye betrayed him. "I said something that maudlin? I must have been foxed."

"Foxed or not"—Simon raised his glass to his lips again—"you were right."

Ben sent a glance toward the garden doors and gave his head a disappointed shake. "Well, you certainly danced with her as if you'd forgotten everyone else in the room. We all had to bear witness to your unveiled expression of love—and her startled realization."

Startled? Simon's smile faltered a little. Perhaps he *had* been a bit too . . . direct. He'd fairly attacked her with the relief at finally voicing what he'd been fighting for months. He should have given her the courtesy of privacy. But when he'd walked into the ballroom and noticed Mr. Rushing hovering near her, all his carefully laid plans had evaporated. He'd been able to think only one thing: *Rescue her.*

Once she took his hand, once he drew her close, every ounce of restraint had abandoned him. "Ben," Simon said quietly. "I love her."

Ben sighed, lowering his glass. "I know." His tone remained devil-may-care, but his expression softened. "And I daresay the two of you will give Ravenscross a fresh start in ways money can't buy."

The mutual affection. The partnership. Something the estate and its tenants hadn't seen in generations. "It's a good start."

"It will have to be," Ben teased, "since her smiles will need to sustain you while the Viscount of Ravenscross mends fences, negotiates with tenants, and haggles with tradesmen, instead of leading the ton in fashionable diversions."

"One of the easiest trades of my life." Simon handed his glass to an unsuspecting Ben, adjusted his waistcoat, and sent his friend a wink. "Wish me luck."

Ben snorted. "Just don't scare her off by quoting me again."

Simon laughed and strode toward the garden doors, his pulse quickening with each step, but just as he reached the threshold, someone grabbed him by the arm. He turned, his smile dissolving as he met the sharp gaze of Miss Selena Hemston. She stood poised in her green gown, arms crossed, her frown so pronounced that it threatened to wrinkle her otherwise flawless chin.

"What a display!" she hissed.

"Display?" Simon raised an eyebrow, glancing toward the ballroom before returning his attention to her. "Do you mean the Ruthtons' decorations? I quite agree, they've outdone themselves this evening."

"You can't be serious, Simon," Selena snapped. "Not even you would throw away your security for some nobody who—"

"I have no interest in discussing my private affairs with you." Simon held a fragile hold on his voice. He tipped his head in a polite nod. "Good evening."

"You're allowing your interest to blur your vision and putting your entire future in jeopardy over"—her voice squeaked—"a country gentleman's daughter with only two thousand pounds?"

The door was tantalizingly close, his future just beyond it. "There are many things in this world far more valuable than money or titles, Miss Hemston."

"And what about reputation?" she countered, her tone unyielding. "Surely, a man with your family history wouldn't wish to further sully the tattered remains of your title. Especially by marrying a woman with a . . . past."

Simon released a slow breath in an attempt to control his rising fury. "Miss Hemston, you are a woman of some means and intelligence, and though I've not desired your company or good opinion, I never expected you to resort to slander, especially toward someone of Miss Lockhart's character."

"Slander?" Selena's lips curved into a saccharine smile. "Oh no, Simon. I wouldn't dare fabricate something so . . . delicious." She leaned closer, her voice dropping to a conspiratorial whisper. "I've seen the evidence myself. Her books, published under a pseudonym. I've even read a letter—to her publisher, no less."

Simon stiffened. *Books? Letters? Ridiculous.* "This is absurd. Mail is private. You can't expect me to believe such nonsense."

"I have many friends in many places, dear Simon. Friends who, with the proper incentive, are quite eager to share what they know." She tilted her head, her smirk deepening. "But consider what a scandal it would be—a lady of society secretly writing Gothic novels. Such behavior would hardly endear her to the ton, or your wealthy aunt."

A chill passed through him. Surely, it couldn't be true. But even as he fought against the thought, memories of conversations with Emme teased alive a hint of doubt. *No. Surely not.* Wouldn't she have confided in him?

Simon shook his head, refusing to let her poison his mind. "Miss Lockhart would never—"

"But she has," Selena interrupted, much too pleased with her revelation. "It may not be common knowledge *now* . . ." She drew out the word like a threat. "But once it is, and if you're aligned with her, any unwelcome attention would only deepen Ravenscross's blemished reputation and, if rumors can be trusted at all"—she slid a finger over her lips—"cripple any benevolent funds provided by wealthy family members."

How did Selena know these things? Emme wouldn't have divulged the information, and he would trust Mrs. Patterson with his life. Could it have been a stable hand? Another servant overhearing private conversations? His blood heated beneath his skin, rising up his neck and tightening his jaw. "You're lying."

"What would I have to gain by making up such a story? You must know me well enough to suspect I would have chosen a tale much more interesting than novelist." Her light laugh oozed with false mirth. "But this will do quite nicely. And I'll be happy to keep it a secret in exchange for a small favor."

It couldn't be true, could it? And . . . if it were true, how . . . how could he move forward with their future? "A favor?"

"Marry me." One manicured brow slipped high. "And I will ensure none of this unfortunate gossip reaches the wrong ears."

"Never," he replied firmly, stepping around her, but she moved to block his path once more.

"It's all very romantic, isn't it?" Her smile tightened into a snarl. "But love doesn't pay debts or shield one from scandal."

Her sentence paused his steps and turned him back around. "Miss Hemston, I seriously doubt what you've said is true, but even if it is, there is no amount of blackmail or persuasion that would ever induce me to marry a woman who finds pleasure in creating pain in others. You are right to say that love cannot pay the bills, but it can certainly create a better future than one built on the vindictive poison of a frightened woman who seeks her security in manipulation, gossip-mongering, and demoralizing those she perceives as beneath her. I will not be your puppet, so no matter what you do with the information you think you possess, you will not gain what you want from me."

Selena's smile twisted into something cold and brittle, her eyes narrowing. "So noble," she murmured. "But nobility won't save you when whispers turn to headlines. Let us see how long your aunt's generosity lasts when she learns of the company you keep."

At that, Simon broke away from Selena and skirted the edges of the room, avoiding anyone else who might have overheard fragments of their conversation. He needed a moment to think, to steady himself. Surely there had to be some mistake. If what Selena claimed was true, then . . .

No. He wouldn't entertain the thought. Not when he and Emme were so close to a future together.

His aunt's insistence upon the need to avoid scandal at all costs drifted back to him. He'd assured Aunt Agatha that Emme's character was beyond reproach. But now . . .

Simon shoved the doubts aside and quickened his pace, pushing through the garden door into the cool night air. The garden stretched before him, bathed in faint moonlight and the softer glow spilling from the ballroom windows—a tranquil scene entirely at odds with the storm inside him.

He'd barely reached the first hedgerow when Emme stepped out from the shadows, her golden curls spilling over the deep red of her cape. His heart calmed at the sight of her, as if her very presence could mend the cracks in his composure.

"I thought . . . I wasn't certain if you'd—"

"I would never leave you without a word again." He captured her hands in his, drawing her close. "I've learned to trust not only your strength but my own a little more since then." His earlier joy flickered back to life as he gave her hands a squeeze. "I'm afraid my excitement at finally being able to ask for your hand may have taken you by surprise."

"It did." She nodded, the moonlight softening her features into something ethereal. But her smile faltered. "And I . . . I don't understand. How can you be free to make such a decision?"

"As I told you, Aunt Agatha and I came to an agreement on what constitutes a 'suitable' bride, and to my astonishment, we agreed." He laughed, still overwhelmed at the prospect of loving her openly and freely. "The money was only part of it. Your sterling character and impeccable reputation were what truly convinced her." He shrugged, adding with a teasing grin, "Though I suspect my admiration for you played a modest role as well."

"My reputation?" The growing smile on her face froze. "Simon, there is something I must tell you."

The look in her eyes stopped his breath, and in that moment, he knew. Selena's claims were true.

"You must understand, I never thought . . ." She pulled her hands from his and glanced away. "It all started before I even met you. And then, on the night you'd planned to propose, I was going to tell you, thinking it wouldn't matter if we kept it a secret." Her voice trembled, every word draining warmth from his body. "But when you didn't come, and I thought it was over, I didn't see the point in confessing."

"No," he whispered, stepping closer, though her words felt like a chasm opening between them. "You're a writer?"

She blinked up at him, her expression raw. "I would never have kept it from you if I'd known—" Her voice broke, and she looked down, twisting her hands together before meeting his gaze again. "Don't you see? When I thought I'd lost you, my secret didn't seem to matter anymore. Writing became my solace. I never imagined . . ."

The impact of her confession struck him like a physical blow, shattering the future he had so carefully envisioned. After all the heartache and loss and misunderstandings, he'd confidently projected the perfect scenario of revelation, proposal, and consequent wedding, but now the unexpected news before him derailed everything else.

"You write what sort of novels?" The question spilled out before he could stop it, absurd and inconsequential under the weight of everything else.

Her brow furrowed as if the question pained her. "Gothic novels. My first three were Gothic."

"Three?" The word burst from him, disbelief mingling with something dangerously close to admiration. "You've published three novels?"

Of course it made sense now. Her cleverness, her wit, her impassioned defense of novels and of women pursuing their own paths—it had always been more than abstract principle. She had been defending herself.

"If I thought giving up writing would change our future, I'd do it without hesitation," she said, her voice shaking. Tears glimmered in her eyes as she stepped closer. "But if the truth of my authorship comes to light, it's too late to undo what's already been done. I've published three, Simon. And I finished a fourth last night."

"You've written another?" How could her words stir both pain and pride? Emme, like the author of *Sense and Sensibility*, had written books that the world read. "And . . . how have they been received?"

She blinked up at him, her brows squeezed together. "Received?" She gave her head a little shake, as if trying to collect her thoughts. And rightly so—her confession derailed all his hopes for their future and he'd, like a fool, asked about her writing? "Very well, from what I understand, but I hope to do better with my future trajectory, if given the chance. My newest story is . . . is more like what you've been reading." Her tears shimmered again as she searched his face. "If I'd known my future held you, Simon, I might have chosen differently."

Differently? Than writing?

His shoulders slumped under the weight of it all. Why should she have to choose? Blast the social rules that made her talent a liability. Blast the expectations that threatened to destroy their hopes. And blast Selena Hemston for her meddling, for her petty jealousy that had exposed Emme's secret, likely already spread through the ballroom.

"I love you, Emme." He reclaimed her hands, holding them tightly. "But I don't know how . . . I don't know what we can do."

"You . . . you still want to marry me?" Her voice trembled with a hope that reignited his frustration at the absurdity of society's expectations.

"Of course." He squeezed her fingers, offering her a smile he scarcely felt. "I'm not surprised that whatever cleverness comes out of that remarkable mind of yours has turned a profit. You've always been extraordinary. This only proves it more so."

"Oh, Simon." Her voice broke, a tear slipping down her cheek like a silver thread in the moonlight.

"But," he admitted, his voice dropping, "I don't know how to fix this for us. In a few years, perhaps Aunt Agatha's funds won't hold such sway, but right now . . . it's an impossible position."

"I know," she whispered, her voice raw with resignation.

"Emme . . . do you understand, the future I'd hoped for us—it all hinged on avoiding scandal. And if Miss Hemston knows . . ."

"Then the truth is already out." She squeezed her eyes closed, giving freedom to a few more tears, and then with a shivering breath, she raised her gaze back to his. Something in her expression stilled him. "I must sever this association your name has with mine, Simon. I must, for your sake and for your family."

What was she saying? She pulled her hands from his and stepped back. "So the timing for my departure is quite providential."

"What?" The word burst from him as her words made it to comprehension. "Departure? You're leaving?"

"I planned to go before I ever knew there was a chance for us." Her hand pressed to her chest as though it might still her trembling. "I thought distance would free you to find a bride—someone without a secret that could harm your family. And now . . ." Her voice faltered, but she pressed on. "Now my presence will only wound you by association. My profession will follow us everywhere."

"Emme."

"You need the chance to find someone else," she continued, a sob catching in her throat. "A woman who brings you security, not scandal. A woman with wealth. I can't be that for you."

"No." He caught her hand, holding it fast. "You are the woman I want. The only one. You're the one I love, Emme."

She sniffled but did not pull away. Another tear traced the curve of her cheek. "I wish love were enough, Simon. But it won't shield your family's name or keep food on your table. I *must* leave."

He pulled her into his arms, holding her tightly as if to tether her to him. "There has to be another way—another solution." His voice grew hoarse as he studied her face, memorizing every beloved line, the curve of her lips, the shimmer of tears in her eyes. Deep down, he knew the truth: There were no solutions. Not yet.

For one moment, she rested her head on his shoulder, her soft sobs blending with the distant murmur of the ballroom. He pressed his lips to her hair, breathing in the familiar fragrance of roses. The heat behind his eyes betrayed him, and he shut them tightly, his arms securing her close in a futile attempt to stop time.

With a wipe to her eyes, she pushed back from his arms, her watery gaze searching his face. If he'd ever doubted her love, the look she gave him stripped away all uncertainty. "Goodbye, Simon."

His shoulders sagged, his head falling forward as he exhaled a long, pained breath. "I don't want to let you go."

"You don't have a choice." Her voice wavered, but her chin lifted in defiance of her tears. "You'll find someone—someone who can give you what you need most. Someone who won't risk your future, who will love your family as dearly as—" Her voice broke, and she stepped farther back toward the garden path.

She paused only once, her gaze lingering on him with devastating finality. And then, with a turn, she vanished into the shadows.

The silence of the garden engulfed him, pressing on his chest. He stared into the darkness where she had disappeared, his breath ragged.

"There is no one else for me but you," he whispered, his words lost in the night.

He raised his gaze to the starry sky, a silent cry clawing for release. Wasn't love supposed to be enough?

But the answer mocked him, echoing in the void she left behind. Life was rarely so simple. Love couldn't mend the burdens of legacy, nor could it conjure wealth from empty coffers. And as the weight of reality settled in his chest, Simon realized the bitter truth: Love alone was not enough to overcome the demands of duty.

CHAPTER 23

God granted Emmeline a rare mercy by having Aunt Bean whisked away from St. Groves the day after the ball. Not only had the entire ballroom discovered her secret by two in the morning, but by noon the next day, all of St. Groves was positively humming with it.

Much to her chagrin, Emme had become the talk of the social season for the second year running—never a promising sign. To punctuate her demise, Aunt Bean delivered her parting words with all the subtlety of a blunt axe: *"Only a miracle could lead to matrimony now."*

Perhaps her future as an independent, unmarried woman had chosen her after all. Her mother's family in Yorkshire would welcome her, and there she could recuperate, let the rumors die down, and focus on writing another novel. Perhaps, with enough time and distance, she could even learn to let go of Simon Reeves.

Oh, but how his words taunted her still, lighting a flicker of impossible hope.

He loved her.

And the way his eyes had gleamed with admiration at the thought of her writing—it had been nothing short of astonishing. Almost as if he were proud of her. She tipped her gaze heavenward.

Dear God, how could I ever give up such a man?

"I still can't believe it." Aster's voice broke into her reverie. She stood by Emme's bed as Emme placed her garments into the trunk. "All this time you've been an author and never told me?"

Emme laid her favorite gown carefully atop the others, her throat tightening with another wave of tears. But she had cried enough through the night—enough to wake with puffy eyes and a sore nose. There was no point indulging further.

"I thought, in some convoluted way, I was protecting you and Father." She sighed, sitting heavily on the edge of the bed. "But now I see I should have told you long ago. Perhaps then we could have written a different ending to this tale."

Aster joined her, settling close and covering Emme's hand with her own. "I don't care what they say. I'm proud of you." Her smile was warm, her voice unwavering. "You pursued a dream no one else dared, and you succeeded. That's remarkable, Emme."

The praise in Aster's words soothed her, if only a little. But reality was never so easily dismissed. "I only worry how this revelation will affect you and Father. Little Alfie is still unaware of such troubles. But I'd never forgive myself if it hurt any of you."

"Hurt us?" Aster gave an indignant shake of her head, her honey curls bouncing. "You persist in believing we're made of glass, Emmeline. We are not so delicate."

"I do no such thing—"

"You do." Aster raised a brow. "You know Father is proud of you. His reputation will survive. His tenants care only for their work and families, not the contents of ballrooms. And anyone of true importance to us, apart from Aunt Bean, naturally"—she rolled her eyes—"will behave as proper Christians and move on. Writing novels is hardly an unpardonable sin. Stories are in the Bible, after all."

"I hardly think Gothic romances are comparable to Holy Scripture." The urge to laugh bubbled up, a welcome reprieve.

"But the principle remains," Aster countered, her grin tipping with mischief. "Stories have power. They speak to people in unique and profound ways. Perhaps I'll use Paul's missionary journeys to convince Father of the merits of travel."

"I doubt your argument will have the desired effect. Poor Paul's journeys weren't exactly triumphs of leisure." Emme tossed another item into the trunk. "Shipwrecks and floggings are hardly the stuff of romanticized adventure."

Aster gave an exaggerated huff. "Then I must concoct a better scheme to lure Father away from St. Groves."

Emme studied her sister, searching for cracks in her carefree facade, but Aster seemed as unbothered as Father himself. "I only hope my little scandal doesn't deter any potential suitors for you. At least one of us ought to find happiness in love."

"Emmeline Lockhart!" Aster's eyes widened in mock outrage. "If any future suitor is deterred by your novels, then he is plainly not the man for me."

Emme's smile flared. "You're right."

"I am." Aster straightened her spine, a self-satisfied smile on her face.

A comfortable silence settled between them for a moment, but then she tipped her head, her gaze catching Emme's again. "And I'm right about something else. Your writing wouldn't have mattered to Simon. He would have married you wholeheartedly—if not for . . ."

"Money," Emme finished, her voice soft as she looked away. Simon had been so happy, so determined last night, only proving Aster's assertion true. He'd found a way to navigate the demands of his impossible situation to offer her his hand. And she would have said yes. She would have basked in the beauty of being his wife.

But just as in *Sense and Sensibility*, money had proven itself a cruel, life-altering force. "The cog that makes the world go round," she murmured bitterly, shoving a pair of stockings into her trunk with far more vigor than necessary.

"Only in part," Aster replied, deftly retrieving Emme's latest publication from the bed. She waved it aloft like a victorious knight's sword. "Even in these romances—"

PEPPER BASHAM

"They are fiction, Aster."

"But just as I was saying about stories," Aster countered, "these romances are based on truth. And now that I know who the author is, I'm more certain of it." She paused to point the book at Emme like a preacher delivering a sermon. "Once you get past the ghosts and pirates, your stories reveal the strength of the human spirit, the beauty of a generous heart, and the persistence of faithful love. Those things are as true today in your heartache as they were last night during Simon's declaration. The tenets are true."

Oh, how Emme longed to believe that this pain was merely a stopping point on the road to her happily ever after. That the fragments of truth hidden within her fiction could lead to something sweeter than this very real heartache. Tears pricked her eyes, but she managed a smile for her sister. "How is it that you've gained such great wisdom?"

Aster's grin broadened as she held up the book. "Reading." She chuckled. "And watching you."

Emme snatched the book Aster kept wielding toward her. "Me?"

Aster tucked her feet beneath her as she settled on the bed. "Simon's behavior two seasons ago deserved your rejection. I was furious on your behalf. Furious with him." Her frown deepened, and a single dimple emerged in her cheek. "Though you tried to hide it, I knew he'd broken your heart, and I wanted him to suffer for it."

"Aster!" Emme laughed despite herself.

"It's true. I may have even despised him for a time and concocted a plan to poison him. Or at the very least, abandon him in a forest in the Himalayas."

Emme let out a full laugh at her sister's absurdity. "Good heavens! Poor Simon."

"And that's exactly what convicted me most." Aster shot up, gesturing toward Emme. "Your compassion and sympathy toward him when you should have been more furious than I was. Something in

318

the way you believed in him, even when he appeared to be a rake. Well"—her expression softened—"it humbled me. It reminded me that we often don't know the full story of a person. And perhaps kindness is a better choice than vengeance."

"Wisdom, indeed." Emme chuckled. "Thomas would highly approve of your newfound piety."

"Don't let him hear you say that." She leaned closer, lowering her voice to a whisper. "There are still far too many ungenerous thoughts in my head. For example, I briefly redirected my poison plan to Miss Hemston after hearing about her behavior last night."

Emme shook her head in mock reproach. "I'm grateful your plans remain purely theoretical."

"You're one to talk," Aster teased, gesturing toward the book. "You've written about poisons, kidnappings, and murders—"

"For fictional people."

"Ah, well. Semantics." Aster winked and stood, leaning over to press a kiss to Emme's head. "I'll leave you to your packing, but I must confess—I am envious of your journey, even if it's only to Yorkshire."

Yes, her sister's wanderlust was disappointed yet again. "I would prefer a very different reason to leave than this and one in which you could accompany me, I assure you."

"I know." She looked down at Emme, a sad acceptance on her face. "But someone must stay with Father."

Emme nodded. "Perhaps he can come with us next time."

"Perhaps." Aster sighed, leaning her head against the bedpost and staring at Emme. "I will miss you terribly."

Another pang pinched at Emme's already bruised heart. She'd never left home without her family, and certainly never for a long a time as this was likely to be. "I will write to you."

Aster's brows rose in tandem. "Every day?"

Emme laughed softly at her sister's pleading expression. "If there are interesting things to share every day."

Aster grinned, then turned toward the door. "You know how in your books, near the end, things seem hopeless? The hero is on the brink of death, the heroine is succumbing to her injuries, and the storm threatens to bring rescue too late?"

Emme merely raised an unimpressed brow. It seemed drama ran a little too thick in the women of their family.

"But in the end, good prevails," Aster said as she opened the door, pausing in her exit. "Truth wins. The hero and the heroine find each other."

Emme braced herself against the fanciful notion. Simon had to make choices that would determine feast or famine for his family, prosperity or ruin for his name. "Aster, I cannot continue to hope—"

"Your heroine, Lilith," Aster interrupted, her tone firm, "would remind you, dear sister, that there is always a reason to hope."

And with that, Aster left the room, her statement floating in the air like a melody just out of reach of identification. Emme looked down at the book in her lap, smoothing a hand over the dark cover.

Always a reason to hope?

Perhaps that hope needed redirection, because Simon Reeves was no longer part of her future.

⌒�

"Thank you for escorting Emme as far as Derby, Thomas." Father patted Thomas on the shoulder and adjusted his glasses as he looked back at Emme, a few worry lines deepening on his brow. "I'll feel better knowing they made it to the city without difficulty."

"I am happy to be of service, Uncle." Thomas tapped his hat and looked over at her, his expression a mixture of concern and kindness.

Heat swarmed into Emme's eyes again, threatening to spill over, but she steeled herself. Perhaps the carriage would afford her some solitude for a proper cry. Clara, her ever-faithful maid, wouldn't mind—she'd seen Emme cry more than once. Still, the shadowed quiet of the journey promised far more privacy for her battered emotions.

Father leaned close, enveloping her in a warm embrace. "It will all be all right, my girl," he murmured near her ear, his voice steady but strained. The waterworks almost erupted then and there.

Emme pulled back just enough to offer him a wavering smile. "Of course it will. Doesn't it always get better, eventually?"

He smiled in return, though it didn't quite reach his eyes. "You must write to us. We shall want to hear of your adventures."

"I will." Emme turned to Aster, wrapping her younger sister in a hug as well. "I'll write to all of you. You as well, Alfie." She ruffled his hair, knowing he did not anticipate the duty of correspondence with any excitement.

"And send our love to your uncle and his family," Father added, as though determined to prolong the conversation, reluctant to say goodbye.

"Of course, Father."

"And you needn't feel obliged to stay away too long, Emme," he continued. "We're quite content having an authoress at Thistlecroft."

Her tears betrayed her then, slipping down her cheeks as she pulled Father, Aster, and Alfie into another hug. "I love you all."

They held her tightly, murmuring reassurances as if they could physically anchor her to the safety of home. After a few more parting words, Emme stepped back, her breath hitching as she turned toward the waiting carriage. Thomas stood ready, offering his arm as she approached. Clara had already settled herself inside.

Before climbing the first step, Emme paused and turned back to Thomas, a small package tied with string clutched in her hands. "I finished the book."

He blinked, his brows lifting. "The new one?"

She nodded, offering the manuscript to him. "I want you to read

321

it first, as you always do, and tell me if you think it's fit to send to the publisher."

He took the package with the same reverence he always showed for her stories, as if she were handing him some sacred text. "Why wouldn't it be?"

She drew in a deep breath, her focus on the manuscript in his hands. "Because it's not like the other books. It's . . . more of what you suggested."

"And?"

Her gaze lifted to meet his, a small, tremulous smile breaking through. "I've never been prouder of anything I've written. There's more of *me* in there than I ever thought possible to pen—so many loves and joys and characters and . . . life."

His grin stretched wide, and he tucked the manuscript against his chest as though guarding a treasure. "Then it's bound to be a success."

A soft laugh escaped her, though it was tinged with the ache of parting. How was it possible for the human heart to hold such heartache and satisfaction all at once? "It already is—for me."

"And that, my dear cousin, is what truly matters."

She nodded, drawing in a deep breath. "Thomas—if the publishers like it . . . I want to publish it under my own name."

His smile faltered, replaced by something deeper—respect, pride, and no small measure of admiration. "Do you?"

"Yes," she said, her voice steady, despite the weight of her confession. "I'm tired of hiding. If it fails, so be it. But if it succeeds, I want it to succeed as *me*."

Simon recalculated the sums for the twentieth time.

Still impossible.

For two days, he had reworked the figures, consulted his steward, and renegotiated terms with the more pliable businessmen in town. He had pursued every avenue, exhausted every possibility to improve the financial outlook for Ravenscross and his family. Yet no matter how he twisted the numbers, without Aunt Agatha's allowance, it all crumbled.

Of course, if Emme could wait a year—or two—then the business ventures he'd painstakingly begun might bear fruit, giving him the freedom to live without financial dependence. But a year? Two? After everything he'd put her through already?

No, perhaps the best course of action was for Emme to marry someone more deserving.

The thought twisted his insides into knots.

He should be magnanimous, like Emme herself—hope for her to find happiness in the arms of a good, faithful man. Even if that man were the rector.

Simon winced at the very idea.

Magnanimity, it seemed, did not suit him. The only man who should romance Emmeline Lockhart was himself.

Was he selfish? Undoubtedly.

Did he regret it? Many things, yes. Loving her? Never.

He had written to Aunt Agatha, explaining everything—before the news could reach her ears from less sympathetic mouths—but what would she do? Her views on scandal were as rigid as her stays, and an authoress fit her definition of impropriety all too well.

Simon ran a hand through his hair and began pacing the room—for the ninetieth time by his own count. Heaven above, was there no other way?

Charlotte and William had tried to help, of course. Charlotte's suggestion of piracy had been rejected, though not without a moment's genuine consideration on Simon's part. William's equally ludicrous ideas of bank robbery or kidnapping Emme outright had been met with alarm—and, from Charlotte, a highly inappropriate snort of laughter.

Quiet people were sometimes the most unnerving if one found out what all they were really thinking.

Prayer, they had all agreed, was the best—and most legal—course of action.

And Simon made a mental note to inquire with Mrs. Patterson about what, precisely, the children were reading these days.

A sharp knock interrupted his pacing.

"Come in," he called, turning to face the door.

Mrs. Patterson entered with her usual air of brisk efficiency. "You have a visitor, sir."

"A visitor?" A flicker of hope stirred in his chest. Could it be Emme?

"The rector, sir."

Simon's shoulders sagged. Of course. A clergyman. Possibly the very man who would propose to Emme if Simon failed to resolve his circumstances.

"Blast it all," Simon muttered under his breath. "Perfect timing."

Mrs. Patterson took this as assent—or as evidence that Simon was in dire need of clerical guidance—and promptly ushered in Mr. Bridges.

Simon's first thought—not for the first time—was how un-rector-like the man appeared. Were they even sure he was a real rector? Most clergymen Simon had seen in the past proved much older or scabbier or . . . well, not as youthful and fashionable as Mr. Bridges.

The man walked in and greeted Simon with a nod, a small parcel held at his side. "Good morning, Lord Ravenscross. I do apologize for this unexpected visit." And then he paused and looked away before meeting Simon's gaze again. The man's jaw set, his expression focused, and Simon suddenly realized how such a man may very well be a force in the pulpit. "No, I take that back. I am not sorry. I believe this visit is precisely what you need."

Simon examined the man with renewed caution. "Is that so?"

Mr. Bridges stepped forward and offered the parcel.

"What is this?" Simon looked down at the package and slowly took it into his hands. Upon closer observation, he noticed it was a stack of papers tied in twine.

"Emme is my cousin," Mr. Bridges said, his voice steady, his gaze even more so. "We've been like siblings our entire lives. There is no one I know better—or who knows me better—than her."

His cousin? Like siblings? Simon's brow rose—and the tension in his shoulders eased considerably. He much preferred that connection over "beloved."

Mr. Bridges gestured toward the papers. "I was the one who encouraged her to pursue publication, and I have managed the business of her work ever since."

Simon's gaze dropped to the title scrawled in Emme's familiar hand across the top page: *A Ransomed Gentleman.*

"There is no one of my acquaintance with as much generosity of heart as her, and I believe you've seen that," the rector continued.

Simon pulled his gaze away from the title and blinked his attention back to Mr. Bridges. "I have. I know. She is the best of women."

The clergyman studied him for a moment, his expression unreadable. "I don't know what power you have to change your circumstances, or how Providence intends to guide this relationship between you and my cousin. But I do know this: I have never seen her grieve anyone as deeply as she has grieved you. Twice."

The words struck Simon with a dual edge.

"She would have given up her gift of writing for you," Mr. Bridges continued, his voice softening.

Simon's chest ached. She had said as much.

"But she is talented at storytelling and finds joy in these worlds and words she pens." Unmistakable pride crept into his tone. "I understand your situation is delicate. You must think of your family, and there is no shame in that. But I wonder . . ." He trailed off, his gaze sharp. "Have you fully appreciated the woman you wish to marry? To understand the mind behind her kindness, the wit behind her words? To embrace her talents as an authoress—not merely in spite of your love for her but because of it?"

Simon stared at the manuscript, the weight of it settling heavily in his hands. What had been a simple parcel now felt like a piece of Emme herself—vulnerable, precious, and utterly unguarded. He swallowed against the sudden tightness in his throat. "Why are you telling me this?"

Thomas drew in a breath. "Because the revelation of Emme's writing has caused a stain on her reputation among the more sanctimonious of St. Groves—one that most would take as reason enough to distance themselves from her."

Simon's head snapped up, fire sparking through him. "Do you think I would let this change my feelings for her? Are you mad?"

Mr. Bridges raised a brow but said nothing, clearly unshaken by Simon's outburst.

Simon pressed on, his jaw tense. "If I had the liberty to marry Miss Lockhart, nothing—no gossipmongers, no self-righteous social sentinels, not even the ghost of my father—would stop me from making her my bride. If I had the liberty, she would have left the ball last night on my arm—my *fiancée*—and I would have gladly announced it to the world."

For the first time, Mr. Bridges' expression softened, his head tilting slightly as a slow, knowing smile spread across his face. "You hold her newest manuscript," he said. "I just finished it. It's the finest thing she's ever written. And I believe you, in particular, need to read it."

Simon's brow furrowed, his eyes darting down to the manuscript in his hands.

Thomas gestured toward it lightly. "It's one thing to love a woman for the way she makes you feel, but it's another thing entirely to admire her for who she is."

Simon tightened his grip on the parcel.

Thomas inclined his head and began backing toward the door. "Reading that book won't change your circumstances." He paused at the threshold, his hand resting on the frame. "But it might help you understand the woman you love in a way you haven't yet. And," he added, his lips twitching with the ghost of a smile, "you may even find yourself within its pages."

CHAPTER 24

She'd written him as a hero.

Simon turned the last page of the manuscript, his throat tight and eyes burning. Fia played with Blast in the garden before him as he sat in a chair beneath a nearby tree, her little voice creating a background for his thoughts. The day had turned cold in concert with the aging season as fall bent to winter, but Fia didn't seem to mind, and Simon had needed to escape the walls of the house.

To breathe in more space and earth and fresh air, as Emme's story came to life and pierced him through. How could she portray his tortured soul so well and yet still make him out to be a hero?

He shook his head with a chuckle. Only her.

And Emme's writing—her style, her way of bringing out the subtle nuances and shifts in the stories and characters, matched anything from the previous novel he'd read, except this one, Emme's book, seemed to be written just for him.

Of course the hero was not fully him. A gentleman of high rank but not aristocracy; caregiver of two siblings instead of, in reality, five; a broken past, partially of his own making instead of his father's—but the essence of the character was him.

And the way he'd dealt with the heart of the heroine resembled Simon too. A relationship broken because of tragedy that forced the hero into making a choice between his heart and his future.

Yet instead of painting him in the light of a man who'd broken her heart, she'd written about his strengths. His care for his siblings, his willingness to sacrifice, his desire to do right for the sake of his family legacy. His lips tipped. She'd even written a scene where the hero saves the heroine from a fall in a pond.

He gripped the manuscript tightly, his emotions warring for release, the torture painfully acute. Was that how she saw him? Truly? Even now?

Not as the failure, the inconsistent Mr. Willoughby, but as the faithful and noble, though fumbling, hero in his own story? Much more Colonel Brandon than he deserved.

The sting in his eyes intensified.

And Mr. Bridges had been right. She was an excellent writer. Penning feelings and relationships with the skilled hand of not only an author but also an observer of her own world. The strangest combination of pride and humility swelled before him, intermingled with a bit of gratitude and a whole lot of longing.

He'd known only one part of this beautiful woman—a wonderful part—but reading her words gave him a much clearer picture of the lady who held his heart.

She was meant for this.

He lowered the pages to his lap and looked out over the garden. Would she be willing to wait for him as long as it took to earn the funds to become independent? Would she allow him the chance, even if it took a while, to be a part of the story they lived, instead of just the one she created on paper?

Perhaps he could talk to her father. Take out a loan from the bank or from Ben. He stood. Surely there had to be a way to change this fate instead of sitting around waiting for something impossible to happen.

Have mercy! Was this what Emme had talked about—the plight of women having to wait for something to happen to them, feeling powerless? He hated it!

"I approve of the new groom."

Simon jerked his head toward the house entrance to find Aunt

Agatha stepping out onto the veranda, her navy traveling suit billowing like a storm cloud as she approached. He turned in full, blinking in disbelief. She had barely been gone a week—what on earth was she doing back at Ravenscross already?

As though reading his thoughts, she declared, "Women of a certain age are not meant to travel so often. Such extravagance is for the young—or the foolish." Her sharp gaze swept over the garden before she strode past him and seated herself in his vacated chair, arranging her skirts with brisk efficiency.

What was she doing here? He'd expected a letter from her, but for her to travel all the way back from London to St. Groves? Was she so concerned about his welfare? Or, he frowned, about scandal?

"I hadn't expected you to immediately return upon receiving my letter."

She turned her head sharply, her brows arching into an expression of withering disapproval. "And I hadn't thought I would learn that my nephew's intended is the subject of local ridicule. A novelist, Simon? Really? No doubt, she's the laughingstock of St. Groves."

Ah, so that was her game. She wanted a fight. Well, she'd picked the right day for it. "The people who matter most are not laughing at her," Simon countered smoothly. "And you may be surprised how many of the so-called elite find her resourcefulness admirable."

In fact, he'd been stopped just yesterday by Mrs. Cox and Mrs. Sanderson, two stalwarts of the local social scene, who had confessed their secret delight in Emme's stories. *"How brave she is,"* they'd whispered. *"How clever."*

Aunt Agatha sniffed. "A blessed few, I should think." She studied him with an expression that could curdle milk. "You may have inherited your father's looks, but it seems you've acquired your mother's poor discernment in choosing a spouse, if I must judge by your two current offerings."

His jaw tightened. "And what precisely do you mean by that?"

"Isn't it obvious? Miss Hemston was a complete disaster, and now you've gone and given your heart to an *authoress*—a woman who kept this shameful secret from you. Why? To trick you into an attachment?"

Simon barked a humorless laugh. "Hardly. She had no idea I intended to propose at the ball. If she had known of my renewed affection, she would have told me the truth."

"How convenient," Aunt Agatha replied, her tone dripping with disdain. "And yet here you are, entangled with someone who brings neither fortune nor reputation to your already precarious circumstances."

Simon took a deliberate step closer, his frustration rising. "And what of character, Aunt? Or intellect? Or kindness? Do those virtues hold no value to you?" He drew a measured breath. "Miss Lockhart is more than her title of authoress, just as I am more than my father's son. I will not have her degraded in my presence."

Her brows lifted at his tone, but she recovered swiftly. "And yet you persist? You will stand by her? Even now? Even when the world would call you a fool for bringing such a shadow onto an already stained family name?"

He tightened his grip on the manuscript tucked beneath his arm. "I would not only stand by her, but if circumstances permitted, I would marry her tomorrow and count myself the luckiest man alive."

"You're a fool, Simon," she snapped.

He stepped forward, his body rigid with contained fury. "The sum of a person is far greater than their wealth or name, as well you know."

"But both are advantageous—indeed, necessary—in your position. And now, she brings neither."

The blow only ignited his fury even more. "Are you taunting me, Aunt? I had thought you stern but fair. And yet here you stand, spouting cruelty as though it were wisdom."

"Not cruelty. Reality." She leaned forward, her eyes hard. "Some choices in life are hard. And you must still make the right ones by putting sentimentality and passion aside for the good of your family.

Your father, from the very beginning, chose my sister as his wife for her money alone. And then he proceeded to whittle away at her happiness by moving from whim to whim, disregarding her needs or feelings. Do not follow your passions into ruin, Simon."

"I am *not* my father." His voice rose, startling the sparrows in the hedgerows. "And punishing me for his sins will only lead you to alienating the only blood relations who truly care for you." Though his care for her was waning at present. "I love this family deeply—enough to make sacrifices you cannot imagine. But I will not punish myself—or her—for his sins."

Something flickered in her expression—recognition, perhaps, or reluctant respect. Before she could respond, a small voice broke the tension.

"Simon!"

He turned to see Fia sprinting toward him, her dress streaked with mud, her grin wide enough to reveal the fresh gap of a missing tooth. "Simon!"

His frustration ebbed at the sight of her. "What is it, Fia?"

"I found something," she called, holding out her fists as she approached.

"Is it—" Aunt Agatha's voice caught, eyeing the child with visible apprehension. "Is it your little frog?"

Fia blinked over at Aunt Agatha. "He found his family, so I let him go." She frowned and released a long sigh, looking back over her shoulder at the creek. "Simon said it was good for frogs to be with their family instead of with humans, and I wanted Blast to be happy."

"Then what is that you have in your hand for us?" Aunt Agatha clearly wanted no surprises from her little niece, and with Fia's pattern of "rescuing" slimy creatures, it was no wonder. Aunt Aggie was not fond of slimy creatures. In fact, to be such a strong woman, Simon might even go as far as to say his aunt was a little scared of them.

"Oh." Fia looked down at her closed fist, and then her face brightened. "This isn't for you, Aunt Aggie. It's for Simon."

Her shoulders relaxed. "Ah, good. Carry on then, darling."

Something in the woman's countenance had changed a little. Shifted, but Simon wasn't certain how to interpret it, and at the moment, all he wanted to do was leave her alone in the garden with as many slimy creatures as Fia could find. It would serve her right.

Simon tucked the manuscript beneath his arm and lowered himself to a knee, thankful for the distraction from his aunt's criticism. "What have you found, sweetheart?"

She brought her hands closer and turned them over. Simon braced himself for something to jump from her palms as she opened her fingers to reveal . . . a small pile of muddy quartz in each hand.

"I found two handfuls of diamonds this time, Simon." Fia placed her two small heaps of muddy quartz into his one open palm. "That should be enough, don't you think?"

Aunt Agatha made a strangled noise. "Diamonds? My dear child—"

"Enough for what, lamb?" Simon interrupted.

"To marry Emme." Her entire face beamed. "Lottie said you already loved her, and she loved you, but all you needed was money. And we have some in our creek, so it wasn't too hard to find. Diamonds are *very* expensive."

Simon stared at the muddy quartz in his palm, the stones smudging his skin with wet earth. The weight of Fia's innocence pressed against the storm of emotions warring within him. He lifted his gaze to meet her bright, trusting smile, her dimples as deep as the faith she held in him.

He swallowed past the lump in his throat, willing his voice to remain steady. "These are . . . magnificent diamonds, Fia. Truly the finest I've ever seen." Blast it all! He was very near to crying!

Clearly, he was going mad.

"Thank you, Fia." Simon touched her head with his free hand, pressing a kiss into her curls. It bought him a moment to calm the storm threatening to overtake him. "I'm certain Emme will appreciate your thoughtfulness." He cleared his throat, steadying his voice. "Would you be so kind as to run inside and ask Mrs. Patterson to prepare tea for Aunt Aggie and me? I believe she could use some refreshment after her long journey."

Fia tilted her head, studying Aunt Agatha as if weighing the truth of his words, before giving a decisive nod. Her wide grin returned, and with a quick turn, she darted off toward the house, one of the dogs bounding after her.

Simon slowly stood and turned toward his aunt, fisting the stones in his hands until they pinched his skin. "I appreciate what you've done for this family, Aunt Agatha. You have kept us from financial ruin, and I haven't the words to thank you enough."

She regarded him with a measured expression, her gloved hands folded neatly before her.

"But," he continued, his tone sharpening, "I will not allow you to bind me—or Miss Lockhart—to judgments we do not deserve. My father may have been a scoundrel and a cold man, and the wounds he inflicted on this family are undeniable. But I am not him."

Her gaze faltered, her lips tightening.

"And as for Emmeline Lockhart," he pressed on, "she is the most genuinely kind and thoughtful woman of my acquaintance. She is also a talented author, and I am not ashamed to be associated with her. In fact, if your goal was for me to marry someone who could save the heart of this estate, this family, it would be her. Not out of wealth or position, but out of sheer generosity of spirit."

A sharp breath escaped him as he laughed. "She could write a thousand novels, filled with pirates, vampires, or whatever she pleases, and I would bask in the joy of calling her mine."

He stopped, his chest heaving slightly, the weight of his words hanging in the charged silence. Then he saw it—a crack in Aunt Agatha's steely composure. Tears glistened in her eyes, and the taut line of her mouth trembled, a hint to her struggle for control.

Slowly, she pushed herself to a stand, attention unwavering. "I have been a blind and fearful fool, Simon." She pressed her fist to her chest and swallowed, her breaths halting. "Watching my sister wither away after being treated so cruelly by a man who'd won her heart with his charm and false promises—I couldn't bear to see it happen again. Not to you. Not to these children."

Simon blinked, his anger giving way to understanding.

"You look so much like him," she continued, her voice breaking. "The firstborn, his spitting image. And when Miss Hemston arrived, with her charm and wealth, I thought I was watching history repeat itself. She was the type of person I feared would woo you with her words and money. Then came Miss Lockhart and the revelation of her books. I feared you were being drawn into yet another trap—this time by a woman who might be as disingenuous as the last. And instead of becoming your father, you'd fall victim to the long and painful illness of being wed to a manipulative and selfish person."

Like Mother.

All anger fled and he saw her clearly now. Her stubbornness and her ultimatums were birthed from an unfettered fear of watching a second generation of the Reeves family self-destruct. In her own way, she'd given herself the assignment of reforming and saving the family by whatever means within her control, and in the process, the fear had blurred her vision as much as Simon's.

"I am the only family left to you." Her voice quivered, those eyes—stern only a moment ago—had transformed into pale pools of liquid tenderness. "I took it upon myself, uninvited, to guard you. To keep you safe. And in the process, I—"

"Aunt Aggie," he said gently, using her nickname to rebuild the intimacy he'd once known with her. "Perhaps you couldn't trust me to make the right decision a few months ago. But you can now. Marrying Emme may not be the easiest path, but it is the right one—and a very good one."

As if working through the kinks, her worry-wrinkled brow and tense features finally bowed to a smile. "You're right," she admitted quietly. "You are not your father. And Miss Lockhart . . ." She paused, inhaling deeply. "She is nothing like the women I feared."

Simon smiled, taking her hand in his. "Thank you."

She looked away, tugging her hand from his, attempting to compose herself. And then she turned her gaze back to him, a glimmer in her eyes. "Is she a good writer?"

His grin tipped. "Very good. Excellent, in fact." He shrugged a shoulder. "Though her judgment may need some strengthening."

Aunt Agatha tipped her head in silent question.

He raised the manuscript to her view. "She wrote me as a hero."

"Did she?" His aunt's brow rose, and with a click of her tongue, she added, "If she's written you as a hero, I expect you to live up to it."

"I'll do my best." He offered her his arm, turning them toward the house. "But I'm fairly certain I'll still need assistance from my very helpful and extremely vocal family."

"Yes." She nodded, giving him a thorough look of appraisal, her lips tipping ever so slightly. "Thank heaven, we are here to help you, poor man."

His chuckled warmed over the previous tension. "Thank heaven, indeed."

They'd taken only a few steps when Aunt Aggie paused him with a squeeze to his arm. He looked down at her, her expression gentle yet filled with conviction. "I don't have diamonds, Simon," she said with a rueful smile. "But I do have the ability to try to set things right."

CHAPTER 25

Late autumn had always been Emme's favorite time of year. The leaves still blazed in glorious colors, the air carried a crisp promise of winter, and the scent of hearth fires lingered on the breeze. Christmas lay just ahead—a season of light and joy she usually faced with unbridled anticipation. Yet tonight her heart felt as heavy as the leaden clouds that had threatened rain all day.

She wrapped her cape tighter around her neck, stepping away from the house and its ever-present bustle of conversation and laughter. Aunt Meredith's dinner party had been a roaring success, but even the warmth of her family's company could not banish the ache that had taken root within her.

Uncle John and Aunt Meredith had welcomed her into their home, offering solitude or company, as needed, and her cousins—all younger than she—provided ample entertainment.

Time would help. Comfort certainly did.

And she'd survived heartbreak before.

Only this time, she'd broken her own heart.

Thomas's letter from a few days before praised her newest manuscript, offering his confidence in the publisher acquiring it without hesitation. And writing such a story, so real to her everyday life, kindled another, of which she'd only penned a few pages, but she already adored the travel-loving heroine.

Oh, how she hoped her sister's road to romance led her down much easier and more fulfilling paths.

She settled onto the small stone bench in the garden, letting her gaze drift skyward. The stars shone bright, their pinpricks of light a silent reminder of the vastness of the world—and perhaps a much greater Storyteller's work.

It had been a week since they had parted. Seven days, and yet the ache had not lessened. Every knock at the door still sent her heart racing. Every creak of carriage wheels made her foolishly hopeful. But Simon had not come, and she could not fault him.

At some point, she would stop crying.

And at some point, the deep laughter of someone nearby wouldn't immediately make her think of him.

She closed her eyes, willing herself to stop this nonsensical pining. Simon was bound by duty—he had honorable obligations that she could not resent, even if they kept him from her.

Despite Emme's internal fortitude to be like Elinor Dashwood in her acceptance of her situation, she'd spent a few quiet evenings crying in her room as she'd read over the three letters Simon had sent her two years before. Of course he shouldn't have written her until they were engaged. And she shouldn't have kept them for the same reason, but somehow—she laughed at the absurdity—in a tortured sort of way, they comforted her. His writing, his words, his affection had all been real and genuine . . . and lasting. There was such comfort in the knowledge that he had loved . . . *did* love her, and much like the tenderhearted Edward Ferrars caught in a web of his own making, Simon's desires had been for her, but social expectations and the power of money changed everything. No, Simon had never been Willoughby. Perhaps in a cursory look from the outside, but never at heart. He'd been faithful to his first love. *Her.*

Her smile peaked. Perhaps he was a Colonel Brandon after all.

She stood from the bench and approached a few lasting roses intermingled in the hedgerow. Red roses. Her lips tipped. Passionate love.

The sound of approaching footsteps broke the stillness, their measured pace soft against the gravel path.

"Don't you think it's a bit cold to be studying roses out here by yourself?"

Emme startled, her eyes snapping wide. That voice—it couldn't be. She turned, and her heart seized as the familiar silhouette stepped into view. The light from the house framed him, casting his face in shadow, but she knew him.

Knew his stature. His gait.

She attempted to respond, but all the words in her head disappeared. Nothing but a puff of translucent air emerged from her open mouth, creating a tiny cloud in the night. She pinched the collar of her cape, just to have something to hold on to, as he stepped nearer.

"Speechless, are we?" His teasing tone carried warmth that wrapped around her like a second cloak. "I must say, I'm honored to have rendered an author incapable of words."

His next step brought him close enough for the moonlight to reveal the unmistakable curve of his smile. Her breath caught. He was here. In Yorkshire. Smiling?

She blinked, struggling to reconcile the man before her with their last encounter.

"How—" But words proved as intangible as breath.

"By the fastest carriage ride in recorded history." His grin tipped wider.

A voiceless laugh broke from her—was it relief or disbelief?—before she managed to say, "I hope you rewarded the horses and driver handsomely."

"I was rather preoccupied with finding the woman I mean to marry." His gaze held hers. "But if you'll remind me later, I shall see to it that the horses receive their due praise and the driver a generous tip."

"Marry me?" she repeated faintly, the words shaking as they left her lips. "How can—"

"You're proposing?" His teasing tone softened, but the glint of mischief lingered in his eyes. "Then I accept. I *will* marry you."

Another laugh shook free from her. "Simon, this—how is this even possible?"

"It's quite simple." He stepped closer, his voice dropping to an intimate timbre. "If you don't marry me, my family may revolt and lock me out of Ravenscross for the rest of my life. Believe me, Lottie and even Will are not to be underestimated."

The slightest crook in his grin pulled her attention to his lips, and her throat went dry. When her eyes met his again, his expression had shifted, the teasing giving way to something deeper, rawer.

He breached the distance between them and slid one palm across her cheek, the pad of his thumb trailing over her lips. "Will you let me love you for all the days of our lives, Emmeline Lockhart?"

The heat building in her eyes liquified, and in one swift movement, he captured her mouth with his. She melted against him as his arms pulled her nearer, encapsulating her. Oh, she'd dreamed of another kiss. Another opportunity to relish the feel of his lips against hers.

And this time, she was ready—ready to embrace the moment and all that came with it. Her hand fisted the front of his coat while the other ventured upward, tracing the firm plane of his chest to the strong line of his jaw. His breath caught as her fingers brushed the curve of his ear, and a deliciously deep sound escaped him when her hand slid into the soft waves of his hair.

No fantasy could compare to this—the reality of his lips, his strength, his scent. The romance of paper and ink, no matter how eloquent, held no candle to the fiery truth of him.

He broke the kiss first, his forehead resting gently against hers as their breaths mingled in the air.

It was all too . . . much.

Her fingers trailed from his hair to his cheek. A smile she'd kept locked away for too long finally bloomed, accompanied by a quiet, almost disbelieving chuckle. "What happened to change things? I'm still an author, and your aunt . . ."

"She's reevaluated her priorities and found them misdirected." He brushed a stray lock of hair behind her ear, his touch lingering. "And once I was free to act, I went directly to your father. Not only did he give his blessing, but he also supplied explicit directions to the Spencers' house. I must say, he was remarkably efficient."

A laugh bubbled up from her, lighter than she'd felt in weeks. "Efficient, was he?"

"Indeed. As we shall have to be as well, given the need for frugality. But if you're willing—"

"I'm willing," she interrupted, rocking up on tiptoe to touch her lips to his. "Happily willing."

Her brief touch must not have been enough for him, for his arms pulled her in once again to indulge in another lingering taste of her lips. Her hold on his coat likely prolonged the delightful embrace longer than he'd originally intended, but he didn't seem to mind.

"And Simon," she began, her fingers smoothing over the fabric of his lapel, as his mouth breathed another kiss against her temple. "I do have some funds of my own, other than my dowry. It's not much compared to an estate, but it may help."

His lips took a gentle detour to her cheek, then her ear. "Do you?"

Her eyes flickered closed at the blissful caresses, his whisper so close to her neck, it shot a fire of tingles over her skin. She'd never known such delightful flutterings. Her fingers fisted his coat again, more to stay upright than anything else. She waded through her blurry thoughts to rediscover what she'd said. "Yes," she breathed, as his lips found her jawline. "I . . . I have almost three thousand pounds in the funds."

He jerked back, his eyes wide. "Did you say you have three thousand pounds in the funds?"

"And I'm assured of more with a fourth book," she admitted, her uncertain smile gaining more confidence in the light of his appreciation. Perhaps three thousand proved impressive, even for a viscount? "And continued royalties from the first three."

"Three thousand . . ." He gave his head a shake before reexamining her. "Why on earth didn't you mention this sooner?"

"Because to reveal the funds, I would have had to reveal my writing. Without assurance of a future with you, I . . . I never thought of them as a solution."

"It's extraordinary, Emme. What a testament to your brilliance." His palms rose to cradle her shoulders and his expression sobered. "But we can't use that money for Ravenscross. It's yours, and I want it to remain yours. You earned it."

"But if it *is* mine," she countered, her own hint of mischief curving her smile, "then I may do with it as I please. And I choose *us*. If Ravenscross is to become my home, then I want to be a part of its restoration."

His laughter was warm as he rested his forehead against hers once more. "You have been reforming Ravenscross—and me—long before tonight."

"Then let us finish the work together." She tugged on his coat, drawing him closer. "As man and wife?"

"My new favorite phrase," he murmured, capturing her lips again, lingering with caresses both gentle and searching. *Heaven and earth, she loved him!*

As they began the walk back to the house, her hand tucked securely in his, he glanced at her, his lips curving into a crooked grin. "I feel as though we've come full circle."

"Do you?"

"Indeed. I had intended to propose to you in a garden two years ago." He waved toward the space of flowers and hedgerows. "And now, you've proposed to me in one."

"I did not propo—"

"Shhh." He raised a finger to her lips, his expression playfully severe. "Let us not ruin the moment." He resumed their walk at a slower pace. "I shall regale our children with the story of the time their mother broke all propriety to propose to their father."

"Simon!" She laughed, swatting at his arm, but he caught her hand and pressed a kiss to her palm, his gaze catching in hers.

She could drown in that admiration.

"You know, this scene is almost an exact replica of the ending in a recent book I read from a new favorite author of mine." He raised his brows, tucking her arm within his and taking his time guiding them back to the house. "Only the man proposed to the woman in that story, but I'm willing to overlook the difference."

He was wonderfully ridiculous, and she'd missed this lighthearted side of him. Could it be that their shared love lightened his burdens a little, enough to allow the carefree and teasing Simon back to the light again? But his gravity of character suited him well too, his deep and abiding love for those under his protection. For her.

"But Elinor and Edward don't reunite in a garden."

"Ah, no." He looked up at the sky as if in thought, but the slightest twitch to his lips gave away his humor. "I was referring to a brand-new novel I read where the hero proposes to the heroine in a garden at night after their possibility of marriage seemed all but lost."

"You read a story with that ending?" She searched her thoughts for the title of such a story.

"And the hero had two younger siblings instead of five."

What was he talking about? "But you—"

"And the worthless hero had to grow into his status as hero after fumbling around like an idiot for a good half of the book." He narrowed his eyes at her, pausing their approach to the house just within the shadows of the doorway. "I really do feel you were basing this character on someone you know."

Her breath caught as his meaning became clear. "You . . . you read my book?"

"Devoured it," he corrected. "It was marvelous, so much like its creator." He captured her chin with his finger and thumb, his look so filled with adoration that it took her breath away. "I'm so proud of you, Emme. And even prouder to be the man you've chosen."

She basked in the knowledge of his love for her, of his appreciation of her gifts. Of the fact that after all this time, they'd finally found each other again and were both better people than they'd been before. "Our romance does make a very good story."

"Indeed, it does." He took another quick kiss, his fingers still lingering on her chin. "But I'd much rather live this one than read about it."

"Oh yes," she said, sighing against his lips, embracing him, his love, her stories, and this beautiful ending to a very long journey to find each other again. "I look forward to the adventure."

CHAPTER 26

The phaeton trundled over a dry road on a sunny April day, carrying a couple in elegant dress and a pleasant-faced driver. Adorned in strings of flowers with a few bells dangling off the back, it created a merry sight among the cottages speckled along the back way toward Ravenscross.

More than wildflowers framed the road on this day.

In front of each cottage waited its occupants, each holding a welcome bouquet or simple gift from their home to celebrate the wedding of their lord and bride.

Lord and Lady Ravenscross.

Emme could scarcely believe it. Within six months, she had gone from a rejected woman, retreating in order to free her suitor from a match they could not have, to a bride on the arm of the man who had always held her heart.

With a laugh, she waved toward Mrs. Anna Campbell as the carriage stopped to receive their simple gift of produce from their first spring as Ravenscross's tenants. Mrs. Campbell's beaming smile and her burgeoning middle promised that much more than the fruit of the land would greet their home very soon.

"She looks happy," Emme said as she turned to her—dare she say it?—husband as the carriage drove on.

Simon, who had scarcely let go of her since they left her father's home, tightened his hold on her waist. "You are welcome to visit her and confirm it," he answered, voice warm. "As lady of the manor, you have full authority to dispense visits as you see fit."

"Lady Ravenscross," she repeated, as though trying the title on for size. "It feels rather grand."

"Not grand." Simon leaned close. His breath teased her ear, sending delightful shivers down her spine. "Perfect."

Their departure had come after hours of festivity, followed by a lively family dinner at her father's insistence. The younger Reeves siblings had departed with Aunt Agatha, leaving Emme and Simon alone in the fading light of the day for their first journey to Ravenscross as husband and wife. As if in sweet benediction to the day, the sky began to bow to the burnished hues of sunset. The estate—theirs now—lay just beyond the horizon, the distant towers of the house like a promise in a storybook of everything yet to come.

The drive had afforded a wonderful and lengthy time of privacy, just the two of them, as Emme attempted to take in her new life, her new future. And he'd peppered the moments with sweet endearments and tender kisses, almost as a prologue of a scene yet to come.

"Well, as the new mistress of Ravenscross, I should like to get to know all *our* tenants." She smiled up at him.

"*Our* tenants," he echoed, and without further hesitation, he leaned close, his nose sliding over hers in a playful gesture, before his warm lips claimed her cool ones.

This kiss, firm and earnest, was more than a thrilling flirtation or a gentle admiration. It was a lover's kiss, a promise. And the warmth of it emanated through her to her very soul. She belonged here, with him.

She raised a palm to his cheek, answering his unvoiced request with her own. She'd made a promise too. Before God and those she loved.

She was Simon's and he was hers.

As they capped the hill nearest the house, Emme's gaze traveled beyond the pond where she'd taken an unintentional swim and settled on a distant roofline beyond the treed boundary of Ravenscross. An edifice of stone and modern pillar caught fading daylight, and her smile faltered.

The former Hemston estate.

Emme hadn't particularly liked the Hemstons, but she'd not wished their fate on anyone. Only two months after she and Simon had announced their engagement, a great scandal eclipsed the future marriage of a struggling viscount and a tainted authoress. Mr. Hemston, on the advice of his partner, Mr. Chambers, had sunk his entire fortune into a doomed business venture. Chambers had vanished soon after, leaving Hemston to face creditors and ruin alone. The estate was sold, the family scattered, and Selena Hemston, in what could only be called a desperate act, had run off with Chambers himself.

According to rumors, she and her notoriously profligate lover disappeared in the direction of the West Indies, lured by the promise of lucrative trade and sugar plantations. But such ventures were not for the fainthearted—or the foolish. Within months, word filtered back of their utter ruin. Chambers had squandered what little wealth he'd stolen in ill-fated schemes, leaving Selena stranded in an unfamiliar land. She was last seen attempting to charm her way onto a merchant ship bound for anywhere but there.

However, who could trust rumors?

Cool evening air fluttered toward them as the phaeton turned up the drive toward Ravenscross, its jagged stonework creating a formidable silhouette against the backdrop of dwindling, fiery daylight.

"I had some of the men bring your belongings ahead," Simon said, shifting so that his fingers entwined with hers.

"Thank you." She bathed in his smile, his look, feeling very much all the things she read that brides should feel . . . and more, she thought. More than words could describe. "I'm certain Clara will have everything in good order by the time we arrive."

His attention skimmed her face before dropping to their braided hands. "If I could have afforded a honeymoon trip right now, Emme, I would have—"

She silenced him with her lips, and when he was sufficiently distracted—which she inferred by the way he'd pressed her back against the seat of the phaeton and nearly kissed her senseless—she drew back, holding his gaze as she did. "Will you be with me?"

"Always" came his quick vow.

"Then that is honeymoon enough for me."

His gaze searched hers, his emotions raw, his smile faltering, only to grow brighter. "Welcome home, Lady Ravenscross," he rasped.

She smiled as the carriage came to a stop at the steps of the grand house. Simon pressed a kiss to her cheek, lingering as if savoring the very essence of her.

She leaned into his affection, his love.

Ravenscross had never felt so large or so beautiful as it did bathed in molten sunset and ushering her forward as its new mistress. She would embrace the estate and the storied weight of generations who'd lived, worked, and died there.

They hit the steps together, her hand tucked in his elbow, but before she could cross the threshold, Simon swept her into his arms. With a swirl of white lace and laughter, he charged forward into the house as merry as a child.

The dour-faced butler gave an indifferent nod as he held the door, but Mrs. Patterson beamed, her smile following them all the way up the grand staircase until Simon deposited Emme at the entrance of a large wooden door.

"Our room," he whispered, taking her lips again as he opened the door.

Wrapping his hand around hers, he led her inside, never straying far enough from her to release his hold. She felt his gaze on her as she took in the room—his smile so bright, she couldn't help but respond in kind. Every comfort adorned the space, from new rugs to elegant curtains, and a bed large enough to rival a royal chamber.

And then she saw it. Tucked away in one of the turrets connected to their room stood a small desk flanked by windows, and on the opposite wall waited two massive bookshelves.

"I thought you might like a place to write," Simon said, gesturing toward the cozy nook. "Morning sunlight, a fireplace for the evenings—it seemed perfect for you."

She turned into him, wrapping her arms around him and resting her cheek against his. Warmth crept beneath her eyelids as she clung to him, words insufficient to express his thoughtfulness. His arms came up to encapsulate her, his lips pressed to her hair.

"I love you, Simon." She touched her lips to the skin just above his collar. "Thank you—for all of this."

Simon drew back, his hands cradling her face, his expression tender and unguarded, drawing her near. "This is only the beginning of our very own story, Emme." His whisper brought his lips close again. "A story worthy of a thousand novels."

Her breath caught in anticipation of the next scene and the next chapter. She had a feeling that once their kisses began in this intimate space, they would continue for a very long time. She smoothed a hand around the lapel of his jacket, ready to experience a brand-new part of their story. "Then let us write it together, my dear Simon."

And without another hesitation, he breached the space between them, his lips doing much more than stealing her breath and quickening her pulse. They sent her a promise. Not that everything in their story would always be easy or beautiful. Heartache and fear may yet wait within the pages.

But above it all, she knew.

They'd begun a story with the certainty of a happily ever after.

AUTHOR'S NOTE

Thank you so much for celebrating Simon and Emme's story with me! As my first foray into writing regency romance, I had to do some research apart from just reread (or rewatch) Jane Austen books/movies over and over again. 😊

St. Groves is a fictional place but is based on smaller spa towns of the time, particularly those that were less well known, such as Matlock Bath and Buxton (both in Derbyshire). Derbyshire is one of my favorite counties in England, and I love placing as many stories in that part of the country as I can.

I first read Jane Austen in high school. At the time, she wasn't an easy read, but I'd fallen in love with British literature from my first reading of *The Secret Garden* in sixth grade, so when I read *Pride and Prejudice* . . . I fell in love. Not so much with Darcy, but with Austen's style, her worlds, and her banter. Oh, the banter! There's so much wit that even now as I type this, I grin.

Clearly, Jane Austen's novel *Sense and Sensibility* is showcased in this story, and while it features romance, Austen's classic also looks at family dynamics (particularly siblings) as well as parent/child. I loved getting to bring those particular relationships to light in *Sense and Suitability*. I am frequently in awe of Jane Austen and her wit. It's one of the things that made me fall in love with her as a teen reading her books for the first time . . . and that adoration has only grown as I have. I hope a little of her wit shines in this story, because if her inspiration could be "seen" in this book, it would be found on every page, I'm sure.

AUTHOR'S NOTE

Thank you so much for reading my books. I appreciate y'all so much and hope this story brings a smile!

I have an entire shelf of regency research books now that have helped me create this story world. If you'd like to learn more, I've listed a few of them.

Elegant Etiquette in the Nineteenth Century by Mallory James
Georgette Heyer's Regency World by Jennifer Kloester
Jane Austen: The World of her Novels by Deirdre LeFaye
The Time Traveler's Guide to Regency Britain by Ian Mortimer

ACKNOWLEDGMENTS

This story would not have become reality without the encouragement and faith of my amazing editor Becky Monds. She encouraged me to "try" writing a regency story, and here we are. I never realized how much I'd love writing in this time period, but I should have known, with my love of Jane Austen, I'd also love writing in "her world," so to speak. It has been amazing to uncover more details about the regency era, people, and culture to make this story come to life. Thank you, Becky.

Thanks to Ashley Clark. When I was first asked to write this story, I called her and said, "I don't know if I can do this. I mean, there are already so many great regency authors out there. They don't need me." And she very calmly said, "You can do this. You have to do this."

Thanks so much to the amazing authors Julie Klassen, Sally Britton, Eric Vetsch, and Grace Hitchcock who welcomed me into the regency fold and gave me the gentle nudge I needed.

As always, behind every author is a group of bedraggled encouragers trying to keep the author from calling it quits. I want to send a special thanks to Beth Erin, Joy Tiffany, Laura and Sierra Wiersma, Tiffany Wade, Lisa Kelley, Andi Tubbs, Deena Peterson, Andrette Herron, and Katie Combes!

I'd also like to add a special thanks to the amazing and wonderful Debb Hacket, who never fails in her willingness to read my books in order to check my English-ness. ☺

My street team are ever the wonderful support group, and I'm so grateful for them!

ACKNOWLEDGMENTS

And to my agent, Rachel McMillan, who is always ready to quell my concerns with her encouragement and support. I hope I continue to get to pay your phone bills for a long time.

I will never cease to thank my mom (and my dad) for their support in this writing process. If faith and encouragement could make dreams happen, theirs did.

And I am ever-grateful for the support, love, and sweetness of my family. As my kids grow, our conversations change and grow along with them, but I can't imagine having a more willing group of cheerleaders. Many of my "family" dynamics and especially sibling dynamics come from living life with them.

As ever, I am grateful that the Great Storyteller gives me the love and desire to create stories for His glory. Whether overtly faith-filled or more covertly, I hope to incorporate within the pages love, hope, and joy because of what God has given to me.

DISCUSSION QUESTIONS

1. Can you recall one "marriage tip" given by Aunt Bean that you found the most humorous?

2. Social status plays a significant role in disrupting Simon and Emme's romance. What are some other books from the regency era that show these dynamics? Can you think of any by Jane Austen, in particular?

3. Having children in novels is sometimes a difficult balance of being realistic and engaging. What elements of involving the Reeves's children in *Sense and Suitability* did you enjoy? Not enjoy? Why or why not? How do you think their involvement deepened the story? The characters?

4. What are some assumptions we can make about Simon before he became viscount and guardian to his siblings? How about after? How do the trials from his circumstances make him stronger? More grateful?

5. Sibling relationships play a large part in this story. What are some positive elements among the siblings that you noticed? What were some negative ones? How could you tell that the siblings loved one another?

6. It's easy to jump to conclusions and judgments when we've been hurt, and Emme is right to feel hurt and angry at Simon's initial actions toward her. How does finding out the truth about Simon change Emme's behavior toward him?

7. Though Aunt Bean and Mr. Lockhart are siblings, they deal with conflict very differently. Mr. Lockhart is a peace faker (faking and/or fleeing conflict) and Aunt Bean is a peace

breaker (encouraging conflict to happen). What are ways peace faking and peace breaking can hurt relationships? What is an example of healthy peacemaking you've experienced or read about in this story?

8. Forgiveness is an interesting part of *Sense and Suitability*. How does Emme's forgiveness of Simon impact him? How does Aunt Bean's unforgiveness (if it can be called that) impact her relationship with Aunt Agatha?

9. Good friends are sometimes hard to find. How does the presence of Ben Northrop in Simon's life and Thomas Bridges in Emme's life add to the story?

10. What were some of your favorite parts of *Sense and Suitability*? Did you have a favorite character? Why or why not?

ABOUT THE AUTHOR

Michael Kaal @ Michael Kaal Photography

Pepper Basham is an award-winning author who writes romance "peppered" with grace and humor. Writing both historical and contemporary novels, she loves to incorporate her native Appalachian culture and/or her unabashed adoration of the UK into her stories. She currently resides in the lovely mountains of Asheville, North Carolina, where she is the wife of a fantastic pastor, mom of five great kids, a speech-language pathologist, and a lover of chocolate, jazz, hats, and Jesus.

You can learn more about Pepper and her books on
her website at www.pepperdbasham.com.
Facebook: @pepperbasham
Instagram: @pepperbasham
X: @pepperbasham
BookBub: @pepperbasham